Betrayal
Indecision's Flame
Book Four

by JS Ririe

Jan Hill Books

Betrayal - Indecision's Flame
Book 4, by JS Ririe
Publisher: Jan Hill Books
ISBN: 978-1-7326612-4-0
Cover Image by: Yurly Shevtsov/123RF.com

Praise for: Betrayal: Indecision's Flame - Book 4

"So I just ordered the first two books and read them this past week. When will your next book be out? Of course, I'm dying for the end of the story. Great job by the way!" - Kami W.

"I've read all four of JS Ririe's books and each time I find myself turning the pages to find out what happens between Brylee and Jake and the rest of the family. I'm looking forward to Book 5 so I can spend more time with these greta characters." - Maggie P. (Reviewer)

————————————-

AUTHOR'S NOTE: Since the setting for this novel takes place in the Australian Outback, certain colloquial words like "bloody" instead of "very" have been used to set a more authentic flavor. These are deliberate changes.

Please join my mailing list and stay updated with my latest releases and more. The link to join is: http://eepurl.com/dCPYVf.

————————————-

Dedication:

Love is a priceless gift, and I thank my Eternal Father daily for being allowed to be a mother. My children, Jannelle and Jeremy, have a tremendous zest for living and giving. They are my greatest source of love and inspiration.
~JS Ririe

Chapter 1

Morning dawned long before I was ready for it. I had slept fitfully—if at all. My eyes were rimmed with red, my stomach knotted and my head felt like it was being squeezed in a vice, but I had no one to blame but myself for the way things were turning out. I couldn't expect Jake to do all the changing when I wasn't willing to compromise or even give him a chance.

Defining why I felt as I did was impossible. Fear most certainly was part of it, but I had overcome that before by giving up my past way of life and allowing Ben in. I still loved him and the peaceful, fulfilling times we had shared. He was the polar opposite of Jake. With him, I had always known where I stood. There were no games or pretenses, and there had never been a harsh word between us.

But then he had insisted that I come home to face my father. It seemed as if my life had become one disaster after another since the moment I set foot on Australian soil, and every decision I avoided or made came crammed with consequences I did not want to face. Not only had I been forced to accept a new family and learn how to manage the financial affairs of a ranch, but every man who had been a real part of my life was gone—my father, Ben and now Jake.

Maybe I was doomed to spend mortality alone. It was a harsh veracity to face, but as long as I stayed where I was, there would be no happily ever after for me.

I pulled the covers over my head and settled in for another bout of self-pity and tears. Perhaps I had given up on my engagement too fast because, like my cousin Molly, confrontations were hard for me. I didn't want to be dumped so I had done the dumping before Ben's relationship with Jennifer progressed to the point where he would want her more than he wanted me. Everything had seemed so clear that night on the beach when he told me that he wasn't sure where our future would lead because I didn't really trust him. That was why I had released him from his promise, but the regrets had come hard and fast. My falling into Jake's arms for comfort was proof of that. And now I had even alienated him.

Oh, how I hated what I had done to my life. No matter how I sliced or diced it I came out on the bottom. I was still the prodigal daughter—home too late for anything except my father's funeral and the merry-go-round of complications set forth by the reading of his will.

It was too much to deal with, so I closed my eyes as tight as I could and tried to go back to sleep. I could stay right where I was and no one would come looking for me. Ben had Jennifer, LeAnn had Trevor and a baby on the way, and Jake had his waitress in town. All I had ever wanted, even when searching for something more, was to be a good person and show love towards others, but I couldn't even get that right. I had done nothing since coming home but offend and alienate people I cared about. Even Jake, the man who always had an answer for everything, had finally had enough of my platitudes and indecisiveness and had moved on with someone else.

I slept until noon and then crept down the stairs and into the kitchen to get something to eat and drink. It had been nearly thirty hours since I had learned of Jake's encounter in town, and the pain was still so raw I wondered if I would ever get over it, but I was pragmatic enough to understand that life would go on even if I didn't want to be part of it. I had promised my father I would not let his dream die, but doing that without seeing Jake again was impossible. If I could just get away from everybody and everything for a while maybe I could gain some perspective, but there was no place to go or anyone to turn to. I was on my own again and hated it.

Justifying my actions over the next few days was impossible, except to say that I was licking my wounds and couldn't bear to talk to anyone, especially my little brother. How could I pretend that everything was okay, and that Jake and I would be there for him—standing united—when he came home for the weekend? I didn't even know if Jake still planned on being there at all. He might already be making other plans.

I spent most of my time in my room or in the attic with Copper at my side. I loved that little dog. She sat curled up next to me while I cried and never complained when I hugged her too tightly. Jake came into the house several times, but I never went downstairs to talk to him, and he never came looking for me. He drove away from the ranch on Wednesday morning and didn't return that night or even the next day, but I still didn't leave the safety of the rooms I had designated as a safe haven, except to make sure the animals had enough to eat and drink.

My actions were mostly irrational, even to me, but I still made up excuses for why I couldn't see him. It wasn't as much for what we had lost as it was for what might have been if one of us had been willing to make more than minimal concessions. But as the hours wore endlessly on, I came to more fully understand that what had happened between us was as much my fault as it was his. I was rigid in everything I did, especially in my expectations about my future husband.

Ben was everything I had dreamed of having, and I was constantly comparing Jake with him.

That wasn't fair, and it wasn't what the Savior would do. Jake had no idea where I was coming from because religion, or even the concept of spirituality, had never been part of his life. I had been much the same way when I first met Becky and Ben, and it had taken months for my heart to soften enough to do more than act resentful and contemptuous every time she talked about family and wanting to be with them forever. I hated my father and my mother was dead, so there seemed little point in even listening to anything she said. It just made me more angry and bitter.

Still, no matter how many times I replayed the issues and possible solutions to my predicament in my head as I slowly resumed simple household tasks, it always came back to the same thing. I might be falling hopelessly in love with Jake Johnson but was terrified of taking a risk because I knew what would happen if his heart didn't soften as mine had done. There would be an even worse ending to our relationship that could mean the loss of everything to our entire family.

The emotional turmoil of relentlessly hiding from him and yet wanting to run straight into his strong, protective arms was making me ill, so I called Emma on Thursday afternoon to see if she would cover for me with Trevor on his expected visit home for the weekend. It wasn't a lie that I was sick. I had lost my ability to move forward. I still wanted to be there for the people who needed me but, like LeAnn, I had experienced too much loss, and until I was able to replenish the emptiness inside, I would never be able to help anyone again.

"This isn't like you," she said, after listening to my short outburst of garbled feelings. "You have only talked to Trevor once this week and now you are asking me to make excuses for why he can't come to the ranch this weekend. He will never understand. All he talks about is you, Jake and his animals. I think you owe me an explanation since I am the one you expect to get in the middle of this with him. The last time we talked, you seemed more hopeful than you had in a long time."

"Well, I have lost all hope now," I responded. "All I do is destroy everything I touch. Even the heavens seem closed against me."

Her intake of breath was sharp. "You know that's not true, Brylee. God never leaves us to endure more than we can handle, and whether you believe it or not, you are not alone."

"But I feel alone, Emma," I sobbed as a floodgate of tears opened again. "There isn't one single person who would not survive just fine if I left and never came back."

"That is utter nonsense, and you know it," she protested. "There are a great many people who love you. Did something happen with Jake I should know about?"

"Yes," I retorted. "He has moved on with someone else because I couldn't, or wouldn't, let him into my life."

"Oh, my," she sighed. "I suppose we both knew that was a possibility once you took a firm stand . . . ."

"But he didn't have to sleep with a waitress just a few hours after telling me that if I didn't want him he would find someone who did?" I interrupted.

"So that is what has your knickers in such a knot. Jake is a passionate, attentive man who is used to getting what he wants. That is one of the things women love most about him."

"No kidding!" I replied with more anger than was necessary. "Beth called an hour after he left her. She wanted to make sure I knew they had spent the night together."

"Have you talked to Jake about it? She might only be trying to get you to stay away from him. It is pretty much obvious to everyone who sees the two of you together that there is more going on than simple friendship."

"Not anymore, and our relationship was never simple. I have avoided him since he flew Trevor into town on Sunday after what was supposed to be a very special day. I even missed church so he would know I was capable of making compromises. Now I can't bring myself to even look at him his betrayal hurts so much. That's why I need to put some distance between us before I fall completely apart."

"You can't run away from your problems, Brylee. They will still be there when you get back."

"Then maybe I won't come back!" I told her.

Her quick intake of breath was more than obvious. "You aren't planning on doing something foolish, are you?"

"No," I replied, sinking onto the stool that had been placed underneath the wall-mounted kitchen phone. "But I don't know what else to do. Jake and I can't even be in the same room right now, and I am not sure that will ever change."

"I am not trying to minimize your pain or concern, Brylee. There are some very serious issues that need resolution and it is doubtful that will happen overnight, but you cannot let your personal problems affect Trevor. He has been through so much the past few months. If you leave now, he will spend the rest of his life believing that you never really cared."

"But that's not true, Emma! Trevor means everything to me."

"Then maybe you will have to treat the situation with Jake like a less-than-amicable divorce until you can figure things out. He called here earlier today to say he would pick Trevor up after school tomorrow as planned. I don't know what he intends to do after that, but it gives you twenty-four hours to decide what your response is going to be. Can you be there for your little brother this weekend or not?"

The tears were flowing freely now. "How can I be there for him when my own life is such a muddle? What if Jake brings Beth with them, and what if he doesn't even bring Trevor back to the ranch?"

"You sound plumb loco right now. Jake is not the kind of man to throw any relationship in your face, but you are never going to know the truth about anything unless you are willing to talk to him. I know you feel that is impossible, but this situation is bigger than the two of you. There is a little boy to consider who needs both his sister and his uncle to provide some stability in his otherwise unsettled life. You simply can't let him down again."

"But what about me?" I cried out, hating the fact that I had allowed the darkness to enter my heart, but Satan was a cunning demon hitting below the belt when a person was already down. He could twist everything that was good until the truth was completely obliterated. "I can't see Jake again. It would tear me apart."

"Better you, than Trevor. He is too young to understand what has been going on. All he knows is that the one person who has consistently been there for him since this string of tragedies started is you, and now you are talking about bailing. It won't matter that you and Jake are on the outs. He will only see it as another rejection."

"Then maybe he should go away with me. Missing a little school shouldn't matter that much at his age."

"Listen to yourself, Brylee? You cannot rearrange other people's lives just because yours isn't going the way you want it to. That is not the way God expects us to act even in the face of difficulties."

"These aren't just difficulties, Emma," I defended myself. "I have lost my father, the man I was going to marry, the life I planned on living, and the man I was starting to really care about. And that doesn't even include finding out about my father's infidelity, a brother I never knew I had, a new half-sibling on the way and a will that ties me to everything that goes on out here unless I am willing to relinquish the last thing my father left to me. I would say I have more than a little bit to be confused about."

"I'm not saying you haven't received your share of trials and disappointments. You have been through a lifetime of sorrows in a very short amount of time, and it might take the rest of your life to fully recover. But make no mistake, I am no stranger to misfortune, lost hopes and dreams myself. If you think it was easy never being able to have children and never knowing the reason why, you are sorely wrong. But I have come to understand that we don't always see the bigger picture. We are too busy muddling through our own valleys of sorrow to realize that what we are learning must be necessary for our personal growth, or it wouldn't be happening."

"But I didn't ask for any of this. I just want to be happy."

"So welcome to the human race. That's all any of us want, but sometimes we have to make our own happiness."

"And just how would you suggest I do that when there is nothing left to build on?"

I was so tired of trying to be strong and pick up the pieces left over by everyone else's selfish decisions. I needed time away from the ranch to decide if fighting for what my father wanted for me was worth all the pain and heartache involved. There were far too many unhappy reminders of everything I had already lost.

"You do it by getting over yourself and thinking about that little boy you claim to love so much. He might not be able to fill the void a lover or husband could, but he can certainly shower you with affection and acceptance. That doesn't sound so bad to me."

Her assessment of the situation did little to calm my troubled spirit. "I do love Trevor with all my heart, but how am I supposed to face Jake after what's happened? He has made it abundantly clear that he doesn't want to see me again either."

"And how would you know that? You said you hadn't spoken since Sunday. Perhaps he doesn't know what to say any more than you do. His pride has been hurt."

"And mine hasn't?" I snapped back. I needed sympathy, not some futile attempt to help me see the situation more clearly before I was ready. Maybe I should tell her about having been raped. It was the one event that had ruined my ability to trust, and unless I could get past it, I might never be part of an intimate, loving relationship again. But something kept me from doing it. "I was just trying to do what's right." I said instead.

"And you think loving Jake is wrong?"

Her question startled me, and I gulped back another sob as I stared blankly at the kitchen walls with their nail holes and faded paint. They needed sprucing up like everything else on the ranch.

"Not wrong, but certainly not right for me. It would have been so much easier if the contempt we felt for each other in the beginning had remained, but how could I not grow to love a man who cooked me breakfast, brought me wildflowers and was always there when I needed him?"

"If that's what he has been doing, then he is already starting to reform. Jake was always a *love'em* and *leave'em* bloke; going into town every weekend to see what willing girl he could find in hopes of easing some of the disappointment in his own life. He has only let two women get close to him other than his sister—his fiancé who cheated on him with his best friend and you. LeAnn said he has been more content these past few months than he has been in his entire life."

"I don't see how that could possibly be true. He needled me all the time, making my life almost unbearable."

Why was I still beating this dead horse into the ground? Jake had changed in so many ways, but I was still pushing him away because I feared he would never be capable of becoming the man I wanted him to be.

"He did that because you were different and wouldn't fall into bed with him at a moment's notice."

"That's not a very good character reference, Emma, but I suppose he was used to it."

"Bloody right, he was! Jake's a charmer. He has been that way since he was a wee ankle biter, and women seem to love the kind of attention only he can give them."

"Not me," I countered. "I like to know where I stand."

"I think Jake told you where you stood with him."

My memory darted back to the night on the porch less than two weeks earlier when I had inadvertently said *I love you* when he threatened to leave because I couldn't seem to make up my mind about there being an actual us. He had let me know he felt the same way and had promised to give me time. But I was so afraid of losing control and doing something stupid that I hadn't even tried to relax and let time gradually ease us into what was meant to be. Was my fear of intimacy after what Jon had done to me the reason, or was it my commitment to God that kept Jake at arm's length? Without knowing that, I might remain in a state of limbo forever.

"I suppose he did, and I had to wreck it all by getting in over my head before I was ready. LeAnn is going to hate me when she finds out what happened. Some missionary I turned out to be."

Emma laughed. "Missionary work isn't linear. Sometimes many seeds have to be planted before one of them takes root. I can't tell you how many times I had to be exposed to the message the missionaries brought. We Aussies are a stubborn bunch, but eventually we do get the point."

"Even the wrong one?" I lamented. "I never meant to drive Jake away. I just needed more time."

"I doubt all the time in the world will change how you feel about Jake or the church. You are a fiery woman, Brylee, and you weren't meant to spend your life alone. But you were also given the gift of knowing Christ in a personal way, and that comes with certain responsibilities."

I shook my head, even though no one was around to see. When I first joined the church everything in my life had been radiant. Not only had I found the truth, but I also had Ben and the promise of an eternal marriage. That was gone now, and it seemed there was nothing left but darkness.

"So where do I go from here, Emma?" I asked. "Jake will never change his mind. He has proven that already."

"Miracles happen every day, but I think you need to ask yourself a couple of very important questions before making a rash decision that cannot be undone."

"And what would those be?" I challenged.

"First, you need to decide why you love him? And once you have answered that, you need to determine how your religious beliefs actually add to or complicate the situation."

"I don't see how answering those questions makes any difference now since he is the one who walked away."

"Just think about it. We love people for many different reasons, and not all of them are meant to be romantic. Are you feeling the way you do now because you really want to be with Jake for the rest of your life, or are you just hurt because he is with someone else?"

I had little idea what she was talking about. I had never gone on many dates until I met Jon. He was handsome, charismatic and knew all the right things to say to make a shy girl feel beautiful. But then he raped me—it was amazing how I could finally say those words—destroying every ounce of confidence I had gained by knowing him in the first place. Ben had come into my life like a breath of fresh air nearly two years later. He was more than physically attractive. He was kind and patient and did everything in his power to make me feel safe and secure, even though he didn't know what I was hiding— that horrible secret that had ruined everything.

Jake was a total enigma. He was strong, virile, passionate, dangerous and captivating, but he was also loyal to his family, hardworking, understanding and willing to put aside his wants if it meant injuring someone else. No wonder I was both fascinated and repelled by him—leaving little doubt that I would eventually find myself falling in love with him.

"I do love Jake," I told her. "He is the most decent guy I know, and he loves Trevor every bit as much as I do."

"So there is only thing really holding you back. No wonder he is reluctant to discuss religion. In his mind, it is the only thing keeping the two of you apart."

I closed my eyes and leaned my head against the wall. How could I tell her how utterly hopeless I felt inside without revealing more of my past than I felt capable of doing right now? I didn't want anyone looking at me with pity simply because I was damaged. I wanted to be the strong and capable woman God intended for me to be.

"I'm not sure he loves me anymore," I said.

"Because he got involved with someone else?" was her instantaneous reply. "He and Beth have been friends for years. If something romantic was going to happen between them, it would have happened long before now."

"Then why did he spend the night with her, and why didn't he come home last night? It seems quite evident that I am out of his life for good."

"If that is how you really feel, and if getting away from the ranch is the only way you can make a truly informed and righteous decision, then I will support you as best I can. You are more than welcome to use the beach house if that will give you the privacy you need. Just don't stay away too long."

"I would never do that to Trevor. I just need a few days to think."

"In that case, I will have the key ready whenever you come to get it. And I will do what I can to help Trevor understand that you are not deserting him permanently by needing some space for a couple of days. I only want you to be happy, but please do not make a liar out of me."

"I won't and thank you," I told her. "I also promise to give careful consideration to everything you have said. I just feel completely empty right now and have nothing left to give, even to my little brother."

I thought about all we had discussed as I prepared for bed that night. I was a sum total of my entire past, not just the parts I chose to, or even could, remember. Secrets, lies and betrayals had eroded my very foundation. If I really loved Jake as much I thought I did, I would be willing to give him the time he needed to learn what I had in the right way—without all the preaching and backpedaling when it came to giving us a chance.

There had to be something fundamentally wrong with me, or at least with my thinking. I had shared the most agonizing experience of my life with him, and he had not betrayed my confidence. So why couldn't I trust him with my heart? Until I knew the answer to that, it wouldn't matter how many women he sought comfort with, I would never be able to let him into the part of me that was most vulnerable. We both deserved far more than that.

I fell asleep listening for the sound of his plane, but it never came.

Chapter 2

When I awoke the next morning and slipped from my bed to my knees, I realized that nothing had changed except the coming of another day. I was no closer to knowing my own heart than I had been the night before. I wanted Jake in my life, but it still had to be on my own terms. Expecting him to wait patiently until my past had healed and he was ready to believe in God and all the blessings he had in store for his children was unrealistic and cruel. Besides, I didn't even know if he still wanted me.

He had Beth, and from what I had seen, she was attractive, alluring, and definitely willing to do anything necessary to be with him. I wasn't that kind of girl. I respected the woman I had become too much and still wanted my first experience— after the horror of being raped—to be with my husband. It didn't seem like such a mammoth thing to ask for, but the world saw things much differently than I now did. Sex was just something people did for entertainment like going to the beach or having dinner with friends. It didn't even mean that the couple actually liked each other.

These thoughts, and more, made the idea of speaking to Jake impossible. How could I search him out for a conversation when I had nothing different to say, and I certainly didn't want to hear confirmation that what Beth had suggested over the phone was true? We would only end up in another argument that would hurt Trevor more than my avoidance all week had done. He was already confused and hurt. How would he feel when he saw only bitterness and enmity between his uncle and his sister?

So I made up my mind to go to the beach house while I sorted through the shambles of my tattered life. It was far from an ideal solution, but it was the best chance I had at coming to terms with a situation that would only go from bad to worse if I stayed.

I fed and watered all of the animals before packing my suitcase, but I didn't think about going into the den or calling Uncle Ned to tell him I would be gone for a few days. Things might have turned out much differently if I had.

I simply scribbled a note to Jake telling him I was sorry for being a coward and running away without talking to him, but I hoped he would be happy in whatever he chose for his new life. I assured him that I had every confidence he could run the ranch by himself until I figured out what I was going to do. Although I wasn't sure he would do it, I asked him to tell Trevor that I loved him with all my heart and would contact him as soon as I could.

I didn't mention anything that had happened between us or tell him that I wanted another chance to see if we could make things right. That wouldn't be fair since I had pushed him aside every time he tried to get close, but the dreadful truth was that I had never really given him a chance. I was far too afraid of losing my relationship with God to risk finding possible happiness with him.

My hastily written and pointless note was placed underneath his favorite coffee mug on the kitchen table where he would be sure to see it when he brought Trevor home for the weekend. I hated the idea of bringing more pain into my little brother's life, but my own fragile world had been turned upside-down too, and I had to do something about it before there was nothing left inside besides grief, anger and emptiness. By tonight, he would likely believe I was like every other adult in his life, except for his uncle, breaking promises I had only meant to keep.

I remember nothing about the drive into town over unevenly surfaced roads and through dry, mostly colorless countryside. My mind was consumed with thoughts that bounced from one dilemma to another so quickly I missed the cutoff road that shaved thirty minutes from my trip making me even later getting to Emma's than anticipated.

None-the-less, I had the presence of mind—or enough innate guilt—to stop at the toy store to get an action figure and a game for Trevor before picking up the beach house key. I even purchased a card and wrote a note inside telling him that I had been sick all week and didn't want him exposed to anything, but I knew he would have a great time with his uncle anyway.

It was an intentional act of deception, but I had been sick all week. And while Trevor could not physically get what I had, he deserved better than my continual bouts of tears and a possible confrontation between Jake and me. I didn't really believe that would happen in his presence because both Jake and I knew better than to argue in front of a child, but the silence and discomfort would be deafening and my little brother was far too astute not to notice. I would come back when I felt capable of being around Jake again and not a moment sooner.

Emma opened the door when I got to her house. She was still in her housecoat—something many older women wore when they didn't have errands to run. She looked tired and discouraged. It bothered me considerably that I was bringing more worries into her life when she was already taking care of my family for the better part of each week, but I was still determined to take the path of least resistance.

"I'm sorry," I said as tears slid down my cheeks. "I wanted to talk to Jake, but he never came home."

She didn't say anything to dissuade me from the course I had set. She simply invited me in.

"Come to the kitchen with me, and I will make eggs. You look like you haven't eaten in days."

I looked down at my well-worn clothing. They seemed to be almost hanging off my frame, but how could I eat when there was a constant gnawing in my stomach that had nothing to do with a lack of nourishment?

"You don't have to do that," I said as I followed her down the hall into her small, but brightly colored kitchen with its red curtains, yellow chairs and blue canisters. "I guess I've had other things on my mind besides food."

"I'm not criticizing, love," she replied, pulling a carton of eggs and a bunch of vegetables and cheese out of the fridge. "I know you are not in the best place right now, but you have to believe that life will get better. When God closes a door, he really does open a window."

"Then where is my window?" I asked, slumping down in a chair and putting my elbows on the table so they could support the weight of my chin. "I am just so tired."

"You have every right to be tired since you have been trying to be a super woman for months. Our bodies and minds can only take so much."

"But I'm young! I should be able to handle anything."

She sat down beside me and put her hand over mine. "We all should be able to do a lot of things, but that doesn't mean we can. You've hit a point where you have nothing left to give. I get that now, and it doesn't mean you are unrighteous, lazy or unlovable. It simply means you need time for yourself to refuel."

"But I have time! Trevor is in town with you all week. Jake doesn't need me for anything, and I can have the chores done in less than two hours."

"I'm not talking about a few hours of silence at home where you are still worried about everyone and everything that is going on around you. You need a spiritual retreat where you can fortify your testimony and remember just how much God loves you."

I wiped at my tear-stained cheeks. I loved Emma so much. She was my rock of reason and my best friend. But I was over fifty years younger, and I still wanted what she'd had—life with a man I loved.

I finished my omelet and toast and went into the bedroom to see LeAnn. Her belly was growing fast, but that was to be expected. She was well into her eighth month now and so far, the bed rest was working. In a few weeks, the baby would arrive—due in part to the sacrifices we had all been willing to make. I loathed the fact that I was reneging on mine now, if only for a few days.

"You look really pregnant," I told her, trying to disguise the sting in my voice. I wanted to be having a baby of my own, and if things had worked out with Ben the way we had originally planned . . . . Well, lots of babies were conceived on wedding nights. It had certainly happened that way with LeAnn.

"And you look sad and tired." She extended her hand in my direction. "Come sit by me. We haven't had a good talk in the longest time."

"Things are always chaotic when I bring Trevor back to town. How is he?"

"Confused about why you are not being yourself. What's going on? I know you would never hurt him intentionally, but he is going to be devastated when he finds out you won't be at the ranch when he gets there."

I took a deep breath and sat down in the green and rose-colored floral chair by her bed. I didn't want to lie to her about what was going on, but the entire truth wouldn't be good for her. Besides, everybody lied, if only to keep the peace or not hurt someone.

"Maybe I have just allowed myself to become overwhelmed with all the changes that have occurred lately. Getting comfortable with overseeing the finances of one ranch was difficult enough and now I have Uncle Ned's to account for. Aunt Nora has been amazing, but there is still so much to absorb."

She frowned and touched her chin as if she didn't quite believe me. "I'm sure it is all very confusing. I will even admit I wasn't overjoyed about the idea of rejoining the ranches when Ned came to see me this week. I know your father wanted him to have that land, or he wouldn't have given it to him."

"Uncle Ned and Aunt Nora want more free time to spend with their family, especially now that they are going to be grandparents."

LeAnn rubbed her swollen tummy tenderly. "Not to speak ill of any of God's greatest blessings, but children shouldn't be having babies."

"Molly's twenty."

"But she is still so young and was never fond of babies. She avoided Trevor until he was almost six."

"That doesn't mean she won't be a good mother to her own child."

Why was I defending my cousin? She was the ultimate college partier and flirted with every man she saw, including Jake. More importantly, she was getting the blessings I wanted without having to pay a single price for them.

"I know this has to be hard for you," LeAnn said. "I don't suppose you have heard anything from Ben."

"He sent all my stuff back. That is about as final as anything gets."

"But you're still not over him, are you? I can see such pain in your eyes. I hope both of us haven't lost the only men we will ever love."

I knew she hadn't meant to be unkind, but unless I could straighten out my own life and discover what God had in mind for me, I would be eternally miserable. Emma was so right! I needed a spiritual retreat to come to know God and my Savior again.

I kept the visit short so there would not be time to talk about Jake, but I suspected that Emma had already given her a shortened version of what was going on between us because she didn't bring up his name either. I kissed both women goodbye before leaving, but I didn't allow their support or concern to stop me from moving ahead with my plans.

Despite many misgivings about the advisability of running away again, I made a quick stop at the bank before leaving Edna—something I had not done since coming home—and withdrew two hundred dollars from the ranch's account. It was an emotionally draining experience since I didn't want my father to be disappointed in me, but my own account in Los Angeles was nearly depleted, and I couldn't get to the coast without gas or survive without something to eat. I looked down at the money the cashier gave me and nearly burst into tears yet again. Even after all the months I had spent working on the ranch, it didn't seem quite right to be taking it.

But distance has a way of changing perspective in even the most difficult circumstances, and by the time I made it from Edna to the busy four-lane highway leading up the coast, I felt like I could actually breath. I had only been off the ranch a handful of times since coming home, and that wasn't healthy. Even Trevor was enjoying the new experience of attending public school. I needed this time alone, if only to figure out who I was now that both of my parents were gone, and I was responsible for carrying out their legacy.

It was early evening when I got to the beach house. A distinctly cool breeze was blowing in from the ocean, and the gulls and other birds were calling out to each other in the brilliant expanse of blue overhead. I could see the white lighthouse trimmed in a glowing red through the kitchen window with its beacon of brightness that protected both watercraft and sailors and tried not to think about what had happened with Jake the last time I had been here.

Perhaps I should have come up with a different place to go, but Emma's suggestion made perfect sense at the time. I put a few purchased groceries away and then carried my suitcase up to the loft. Using the bedroom LeAnn had occupied would only bring back further memories that were best left alone until I felt more in control. I wasn't sure there was even a place to sleep upstairs but was pleasantly surprised when I got there.

The room was spacious with large windows at both ends and two single beds fitted against opposite walls in one portion of it. The other area had been turned onto a family room with a television, a desk and a comfortable sectional. It was absolutely perfect for a retreat. There was even a small bathroom with a shower and walk-in closet.

I unpacked my suitcase, sat down on the sectional and pulled my knees up to my chin. Remembrances of my first night in this house were more than bittersweet—LeAnn's announcement, my breakup with Ben, Jake's kiss and my fall. It seemed a lifetime ago, but it was the night I first realized I was falling in love with my stepmother's brother and the danger that brought. I loved his unpredictability, his passion for life, his strength, courage, need for adventure and love of family. I also loved his kind and gentle nature when he knew I needed him, the way his lips curved and the deep soulfulness I found in his eyes when they met mine.

I had been living in a dreamworld with Ben—an existence where my own family did not exist. I had told him very little about them because I was afraid he would not understand all their nuances and faults. If he hadn't insisted I return home and make things right with my father, I would have lived the rest of my life not knowing what had happened to anyone from my past. And I would never have felt like I did now.

Nothing had turned out in the expected way. I had lost my father and gained a new family, but apparently I couldn't talk to them about what I now believed without sounding condescending or judgmental. I couldn't even lead by example because all I did was hurt the people who had come to mean everything to me, especially my little brother. What I was doing to him now was unconscionable, but I didn't have the inner strength to go back and make things right. I just wanted the pain and disillusionment to go away.

Sitting there in such quiet and pleasant surroundings, I suddenly realized that it wasn't God who had moved away, but me. Other than teaching Trevor the words to *I am a Child of God*, taking him to church a couple of times, and giving him the copy of the *Book of Mormon* I had purchased for my father, there were no reminders in our house of anything religious, not even the crucifix my mother had once hung on my bedroom wall. There were no pictures of Christ or of anything related to what I now believed. We never prayed together and never had what I had come to know as Family Home Evening activities that might bring us closer as a family. We never even listened to what could loosely be called inspirational music.

How could God's spirit be present in a place where there was nothing to remind me of him? My mother had been gone for six years, and the majority of the house still stood as a mausoleum to her memory, regardless of the fact that LeAnn had been living there for several years. Her things were scattered everywhere, most of them useful, but some, like her paintings and knickknacks, could be stored elsewhere until I had a home of my own where they could be displayed without feelings of discomfort or remorse.

The fact that my father had never really closed the door to his life with my mother had to be disturbing to LeAnn, and now that the house belonged to her, she should be able to do with it exactly what she wanted. I didn't know how her changes might affect me, but unless something was altered, even a new baby would not bring joy into a place where so much sorrow had been known.

It truly was time to move on! I knew that with every inch of my being. It was time to bring the right kind of music and a great deal of laughter into the house of my youth and make it a testament to the living, not the dead. And while I would never do anything without LeAnn's permission, I knew she would not object to me hanging some of the pictures Ben had sent—pictures of temples and prophets and words of inspiration—if only in my own room.

I fixed something light to eat for dinner and then sat outside on the whitewashed deck looking at the crashing waves for hours as I thought about the things in my life that needed to change, and my past relationship with Jake was only part of it. I needed to learn how to forgive and accept, not only others but myself. We all lived imperfect lives, and could not be considered failures unless we quit trying. Well, I wasn't willing to quit trying quite yet. I just needed a jumpstart so I wouldn't regress any further into past negative and debilitating behaviors.

Without any warning, I suddenly remembered the small package Ben had included when he returned all my earthly possessions. It was meant as a Christmas gift and had been tucked away in the back of a drawer for over a month, but for some reason I had brought it with me. Now felt like the perfect time to see what it contained.

I retrieved it from my attic oasis and sat on the white, sandy beach as I removed the colorful paper. Inside a small, white box was a silver charm bracelet commemorating the Young Women's Values. As I turned each small talisman over in my fingers, I could see Ben's face and hear his voice as he brought me out of the baptismal font at the stake center.

"You are on your way, Brylee Hawkins. Nothing will ever stop you now."

How radiant I had felt as my life was cleansed from past sins. I was a new person—a true daughter of God—with all the talents and abilities necessary to become exactly what he wanted me to be. I was even free from having been raped. All the guilt, anger and horror of that incident had been cleansed by the Savior's Atonement. Why had I let it back into my life to cloud and destroy again?

It was time to quit hiding my light of devotion underneath a gauze of fear because I was so afraid of offending someone. It didn't matter if others believed as I did or even made fun of it. The only thing that mattered was my personal joy at having learned what needed to be done before returning to my heavenly home.

I could rejoice that my little brother was allowed to attend church with me, and that I would soon have a baby sister or brother. The way my new family had come into my life no longer mattered. This baby was God's gift to all of us, a part of our husband, father and friend that could enhance our lives now that Jack Hawkins was no longer here. I had also found a great friend and confidant in Emma. She had most certainly been brought into my life as an anchor for my soul.

I needed to stop dwelling on what I didn't have and show more gratitude for what I did. I could listen to church music and hang a picture of my Savior above my bed. I could have personal, meaningful prayer each morning and night, read the scriptures daily like I had once committed to do. I could say my own blessing on the food, and even hold Family Home Evening with Trevor before I took him back to town on Sunday afternoon.

Why hadn't I realized all of this before? My narrow-minded vision had centered on losing Ben and not wanting to make a mistake by falling into Jake's arms. If those were the only two things I thought about, I would never be happy again.

I had to let Jake go without resentment, hatred or feelings of betrayal. He had never belonged to me in the first place, and if he ever came back it would only mean that he was finally where he truly wanted to be. If he didn't, then God would help me through the pain just as he had always done—even before I knew he was literally my Eternal Father.

I fastened the charm bracelet around my wrist. "Thank you, Ben," I whispered into the night air. "I hope you can feel my love tonight. You gave me the gift of coming to know my Eternal Father in Heaven and my Savior, Jesus Christ. Now, it is time for me to give that knowledge to someone else."

Despite a great deal of emotional duress, I slept better that night than I had in months. So well, in fact, that it was nearly one the next afternoon before I stretched and then walked down the stairs into the sunny kitchen. I drank a small carton of orange juice and ate a cinnamon-sugar bagel—something I hadn't done since leaving Los Angeles. And then for the first time since coming home, it finally registered that I could think about my past without grieving. God had simply sent me on a different mission than the one I had been anticipating with Ben, and it was time for me to get out of his way so I could accomplish it.

I dressed leisurely, letting the quiet and the calm of the seaside resort wash over me. With my sunglasses to keep the reflections off the water from bothering my eyes, I took an extended walk along the beach. I watched as children played in the crystal blue water and buried each other in the sand, laughing happily. I ran into the waves myself and let them crash against me. I turned my face to the wind and rejoiced that I was lucky enough to feel it against my skin and see what treasures it brought from the ocean depths for people to take home with them.

My new family needed to see me happy because I had never been that way since coming home. How could I ever expect them to embrace the gospel when I went through the days with a heart so weighted down with worldly cares that the light inside of me couldn't escape?

But I was getting stronger. These few hours away from the normalcy I had come to expect were bringing much needed clarity. I had so much to be appreciative of—the light of the Christ's gospel, my unexpected and rediscovered family, a few trusted new friends, my healthy body and mind, my work on the ranch, and my ability to learn, reason and talk to God—with complete faith that he would answer my prayers in his time. All I needed was the courage to embrace each day for the opportunities it might bring.

I decided to walk the few blocks to the Pizza Palace I had passed on my way to Emma's to order a small pizza for dinner. For the first time in over a week I was hungry, and I was no longer ashamed of being seen in public alone. People weren't out to hurt me, but I was definitely hurting myself by giving in to Satan's taunting until it took every ounce of happiness away. It was what my mother had done her entire life—never being content with what she had and always mourning the things she had lost. I had become just like her without even knowing it.

I thought about both of my parents as I read my scriptures and pondered over what I was reading later that evening. They weren't the parents I envisioned as I read about Lehi and Sariah, Adam and Eve, Mary and Joseph or any of the other parents in the scriptures, but they had been good, honest people, and I loved and missed them dreadfully.

On Sunday, I went sightseeing and stopped at a small gift shop to buy a t-shirt for Trevor and a rattle for the new baby. I knew I shouldn't be purchasing anything on the Sabbath but figured God would understand. For the first time since learning of LeAnn's pregnancy, I was genuinely excited for her child to be born—a helpless, innocent and trusting infant straight from God's arms to ours. It couldn't be left alone or taken with us when there was work to be done on the ranch, but it would unite us a real family because it would have no baggage. I didn't want to miss that, even if it meant more personal pain for me.

The phone ringing caught me by surprise when I got back to the house. I dropped my package of gifts on the sofa and answered it.

"Hi, sweetie," a familiar voice said. "I hope you don't mind that Emma gave me the number, but I really need your help."

"Anything, Aunt Nora," I said, confused as to why she would be calling me unless something truly awful had happened. I didn't want to be forced back into a world of chaos after such a brief respite. It would take a while longer for my resolves to take hold. "I am sorry I didn't call to say I would be gone for a few days."

"No worries! Emma explained all that. We were all relying on you too much. I told Ned we should have given you more time before bringing up the idea of incorporating the land, but like all men, he couldn't wait."

"It is a sound business decision."

"But we could have waited a few weeks before springing it on you. It's just that Molly's news took us by surprise. All I could think about was becoming a grandmother and not wanting to miss a moment of the baby's life."

"How are Molly and the baby?"

"That's why I called. She and Bradley had a huge fight and the wedding was called off."

"I am so sorry," I told her, not in the least surprised by her news. Molly had a flare for the dramatic, and things moved way too fast in her world. I hadn't even known there had been an engagement.

"So am I, but that is the least of my worries right now. Molly said she doesn't want the baby, and I am afraid she has done something really stupid. NJ called last night . . . . Oh, how do I say this? My baby girl is in the hospital in Sydney. She tried to slit her wrists."

My body went limp like a rag doll, and I sank to the floor since there wasn't a chair nearby. Molly had always been impulsive—the epitome of a pampered princess. But how could she even think about ending her life, and the life of an unborn baby, just because she'd had a fight with the baby's father?

"I don't know what to say, Aunt Nora, but I will lock up the house and be on my way in thirty minutes."

"I hate asking you to do that, but I could really use the support. Ned and Jake have everything under control here, but I have to go to Sydney to see her, and I am terrified of going alone because I don't know what I will find when I get there."

"Then I'll go with you," I told her before she had time to ask. "I can meet you at Emma's in a little over three hours if I hurry. Is there anything else I can do?"

"Just pray for her and the baby. I know God will listen to you."

Chapter 3

I pondered what Aunt Nora had said on the drive back to Edna. God listened to all of his children's prayers, so why would she specify that listening to mine was any different? Perhaps her heart was softening towards the message I had yet to deliver. Tragedy had a way of doing that if the right groundwork had been laid. Otherwise, it was very easy and convenient to blame others, especially a higher power, for everything that went wrong. I had been guilty of doing that myself until I understood how many of life's difficulties we brought on ourselves.

While we traveled the long distance to Sydney in the dark of night, Aunt Nora explained about Bradley's father demanding a paternity test to make sure the baby was his before the wedding took place. Molly had refused. Apparently, there was reason to believe the baby might belong to someone else. She had begged and pleaded for him to trust her. When he sided with his father, she pulled the ring from her finger and threw it in his face.

Her roommate found her a few hours later, lying in the bathtub with razor blade cuts from her wrists to her elbows and her knees to her ankles. She had been frightened beyond belief when she couldn't get Molly to respond, but had the presence of mind to call NJ who was able to get her to the hospital where her wounds were treated and she was placed on suicide watch. No one outside the immediate family was allowed to see her and no one else had been told, not even Bradley.

"I just don't understand how she could have done this? Suicide is a sin," Aunt Nora lamented as the tires finally quit rotating and we parked their Land Rover in front of St. Peter's Hospital. I had left ours at Emma's so neither of us would be traveling alone.

She climbed out immediately, leaving me to follow behind, but it took a few moments before I felt like I could stand without collapsing. I was emotionally and physically drained having been behind the wheel for nearly eleven hours with only two short pit stops for gas. It was now well after midnight, and we weren't sure if either of us would be allowed to see Molly, but my aunt was determined to try.

NJ met us in the waiting room on the psych floor. Aunt Nora threw her arms around his neck and started to cry. "Where's my baby? I need to see her straight away."

"Calm down, mum," he said. "She is sleeping peacefully. I told the doctor you would be coming. He said you could sit with her as long as you didn't ask any questions until she was ready to talk. She is in a very delicate state right now."

"I can wait for answers. I just need to see that she is okay for myself. Please take me to her NJ," Aunt Nora pleaded. "She might not realize it, but she needs me."

I sat down in a chair in the corner of the waiting room to wait for my cousin's return. It was deserted and smelled of antiseptic and cleaning solvents.

How could Molly have been so foolish? Couldn't she see how lucky she was, despite an argument with the man she was supposed to marry? She had parents who adored her and a family who would always be there, but then she had always lived life hard and fast—never believing her actions might have consequences she couldn't control. I understood that in my own way because I was certainly paying for some of the choices I had made.

"This is a hell-of-a-way to see you again, cuz," NJ said after he had taken his mother to Molly's room and was sitting down in the chair next to me. He looked more haggard and worried than I had ever seen him. There was a stubble of fair whiskers on his chin and his eyes were bloodshot. I wondered if it were from lack of sleep, or if he had been sneaking off to one of the local boozers while his sister slept. He pushed his hair from his forehead as he slumped backwards.

"I always thought Molly had more bloody sense than attempting suicide because some bloke challenged her. I would kill that bugger with my own hands if I had the chance."

"And what good would that do?" I asked.

"Ease my bloody mind a bit. I know my sister is a little too generous with her affections, but damn-it-all, she's my twin. Two people can't get any closer than that."

I wanted to reach out and comfort him but didn't know how. We had never been close as children, and I certainly didn't know the disheveled man sitting in next to me now. A relationship with my cousins was something else I had forfeited by running away.

"Maybe it was simply a cry for help," I said. "Do you really think the baby might not be Bradley's?"

"Anything is possible! Molly loves attention, but you already know that from the way she acts around Jake."

A knot of agitation hit the pit of my stomach, but getting away from hearing his name was impossible. He was part of my life forever because we belonged the same messed up family.

"I doubt guys ever back away from her attention," I said. "She is beautiful, charismatic and definitely not afraid to go after what she wants. Sometimes, I wish I was more like her."

I looked at NJ from the corner of one eye. He had been a cute child with freckles and a mischievous smile. Now, he was an attractive young man, in spite of the way he looked right now and who—I had no doubt—had broken his share of female hearts.

"You can't be serious," he responded. "I admire the woman you have become—so strong and sensible. I never would have believed someone could change so much if I hadn't seen it with my own eyes. You were the shyest and loneliest kid I have ever seen."

"We didn't do much socializing back then."

"Well, damn it, we should have. I always had Molly, so I never really thought about what it must be like for you. But I got a brief dose of that last night. I really thought my sister was a goner. She had lost so much blood by the time I got to her apartment. The doctor said she would have bled out if we hadn't gotten her to the hospital when we did. I simply don't understand how she could go all troppo like that." He put his head in his hands and closed his eyes. "Doesn't that foolish lass understand that death doesn't solve anything?"

I wanted to reassure him, but the right words of comfort escaped me. What Molly had done was more than stupid, regardless of the reason.

"She must have been very frightened, but lucky for her, she has a brother who loves her very much," was all I could think of to say.

"I do love her, Brylee, but I am afraid I have hidden more from our folks than I should have. Molly has been getting into one bloody scrape after another the past couple of years. You have to promise that this will go no further because the oldies would kill us both if they knew, but she had an abortion her first year here. Got preggie by the married professor she was seeing. When he found out he gave her the money to get rid of the problem and then took a post in Darwin, taking his wife and two offspring with him. It nearly destroyed her. I think she really loved the bloke, but once again, she was just being Molly-like, reacting without considering the options or the consequences. She got rid of the baby before anyone knew about it, even me."

I just sat there feeling sick to my stomach. My younger cousin was famous for her tantrums as a child, but taking the life of an unborn child went far beyond anything I could comprehend. The world might proclaim that a woman had the right to decide what she wanted to do with her own body, but I didn't agree. Life was sacred, even an unborn one.

"Don't look so shocked, cuz," NJ said. "Girls do it all the time. It's not like it is against the law or anything. It's just that I know Father Frederick and mum and pops would go ballistic if they knew."

"I suppose they would," I said, biting my bottom lip. But how could I cast stones at anyone after what had happened to me. God was the only rightful judge because he knew exactly what was in our hearts. "How did you find out?"

"Even my dear sister can't keep a secret forever. She just blurted it out one night when she'd had a little too much to drink. You won't tell anyone, will you? I know it's a lot to take in, but I really need your promise on this."

"Your secret is safe with me," I replied, putting my hand on his shoulder. "But it does lead to more questions about why she tried to end her own life after what she had already been through. Why not just have another abortion?"

"I can't answer that, love. Maybe she was trying to punish Bradley for doubting her. Who knows what goes on in that rickety mind of hers? All I know is that she had decided to give that wee one a fair go and then changed her mind the moment her relationship with Bradley hit snag—huge as it was. She didn't give one thought as to how this would affect mum after learning she was going to be a grandmother. It was always 'Molly this and Molly that' with her, and she has the old man wrapped around her pretty, little finger. In fact, she has all of us eating out of her hands, and then she does something truly idiotic like this."

I felt fingers of cold travel up and down my arms despite the warm night. What made anyone want to end his or her life? I could remember wishing I were dead for a time after what happened with Jon, but then Becky and Ben eventually came to my rescue and life seemed worth living again. The same thing could happen to Molly, if she survived.

"I guess we are lucky that God sees into our hearts, instead of judging us from the way we behave at times," I said. "Do you think there is any chance she and Bradley will get back together? He must love her, or he wouldn't have ask her to marry him."

NJ cleared his throat before responding. "I'm not so sure anyone would be willing to take a chance with her after the stunt she pulled. I mean no disrespect but Molly must be totally off the old rocker to do all that cutting. There are bound to be scars, and a whole lot of them from what I saw. It wouldn't surprise me if Bradley let her have a go of it alone, even if tests confirm the baby is his. He has dozens of young things flocking around him. His old man is loaded and young Bradley stands to inherit everything, as long as he doesn't step out of line. Girls go for things like that, even if the bloke treats them like trash once he is through with them. Daddy expects him to marry wisely."

"Oh," I replied as my frown lines deepened. "I cannot begin to imagine the amount of pain it would take to even consider ending my life. Molly is going to need all of us to help her through this."

The way his jaw moved let me know that NJ had already considered just how much more of his sister's shenanigans he could take.

"Well, I don't know if I can do that," he said. "She's my twin and I love her, but I am not sure I will ever trust her again. It hurts too damned much. You have no idea what it was like finding her in that bathtub with blood splattered and pooled everywhere. I had to shower and change before coming back to the hospital. Mum would go bonkers if she knew how really bad it was. We could have lost her before I even arrived. I still don't know why her roomie didn't call the ambulance straight away, but I guess she got scared."

"I'm sure it was an awful scene and not one that will ever be completely forgotten."

"You're bloody right about that, cuz. I'm not sure I will ever have another decent night's sleep wondering if she will try it again. Why can't she understand that her actions affect everyone who loves her? Even if she has the baby, there will be others blokes in her life. It's not like Bradley is God's gift to every woman—although he will likely inherit millions if his father doesn't disown him first."

I thought about trusting other people as we sat near each other in the waiting room on the psych floor of the hospital. It was eerily dark outside, and the lighting inside the building was so dim it would have been difficult to read anything by. I had my scriptures in my purse, but they stayed there as we stood vigil waiting for word on how Molly and the baby were doing.

NJ finally rested his head against the wall, propped his feet on a worn end table and fell into a troubled asleep. The soft rhythm of his breathing when he wasn't thrashing around was oddly comforting. I wasn't alone any longer, although it felt like it most of the time. I had my family, and while our lives had taken very different directions, we still supported each other in times of crisis. Perhaps someday, we would share a few of the joys of living as well.

The sun had made its appearance in the sky when Aunt Nora came through the double doors leading to the patient's rooms. She was a tall woman, five feet and eleven inches, but she looked much shorter and infinitely more tired than she had a few hours earlier.

"How's Molly?" I asked, taking her arm and leading her towards the sofa next to where NJ was still trying to sleep.

"My poor baby," she moaned, starting to cry. "She looks so small and helpless."

"But NJ said she would be okay."

"Physically, but I don't know about her mental state. How could she consider taking her own life, and the life of my grandchild? I must have failed her miserably as a mother."

"This isn't your fault, Aunt Nora."

"But suicide, Brylee. What if she had succeeded?"

"We can't think about that right now. We just have to thank God that both she and the baby are still with us."

I knew my words rang hollow. Molly wasn't out of danger yet and neither was her unborn child. That was bad enough, but if my aunt knew the secret that was being kept from her, she would never be able to leave her daughter alone again. I hated that I had been drawn into such a repugnant deception, but breaking my promise to NJ would only make matters far worse than they already were.

He suddenly stirred and opened his eyes as his feet hit the floor. "How's she doing? I could have sat with her, mum. You look like hell."

I frowned at him, but Aunt Nora didn't flinch.

"She is still sleeping. The doctor should be here soon. I thought I might wash my face and get a cup of coffee before he comes."

"I'll get the coffee," NJ volunteered. "How about you, cuz? Coffee or tea?"

"Neither, I'm good," I told him. I had purchased an apple and some orange juice from the vending machine in the waiting room. It was the only thing that had kept me awake through the night.

"I should have insisted you go on to a hotel, but I couldn't leave Molly," Aunt Nora said after NJ left. "People think she is spoiled and sleeps around, but she is really just a little girl who wants to be loved and accepted. Now, her wedding is off, and she told me when she woke up for a few minutes that she wants to give my grandchild away if it survives. She can't bear the thought of seeing it everyday."

"People say lots of things they don't really mean when they are hurt and angry."

"I tried to tell Molly that, but she insists it is over. She said she wouldn't have Bradley back now even if he begged and pleaded. He called her a 'white trash whore'. How can a bloke say something like that to a girl who is carrying his child—a girl he asked to marry him?"

I had no answer for her. Molly was learning the hard way, as I had done, that actions have consequences. I could never condemn nor judge her for the mistakes she had made. She was just trying to muddle through life like the rest of us, only she didn't have a spiritual foundation to help show her the way.

"Would it be okay if I went in and sat with her while you wash up and drink your coffee?" I asked my aunt. There was nothing I could say to make the situation better for any of them, but maybe giving her a little time to digest what had happened would help.

"I suppose that could be arranged since you are family," Aunt Nora replied. "Maybe she would be more willing to talk to you than her brother or me. She is more than confused right now."

The nurse on duty gave her okay, and I made my way to Molly's room while Aunt Nora washed her face. My cousin tried to sit up in her white, metal bed when the door creaked open, but heavy straps around both her wrists and her ankles prevented it. I had never seen her looking less-than-perfect before and had to avert my eyes more than once to keep from staring. A baby bump was clearly visible underneath the light covering. How could she not have suspected she was pregnant until two weeks ago? Her body was changing so rapidly.

"Go ahead and say it," she retorted as I approached. "I have been a selfish boob for worrying everyone. Though I don't know why anyone cares. My life is over, whether I have this baby or not."

It seemed pointless to avoid the topic at hand since she seemed so willing to bring it up. "I am sorry for what happened, Molly, but you know your life isn't over."

Her narrowed eyes let me know that at least her interest had been aroused.

"I thought you would be happy to find out I am in the family way. I deliberately flirted with Jake because I knew he liked you."

"Jake and I aren't together. We never have been."

"Well, you should be. I was so jealous of the way he looked at you. I just wanted someone to look at me like that."

"But you're beautiful, Molly. You have guys falling all over you."

"Only because they want something and know I will give it to them. That's why Bradley doesn't trust that the baby is his. He knows I sleep around, but then so does he. I hate the double standard between men and women. If a girl sleeps with a lot of blokes, she's a slut, but if a bloke sleeps with lots of women he is known as a stud. The whole thing makes me sick."

"We all make mistakes. It's part of living."

"Not you, Brylee. You are so calm and collected. I don't think anything could rattle you."

Her assessment of my character was surprising. "You seem to forget that I ran away from home after my mother died, and I have done lots of other things I am not so proud of."

She frowned. "But Jake is still crazy about you, and he is every girl's dream."

"Our relationship is complicated," I said, hating the words as they slipped out. Everything was complicated now days. It was one of those phrases that had been used so often it no longer had any meaning, but it still seemed appropriate for so many situations.

"Life really sucks," Molly said. "You have the sexiest bloke in the world wanting you, and yet you do nothing about it. I get pregnant, and the bloke I'm with wants a paternity test. Just how messed up is that?"

"Is there any reason to believe the baby isn't his?" I asked.

"There's a fifty-fifty chance. I only slept with one other guy after we became exclusive. I couldn't help myself. Evan and I have been friends forever, and when Bradley and I had a fight, I turned to him because I knew he would always be there for me. And now one stupid mistake has ruined my life. I will never find anyone else who can give me what Bradley can."

"Are you sure what he can give you is what you really want?"

She looked at me with confusion. "His father is loaded, and everything will go to him someday. I would never have to work a day in my life and there would be someone around to fill my every need. It is the only kind of life I have ever wanted."

"Maybe you can still have it," I said. "If you have the paternity test, and the baby is Bradley's, you could get married as planned."

She settled back on the pillow, pouting like a child. "But he called me a slut, Brylee. How can I forgive that? I am good enough to sleep with, but not good enough to marry, unless he has proof that the baby is his. I hate all of them!"

I sat with her until she fell asleep again. My compassion for the condition she was in was rather astounding. Notwithstanding her flaws and mistakes, Molly was in pain, and I wanted to help her. If the state of affairs with Bradley didn't change, I was afraid of what might happen to all Uncle Ned's family.

NJ took me to Molly's apartment later that morning so I could rest. Aunt Nora refused to leave the hospital after the doctor informed her that Molly would have to stay where she was until she was no longer a threat to herself or the baby. She was to begin therapy that afternoon, and once she was released, someone had to be with her around-the-clock, likely until after the baby was born. I knew Aunt Nora would not be returning to the outback with me.

Molly shared an off-campus apartment, just a few blocks away from the hospital, with a girl named Suzette who—aside from calling NJ when she found Molly in the bathtub bleeding —spent most of her time in her own bedroom twittering and texting. According to him, the girls had very little in common, and the living arrangement worked because they had very different tastes in men. I couldn't help but wonder if he might be oversimplifying things. The girls I had roomed with in college had different interests too, but that didn't stop the disagreements. Catfights with name-calling and hair pulling had been a regular occurrence but thankfully, I had never been a part of it.

Suzette wasn't there when we arrived, but NJ had a key and let both of us in. The living area was large and filled with sunlight—very different from the places I had lived in L.A. They had a big screen TV, nice furniture and plenty of food in the fridge.

NJ fell asleep on the settee after showing me which bedroom belonged to his sister. He asked me to wake him by 3:30 so he wouldn't miss another class. Despite his insistence that he would never sleep again, he seemed to be doing plenty of dozing.

The first thing I did after promising him that I would make sure he wasn't late was to fall on my knees by the side of

Molly's queen-sized bed and ask God for guidance in knowing how to help her. She had confided in me before I left her room that she really liked the guy named Evan better than Bradley, but he couldn't give her the kind of life she wanted. I decided against telling her that money couldn't buy happiness. That was something she would have to discover for herself.

I closed my eyes until the alarm I had set went off, but I needn't have worried about waking NJ up. He was pacing back and forth across the living room rug when I left Molly's bedroom.

"Did you get any sleep?" he asked me.

I looked into his red-rimmed eyes. "About as much as you did, I would surmise, but you have to believe that everything will turn out alright. Molly isn't stupid. She just found herself in a very difficult situation."

"I know I can't blame her entirely for getting into trouble again. If I would told mum and pops the first time this happened, they would have cut her off financially and insisted she come home."

"I'm not sure that would have solved anything."

"You are probably right. My sister is definitely a free spirit, and Jake would not have stood a chance if she had been around the past couple of years. Come to think of it, that was one of the reasons our folks practically dragged her away from the ranch kicking and screaming in the first place. Molly has never been afraid to admit that she has the hots for him, even when she was jailbait."

I didn't want to think about Jake becoming involved with my younger cousin. I was having enough trouble dealing with the fact that he now sleeping with a waitress who wasn't about to let him go.

"Jake is his own man," I responded, hoping my tone didn't give away the complexity of the situation I was trying to escape. "I have never known him to do anything he really opposed."

NJ laughed. "He was always my idol, getting every girl in town. I wanted to be just like him when I grew up."

"Are you like him?" I asked.

"Likely as close as I will ever be. I can get plenty of girls, but have to work at it occasionally. With Jake, it comes naturally."

He looked at his watch and decided he had spent enough time talking to me. "I will see you at the hospital later. I have a test to pass if I don't want to wash out of a very difficult class."

He had only been gone long enough for me to get a drink of water when someone knocked on the door. When I drew it open, I found myself facing a young man who seemed genuinely surprised by my presence. He looked back down the hallway as if to make sure he had rapped on the right door.

"Is Molly here?" he asked with a frown on his pleasant-looking face. He reminded me of a much younger Uncle Ned. He was tall and broad-shouldered with light brown hair and sparkling blue eyes.

"She isn't home right now," I told him.

He shifted his weight from one foot to the other. "Could I wait? There is something I really need to talk to her about."

It was my turn to feel uncomfortable. Just how much should I tell a stranger about my cousin, but I couldn't just slam the door in his face. "She might not be back for a few days, but I could give her a message when I see her again."

"That won't work," he said as the lines deepened between his eyes. "I have to tell her myself that it doesn't matter what she decides about the baby. I will always be here for her."

His honesty touched my heart. I didn't know who he was, but he obviously cared a great deal about my cousin.

"Would you like to come in for a few minutes?" I asked, stepping away from the door. "I'm Molly's cousin, Brylee."

He walked past me into the living room and sat down on the sofa, clasping his hands together around one of his knees. I sat down in a chair across the room from him wondering what

I could say that might dispel the awkwardness that seemed to surround us.

"I don't mean to speak out of turn, but since you are family, I am just going to say what I have been thinking about for weeks," he said, staring at a spot of something on the carpet. "I don't think it would be such a bad thing if I turned out to be the father of Molly's baby. I may not live in a fancy house or have unlimited pocket change, but I love her and will do whatever it takes to make a home for her and the baby. Heck, I don't even care if the baby is mine. I just want to be part of their lives, if they will have me."

Tears clouded my vision without warning. This had to be Evan—the young man Molly had told me about. No wonder she said that she loved him. He was warm, tender and sincere —qualities a girl doesn't often consider until she is involved with, or married to, the wrong man.

I looked over at him and smiled. "Molly mentioned you when I talked to her this morning."

"Then she is in town," he said. "Please tell me where she is."

Would I be betraying my cousin if I told him what had happened and where she was? Or was he the one person who could convince her that the world wasn't so bleak and dismal after all? I weighed my options and quickly decided to tell him part of what I knew.

"Molly is in the hospital."

His look was one of agony. "I knew something was wrong. I should have come to the apartment last night. Is she alright?"

"Molly and the baby are both fine."

"Then why are they in the hospital? She was in good spirits when I saw her the day before yesterday."

"I suppose you could say that she had an upsetting experience."

"If Bradley hurt her in any way! The rich, lying . . . . Well, I won't tell you what I really think of him."

"They broke up," I said and then watched as his eyes narrowed to thin lines.

"I hate saying I'm not surprised, but Molly is not the first girl he has used and tossed aside for the very same reason."

It was my turn to frown. What kind of a man was this Bradley anyway? If Evan was right, she would be better off without him because he would only break her heart again if she went back to him.

"Did you really mean it when you said you would stick by Molly, even if the baby isn't yours?" I asked.

He didn't even hesitate. "Absolutely! It's not like a bloke gets to raise his own kids that often anymore. It's more about love than biology."

"If you really feel that way, then maybe you should go to the hospital and see Molly. She is a very confused young woman right now."

He didn't ask me why she was there, but then perhaps he knew her better than any of the rest of us did. I stood up when he did, and escorted him to the door.

"Thank you," he said, giving me an uncomfortable hug. "I will help Molly see that there is more to life than having money."

"I'm sure you will," I replied as he turned, walked down the hall and disappeared into the sunshine outside.

I liked Evan a lot. He was down-to-earth and friendly. Molly could do a whole lot worse than being with a man who so obviously adored and accepted her for the person she was now, not the person he might wish her to be. It made me think about Jake, and the fact that I couldn't seem to accept him without going through some makeover. No wonder he had determined it was time to move on with someone else.

Chapter 4

When Aunt Nora walked through the apartment door a couple of hours later she was a changed woman.

"I feel like celebrating," she said, giving me one of her warmest smiles. "I don't know how Evan found out where Molly was, but talk about a God-send. My little girl was laughing when I left."

"I am so glad," I responded as the corners of my lips found their way upwards. This was the closest thing I hd seen to miracle in a very long time. "I like that young man."

She sank down into the chair I had just vacated. "So you were the one who told him where he could find her. Molly has decided that she is not going to have the paternity test right now, and you will never believe what happened after that. Evan proposed, right there in the hospital room, and she accepted. I have never seen anything more romantic."

"Wow," I said, not wanting to dampen my aunt's spirits with my doubts about rebound relationships and timing after what I had been through with Jake. She deserved to have something restore her peace of mind.

"I know it is sudden," she continued. "But the moment he walked into the room, Molly just came alive. He walked straight over to the bed, took her in his arms and held her while she cried. He didn't even ask about the bandages on her arms and legs."

"He seems very genuine in his feelings for her, but it does surprise me that she is not going to find out who the father of her child is," I said, wishing I was a good enough person to be happy for her without wanting a little happiness of my own. "What if Bradley changes his mind?"

"She says she will cross that bridge when, or if, it ever comes. And if the bum turns out to be the father, she will demand child support. I am really not surprised by anything he says or does. Molly told me that he already has another child, a little girl that he is not claiming. His parents are paying out a great deal of money to avoid a scandal. They want a legitimate heir from a girl with good breeding. I say, good luck finding it with a son like the one they have. He will never find a girl better than my Molly."

I was grateful things had turned out so well, but it was hard not having a few doubts since everything had happened so rapidly. Molly could just as easily change her mind again before morning.

NJ joined us for a late dinner. His test had gone well. Aunt Nora talked to Uncle Ned several times during the course of the meal, but they only discussed Molly, the baby and Evan. It was now Monday night, and Trevor would be back at school. I wondered if he had missed me over his weekend at the ranch, or if the waitress from the diner had kept him company during my absence. But I was too scared and embarrassed to bring up the subject with anyone.

Aunt Nora paid the bill at the restaurant—refusing to let either NJ or me do it—and we went back to the hospital. Molly was sitting up in bed, and Evan was stretched out beside her. She had a pad of paper on her lap and was twirling a pen around in her fingers. They gave us co-conspirator looks when we all entered the room. There had been no one in the hallway to stop us.

"And just what is this that we have walked in on?" Aunt Nora asked her daughter.

"Evan and I have been making plans, mum," Molly responded, smiling demurely at the young man who had turned her life so dramatically around. "We don't want to wait until after the baby comes to get married. We want to be a real family when that happens."

I looked down at the floor, not wanting to see the look on my aunt's face. Aunt Nora might be a mother, but she had never been a bride.

"So, I guess that means no long engagement," she said, choosing not to be upset by her daughter's less-than-thoughtful remark.

"Just long enough to make a few plans. Evan graduates in a couple of months and has a job waiting for him in Brisbane. He wants me to go with him."

Aunt Nora dropped into the nearest chair while Molly continued with her news.

"We were thinking about two weeks from last Saturday at St. Marks. He has already called and the church is available. Father Ray will perform the ceremony, and we can have a lovely party at the Bayside Reception Center afterwards. We have already checked and it just happens to be free. How perfect is that?"

"But Molly!" Aunt Nora exclaimed. "What you are asking is impossible! We would never be ready in time. Besides, your families haven't even met each other."

"I called father earlier," Molly replied. "He is fine with it and said he would drive over to meet Evan's family before the wedding. They live right here in Sydney and attend St. Mark's Cathedral. It is the perfect solution to everything, can't you see that?"

She smiled at her husband-to-be, and I felt a jab in my heart. Was it jealousy, or just the sudden thought that my young cousin was only looking for a way out of the mess she was in?

"It helps to have friends in high places," Evan said, kissing her forehead.

"But what about the big wedding you always wanted—the one with champagne, a beautiful white dress, and a dozen bridesmaids? You won't have that if the wedding takes place in less than two weeks. That doesn't even give people time enough to make travel arrangements."

"I might have to make a few adjustments—like calling people instead of sending out invitations—but Evan and I decided we would rather have the money spent on a lavish wedding for setting up our own little home and getting ready for the baby. If that is agreeable with everyone involved, of course. We wouldn't even ask for money, but it would come in handy with the move and all."

"That's it! What have you done with my real sister?" NJ asked, looking at the smiling couple on the bed. "This is not the Molly I grew up with, not even the one I had coffee with on Friday."

"It is the new and improved Molly," his twin responded. "When Evan came to see me everything just fell into place. I want to have the kind of relationship all our parents do—one based on love, understanding and sharing."

There were tears of joy in her eyes as she snuggled contentedly into her future husband's arms.

"I finally realized that I have been chasing the wrong dream. Money doesn't mean anything if I can't share my life with the man I really love. I was afraid to admit that before Evan came to see me looking like I do right now—all bandaged up and such—but I am not scared any more because of him. He is just what I need to be happy, and I really don't mind struggling a bit at first because I will have my best friend standing right there beside me. It can't get any better than that, now can it, dear brother."

Tears were sliding from the corners of my eyes, and I wiped them away with the backs of my hands. For a girl who had sliced up both her arms and her legs less than forty-eight hours earlier—believing that her life was over—Molly had certainly made a miraculous recovery.

"In that case," Aunt Nora said as she wiped the tears from her own eyes. "I guess we have our work cut out. I have never planned a wedding and haven't the faintest idea where to begin."

"Not to worry, Ms. Hawkins," Evan interjected. "I have four older sisters, and my mum has become a pro at planning weddings. I know she will do anything necessary to make sure her baby boy gets married right, and to the girl he has loved since the moment they met. All you have to do is give her a call. She knows the best florists and bakeries in the city."

"Then that is exactly what I will do." Aunt Nora looked over at me. "But I'm afraid I will have to ask you to stay until after the big day, Brylee. It will take all of us working together to pull this off."

I assured her that I would be glad to remain for as long as needed, but inside I was less than enthusiastic. The upcoming nuptials might seem like the perfect resolution to Molly's problems, but there were still far too many questions that needed answers. The first being whether the doctor would even release her from the hospital that soon. She was under psychiatric care and what we perceived as a miracle might mean something entirely different to them.

And the paternity of Molly's baby could still be problematic. From everything I had heard about Bradley, he sounded like a cold, ruthless man who used people for pleasure and then cast them aside at will. But that didn't mean he would not try to make life miserable for the newlyweds if the baby was his. Hurt pride provoked some truly hateful things.

I called Trevor early the next morning to apologize for my actions and let him know that I would be staying in Sydney until after the wedding. I assured him that he was welcome to come and Uncle Ned would be more than happy to pick him up on his way through Edna to the city, but he said he would rather spend his weekends at the ranch with Jake and his animals. I had hurt him with my selfish behavior, and it would take time to repair the damage. He didn't say anything about the waitress, Beth, or if she had spent any time with them. And my asking about it wouldn't change anything.

Calling the ranch wasn't any easier. I didn't want to talk to Jake, but I had family responsibilities that went far beyond my wounded ego or broken heart. If I was really lucky, he would still be in town and I could leave a message, but he picked up the phone on the third ring. I was using NJ's cell since I hadn't renewed the contract on mine. It seemed pointless now that there was no one special to call, even if I could get cell phone coverage at the ranch.

"Hey, there, old man," Jake said in a lighthearted tone. "Are you calling to swap stories on our various lady friends again? I do have a few new ones to tell."

"It's not NJ," I said, willing my voice to remain steady so it wouldn't betray just how much the sound of his voice and his comment hurt me. "This is Brylee. I thought you might still be in town."

"Why should I be? It's the middle of the week."

I wanted to lash out for the anguish he was causing. He did go into town during the week. Hadn't he done that very thing only two days before I went to the coast? He had left on Wednesday and hadn't come back until the weekend. But now wasn't the time to dredge up the past, or the fact that the consolidation of the ranches might never see fruition.

The news of a joyous occasion needed to be spread, and Jake needed to know that I would not be coming back until after the wedding. My staying away for that amount of time should make him deliriously happy because he wouldn't have to worry about seeing me unexpectedly.

"No matter! I just wanted you to know that Molly is getting married a week from next Saturday, and I will be staying in Sydney until after the wedding. Aunt Nora needs my help, and I am sure you can get along just fine without me."

"I heard as much from Ned," he said, ignoring my reference to myself. "It seems a little sudden, but then what do I know about love and commitment."

When I didn't respond, he continued.

"I am sorry for what happened between us, Brylee, especially that the way I presented my decision made even seeing me so distasteful. But whether you believe it or not, I have been worried about you."

"There is nothing to worry about. I'm fine. I just needed some alone time to sort things out."

"Have you done that?"

"Not completely, but I am working on it."

I could see him standing in the kitchen, his shoulder pressed against the wall as he talked to me. Only this time there would be no animation in his face, only the disappointment and anger that had been there the day we went to the cave.

"I read the note you left. I know I can be a real jerk sometimes, but I don't want us to be enemies. We still have Trevor, LeAnn and the baby to think about."

"Those are exactly the people I am most concerned about," I responded.

"Are you sure about that?" he asked. "Trevor missed you over the weekend."

"He said he had fun with you."

"Did he also tell you I found him crying in the attic? He couldn't understand what he had done that made you leave."

"He didn't do anything."

"That's what I told him. I also said that things would be a little different when you came home again."

I held my breath and waited. If Jake had told him about moving on with Beth, Trevor would hate me because I had been the one to break up our rather-strange family again. It wouldn't matter that I had some of my own issues to deal with.

"Don't worry, Brylee," he continued while I was trying to order my dismal thoughts. "I didn't give him any details. But he is a bright kid who can figure things out by himself."

"I really am sorry about everything," I said.

"You shouldn't have to be sorry for standing up for what you believe. I may not understand or agree, but it appears to be the most important thing in your life. That's all that really matters, isn't it?"

Oh, how I wanted him to understand that religious beliefs were for everyone, but how could he possibly grasp my desire to return home to a God he wasn't sure even existed? He was only living his life according to the rules he had always known. They just happened to be very different from mine.

"I guess so," I said, suddenly wishing I could talk to him in person. If I could look into his eyes, I would know if there was even a chance for compromise that might make it easier for us to keep the ranch in the family.

His deep, heartfelt and dramatic sigh, instead of saying something, had a crushing effect on me. If I hadn't known that I loved him before, I certainly knew it now. There was no other explanation as to why I felt like my world was dropping out of orbit again. I had fully decided to be happy and let my inner joy show while at Emma's beach house. But now that I was back in my own dismal and confusing life without Jake in it, I was no better off than Molly who just a few hours earlier had been cutting herself because she no longer saw a reason to go on.

"What is Molly's rich boyfriend like?" he suddenly asked, almost as if he wanted to keep our conversation going. "Ned didn't say anything about him."

"They broke up," was my quick and simple reply.

"But you just said she is getting married in less than two weeks."

"She is, but not to the same guy."

He laughed. "Our Molly is certainly one little vixen. I thought she was pregnant."

"She is."

"And she isn't going to marry the baby's father? I would say that is quite a change of plans."

"Paternity has yet to be established."

I hated discussing family issues with anyone, but Jake was part of the family and would know soon enough whether it came from me or someone else.

"And I thought our lives were thorny. I don't suppose you have met either of the blokes."

"I've met Evan—the man she is going to marry. I really believe he is one of the good guys and from what I have observed, they are devoted to each other."

"As apposed to me," he interjected with distain. "You didn't say anything about love."

"I thought that was implied with the term devotion. I don't think he has left the hospital since he asked her to marry him."

"Then I am happy for both of them. I just wish you weren't going to be away for such a long time. With this change in plans, Ned will want to be part of them, and I could use the help."

"You will be fine without me."

"I'm sure I will. I have been running this ranch practically alone for ages now, but I miss my sparing partner. It is rather dull around here without someone telling me what I am doing wrong all the time."

"I never meant to criticize, Jake. You have every right to decide how you live your life."

"I guess we both do," he countered. "Sometimes I wish I had the trusting faith you do. It is one of your more endearing qualities."

"Should I be saying *thank you*?" I asked. "I'm not sure if that was a compliment or a putdown."

"Maybe a little of both. I hope you know that I would never do anything to intentionally hurt you."

"No," I thought, ending our conversation with a quick goodbye. "But you did it anyway by getting involved with someone else the very day you said it was over for us. You may have thought I didn't care, but I did. And now I am left to suffer in silence while everyone else gets exactly what they want."

To say that the next ten days were a blur of activity was an understatement. The doctor was surprised at Molly's rapid recovery and could find no reason to keep her in the hospital for more than a day or two as long as she promised to attend therapy faithfully until the baby was born. She didn't tell him that she was planning on moving away from Sydney long before then, but I was confident Evan would help her find another therapist in Brisbane if he felt she still needed one.

He was at the hospital with her whenever he wasn't in class. I had never seen such attentiveness and support, and Molly looked happier than she had ever been before. But I had the uneasy feeling that my younger cousin was living in that proverbial house made of straw where one strong gust of wind could cause everything to come crashing down. I believed she should have the paternity test before any vows were exchanged, but no one asked for my opinion and I didn't offer it.

Aunt Nora was in a continual dither of activity. She wanted everything to be perfect for her daughter's wedding.

"I don't know how mum can be so sure Molly won't relapse," NJ said as we sat together at a table in the hospital cafeteria eating muffins on Thursday morning. Molly was being released before noon.

"Your mother says she is doing remarkably well in therapy and some of the cuts on her arms and legs are healing nicely."

"Any girl can be happy for a few days, especially when all the attention is focused on her. I am far more worried about what will happen when everyone goes home, and she is left sitting alone in some apartment with no diversions to keep her occupied. She has missed too many classes to get credit for this semester, and Evan can't be with her twenty-four seven."

"Your mother plans on staying close by until the baby is born."

"And do what?" he challenged. "They will drive each other crazy. Mum can't sit still, and Molly isn't the most motivated lass in the world. Besides, it will only be a few weeks until the happy couple moves north to Brisbane. Mum can't desert the rest of her responsibilities just because her daughter might need her."

"It sounds like you might be a little jealous of your sister."

He snorted his objection. "That is the last thing I am right now. I am simply worried about what will happen if something goes wrong. I know Bradley, and he is not going to take her marriage to Evan well. He might not be inclined to marry her himself, but if the baby turns out to be his, he could make life bloody unpleasant for them. In spite of her faults, I love my sister dearly and don't want to see her involved in anything else she might not be able to handle."

"Then we will just have to pray that things work out for all of them. A baby deserves to be raised in a family where parents love each other and are committed to making their marriage work."

"I'm not exactly a religious man," NJ interjected. "But this is one time I really hope there is a God who will watch out for Molly when I can't be there to protect her."

His admission surprised me. "You are a good brother, NJ, and she is lucky to have you."

"Maybe someday she will recognize me for the great bloke I am and start treating me with some respect, but no more dismal talk right now. Come clubbing with me tomorrow night. You have been in Sydney for several days now and haven't seen anything but the inside of the hospital and Molly's apartment."

"Not true," I told him. "Your mother and I went to the florists and the bakery yesterday, and we are taking Molly to all the bridal shops in the vicinity to look for a dress as soon as she is released from the hospital."

"You can count me out of that little excursion," he said. "I have been shopping with my sister before, and it takes her forever to decide on something as simple as a new shade of lipstick. I hope you are ready for a bloody long day."

"I think I can manage. A girl only gets married once, at least that's the way it is supposed to be, and she wants to look her very best."

"Women and their wedding plans," he scoffed. "If you ask me, it's just an excuse to spend the old man's money. It would be just as legal if they went to the Justice of the Peace."

"And where is the fun in that?" I asked.

"I'm sorry, Brylee," he said, suddenly looking at me with cousinly concern. "All this wedding talk must be bringing back some very unpleasant memories. You would already be married if you hadn't come home to see your father and been roped into becoming a part of all this bloody Hawkins' family drama."

"I wouldn't have missed those weeks with my father for anything, and what happened in the past can't be changed."

"Sometimes the future can't be either. I hate being the bearer of more bad news, but has Molly told you whom she has asked to be her maid of honor, Beth Stanton."

I felt my throat constrict, and I had to swallow to keep from choking. Jake must have told him at least a portion of what had happened between us, or he would not be warning me now. "You mean the waitress from the diner?"

"That very same. They were best friends in high school, although Molly was a year younger. I really thought they had a parting of the way since both of them had it bad for Jake, but I guess true love does conquer all. Molly has Evan, and I understand that Beth and Jake have been seeing each other lately. She couldn't wait to fill Molly in on all the juicy details about them being a couple."

I looked down at the half muffin on the plate in front of me wishing it could open up and devour me. Was there no way I could get away from Jake and is new ladylove?

"Look," NJ said, obviously noticing my distress and reaching out his hand until it covered mine. "I am sorry for letting the cat out of the bag but figured it would be better coming from me since I actually have your back. I always thought Jake and you would get together. There was this unmistakable spark that drove Molly nearly crazy."

"There isn't a spark now," I told him.

"I figured something must have happened because you have both been acting more than a little whacked out lately, but it is not polite to ask unwanted questions."

"I appreciate both your candor and your support, but there is really nothing to tell. What we might have had ended before it even began."

"Then it should come as no surprise that Molly invited Jake too."

"It's her wedding," I said, fighting back the bitter disappointment that was beginning to consume me again.

How could things have happened so fast for them? Jake and I had only been apart for ten days.

"Listen, cuz, like I said before, I am not one to stick my nose where it isn't wanted, but if you ever need to talk, I am here for you."

I knew he was only trying to be supportive, but I would never take him up on his offer because men talked about the women they were seeing. Jake had let me know that quite clearly when I used NJ's phone to tell him I would not be coming home until after the wedding.

We parted a short time later so he could attend class and I could join my aunt and cousin for an afternoon of shopping that would only cause more unwanted feelings to surface. I had come home to make things right with my father and now that part of my life was gone, and I had never even had the opportunity to look at wedding dresses for myself.

Still, notwithstanding NJ's unsolicited information and my own tumultuous feelings, I tried to be happy and helpful because it was the right thing to do. There was nothing modest for sale in any of the shops we visited, but that wasn't a priority for my cousin since she would be getting married in a Catholic cathedral where elaborate attire was more than just encouraged. The opulence of the building alone made it a requirement.

Molly tried on dress after dress. Most of them were strapless and beautiful, but she had trouble deciding on the exact one she wanted. Despite her belief about sex outside of marriage being acceptable, she didn't want to look pregnant on her wedding day. She wanted the guests to know that she was marrying Evan because she loved him, not because she was going to have a baby that might not even be his.

"Beth will be here on Tuesday," Molly said as we were looking through a rack of bridesmaid dresses. "I would have asked you to be my maid of honor instead, but we have been friends forever, and it wouldn't be right to exclude her. I think she is almost as excited as I am."

She gave me an odd look before sliding a satiny, peach-colored dress to the end of the rack.

"You don't owe me any explanations," I told her, but it was impossible not to wonder just how much Beth Stanton had shared about her deepening relationship with Jake. There had certainly been no reservation when it came to talking about him with me.

"I know," she said, pausing before pulling a strapless, yellow, floor-length gown from the rack and holding it up in front of me. "But we are family, even though we don't know each other very well. I was always jealous of you, Brylee, with your big, bedroom eyes and gorgeous figure."

"That's interesting because I have been jealous of you for basically the same reasons," I responded. "The only difference is that guys have always been interested in you. That has never happened to me."

"It's kind of hard for them not to notice since I plant myself right in front of their faces. You are the kind of girl a bloke wants to marry and take care of."

"Well, that didn't exactly work out for me," I carelessly responded.

"I don't know about the guy you were going to marry, but there are plenty of others around if you would just give them half a chance. Even Evan said you were beautiful."

I watched her intently to see if I could figure out where the conversation was heading. I hadn't said more than a sentence or two to Evan since the day I told him Molly was in the hospital and he should visit her. Aunt Nora was a rack away looking at dresses suitable for the mother of the bride.

Molly didn't seem to notice my lack of response to the first compliment she had ever given me. She hung the yellow dress back on the rack without even glancing in my direction.

"Evan is the best chap in the world—and he chose me—so I can afford to be generous with other women now. He said all the Hawkins' women were beautiful, even my mum."

"Your mother is beautiful," I told her. "And all any of us want is for you to be happy."

"I am happy, Brylee. And don't get me wrong, I was thrilled when Bradley asked me to marry him, but I knew it would never work. He has already moved on with someone else. It's like the baby and me never existed, and that is exactly the way he wants to keep it. It's probably a genetic thing since his father has affairs all the time too, but his mother lets him because she doesn't want to lose the big house, fancy cars, servants, and trips around the world. I used to think those were the most important things in life, but Evan has shown me that a marriage without love and commitment would be very lonely. I just wish you could find someone else now that Ben is no longer part of your life."

"I'm sure I will when the time is right," I assured her with a forced smile and misty eyes.

I had lost the three most important men in my life in the past eight months, and it was highly unlikely that my handsome knight would swoop down and rescue me any time soon. But I had to go on living, despite the pain, so I followed my aunt and cousin around Sydney for the rest of the afternoon trying to look happy and engaged when all I wanted was to find a good hiding place.

Chapter 5

With Molly out of the hospital, Aunt Nora booked a suite at the Hilton closest to the university for us. I offered to help pay the bill, but she wouldn't allow it. So we slept like queens at night and scurried around like rabbits during the day to make sure everything was perfect for Molly's wedding. Despite my broken heart, I really did want my cousin to have the wedding of her dreams.

On Friday evening, we attended a barbecue at Evan's family home. Uncle Ned wanted to come, but the ranch wouldn't take care of itself and Jake couldn't run both properties for more than a day or two on his own. Incorporation really was the most viable alternative to our ever-increasing problems, but everyone needed to be there for it to work.

Molly's future in-laws were lovely, gracious people and seemed genuinely accepting of their son's bride and rushed wedding. If they knew about the circumstances surrounding the baby or Molly's attempted suicide, they gave no indication of it. Molly wore a long-sleeved light sweater over her ankle-length sundress to hide the scabs that were starting to form.

After very little deliberation, she decided to wear white gloves that came up past her elbows to her wedding. From what I observed, she was embarrassed by what she had done and didn't want anyone feeling sorry for her or worrying that she might try it again.

We ate pulled pork, fresh fruit and vegetables with all kinds of pies for dessert. NJ stayed close beside me the entire evening, partially because we were the only unattached guests at the party, with the exception of the children who climbed in and out of the pool spraying water at everyone who sat or stood close to it.

"Why don't we blow this gig and head to a club?" he asked as I sat on a poolside chair watching the little ones play. He was restless, even a total stranger could tell that.

"I'm not much for clubbing. You know that." I told him. "Besides, it would be rude to leave right after dinner."

He sat down beside me and pouted. That was something both of my cousins knew how to do well.

"I know you don't feel any more comfortable here than I do, cuz. So what gives? The two of us would hardly be missed in this family crowd."

"Do you really want to know why I am hesitant about going with you?" I asked as he looked over at me with mitigated interest.

"You mean you have a reason other than not wanting to be seen in public with your cousin?"

"I like being with you, NJ. You are handsome, charming and just sulky enough to be interesting, but I made a promise that I wouldn't go to places like that anymore."

"You don't have to drink," he said. "You could have all the ginger ale you wanted and no one would be the wiser. I know you haven't had a drink of anything stronger than lemonade since you got home."

"It's not just the alcohol. I don't like the atmosphere. There is too much smoke and crude language. Besides, people mainly go there to hook up with someone and that just isn't me."

"So Pops and Jake were both right!" he exclaimed while shaking his head. "They said this church you joined has majorly impacted your lifestyle, but I didn't quite believe them until now."

I felt a stab of anger. People should not be talking about me when I wasn't there to defend my personal choices. But instead of saying something unbecoming and futile, I gritted my teeth and pretended to smile. Making a scene at Molly's engagement party would only give like-minded people more to gossip about, but NJ didn't appear to notice my anguish.

"You're young, Brylee, so why would you willingly give up all the good things life has to offer?"

"Because I found something better."

"Better than being young, carefree and might I say, very attractive?"

I blushed for the briefest moment.

"Yes! It is something that will allow me to be with my family forever while keeping me from doing some very foolish things. I can't think of anything more important than that."

He chuckled and shook his head. "I hate to burst your bubble, cuz, but nobody can guarantee that. This life is all we have, and even if it isn't, we shouldn't waste it by becoming old before our time. We are here to have fun while we can."

I knew my rationale for anything I now believed would be lost on him just as it was on everyone else, except Emma, but it didn't really matter. Someday, they would all learn the truth. But until that time came, I had to be strong enough to keep the covenants I had already made regardless of how odd or foolish they might seem to others. The tiniest slip would be enough for any one of them to discount everything I claimed to cherish.

During the next few days, I followed Molly and Aunt Nora from store to store as they picked out china and silver patterns and a trousseau Molly would be able to wear after the wedding while she waited for her child to arrive. No one talked about the baby's paternity or if Bradley had contacted her. It wasn't exactly like walking on eggshells. It was more like if we didn't talk about it, the truth didn't really matter. But I knew from my own past that secrets hurt people—even when they weren't intentional—and they always came out at the most inopportune times. I certainly hoped Molly would be luckier in that respect than I had been.

Beth Stanton arrived the Tuesday afternoon before the wedding as scheduled. She bubbled into Molly's apartment while I sat at the table trying to make seating arrangements for the reception that would be held at the Coastline Reception Center after the wedding.

"You are absolutely glowing," Beth said, hugging Molly and touching her slightly protruding stomach. "If this is what happens when you get preggie, maybe I had better give it a whirl. You get the guy of your dreams and the baby all at once."

I tried not to listen, but that was impossible in Molly's small apartment. What if Beth really meant it about getting pregnant so the baby's father would marry her? Jake deserved better than being set up, but it wasn't my place to inform him. I had lost any right to share confidences by pushing always him away.

"It's not that easy," Molly told her. "But it is definitely worth it."

"When will I get to meet this dashing bloke who has stolen my best friend's heart?"

"Evan will be here after class to take us to dinner. Did I tell you that we will be moving to Brisbane after he graduates? He has an engineering job there."

"Aren't you the lucky one?" Beth said, throwing her head back and laughing like a giddy teenager. "I would be totally jealous if I hadn't found my own dreamboat right in Edna."

I looked down at the sketches in front of me. My hands were actually shaking.

"So how is that charming devil?" Molly asked, escorting her friend to the sofa where they both sat down.

"Fantastic!" Beth said. "Every single girl in Edna is jealous of me. Jake is the most exciting man I have ever known and we are together every chance we get."

"Is that so," Molly said, and I wondered if she wasn't just the tiniest bit envious. After all, she had been making a play for Jake ever since I had come home, but apparently she was over him now. "You simply have to tell me all the juicy details, staring at the very beginning."

Beth clapped her hands together in sheer delight. "I will save the best parts until later, but his very touch sends me right into orbit."

I had heard far more than I wanted to. Despite his many flaws, Jake deserved someone who cared about the person he was inside, not just the outside package or how quickly he could make a girl do what he wanted her to.

Either Beth didn't recognize me sitting at the table, or she was making sure—as she had done over the telephone—that I knew Jake belonged to her now, even if she had to do something drastic to ensure it.

"I'll leave the two of you to visit," I said, getting to my feet and shuffling the papers in front of me into a stack so I could take them with me. "I told Aunt Nora I would meet her at the hotel so we could finalize the flowers and table decorations."

"I'm sorry," Molly said, looking up from her conversation. "I should have introduced the two of you. Beth, this is my cousin, Brylee."

"We've met," Beth said. Her lips were smiling, but her eyes were menacing. "She came to the diner with Jake a long time ago, and in case you have forgotten dear friend, I saw her again at her father's funeral. I think it's nice that she and Jake are family."

I headed towards the door without stopping for a proper greeting, but that wasn't really necessary since Beth had already set the ground rules regarding our relationship. She wasn't about to let anyone get in her way when it came to making sure Jake never strayed from her side, especially a girl she considered a shirt-tale member of his family.

"I hope you will enjoy your stay in Sydney," I said in passing.

"Oh, I will," she replied. "As soon as Jake gets here, everything will be perfect. It is just so lame going to a wedding alone."

Her remark was aimed in my direction, but I wasn't about to let her see how much it upset me. I didn't want to believe Jake had said anything about what had happened between us to her, but desperate women have a way of finding out what they need to know.

"I will see you in the morning, Molly," I said with a smile. Then I almost ran from the room, closing the door behind me a little too loudly. I had known it would be uncomfortable seeing Beth, but her intentional cruelty amazed me. How could anyone be that insecure or heartless? From what she was implying, it wouldn't be long until she and Jake started picking out china patterns for themselves.

Even with all the obstacles we had to work through from planning a menu to picking out bridal attire, the final days leading up to the wedding went remarkably well. I kept to myself as much as possible, making excuses whenever Beth was around so I wouldn't have to deal with her continual gloating. It helped that I wasn't an actual member of the wedding party, or I would have been forced into more unwanted interactions.

I didn't begrudge her happiness with Jake, but I didn't want to be reminded of it several times each day either. If it wasn't for NJ, I would be the only one involved in the festivities who had no one to share the occasion with, but I still wished he would quit pestering me about club hopping. That was something I simply could not do, although Beth's constant jabs provided tempting moments since I wanted to be happy too.

My biggest stressor when it came to wedding preparations was the long list of students at the university Molly wanted invited to either the wedding, the reception or both. Contacting strangers was not my cup of tea, but even with short notice and lack of proper invitations, they all seemed excited about the upcoming nuptials and confirmed their plans to attend. Evan's sisters were making sure every member of their large, extended family were invited as well.

Feeling very removed from the college scene and not wanting to spend any more time than was necessary with Beth, I spent most of my days and evenings with Aunt Nora. She seemed to appreciate my presence and help since Molly gravitated back to her college and high school friends as soon as she found the perfect wedding dress. If Bradley knew what was transpiring, he never surfaced. That was good for both Molly and Evan because it meant smoother sailing as they began their life together.

Aunt Nora insisted I buy a new dress for the wedding since I hadn't brought one with me. It took several hours of walking through stores before finding one I wouldn't be self-conscious wearing. Most of them were strapless, sideless or had plunging necklines that precluded the wearing of much of anything underneath. I finally found one in a deep green with fake pearls stitched into tiny flounces on the skirt. The bodice was simply cut and with a short, cream-colored sweater it would blend in with the colors Molly had chosen for the wedding. I wished I had the ring my father had gifted me at Christmas since I would finally be wearing something fancy enough to show it off.

Molly wasn't overly concerned about what the rest of us wore as long as it didn't compete with her wedding gown, but she needn't have worried. She was both beautiful and animated, and people were drawn to her whether they wanted to be or not.

Still I was grateful when she approved of the dress I had selected because there really wasn't time for further shopping. Beth said her dress was a surprise she was keeping a secret until Jake saw her in it at the wedding. I hated her constant references to him and the fact that she made sure I knew they talked on the phone each night. As much as I didn't want to believe he had gotten over me so quickly, it certainly appeared that he had.

I talked to LeAnn about a family gift for the couple since she was still confined to bed. She relayed my message to Jake —who was more than happy to chip in on something as long as he didn't have to find it. So I purchased an espresso machine— something Molly had been hounding her mother about ever since Christmas. As a shower gift, I bought her a tasteful pink robe that could be worn long after her wedding night when she was living in a much cooler climate. I was more than certain she would receive all the sexy nightwear she could possibly use from her college friends and they didn't disappoint.

Aunt Nora's intention was to stay in Sydney until the newlyweds returned from their abbreviated honeymoon and were settled in a temporary apartment, but the bride and groom had made plans of their own. They would be storing their gifts and personal belongings in Evan's parent's garage and sleeping in his old room until after graduation when they would rent a moving van and head north. That meant there was nothing constructive for her to do once the wedding was over until moving day arrived. She was trying to be optimistic and cheerful, but I knew her concerns for her daughter ran deep. Molly was on an adrenalin high that would not last forever.

Uncle Ned arrived two days before the wedding. Aunt Nora had ordered his tux and even written a toast he could deliver at the wedding dinner. He was glad about that since he was still having trouble with the idea of giving his daughter away to a man he had only talked to on the phone. But he was absolutely elated when Aunt Nora told him she was coming back to the ranch. She had been gone for nearly two weeks, and he wasn't a man who liked to be left on his own. I loved the idea that they depended on each other so much. That was the way it was supposed to be.

Chapter 6

And then her wedding day arrived. Evan's family had been wonderful. His sisters came up with centerpieces and linens for all the tables, and his mother insisted on making the wedding cake since she had done it for all her daughters when they were married. They even arranged for the church and set up an appointment for Evan and Molly to talk to Father Ray.

Aunt Nora and Uncle Ned took care of the reception center, the dinner, the band and the flowers—two large bouquets of pink roses and Baby's Breath with green satin ribbons for the altar, and a basketful of rose pedals for one of Evan's nieces to strew down the aisle in front of the bride. Molly's bridal bouquet matched the floral arrangements, and her maid-of-honor, Beth, would be wearing a strapless flowered dress in the same colors that I had still not been allowed to see. Her other bridesmaids would wear dresses of a similar style but in solid colors.

I was more than grateful I had slipped into the role of wedding planner because it provided plenty of excuses for being busy when the topic of conversation turned to the men in bridesmaid's lives, making champaign toasts to each other's health, happiness and good fortune and then club hopping at night while Molly was still single. I wanted to become more spiritually grounded and accepting of the life Heavenly Father had in mind for me, and yet the few verbal exchanges I could not escape made me feel old, uptight and unenlightened. Like NJ kept reminding me, I was young and needed to be enjoying myself.

Nonetheless, Molly made a breathtakingly beautiful bride as Uncle Ned escorted her down the aisle at St. Mark's Cathedral at four on Saturday afternoon. She had selected a strapless gown with an empire waistline that effectively concealed her condition. It had layers and layers of silk with beadwork on the bodice and along the hemline. She wore long white gloves that covered the cuts on her forearms. No one at the wedding would ever know the trauma she had been through, unless they were a member of the family or a very trusted friend.

NJ made a handsome best man, and even though I hated admitting it, Beth looked lovely. I knew she was disappointed that Jake hadn't come. I didn't know the reason why because she was completely open when it came to her feelings for him. During the few conversation I had been forced to hear, she called him *love* and never seemed to tire of telling him how much she missed being in his arms and could hardly wait to see him again. No wonder he had turned to her when he realized that a future with me would never happen. I just wished it didn't hurt so much thinking about him spending the rest of his life with her, or even with someone else.

Still, Molly's wedding, while lovely and rehearsed, left me feeling somewhat sad. It was held in a beautiful cathedral under the direction of a priest in costly and impressive robes, but it was nothing like what I had planned with Ben. There would be no aisle or flowers or clapping because it would take place in one of God's holy temples. And when we took our vows they wouldn't be just until death, they would be forever if we lived worthy of it.

I stood on the balcony at the reception center after the bridal dinner and watched Molly and Evan and their guests as they laughed and danced and drank toasts to what we all hoped would be a happy and long-lasting union. Everyone looked cheerful, even Jake's new girlfriend was flirting with some of Evan's bachelor friends. I knew I could be doing the same thing, but my heart just wasn't in it. I was a one-man woman who was beginning to believe that the beautiful and romantic part of my life had simply passed me by.

I was fighting back tears of disillusionment when I heard the sound of a deep voice that literally sent chills up and down my spine.

"You shouldn't be standing up here all alone when you could be part of the festivities below."

I willed my heart to quit racing but couldn't turn around.

"I could say the same thing about you. Beth has been talking non-stop about your relationship all week and was nearly beside herself when she thought you weren't coming."

Jake trailed his fingers along the back of my neck, and then he was standing beside me.

"Has she now," he responded. "I wasn't planning on coming at all, but someone wanted to surprise you."

"Someone," I said, pushing back my longings and forcing myself to look over at him. There was only one person, who was not already here, that would be even remotely interested in seeing me.

"You brought Trevor?"

"That I did! He is waiting at the bottom of the stairs, but you need to pretend that I didn't tell on him. He wanted to surprise you."

Without thinking, I threw my arms around his neck. I think it shocked him almost as much as it did me.

"Thank you, Jake," I whispered. "I can't tell you how much it means to me."

"He misses you. When I gave him the option of staying at the ranch for the entire weekend or coming here, it only took him a second to decide. You are a very important part of his life, although he doesn't understand why you have been so remote lately. But then, neither do I. We both knew things couldn't continue the way they were."

"No, they couldn't," I replied as bitter disappointment shattered my brief moment of joy. I thought he might pull away from me, but he didn't. He just stood there with his hands on my waist. If I hadn't known that he and Beth were together, I might have read something more into what was happening, despite his assessment of our situation. Could he possibly miss me as much as I missed him, even if there was no chance of us ever being together?

I fought my desires for an instant longer and then pushed myself away from him. "I'm sorry, Jake. That was very improper of me."

"You can say that again," Beth stormed as she stepped onto the balcony with us. From the angry look in her eyes and the bright color in her cheeks, I knew she had been watching— for how long, it was impossible to tell. She rushed up to Jake and gave him a long and possessive kiss.

"I thought you weren't coming," she said, without looking in my direction again. "How do you like my dress, love? I picked it out with you in mind."

I didn't wait for his reply. I simply hurried away from them and ran down the staircase. When I came to the first landing, I saw my little brother holding a single, white rose. He was wearing his church clothes and looked very uncomfortable.

"I can't believe you are really here," I said, opening my arms to him. He hesitated only a second before running into them and wrapping his legs around my hips, nearly sending both of us sailing down the remaining stairs.

"I wasn't going to come. I was really mad at you until Uncle Jake explained that it wasn't your fault you got sick. He said that a party was the perfect place to tell you that I wasn't angry any more."

He buried his head on my shoulder, and I felt a thorn prick my arm, but it didn't matter. Trevor was my only real family, and I could not believe how much I had missed him.

"I am really sorry for being such an awful sister," I responded, feeling his soft hair on my cheek as tears slid from my eyes. "But I am ever so much better now."

Trevor leaned back in my arms so he could see my face. "Were you really sick like I was when I got the flu and threw up all night?"

I smiled at his innocence. "It wasn't quite like that, but I hurt awfully bad."

He suddenly released his hold on me and slipped to the floor. "This is for you," he said, extending the rose in my direction.

"It's beautiful. I will always treasure it because it came from you."

"It's from Uncle Jake too. He said we should get it so tonight would be special. He knows how much you like flowers."

"Then I will have to thank him too the next time we talk." I held the rose to my nose and smelled its fragrance, trying hard not to think about the man who was now with his waitress. "You are going to break a lot of hearts when you grow up little brother."

"Breaking hearts must run in the Hawkins' genes," Jake said. I hadn't heard his approach, but he and Beth were standing behind us on the next step up.

Tears burned the corners of my eyes at the allusions his words aroused, but I wouldn't let them flow. It would strip away my last ounce of dignity. So, I bit the inside of my bottom lip and looked over my shoulder at them. They were holding hands and Beth was smiling beguilingly, but I knew the implication of his remark was not lost on her.

Maybe I should have taken the higher road and said something to ease her mind, but there was no reason to ruin Molly's day over a simple misunderstanding. It was much better to just pretend I hadn't heard what he said.

"Why don't we see if we can find some refreshments, Trevor? I imagine you are pretty hungry after such a long ride."

I extended my hand and he took it.

"I'm not really hungry," he replied, giving me the strangest look. Everything had to be so confusing for him. His uncle was holding hands with a girl he had clearly never seen before, except perhaps at our father's funeral, and yet Jake had suggested they come to Sydney to bring me a flower. "We went to Maccas already, but I do want some cake."

"Then cake it is," I said as I watched Molly and Evan move towards the small table with an entourage of people following them for the time-honored cake-cutting ceremony. Talk about perfect timing.

"I'm not sure how we are supposed to do this, "Evan was saying when we got to bottom of the stairs and made our way across the sparkling marble floor. It reminded me of the cake with the Styrofoam bottom layer my father and LeAnn had cut at our kitchen table not that many months ago.

One of his sisters laughed a little too loudly and took the cake knife from him. "Can't you pay attention to anything except your blushing bride, baby brother?" she chided, but it was all done in jest and clearly everyone knew it. "And please don't forget that you have to feed each other the first bite. It's tradition."

"Tradition," I thought. Some of it was good when it came to families like cutting cakes at weddings, hanging stockings on the mantel at Christmas and even holding a wake so mourners could share their remembrances of the deceased.

But it was the other pastimes most Aussies shared that caused me concern, like going to boozers and drinking neck oil like it was going out of style, using crude humor, taking the name of the Lord in vain, and sleeping with people just because it felt good or killed time. While those things did not make people inherently bad, they did nothing to promote the values I now held dear because every time I mentioned something of a religious nature I was accused of being judgmental and critical.

I simply did not belong here with people who lived life in the moment, satisfying every urge or desire with no thought to the consequences their actions might bring. I belonged home in Los Angeles with Ben, but I had ruined that. And just like Jake, he was building a life with someone else.

A single tear slid from the corner of my eye, and I brushed it away. If I started thinking about everything I had lost again, I would never make it through the rest of the night. Besides, I had my little brother and a new sibling on the way to think about and a promise made to my father yet to fulfill. Perhaps if I tried hard enough I could live for each moment, individually if I had to, until I more fully understood how to accomplish what God needed me to do.

The cake cutting ceremony was soon over, and Trevor was tugging on my arm.

"Can I have a piece with lots of decorations on it? We never get that at home."

I squeeze his hand and knelt down in front of him.

"I missed you so much, Trevor. You are the best little brother in the whole, wide world, and I am sorry for ever hurting you."

"It's okay," he said, putting his arms around my neck and kissing my cheek.

His gesture of forgiveness meant the world to me because he didn't have to waste valuable time trying to figure out how he was going to offer it. Unlike me, with him it came naturally.

"You are so handsome in your church clothes," I continued, fingering the tie he had worn at our father's wedding and funeral. I kept meaning to get him a different one, but it was just one of the many things I had left undone. "I hope you will save at least one dance for me."

"I don't know how to dance," he immediately replied.

"It's easy," I told him. "All you have to do is move your feet in time to the music. I'll show you how, although I am not very good myself."

I wriggled my nose the way he always did when faced with something he wasn't quite sure of and then let out a heavy sigh.

"Okay, but not until I have some cake," he pleaded, eyeing it hungrily as one of Evan's sisters took the top layer and set it aside before cutting pieces of the center section for the guests to sample. It was a white cake with layers of raspberry and cream cheese filling. I wondered if Molly had selected it, or if it was just another tradition of the family she had married into. We moved into a line that had already started to form.

"You can have all the cake you desire—just for tonight," I said as the band began playing again. "Just don't overdo it. I would hate for you to be sick on your first trip into Sydney because there is so much to see."

I stopped speaking while my brain caught up with my mouth. I had no idea what Jake's plans were and there would be little time for sightseeing since Trevor needed to be in school on Monday and Jake couldn't be away from the ranch for long. Animals had to be fed night and morning and he had already been gone for over nine hours.

"I won't eat too much," he responded, taking a step forward behind people who were moving as fast as the cake was being cut. "Do you think they would let me take pieces home to mum and Emma? I know they would like some too."

I ran my hand over his soft hair. "I'm sure that can be arranged. I saw some little boxes in the kitchen earlier for that very purpose."

"Hey, sport," Jake interrupted, including me with his eyes. Once again, I had not heard his approach because I had been trying so hard to stop thinking about him. Surprisingly enough, Beth was not clinging to his arm in a solely proprietary way. "While you are eating some of that cake, do you think you could convince your sister to dance with me? I promise not to tread on her feet and ruin her fancy, new shoes."

I looked down at the pair of sandals with stiletto heels I was wearing, something I hadn't done since leaving Los Angeles, and wondered what had prompted him to ask such a question with Beth in the room. Dancing could be a very intimate activity, and she would be livid if she saw us together again.

"I'm not sure that is such a good idea," I said without looking up at him. "I was going to dance with Trevor."

"It's okay, Brylee," my little brother responded without guile. "Uncle Jake won't hurt you, and he is a much better dancer than me."

Undeniably, my heart was engaged in a tug-o-war. Trevor couldn't appreciate what was going on, but his encouragement was less than proper now that Jake belonged to someone else. Still, I couldn't deny that I wanted nothing more than to be held in his arms and pretend that we were back to that night on the veranda when we both expressed how we really felt, but once a moment is lost, it seldom returns again.

"Trevor's right," Jake said. "There has been too much hurt lately and I am a fair dancer, even if I don't get much practice."

"Then I suppose it would be very rude of me to refuse," I said as a feeling I wasn't sure I wanted to understand swept over me. "But I don't want to cause any trouble—not tonight when everyone is having so much fun."

"There is nothing wrong with two members of the same family sharing a simple dance. Besides, there are a few things we need to discuss in light of recent changes in our lives."

The brief flutter of anticipation was over. He only wanted to set more rules of engagement. If I returned to the ranch, things would be very different than they had been in the past. There would be no more outings to the movies or trips to the waterfall. I would have to be pleasant, not only to him but to his new girlfriend, especially when Trevor was around. I wasn't sure I could do that, but for my little brother's sake, I knew I had to try.

"We can do that later," I said. "Trevor and I are going to have cake."

"Ouch," Jake replied, touching my arm and making a sliver of chills return. "My charms really must be fading if I need a child to get me a dance with the prettiest girl here."

I felt the color rise to my cheeks. Why couldn't he just leave things alone? Did he simply take perverse delight in tormenting me? He had moved on, but I was stuck in the same dark hole I had been in since the night Ben and I broke up—that same night on the beach when I had been so susceptible to his charms and allowed myself to kiss him back.

Apparently, he had already forgotten what we had shared, but I hadn't. The passionate longings he had stirred came back to me every time I heard his voice or saw his face. But mostly, they just haunted my dreams.

"You already have someone to dance with," I said, refusing the temptation to make more of his idle chatter about my looks than was wise. He was used to flattering women. It was part of his charm.

"Maybe I like to mix things up a bit. Besides, nobody tells me what I can and cannot do. But then you already know that about me, don't you?

I felt the air in my chest constrict. I did know that about him, but he could say the same thing about me. I was inflexible when it came to my personal beliefs, refusing his offer of love because he snubbed his nose at what I both needed and wanted. That was why we were in such a toxic situation now.

I bit my bottom lip quite harshly to help further ground me before speaking. "I suppose I do. In any case, I will look forward to a dance later on."

"You do know I will hold you to that," he responded.

"Wouldn't have it any other way," I replied.

Trevor was watching our interaction with a puckered brow. He had traveled so far to see me and I couldn't ruin his evening, although I knew he had been at least partially manipulated into coming. I just didn't understand why. Perhaps Jake had been planning on joining Beth all along and wanted Trevor to come willingly. That seemed more likely since abandoning him to the little house in Edna—when we had both promised to spend our weekends with him—would put him in the same category with LeAnn and me.

"Why don't we see about that cake?" I asked my little brother as I took his hand and moved a few steps closer to the refreshment table where another one of Evan's sisters was busy arranging small, dessert plates. Evan had four sisters, Eleanor, Roberta, Mattie and Fran. They all looked alike to me, with light brown hair, blue eyes and several children clinging to their skirts, but they were friendly and welcoming, and I was glad they were there to help and support Molly now that she was part of their family.

Trevor looked carefully at each pre-cut slice, searching for the perfect one with lots of white frosting and a sugary, yellow-tipped rose with green leaves that looked even more professionally formed than the ones I had seen in L.A. when allowing myself the luxury of browsing in bakeries as most every expectant bride liked to do.

I felt more tears tickle my nose as I watched Trevor make his selection. I didn't want to think about my lost wedding any more than I wanted to think about how fabulous Jake looked in his white shirt and green tie. The sleeves were rolled up to the elbows, leaving the tattoos on his forearms visible, but they no longer bothered me. I just wanted him to forget about Beth and give us another chance. But my indecisiveness, coupled with my inexplicable need to express my beliefs, had driven him straight into her open arms.

Beth clung to him possessively all evening, whispering in his ear every time they came close to me, and he didn't hang back from her. It was abundantly clear to anyone who saw them that they were a couple—a couple who could very easily be falling in love.

I wanted to quit torturing myself, but my eyes were relentlessly drawn to them. I wanted to hide behind potted plants or even excuse myself because I wasn't feeling well, but Trevor wanted to be part of the celebration, or at least be able to watch the dancing and laughter and champagne sipping. Molly looked deliriously happy with a handsome, new husband standing beside her and well-wishers surrounding them. She hugged Jake tightly and planted a kiss on his lips before introducing him to Evan. Beth didn't seem to mind their exchange. Everyone, except me, seemed to be having a marvelous time.

"So what do you think of Sydney," I asked Trevor as we sat alone at a small round table with a yellow tablecloth and gold fish swimming in a glass bowl in its center. I hadn't missed the disco ball suspended from the ceiling that made everything sparkle or the garden setting that had been created in one corner of the room. It was just the kind of reception I had envisioned for myself until meeting Ben.

"It's okay, but I would rather be at home with my animals. Do you think they miss me?"

"Without a doubt," I told him, my thoughts returning to the animals we depended on so much since every member of the family who could take care of them was at the wedding. "How long are you and Uncle Jake staying?"

"Only until morning. He brought Copper in to stay at Emma's, but Newton had to stay at the ranch. We gave everyone plenty of food and water before coming, even those at Uncle Ned's. Uncle Jake said they would be okay until we got home, but we couldn't waste any time."

I watched his animated movements as he spoke. His eyes were wide, and his hands flailed about in the air almost as much as mine did.

"I'm sure they will be just fine," I assured him, not wanting to remind him that he had school on Monday and Jake would be leaving him in Edna before returning to the ranch.

After our brief refreshments—Trevor had finished his cake and punch, but I had barely touched mine—I asked him to dance.

"I'm scared, Brylee," he said. "What if someone laughs at me?"

"Never going to happen," I replied, sliding my chair away from the table. "Everyone is busy doing their own thing and we won't go very far, but I can't let the evening end without at least one dance with my handsome little brother."

He hesitated, but when I held out my hand to him, he took it."

Molly and Evan were mingling with other couples on the floor. NJ was surrounded by college cuties and doing an amazing job of keeping them all entertained, but it was Jake my eyes focused on as I tried, rather unsuccessfully, to help Trevor keep time to the beat of the music. But he stuck with me until the song ended, and then we went back to our table on the far side of the dance floor. Uncle Ned and Aunt Nora were still talking to Evan's parents. They had been at it all evening, and I hoped that meant they were becoming friends as they supported their children in their new life together.

I wanted my cousin to find complete happiness but knew she and Evan would encounter many rough spots along the way. That was just part of living and they were not starting out with a clean slate. They had a baby on the way whose paternity wasn't known, Molly's mental state could change at any moment and they would soon be living in Brisbane where the amount of family support given in the accustomed way would be minimal.

Like everyone else who knew what had gone on recently, I was praying for a miracle life that might never materialize unless my cousin truly had changed from the flirtatious girl I had always known into a woman who could be happy with just one man.

But still it was hard being happy for someone else when my own life was such a train wreck. I wanted to be noticed by someone who could take my mind off my troubles. I was wearing a new dress and felt more elegant than I had since returning home, but there was no one around to look beautiful for. Other than NJ and his throng of admiring girls, I was the only one in the ballroom—of legal age—who had not come with either a spouse or a date.

When Molly threw her bridal bouquet over her shoulder, Beth caught it. She looked back at Jake longingly and pretended it didn't matter that he gave no response when Molly told her she would be the next one wearing white and getting married to the man of her dreams.

While Beth was still blushing with anticipation and being congratulated by the other girls in the wedding party, Jake came up behind me. I had rejoined Trevor at the table the moment the bouquet was caught. My only reason for being part of the ritual at all was my intense desire not to be singled out for lack of participation and knew my more-than-vocal cousin would eventually say something about it.

"I thought all girls fought to catch the bride's bouquet, but your feet never left the floor," he said, placing his hands on my shoulders. His very touch seemed to sear my delicate flesh through the thin fabric that covered it.

"I guess they didn't have a reason to," I said without looking up at him.

"Nonsense," he replied with a touch of laughter in his voice. "I haven't met a girl yet who didn't want a huge diamond gracing the third finger of her left hand."

I grimaced. I'd had that ring until a few months ago. How could he be so insensitive as to remind me of my loss at my cousin's wedding reception? Tears slid from my eyes so unexpectedly I had no choice except to wipe them away.

"I should be drawn and quartered like the bloody intolerable jerk I am," Jake said, immediately dropping his hands and taking the chair next to me. "I didn't mean for it to come out like that. I was only making a general comment about girls and weddings."

I knew he was being sincere, but that didn't stop the pain in my heart. I was a two-time loser when it came to love.

"Don't give it a second thought," I replied, biting my bottom lip again. "Weddings should be happy occasions. I am sure you will find that out for yourself soon enough."

"Not me," he replied with a scorching look of distain. "I enjoy my freedom far too much to be saddled to just one girl."

I looked over at Trevor who was fidgeting in his chair. Grownup talk was distressing him again, and I was at least partially responsible because I could not let go of the past. My little brother might not be able to fill the emptiness left by my broken engagement or Jake's purposeful rejection, but he knew how to love without guile or pretense.

"Don't be sad, Brylee," he suddenly said. "I will marry you when I get big so you won't have to be alone."

His sincerity, as ridiculous as it was, broke the melancholy mood I was in and forced a tearful smile.

"That is not exactly how it works, sport," Jake told him, fighting back laughter so he wouldn't embarrass his nephew. "Brothers and sisters can't get married."

"Why not?" Trevor asked.

"It's a little complicated. Let's just say that it's the law."

"Then you marry Brylee, Uncle Jake. She likes you better than anyone else, and I don't like that other lady. She laughs too much and acts silly."

I felt the heat rush to my cheeks in a most unbecoming way, but I couldn't blame Trevor for saying what was on his mind. I had been wondering myself just how many people at the reception suspected a triangular relationship. I had been trying to be discreet and keep my emotions in check, but Jake kept approaching when I least expected him to. And there was little doubt that some of the people around us heard what Trevor said.

The muscles along Jake's jaw line rippled as he looked down at his nephew. I loved that my little brother's loyalty was with me, but his comment about Beth had to hurt since I was sure Jake wanted Trevor to like the woman he had chosen to spend his time with—even if he did not intend on it becoming something permanent like Beth did.

"Why don't you go ask your Uncle Ned and Aunt Nora where we can stay tonight while I talk to your sister?" he finally said. "We need to get an early start for home in the morning."

"But I want to go back with Brylee," Trevor countered.

Jake's patience was being tested, but he rose to the occasion at my expense.

"I'm not sure when she will be coming back. She is part of the wedding party, and that means she has specific duties to take care of. It might be a few days, or even longer before she leaves Sydney, and you have school on Monday."

"It won't matter if I miss school just once."

"I'm not sure your mum would agree. She was a stickler about school when I was your age. If she caught me playing hooky for any reason it was bread and water for at least a week, and I wasn't allowed to see any of my mates. You wouldn't want that happening to you, now would you?"

Trevor laughed. That meant he had already forgotten about his confusion over who could and could not get married.

"Mum wouldn't do that to me."

"I wouldn't be too sure about that, sport. Your mum believes education is important."

He was thoughtful for a moment. "Are you still going to dance with Brylee before we leave? I already did, and you promised."

"In that case," Jake responded. "It would be very ungentlemanly of me to renege. But I'm not sure Brylee will agree to it. She has already danced with the best partner here."

He was giving me a way out, and I should have taken it. But this was the most opportune time to resolve some of our issues before returning home because we couldn't let our conversation get heated or emotional with so many people around. So, I handed Trevor the white rose he had given me earlier for safekeeping. Its stem had been capped with water, but its petals had taken a beating. I would press it between the pages of a book as soon as I could. I needed something positive as reminder of this evening because my life, of necessity, would take on a new kind of normal once it was over.

Jake took my hand without saying anything more and led me onto the dance floor. It was social suicide when it came to Molly's friends, especially Beth, but I needed to be held one more time before this chapter of my story ended. A slow song was playing when I put my hand on his shoulder and felt him draw me closer than was necessary or prudent.

The beating of his heart was in rhythm with mine, just as it had been that night on the beach when I had bared my soul to him and then found comfort in his strong embrace and intoxicating kiss. I wanted to feel his lips pressed into mine as his fingertips burned trails along my cheeks and neck again, but wishing the hands of time could be rewound wasn't going to make it happen. He was only dancing with me because he had something important to say that could not be left until later.

That cold douse of reality made me pull away from him, and I could almost feel the eyes of others in the room judging us for being in each other's arms when he and Beth had been dancing so happily together for over an hour.

"I'm sorry Trevor does not understand your relationship with Beth," I said in hopes of bridging the awful gap between us.

"Don't let that concern you," he responded. "Though I suppose one of us should set him straight about who is together and who isn't. He is too young to appreciate the fact that certain people only hurt each other when they try to move past certain immovable obstacles."

"How did we ever get to this point?" I said a little too fervently.

Try as I might, I could not stop my mind from drifting back to everything positive we had shared since our ill-fated meeting on the road leading to the ranch when he had demanded to know who I was, and I had told him it was none of his business. We had loathed each other then, mistrusting every word and action. He believed I was there to take away my little brother's birthright, and I believed he was the most arrogant and unpleasant man I had ever met who was keeping more than his share of unsavory secrets.

"I wish I could answer that," he whispered into my ear since the music was too loud for a normal conversation. "I just hope your father isn't overly unhappy with us. I know he was hoping for more when it came to both our personal and working relationships."

"It wasn't all bad, was it?' I asked.

"Hell, no," he responded. "Not that you have ever made anything easy, but I can't fault your determination when it came to keeping the promise you made to him. I always figured you would bail at the first sign of real trouble, but you have proven many times over that you have the grit to be an outback rancher if it is what you really want to do with your life. No other woman I know of would have helped deliver a calf when the very thought of getting her hands dirty was revolting, rid an outhouse of spiders during the aftermath of a flood when there was no way of knowing if they were poisonous, or plan a wedding for her father's mistress and then take over all of her responsibilities so she could bring another half-sibling into the world."

"I'm not some heroine, Jake. I am just a girl who did what anyone else would under the same circumstances."

"Not true!" he exclaimed. "You are the strongest, most loving and capable woman I have ever known. It's just too bad certain things had to get in the way of . . . ."

"Don't say it! Not tonight," I interrupted.

Using my religious beliefs or my inability to commit as an excuse for sleeping with Beth the very night he walked away from me wasn't fair. It would take away all of the memories I wanted to cherish—him pushing me on the swing in the loft of the barn, the necklace he had made and hung around my neck at Christmas, the spark of arousal when I had bathed his arm after he got hurt on the trail while we were herding sheep and so many more. I needed those remembrances so I would not grow to hate him.

"I know life would be easier for everyone if I didn't believe what I do, but I can't go back to the time when I didn't believe in anything."

"Like me?" he questioned, leaning his back so he could see my face.

"No, Jake, not like you," I said. "I think you believe things very deeply."

His face was a study in contradictions. His eyes told me that he wanted to believe in something greater than what he already did, but the hard line of his lips reaffirmed the fact that he was still fighting demons I knew nothing about.

I wished with all of my heart that he could see himself the way I did—the way God did—because I truly believed that the only thing stopping him from becoming the man he was destined to be was the fear of change. He was comfortable, if not satisfied, remaining exactly where he was and indulging in all the things that were familiar to him, but I knew him better than he thought I did. He wanted to feel truly alive again, just as I did, but with that aliveness came the possibility of more betrayal and pain like he had suffered with Wendy. He might pretend that was all in the past and had never really mattered, but it had.

"You're an amazing man, Jake Johnson," I said without realizing it. "No matter what happens, I never want you to forget that."

The tension in his jaw only increased. "But not amazing enough for you, is that what you are trying to say?"

"No, Jake, it isn't. I think we were the victims of bad timing, coupled with a whole lot of misunderstanding."

"Maybe so," he admitted. "But there comes a time when a man simply has to give up or lose himself in the process. I am not willing to let that happen to me again."

"I would never ask that of you."

"But you did! It was either your way or the highway, and I learned a long time ago that people should be accepted for who they are at present, not for what they might become someday."

I was sobered by his insightful remark, but before I could respond, I felt a hand pressing down on my shoulder that made my stomach lurch. The new object of Jake's affection was standing so close to me that I could see every pore on her face, along with the malevolent look in her eyes that assured me she would do anything necessary to keep what she viewed as being hers.

"I'm here to take my man back?" Beth said in a controlled, but chilly tone. She was holding the bridal bouquet in one hand as if it was a trophy proving just how much she had already won.

Reassuring her that she had nothing to fear from me was pointless, so I merely removed myself from Jake's arms and walked away. He didn't protest as I thought he might. He simply took her hand and led her away from me.

I spent the rest of the evening with Trevor trying to make him smile and laugh by telling him anecdotes from my youth that still seemed to amuse him. When most of the guests had gone and it was time for the bridal couple to leave, I sent him to ask Jake if it would be okay for him to spend the night at the hotel with me. I couldn't bring myself to approach him again since Beth never left his side.

We helped Uncle Ned, Aunt Nora and Evan's family load presents into cars so they could be stored until the new couple returned from Tasmania—the island they had chosen to visit for a brief honeymoon. I might have enjoyed seeing what they received but was grateful the evening was almost over. Trying to remain positive when all I wanted to do was scream had consumed every ounce of energy I had left after a very demanding and soul-searching few weeks.

Aunt Nora was more than emotional when she kissed her daughter and told her she would be back to help with the move to Brisbane. There were tears in Uncle Ned's eyes as he shook hands with his new son-in-law and told him to take good care of his little girl, but he broke down completely when he hugged Molly.

"You be safe, little girl, and if you ever need anything, all you have to do is call."

"I will," Molly said as she stood on tiptoes and kissed his leathery cheek. "But everything is going to be okay. I love

Evan. I truly do, and I know he loves me. And in just a few months we will be a real family."

"God willing," Uncle Ned told her.

"I'm not going to do anything else that is stupid," she responded. "No matter what happens with the baby, Evan and I are determined to make our marriage work and give our baby boy the best life he could possibly have."

"Are you telling me I am going to have a grandson?"

"We found out yesterday, and I hope he looks just like you, father."

Uncle Ned didn't even try to muffle a giant sob. "Don't wish that on the little bloke. Does that mean Evan is the baby's father?"

I was standing too close not to hear the conversation and was grateful that Trevor had gone with Jake to get his backpack from the truck so he could stay at the hotel with me. He didn't need to be exposed to anything else he was too young to understand, and Beth wasn't about to let Jake out of her sight, especially now that he would not be babysitting his nephew.

"We haven't taken the paternity test, and we are not going to," I heard Molly say. "Evan will be this baby's father in all the ways that really matter. It doesn't matter whose blood he has."

"It sounds like my little girl has turned into a woman with a first-rate head on her shoulders," Uncle Ned responded.

"Cutting myself was just a cry for help. I thought I couldn't get over being dumped, but the truth is that I didn't know what I really wanted until Evan came to the hospital to see me."

She squeezed her husband's hand. "He has been my best friend and confidant for two years, and I love him with all my heart and always will."

When it came time to say goodbye, Molly pulled me aside quite unexpectedly. Since she had paid relatively little attention to me during the nearly two weeks I had spent helping to plan every aspect of her wedding, it was almost worrisome.

"I'm sorry for being such a brat since you came home, Brylee, but I have always wanted what I couldn't have. I was jealous because Jake liked you better than me."

"That is certainly something you don't have to worry about now," I told her with a sad smile. "I just want you to be happy, and I hope you know that if you ever need anything, I am here for you."

She gave me a sudden hug. "I know that. After all, if you hadn't told Evan where I was this day never would have happened."

"You would have found your way to each other eventually."

"Maybe! But I am happier than I ever thought I could be and want you to be that way too. I have seen your misery since you came to Sydney, and it isn't just because of a broken engagement. Mum said that you and Jake have been having issues, but you don't have to worry because she didn't give away any particulars. I can see for myself how wretched both of you are. I can't believe I am going to say this, but the two of you belong together, even if you are having a few difficulties right now."

"What about Beth? I thought she was your best friend."

"She is, but Jake doesn't love her. He is in love with you and has been for a very long time."

I felt my stomach knot. "But he chose her."

"Maybe you backed him into a corner and he was just reacting. I love Beth like a sister, I truly do. We have been friends forever, but love can't be forced. She has been after Jake for years. Why else would she stay in a place like Edna? It's Dullsville compared to the big city, but she kept clinging to the idea that if she waited long enough he would eventually come to her."

"And he has."

"Really, Brylee," she said, grabbing both my arms with hands that were still covered with gloves. "I don't know what happened between the two of you, but I do know what I am talking about. You will never be happy until you are willing to open your heart to the right man. You might have to give up something you thought was important—like I did with Bradley —but there is nothing more intoxicating or fulfilling than being with your soul mate. That amazingly wonderful person who knows everything about you but loves you in spite of your faults—even new religious beliefs that no one understands anyway. Just promise me that you will give it some thought. I know how intimidating Beth can be, but don't let her get the upper hand if you have any feelings at all for Jake. He won't be happy with her for the long run. He is just nursing a bruised ego and a broken heart right now."

"I'm afraid it is not that simple, Molly."

"Sure it is," she responded. "You just have to decide if he is worth loving for the rest of your life. I know most everyone who has even an inkling of what happened with me thinks Evan and I won't make it, but I have faith that everything will be all right no matter how many rough times we might have to go through."

"I promise to think about what you said," I replied, suddenly very aware that every pair of eyes left in the room seemed to be focused on us. Even Jake and Beth were watching our unusual exchange. Trevor was holding his uncle's hand and looked like he was almost asleep standing up. "Just enjoy your honeymoon, Molly, and don't worry about anyone else. We will figure things out just like you have."

Molly's words were stuck in my mind as Trevor and I drove to the hotel. Uncle Ned had reserved his own room when he arrived, and he and Aunt Nora had insisted that I stay where I was until it was time to leave. That meant Trevor and I had a suite of rooms to enjoy, but he was so tired he barely glanced at the furnishings or the spectacular view of the harbor. He was out before his head even hit the pillow, and I decided there were worse things than allowing him to sleep in his church clothes. They could always be washed and ironed later.

I tried not to think about Jake and Beth. I knew she'd had too much to drink but wasn't sure about him. At any rate, he was a man and I doubted he would resist her advances, even if what Molly had said about him still loving me was true.

NJ met us at the hotel for an early Sunday brunch. It was easy to tell that he had been out clubbing after the reception. His eyes were bloodshot and his face drawn, but he was cheerful and ready to eat with the family. He assured his parents that the bride and groom were safely on their way to their honeymoon destination. He had already received a text from Molly saying how amazing her new husband was and how happy she was just being with him. I wondered if the same thing would ever happen for me.

Chapter 7

Emma was relieved to see all of us when we arrived at her home in Edna. She had dinner ready to put on the table, but Uncle Ned and Aunt Nora declined her invitation. They had work to do on the ranch and my aunt was especially eager to get home since she had been gone for nearly two weeks. So I returned the keys her Land Rover since she had ridden back to Edna with Uncle Jake, and then said my goodbyes since it was rather unclear as to when I would see them again.

It was almost nine when we finished eating. Emma had already asked me to spend the night because she didn't want me on the road after I had already driven most of the day. I was grateful for her kindness. She knew the struggle I was having with Jake, especially since I had been made so painfully aware of his relationship with Beth. He had stopped by to pick up Copper earlier in the day so Trevor would not have to tell her goodbye again.

I hated the fact that what he did and who he was with mattered so much to me. Nothing would change unless I was willing to make some major concessions. But even if I did it might not be the right thing for me, and it certainly wouldn't be fair to Beth. She deserved the chance to see if she could win Jake's heart, not just a place in his bed.

As I drifted off into a troubled sleep stretched out on the sofa in the dark at the foot of the stairs, I knew that I had finally run out of excuses and options for sidestepping family responsibilities. Running away had not solved anything since what had happened between Jake and me was inevitable. From now on, we would live parallel lives. We would see each other because we had promised to save the ranch, and we would be pleasant while doing so because we had to. Trevor, LeAnn and the new baby needed a secure life, and we had promised to make that happen.

I took Trevor to school the next morning, promising him that I would check on Newton and his other animals as soon as I got home, and that I would plan something special for us to do when he came home for the weekend. Then I did something very unlike me. I decided to go shopping for clothes.

I had been in Australia for almost nine months and had purchased nothing new to wear except the dress for Molly's wedding that was much too fancy to even be worn to church. My personal life had evolved into nothing short of a mockery of what it had once been, but I had to trust that God had something more important in mind for me than learning how to endure even more heartache and loss while trying to pretend that I was doing so okay.

So instead of looking at shorts and sleeveless tops like I had done in the past, I hunted for clothing that could be worn as I worked around the ranch, along with a new Sunday dress that would be appropriate for the kind of life I was still committed to live. I simply could not walk away from the concept of being with the man I loved forever and what it would take to have that happen. My heart might scream out for all the promises of love that had vanished by giving Ben his freedom and walking away from Jake, but I had to be strong enough to get past both of those awful letdowns.

Copper came running to me, wagging her tail, when I walked into the kitchen at the ranch late that afternoon. I picked her up as soon as my packages had been dropped onto the table.

"It's good to see you again," I told the little dog as she nuzzled her nose into my cheek, and forced me to laugh. Why couldn't people be more like her? She loved completely with no questions, no complaints and most certainly no complications.

I was glad she had been there to welcome me home, but it was a bittersweet return after all that had happened during the past few weeks. I loved everything about the ranch from the indigenous plants and animals to the memories I had about time spent with loved-ones. But it also made me realize just how utterly alone I was with Trevor and LeAnn in town and Jake involved with someone else.

I knew he had been there recently because Copper and all the animals in the barn had been fed and watered, but his truck was gone, and I had no idea where he was or when he would be back.

After talking to Trevor, I washed the clothes I had taken with me and fixed something to eat. Then I went to the cemetery to tell my parents about Molly's wedding and what had happened between Jake and me. I needed to feel connected to the land and people I loved, regardless of the fact that everything familiar was gone.

It was still hot in the house when I got back. The AC had been turned down during my absence, and it would take time for the air to fully circulate, especially upstairs where my bedroom faced west, so I decided to sleep in the den where I could get a cross-breeze during the night and hopefully a little sleep. That was when I discovered the note that might have changed everything if I had found it before driving to the coast. Jake had written it and put it in front of the computer screen where he believed I would find it since the den had become my sanctuary—just as it had once been for my father.

"Dear Brylee," it began. *"I have so many regrets for the things I said on Sunday. I was frustrated and hurt that you couldn't see past your new religion into my heart. I think I have loved you from the moment we met. You were so damned beautiful standing in the middle of the road with your hands on your hips, demanding to know what was going on. But even more than that, I saw your courage, compassion and strength as you dealt with your father and his new family.*

"Most of the women I know would have gotten angry and stormed away, but not you! You have so much love in your heart to give. All I could think about when I found out you were engaged was 'why in the hell aren't you here with her'. I would never have let the woman I loved go off on her own to settle family differences. I hated the bloke I rather haughtily dubbed 'your surfer boy' for his indifference and selfishness, and because you loved him and were able to overlook all of his faults, something you were never able to do with me.

"I am a very passionate man and can be incredibly self-centered. That was abundantly clear the night you broke up with him and we shared our first kiss. I had wanted you for so long and thought I might have a chance with him out of the picture. But he wasn't the only thing that stood between us. That bizarre religion he introduced you to had consumed your life so completely that you couldn't see what was right in front of you—me, loving you.

"I really thought we could work through our differences if we cared enough about each other, but maybe things were more one-sided than I thought. I guess I just got tired of trying to fight something I couldn't see or understand, so I ran back to my old behavior—momentary pleasure without emotional commitment. I am so incredibly sorry for that single lapse into weakness because it took me away from

what I really wanted. I still love you, Brylee. Perhaps if I had been able to say that to you in person again things would not have gotten so out of control. I want us to start over again if you feel you can ever forgive me for being much too human.

"I will listen to what you have to say about religion. If it's the reason you have become the woman you are then it can't be all that bad. And I could certainly use further grounding in my own life.

"Ned needs my help for the next few days so I will be staying there at night, but you can call me for anything. My thoughts, and yes, even my prayers—if there is a God who listens—are always with you. Love, Jake"

I held the sheets of papers tightly in unsteady hands as I reread his letter time and again trying to understand why I hadn't come into the den before leaving for Emma's house on the coast. I went there everyday to sit in my father's chair and reflect on the blessing of making it home in time to repair some of the misunderstandings between us. But I had left early that Friday morning, my heart so filled with grief over finding out that Jake had spent the night with Beth that I had abandoned my daily practice in favor of getting on the road before changing my mind.

I should have taken Emma's advice and talked to him before leaving. It was the right thing to do and would have saved so much misery for a great many people, but pride and grief are a lethal combination, and I had chosen the easy way out. If he had taken the note I left for him underneath the coffee mug he always used as a reaction to the one he had left for me, it would certainly explain his seemingly besotted interest in Beth and his mixed reactions to seeing me.

And yet, despite his declaration of love, and his belief that I had rejected him as a man who was willing to listen and even believe, he had been kind to me at Molly's reception. That had taken far more strength than I possessed. There had to be a way of undoing some of the damage I had caused without destroying someone else's happiness in hopes of finding my own. Besides, there were no guarantees that Jake would even want me back after all the turmoil I had caused in his usually well-structured life.

If he returned to the ranch during the next few days, he did it under the cover of darkness because I never saw him. I got up early each morning to make sure all the animals were fed and watered, but the rest of my days were spent in a state of suspended animation trying to make minor repairs to the barn, the house, the fences and corrals—anything that I was capable of doing on my own.

I wanted desperately to talk to him and tell him that I hadn't found his note until after Molly's wedding—that supposedly happy affair where I had said or done nothing to indicate that there was anything left between us—even the slightest hint of friendship. But I couldn't pour out the feelings in my heart over the phone? It was too impersonal. I needed to see his face to know if anything I said would even matter now.

Trevor phoned every afternoon to tell me about his adventures at school, and Aunt Nora called to check in with me every few days. We talked about Molly and Evan and LeAnn and the new baby, but neither of us mentioned Jake. I surmised that he was still staying with them, if he wasn't in town with Beth.

My suspicions were at least partially confirmed when she called on Friday morning to say that Jake would not be able to fly into Edna to get Trevor because he and Uncle Ned were taking the plane into Sydney to meet with other small ranchers about the encroachment of corporations in the outback.

I wondered if they were intentionally leaving me out of these meetings because of my rift with Jake, or if they both believed that I was no longer interested in honoring our new arrangement. It seemed as if my one lapse in judgment had destroyed most everyone's faith in me, and it wouldn't be easy proving to any of them that I had no intention of acting like a ninny again.

I tried to make the weekend fun for Trevor. Before leaving Edna, we saw a movie and went to Macca's for dinner. It seemed like a lifetime since we had met Mary and her children and planned a play date with them. Jake and I had been at odds even then, but I couldn't help but feel that hostile situation was far preferable to the silent war that existed between us now.

We saddled some horses rode over to have lunch with Aunt Nora on Saturday. She had just heard from Molly and Evan. They were home from their brief honeymoon where they'd had a wonderful time, buying so many souvenirs for their new home that they'd had to ship them since there wasn't enough room in their suitcases.

It was hard not being envious of my cousin. She hadn't lived a particularly admirable life, yet that hadn't stopped her from finding the man of her dreams who was willing to forgive any indiscretion. She was even having a baby—something I might be doing if my marriage to Ben had taken place like planned. And if that wasn't enough to make me a little bitter, I knew both she and Evan would have the opportunity to learn the true meaning of life when they were ready.

"Trevor," I heard Aunt Nora say. "Why don't you run out to the barn and see the new baby chicks and pigs? Just be careful not to let any of them out, or we might spend the rest of the day chasing them."

He scurried away from the table, and Aunt Nora refilled my glass with cold lemonade. Then she escorted me to the covered back porch where the flying insects would not eat us alive. It was time for another talk, but it was too late to run after Trevor.

Aunt Nora took a long drink of iced tea while I sat uncomfortably on a chair almost dreading what she might say.

I had neglected far too much, and there would be a price to pay.

She cleared her throat and looked at me. "You know I try very hard not to meddle in other people's lives."

I nodded my head in the affirmative.

"But this thing with you and Jake has to stop!"

My eyes opened wide, mostly to stop further tears. Aunt Nora was known for her honesty, and I had just received a double portion of it—no sugary coating added.

"You are both so damned miserable it breaks my heart. Uncle Ned and I promised your father—on his deathbed—that we would make sure you were okay. I kept thinking that you and Jake would figure things out on your own, but I watched the two of you interact at the reception, and you are barely talking. How can you resolve anything if you refuse to communicate with each other?"

"Jake and Beth are together," I jumped to my own defense. "You saw that for yourself."

"What I saw was two people who belong together but who refuse to do anything about it. Jake isn't interested in Beth in any of the ways that really matter."

"But they are sleeping together. That's a pretty big commitment."

I didn't want to tell her about Jake's letter. Its contents still haunted me, but changing what had happened in the past was impossible.

"Jake's a man who is used to the attention of many women. In our society, sleeping together doesn't mean anything. It's a biological urge being satisfied. That is the only thing going on between them."

"Not according to Beth. She is very much in love with him and willing to do whatever it takes to keep him."

Aunt Nora sighed. "I feel sorry for the girl. She has called here every day looking for him. I give him the messages—not because I want to—but because it's the right thing to do. I don't know if he is getting back with her."

I looked down at the wooden planks that made up the floor of the enclosed porch and frowned. I wanted to say that it wasn't right to sleep around just because everyone was doing it, but few people saw life the way I did. Aunt Nora wasn't married to Uncle Ned, my father and LeAnn had begun an affair long before my mother died, Molly didn't know who the father of her baby was, and according to Aunt Nora, Jake was sleeping with Beth because his feelings had been hurt. Maybe I was the one who was out-of-touch with reality, but some things were just too obvious to be ignored.

"Well, if he isn't returning her calls, he should be," I retorted with more vehemence than I felt. "No one deserves to be treated poorly just because they fall in love with the wrong man. Besides, they seemed like a real couple in Sydney, and since Trevor spent the night with me . . . ."

"I don't know what happened in Sydney," Aunt Nora broke in, clearing her throat again. "But I'm not sure you could call what was going on between them mutual. Jake was resisting her every advance."

"They were laughing and dancing and holding hands."

"And he was watching your every move. I could see the pain in his face. He might say he has moved on with Beth, but I am more than certain his heart is still with you. That's why he can't go back to the ranch. Being around you is killing him."

"It's killing me too," I said, suddenly wondering just how much she had been told and how much of what she was saying came from simple observation and inherent intuition. "But what can I do to make it better? I don't want to hurt Beth, especially since I am not sure Jake and I could make it together even if we tried. There is just so much stacked against us."

"Don't sell yourself short, or Beth either. She might think she can't live without Jake, but can you imagine the pain if they got married and then she was forced to accept that he was in love with someone else?" Aunt Nora's demeanor abruptly softened. "I know you have lots of doubts about everything right now, love, but you are a smart girl with plenty of common sense."

"I'm not so sure about that, Aunt Nora. I have made more mistakes lately than I care to count."

"Who hasn't?" she responded. "It's easy to set a clear course and stay there if the heart doesn't become involved. Once that happens, everything changes. I have all the confidence in the world that you will figure things out."

I wished I could be as sure of myself as she was. Everyone I talked to said the same thing. Jake and I were meant for each other, and if the gospel weren't part of my life, I would have to agree. He complimented me on every level. Together, we could be dynamite.

Trevor was thrilled with the new animals. I joined him in the barn and held a yellow chick in my hands while he talked to the fat, pink piglets that devoured everything he put within their reach.

It was a pleasant afternoon, despite my conversation with Aunt Nora, but it was still early when we got back to the ranch. So we took the four wheelers out for a ride before fixing dinner, and then we sat at the table playing checkers once the dishes had been washed and put away. The house seemed so silent—almost dead—without Jake's presence. Even Trevor commented on how things were so much more fun when his uncle was with us. He wanted to know when he would be back from Sydney and if we would all be together when he came home the following weekend. My answer was far from convincing but he fell asleep listening to stories anyway. He deserved so much better from the adults in his life.

Chapter 8

My heart was still heavy when we left for Edna on Sunday morning. Trevor liked going to church. He reminded me of myself when I first started attending meetings with Becky and Ben—a sponge absorbing truth I had never known existed before. But he was still a child, and once the baby was born and everyone returned to live at the ranch, he might not be as excited to go with me as he was now.

I stayed for lunch at Emma's. If Jake had been around I might have stayed the night in town again, but the animals had to be cared for, especially Copper. She had been neglected terribly lately and that wasn't fair.

LeAnn was more than optimistically excited when I went into her bedroom for a short visit before turning the Land Rover in the direction of the outback. She had decided that she couldn't wait until the baby was born to find out if it was a boy or a girl. So at her last appointment, she asked the doctor.

"I'm going to have a daughter, Brylee," she said when I sat down on the chair near her bed. Trevor had gone up to his attic bedroom to play. "And I'm going to name her Jackie after your father, if that is okay with you."

"Wow!" I replied as tears tickled the end of my nose. I had thought about naming my first daughter Jackie; and Jack if it happened to be a boy. But that would be impossible now. I was disappointed but tried not to let it show. "It will be wonderful having a baby sister, and I think Jackie is the perfect name."

"So do I," she said, nestling back into the pillows on her bed.

I didn't begrudge LeAnn giving my father another child—even if he wouldn't be around to watch her grow up—but the heaviness in my heart defied description. I wanted to be a wife and a mother more than anything else in the world, even if I couldn't name my daughter after my father.

"Don't look so sad, Brylee," she said, reaching out her hand to me. "I know none of this is easy for you. If you had never come home, you would have been married months ago and would likely be expecting a baby of your own."

I forced a sorrowful smile. "Things turn out the way they are supposed to, even if we don't understand or like it. I really am happy for both you and Molly, but part of me still hurts."

She squeezed my fingers in a kindly way. "You have sacrificed so much since coming home, but you have to know that it hasn't been in vain."

"I know that," I said with a shrug of my shoulders. "I found you and Trevor and Emma, and now I am going to have a little sister."

"A little sister who will be young enough to be your own child. I noticed that you didn't include Jake in your list of blessings. Do you mind if I ask why?"

Her brother was the last person in the universe I wanted to talk about after my conversations with both Molly and Aunt Nora. The state of our relationship hurt almost more than anything else in my life right now.

"It's complicated," I told her. "I wouldn't know where to begin."

"Maybe I can help with that," she said, leaning back on the pillows stacked behind her shoulders and head. "Jake has been to see me several times, and it was like pulling teeth with eyebrow tweezers to get him to open up about what has been going on, but eventually he let a few things slip."

"Like what?" I asked.

"Like the fact that he loves you with every fiber of his being. Now, even more than when he thought you might have a future together. I always wondered about the old adage of absence making the heart grow fonder, but in your case it certainly applies."

My lips puckered in that unflattering way they did whenever I was on the verge of crying.

"I never meant to hurt him, or anyone," I said as my voice cracked with a longing I wasn't sure I could explain. "I love Jake. He has taught me so many things and has always been there when I needed him, but I also love God and I simply cannot turn my back on him after all he has given me. And that doesn't even touch on the fact that Jake has Beth in his life now, and she is very much in love with him too."

She reached out her hand again and placed it on my knee since my shoulder was too far away to reach.

"You shouldn't have to be in so much pain, but I do understand your misgivings. Beth is a sweet girl, but she isn't you. Perhaps if you had never come to Australia things might have worked out for them. But you did come and have given my brother something he has never had before."

I looked up at her with a mixture of confusion and surprise. "I'm not sure aggravation, indecision and more than a little heartache apply."

"Those things are just part of living. What I am talking about is the fact that you have given him something to fight for. Women have always come too easy for him. All he had to do was smile, and they would melt into his arms. Beth is a pretty little distraction, but she was too easy and he is easily bored."

"That doesn't say much for his character."

"Maybe not, but that's the way most men are. They want what they cannot have."

"All that tells me is that Jake would eventually get bored with me if we did get together."

"You're missing the point, Brylee. You are Jake's intellectual equal. You challenge him in everything. He doesn't love you because you love him. He loves you because of the person you are inside—a person he wants to be worthy of, only he doesn't know how."

"I have tried to tell him how I feel, but everything comes out wrong."

"Maybe you are trying too hard! People need time to decide what is right for them."

I knew she was only trying to be helpful, but how could she possibly understand how I felt? I couldn't have life both ways. It was the gospel or Jake, and I couldn't risk everything on the slim hope that someday he might be willing to seriously listen to what I had to say. Even the sentiments in the note he left for me might not apply now. Love could very easily turn to hate.

"But what if that time runs out, LeAnn? I can't afford to gamble like that. I don't expect you to understand, given the fact that you think I am a little crazy with all my talk about religion anyway."

"People change and so do circumstances," she said. "I've had plenty of time to think these past few weeks, and I believe I understand more than you think I do. I have been reading the *Book of Mormon* and talking to the missionaries."

The room with its rose-colored walls and patchwork quilt began to spin, and my hands flew to my mouth as I struggled to take in enough air to keep from slipping into a dark abyss. "The missionaries?" I asked.

LeAnn smiled, and her face literally glowed like mine had done when first hearing about the amazing Plan of Salvation—

or the chance to be with my family forever and so many other wonderful things.

"Don't look so shocked," she said. "I have been watching you very closely since you came home to see if you could really live what you professed to believe. I wanted you to have feet of clay and fall because I knew if you didn't, I would have to find out for myself if what you believed was true."

My world quit reeling, leaving me with a free-floating sensation that God had literally answered one of my most fervent prayers, but I was still too overcome with emotion to speak.

LeAnn smiled again. "I wanted to ask you so many questions from the very beginning but knew I would have to give up my entire way of life if I did. We Aussies are a stubborn lot who like our tobacco, alcohol and crusty talk, not to mention taking our pleasures where we find them. But since I have been here with Emma, my whole attitude has changed. I decided I wanted what the two of you have, so I started asking questions.

"I was skeptical about Joseph Smith and that whole vision story at first, but when she talked about eternal families and knowing for sure that she would be with Robert again, something in my heart changed and I knew she was speaking the truth."

Tears were sliding down her cheeks, and I handed her a tissue from the box on the nightstand and took one for myself.

"I can't believe this," I said between sniffs. "I have wanted to share what I know with you so often, but every time I said anything of a spiritual nature people I love acted like I had lost my mind or were judging them."

"That's true!" she admitted. "Few people want to give up a life they are comfortable with, or accept the fact that what they have believed their entire lives isn't quite right, but when the spirit touches a heart, it doesn't leave much of a choice but to listen and eventually believe."

I looked over at the pregnant woman lying between white sheets in the guest room of another person's home. Her entire demeanor had changed. She didn't look angry or confused or even half-crazy with heartache anymore, but she was still the last person in the world I thought would come to accept what I had. She was—at least in part—responsible for destroying my family, but apparently God had other plans for all of us. If he could wipe her slate clean, then so could I.

"This is just so unexpected! I think someone needs to pinch me so I will know I'm not dreaming."

"Well, believe it, Brylee. Once Jackie is born I am going to church with you on Sunday. Heck, maybe we will even come in on Saturday so we can spend the night with Emma. I always knew she was a special woman, but not how special until she let me move in with her this last time. She has saved my life in so many ways. I can't begin to thank her enough."

I got out of my chair and sat down beside her on the bed. We hugged each other tightly, and for the first time since coming home, I knew that God truly was in charge of everything. I had never entertained the thought that my father's mistress would be the first one to accept the Restored Gospel of Jesus Christ, but in a way, it was fitting. She ad certainly been a catalyst for change in all of our lives. If she could alter her life so completely, there had to be hope that others could do it too.

"So, you see," she said, after our hug had ended, "I do understand how you can love my little brother and still not be willing to get involved with him. You want your marriage—whenever it happens—to last forever, and you want your children to belong to you for always."

"That's exactly what I want."

"Then you have to exercise more faith. My brother may be stubborn and proud, but he is not a fool. When he comes to understand that wedding ceremonies don't need to have a divorce clause written into them he will come around. No matter what he has done, or what he might still do, please don't give up on him, Brylee. You will have that marriage and family, and when you do, you will forget all about the past because there is nothing more glorious than having a child with the man you love and knowing that you really can be a family forever. It is what I always wanted with your father."

Oh, how lighthearted I felt on the long drive back to the ranch. I had to pull off to the side of the road more than once to wipe away tears of joy so I wouldn't be a menace to myself or any other motorist on the highway.

I no longer had to hide what I believed from everyone for fear of chastisement or hurting someone's feelings. We might be a rather unlikely lot—LeAnn, Trevor, Jackie and me, but we were a family. I wasn't sure how both of my parents fit into the mix quite yet but God would sort out all the complications, including those surrounding my messed-up relationship with Jake.

I took care of the chores and set the house in order before heading up the stairs to bed. For the first time in months, I wasn't quite so worried about what was happening with Jake because I knew he was in far more capable hands than mine. God loved all of his children equally, even the clearly rebellious because they needed his love and grace most.

After changing into my pajama pants and a light t-shirt, I lay down on my bed in the guest room and stared at the ceiling for the longest time. It was a silent night, only interrupted by an occasional owl's hoot or the call of some wild animal that I hoped was a good distance away from the house. I hadn't truly thought about being alone on the homestead until now, but while my loneliness was acute after leaving the people I had grown to love in town, I felt great joy as I thought about LeAnn's revelation. It meant I could hang pictures of the Savior, temples and prophets on the walls without fear of being reproved, and I could pray openly and listen to church music any time I wanted because I would no longer be judged as being overbearingly devout when it came to a something no one else was even willing to talk about.

Ben had loaded my IPOD with tons of church music—hymns by the Tabernacle Choir, Primary songs, the work of contemporary church artists and everything in between. I had grown to love singer/composers like Michael McLean, Afterglow and First Light who wrote songs about church beliefs in a way the Christian world could understand without becoming offended.

Since it was still early and all thoughts of sleep had fled, I went to the den, turned on my father's computer and subscribed to the Friend for Trevor and the Ensign for LeAnn and me. I even ordered pictures of the First Presidency and the Salt Lake Temple—the most well-known building of all in the Latter-day Saint culture—and several others by church artists like Liz Lemon Swindle, James Christensen and Greg Olsen that depicted the Savior loving and serving others. My favorite was the woman in the red dress kneeling at the Savior's feet.

I knew she was pouring out her heart to him the way I had done so many times the past few months. I marveled each day that God could still love me when all I seemed to do was doubt his timing, but I was beginning to understand that while mortal vision was limited, God knew the end from the beginning. And he definitely knew what I would have to pass through before I was ready to accept what he had in mind for me.

After that I found a strong flashlight, just in case I needed it, and went to the cemetery to share the news about LeAnn accepting the gospel with my parents. Not that they had even discovered it yet, but they would in time and LeAnn's conversion meant that Trevor could be baptized when she was. I could hardly wait to see them come out of the water knowing that a new life would begin for both of them. My only regret was not being able to share this amazing experience with Ben.

Without him, none of us would know that families really could be together forever.

As I sat on the dry, prickly grass in the place where so many of my ancestors had been laid to rest, I suddenly realized that I could hardly wait for my little sister to arrive, regardless of the fact that I was old enough to be her mother and wanted a child of my own. She would bring joy and laughter into a home that had always been weighed down with too much sorrow. I hoped she would look like my father because that meant she would look a little like me. I knew with complete certainty that both my mother and my father were spending time with her now, and that I no longer had to worry about how we would all fit together once mortality ended.

When I returned to the house, I knew I would be able to sleep, and I did. I woke up the next morning with a new determination to give my own past the burial it needed so I could go on with living.

I talked to Trevor, LeAnn, Aunt Nora and Emma every day after that. It made the time alone go by faster. Copper was always in my lap when I was sitting down or treading close behind when I went anywhere on the ranch where it was safe for her to follow. I was even letting her sleep with me since I knew she would return to Trevor's room the moment he stepped through the door, and in no time at all my entire family would be back where they belonged.

Being determined that my days would count, I got up early each morning to feed and water the animals in the barn and make sure the horses and other animals in the pasture had what they needed before moving on to something else. I picked one large job to do each day like cleaning out the tack room or re-stacking the hay. Physical exertion was a blessing. It meant I would sleep better at night because I was too tired to do anything else.

Despite being left out of the meeting in Sydney, it was full steam ahead in merging the ranches back to the way they had originally been. While Uncle Ned and Jake were still gone, LeAnn and I signed the papers Buck Henry had prepared. Some of the jargon was confusing, but it would allow more flexibility in solving the problems that came along, especially with the corporations who were still trying to force all the small ranchers to sell out and go away.

I couldn't help but wonder what was taking them so long. It wasn't like Uncle Ned to be away from his responsibilities for more than an occasional day at a time. Perhaps there was more to their trip than just business, but Aunt Nora never said they were involved with anything more than the obvious. Rather than press for answers she wasn't ready or willing to give, I called NJ to see if he had heard anything more than I had. He and Molly had the most to lose if things went south, but he assured me they were both excited about the proposal because neither of them planned on returning to the outback to live.

When I wasn't busy with work on my part of the ranch, Aunt Nora and I were integrating the accounts on paper so I could manage the finances while she was spending time with her children and grandson that would arrive in less than six months. In truth, that was all she wanted to talk about now, and I couldn't blame her for how she felt. Family was everything, but it still took a certain amount of solvent income to survive, and trips away from home were expensive. Especially since I already knew how much she was planning to spend in helping the newlyweds get settled in their new life in Brisbane.

I was genuinely happy for everyone involved but knew that working with family was dangerous under the best of circumstances. Feelings could easily get hurt—as I had already discovered—and differing opinions could ruin just about anything. To make what I was doing even more uncomfortable, there was a continual nagging fear that another catastrophic situation from weather to disease to a drop in the market could force the combined ranches into ruin anyway. If that ever happened, I didn't know what any of us would do.

I was meticulous in my record keeping, but with no money coming in from the sale of wool or animals, I was mostly watching our limited assets drain. Jake was still receiving his salary, and Aunt Nora and Uncle Ned had a formula in place as to how they would receive money from the account. But I was still not taking anything for myself, and LeAnn hadn't asked for much besides help in buying food and paying for utilities while she stayed with Emma.

The thing that frightened me most was the number of doctor and hospital bills that kept accumulating. There was no health insurance, and I couldn't bother LeAnn with financial details in her fragile condition, so I prayed daily that things would go smoothly and she would not have to stay in the hospital for more than the days allotted for a safe delivery. I wanted my father to be proud of me for the way I was taking care of his legacy, but life was uncertain at best, and I was having trouble trusting the business decisions I was being forced to make. My degree had given me the tools to succeed, but ranching was a complex operation, especially when I knew so little about it.

To combat my inadequacies, I started paying attention to details. I walked nearly every inch of the compound where the house and buildings stood, taking notes on things that needed repair and what assets were available for use if the need arose. My discoveries were both discouraging and surprising.

In the tack room where the saddles and bridals were kept, there were numerous items that belonged in a museum. Plows that had been pushed by hand, bellows and forges, harnesses for teams of horses, and strips of metal for cutting and bending into horseshoes. There were saws, clippers, wire cutters and square-topped nails. And there were dozens of things I didn't recognize and had no idea what they had been used for.

On the far side of the barn was a building that was still used to store the grain we got from Uncle Ned. I sneezed as I walked through the almost empty rooms that would have made an amazing playhouse had I been allowed to go there as a child. My feet stirred up little clouds of dust that had likely been there for years, but it was structurally sound as far as I could tell. That was something I couldn't say for many of the other buildings on the ranch. It would take more than wood, paint and nails to get things back to where they needed to be. It would take a great deal of money and backbreaking determination, both things we were desperately lacking at present.

I was very careful as I did my thorough inspection, wearing heavy boots and leather gloves. I had not forgotten my experiences with the Eastern Brown and the spiders that inhabited the outhouse. And while I hadn't seen any wild cats, dingoes or crocodiles near the house, I knew they could travel anywhere, and they weren't opposed to eating humans if they were hungry enough.

When I had told people in Los Angeles that I was from the Australian outback, they brought up how nice it must be to see kangaroos and Koala bears in the wild or even an aborigine or two. But that was so far from reality as to be laughable. No one saw things like that unless it was by accident, especially the locals who lived and worked there. Australia was a massive continent with many extremes and much of it was humanly uninhabitable. But if one had never been there, it was almost impossible to describe the diversity and loneliness to be found in a place as old as time.

With the lists I had made in my pocket, I saddled Rupert on Thursday morning to ride over to Aunt Nora's and get her advice on which repairs needed to be done now and which ones could wait. I also wanted to ask her about the artifacts I had found and see if I should leave them where they were, move them to a more prominent place on the ranch, try to sell them or just give them away.

Other than Jake's plane, four motorcycles, two four-wheelers, an old John Deere tractor and an ancient pickup truck that was in need of more than overhauling, nothing I found was of any realistic use. Horses were no longer needed to pull the plows, and gas-powered combines and bailers were used to bring in the crops. Uncle Ned had those types of machinery in the barns on his part of the ranch since it was the best suited for crop cultivation. We were more in need of barbwire, tin snips and hammers since we took care of the majority of the animals.

Aunt Nora was in the yard behind the house when I arrived.

"I didn't expect to see you this morning," she said, pushing herself to her feet and stretching her back. She had been on her hands and knees weeding one of her many flowerbeds that had been carefully brought back to life after the flood. "Ned called earlier. He and Jake are coming home today."

My heart began to race just hearing his name.

"Did they take care of everything that needed to be done?"

She took off her gardening gloves and draped them over the rim of her bucket.

"I'm not sure what they accomplished by going. Any way you slice or dice it, small ranchers aren't going to have it easy. But here is the real kicker. There is more talk of gold in the outback."

"Really," I said as a shiver of fear traveled the length of my spine. I hadn't thought about the cave or what Jake had shown us since leaving the mountain. I had been too busy dwelling on the pain of no longer having him in my life.

"Yes," she continued, seemingly unaware of my heightened senses. "I hate it when that happens. The local ranchers can't afford to mine it, and they don't want to sell out to the corporations who can. That leaves all of us right in the path of trouble. Once ruthless groups of people smell money, they will stop at nothing to get it. Ned said that one of the ranchers on the other side of the mountain, John Sutter, was killed a few days ago trying to defend his property."

A knot of sorrowful dread formed in the pit of my stomach. If a man had been killed due to an outbreak of gold fever, it could mean that someone had discovered the cave while we had been away doing other things. If that had happened, we could be in more danger than anyone realized.

"Did you know him?" I asked, frowning with both remorse and apprehension for keeping such a potentially volatile secret from them. Jake and I should have told them about the cave, the drawings and the gold flecks in the stone walls when the idea of incorporation first came up.

"Not well, but don't look so worried, Brylee. There isn't any gold on the Hawkins' ranch. If there was, someone would have found it by now."

Someone had found it, I mused, and had shown it to both Trevor and me. What if my little brother had innocently mentioned it to someone in town? We hadn't specifically told him not to say anything.

"I'm not worried," I told her, wishing I knew what to do. She had the right to know what we had found, but I couldn't say anything until I had talked to Jake.

The opportunity for that discussion came later that afternoon when Jake walked into the kitchen where I was baking apple and cherry pies for Trevor when he came home for the weekend.

"I'm glad you are here," he said without fanfare or explanation when he saw me standing at the sink peeling and slicing the apples I had brought home from Aunt Nora's. "We need to talk."

Without saying anything in return, I ran water over the apples so they wouldn't turn brown and sat down at the table with him. He didn't ask for his usual cup of coffee, and I didn't offer him anything.

"I saw Aunt Nora today," I said through lips that were beginning to tremble. "She told me about the rancher that was killed."

Jake ran his hands through his thick, dark hair but kept his eyes from making direct contact with mine.

"Then you know we are not sitting in a very good place. The rancher who was killed lived straight through the mountain from the cave I showed Trevor and you. I don't know if our tunnels come to an end or lead into some of theirs. I haven't had the time to thoroughly explore them, but even if what we found is self-contained, it won't take long before someone starts snooping around and finds it."

"What are we going to do?" I asked, biting the inside of my lip. My hands were clenched tightly together underneath the tabletop so he wouldn't see them. I didn't want him to know how really frightened I was, especially since Trevor would be coming home the following day.

"That's what I have been trying to decide. Technically, the cave is on your father's land, but since this consolidation thing, Ned does have a right to know."

The telephone rang quite suddenly, and Jake literally jumped to his feet to answer it. I sat silently at the table chewing my lip and wishing life didn't always have to be so problematic.

"I just got back a few minutes ago," I heard him say. "I'm sorry, but it couldn't be helped. Ned and I had a lot to do in Sydney and there wasn't time to call. I know it was inconsiderate, but I promise to make it up to you."

It was Beth on the other end, and she had been desperate enough to use the landline at the ranch in trying to reach him.

Nothing had changed in that department, no matter how many people told me otherwise.

"No, I won't be in tonight either. Something has come up out here, and I have to take care of it, but I will call you later. I really am sorry." There was a brief pause, and then he said, "me too" and hung up.

Further clarification was unnecessary. They had been planning something, and the gold in the cave had spoiled it.

"Sorry for the interruption," he said, when the receiver was back on the wall. "What were we talking about?"

I tried not to let my emotions surface. Just talking to her had made him forget I was even there. So much for believing what certain others had told me about their more than blossoming affair.

"We were trying to decide whether or not we should tell Uncle Ned about the cave. I for one, don't care about the gold. We don't even know if there is enough to worry about. But I do care about the safety of those drawings and that one man has already been killed. They are priceless and need to be preserved, and the madness that comes with gold fever needs to be stopped before it spreads any further. The problem is trying to make the right decision when we don't have all the facts."

Jake slammed his fist on the table as he sat down beside me. "I couldn't agree more. That is precisely why I haven't said anything to Ned, Nora or LeAnn about it. I was hoping it would just go away. But in light of the fact that a rather large nugget has been found so close to the ranch, I don't suppose we have any other choice. We need more information, and the only way we are going to get it is by going up there again."

He looked more than just tired and concerned. He almost looked defeated, and that was only natural since he carried the greater load when it came to keeping the corporation we had just formed going. My being supportive was what he needed now, but I wasn't sure how to go about it without letting my heart get in the way.

"It's too late to make that trip tonight," I told him. "And one of us needs to pick Trevor up after school tomorrow. We could all go together on Saturday."

He looked at me with genuine surprise. "You have got to be kidding! It's too dangerous! If someone else already knows about the cave, I hate to think about what might be coming."

"I haven't told anyone," I said. "I would never break a confidence like that."

"I know you wouldn't, but I am worried that Trevor might have said something unintentionally. You know what it's like when you are young, always wanting to have something a little bigger or better than anyone else to share."

"I had the same thought," I reluctantly admitted. "I love Trevor with all my heart, but he is still just a little boy who knows nothing about the value of gold or ancient drawings."

"Then you can understand why I don't want either of you anywhere near that cave. Now that the story about the possibility of gold has leaked out all the unscrupulous people in the country will be drawn here like flies to honey. I even worry about having you at the ranch given what happened to John Sutter. Maybe you should stay in town with Emma until this whole bloody thing blows over."

I didn't want to take exception to what he had said, but I wouldn't be driven away from my home. Trevor's safety was another matter.

"Don't take this wrong, Jake, but I can take care of myself."

His frown was instantaneous.

"I know you consider yourself an independent woman, but you haven't met the kind of men I am taking about. They don't care who they maim or kill if it means getting what they want."

"Then I guess we need to proceed carefully, but before we do anything else, we have to tell Uncle Ned and Aunt Nora about the cave."

He slowly filled his lungs with air before speaking. "I suppose they do have a vested interest in what happens on our side of the ranch now, and in all fairness they know more about the land and the people than we do. I could drive over and talk to them while you finish your pies."

"The pies can wait, but talking can't," I said, standing up. "I need to be part of this, and I promise I won't run away again, regardless of how bad it might get. This is my home—or better or worse—and I want to be included in everything that goes on around here from now on."

Jake didn't object as I thought he might. He simply got up and helped me put the apples in the fridge and cover the pie crusts I had already rolled out on the counter.

"I like seeing you this way," he said as the refrigerator door slammed shut. "I have missed the feisty Brylee who was always putting me in my place."

"And I like the fact that you still feel protective towards us. So many things have changed since I came home."

"And so many haven't," he replied.

Jake backed his pickup truck out of the shed while I called Uncle Ned to tell him we were coming. I said very little on the short drive to their part of the ranch. It was too tempting sitting just a few inches away from him, but now wasn't the time to discuss anything personal, not even the letter he thought I had known about. We were in another crisis. I couldn't count the number of those we hd been through the past few months, but I did know one thing for certain. Jake was as committed to family as I was.

Uncle Ned and Aunt Nora were waiting for us on their new front porch. He was making smoke rings as he puffed on a fat, brown cigar. They each had a can of cold beer in their hands and a few extra cans in a bucket of ice on the table. They had been considerate enough to put a pitcher of lemonade and an empty glass out for me.

"Grad a cold one and sit down," Uncle Ned instructed as we climbed out of the truck at the same time. "It's a fine night for a drive, but I get the distinct feeling this isn't a social call. Things are really heating up right now."

I heard the tab on Jake's beer can pop open as I filled the glass with lemonade and sat down next to Aunt Nora. All pleasantries aside, this was going to be a very difficult evening. I was glad Jake would be the one telling them what we had been hiding since there was no way of knowing what their reaction might be.

"Have you heard from Molly today?" I asked, wishing we didn't have anything except pleasantries to discuss.

"As a matter of fact," Aunt Nora said. "Molly called not long after you left. She loves Evan's family. They went looking for baby things today."

I wanted to ask her what they had purchased, but postponing the inevitable wasn't wise.

"I can't believe my little girl is going to make me a grandfather," Uncle Ned's booming voice was filled with pride. "I don't know how I am going to keep Nora way out here after that child arrives. I bet you didn't know that she has already purchased everything that baby will need for its first year of life. My credit cards will be maxed to the hilt."

"You hush up, Ned Hawkins," Aunt Nora said with a bright smile. "I have left a few things for Evan's family to buy. You would have done it yourself if I hadn't beaten you to it."

Uncle Ned laughed. "That's how you know you have been together a long time, kids. You finish each other's thoughts and know all about each other's behaviors, but I wouldn't trade what we have for anything."

He reached across the table and took her hand. She tried to make light of the compliment, but the tears floating in her eyes told a different story. She loved my uncle every bit as much as he loved her.

"So," Uncle Ned said, turning his attention back to us. "Let's discuss what we need to so we can get back to having a pleasant evening."

Jake took another swallow of beer. "I made a discovery a few months ago that I should have told you about sooner, Ned. There is a cave behind a waterfall."

My uncle didn't flinch.

"There are lots of caves on this property. I have found a few of them myself. Jack and I used to play in them as children."

"I'm not sure you found this one," Jake replied. "It has aborigine paintings on the walls, and if you go further back, there are veins of what appear to be gold."

"Well, I'll be damned," Uncle Ned said, slapping the table so hard it made the beer cans jump. "Old Ishmael, the aborigine who worked for us when we were kids, told us about it, but we thought it was just folklore."

"Oh, it is real enough," Jake replied. "You can ask Brylee if you don't believe me. I took her and Trevor there."

"Now, isn't that interesting," he said as his eyes bored into mine. It was impossible to tell just what he was thinking. "I suppose it's on Jack's part of the property."

"It is!" Jake responded. "I found it quite by accident a few months back. I had taken the plane out and saw a small, but magnificent, waterfall from the air. So I checked coordinates and rode up to take a closer look. I had no idea there was anything more to it until I found the cave."

"But you kept it a secret. Do you mind if I ask why?"

"There didn't seem to be any point in mentioning it at the time. Jack was sick, and when he died, everything was pretty much put on hold."

I knew I should be adding something, but just watching my uncle's jaw move slowly back and forth was making me nervous. It was like the quiet before some major storm broke.

"I never meant to leave anyone out," Jake continued. "It just didn't seem important until now."

"But you did leave us out of it," Uncle Ned said. "And so did you, Brylee. We have been working on the consolidation of the ranches for weeks now. It seems to me there has been plenty of time to mention the existence of a cave, especially one that might have gold in it, unless you had other plans."

I looked down at the glass of lemonade in my hands. Uncle Ned had every right to be annoyed. We were partners in everything now.

"Don't blame Brylee for any of this, Ned," Jake said. "I asked her not to say anything because I didn't want news of it getting out before I figured out what should be done. A find like this could disturb the balance of nature. People would come out here in droves to see the paintings and try to discover if there really was a gold mine further back in the mountain."

Uncle Ned ran his hand over the top of his head just like my father had always done when he was thinking. Then he looked across the table at Aunt Nora.

"So why tell us about it now?"

"Because the cave is straight through the mountain from John Sutter's ranch," Jake said without hesitation.

Uncle Ned put his cigar in the ashtray in the center of the small table and took a long, deliberate breath of air. Aunt Nora was watching him attentively.

"It appears we have a problem then," he finally said. "And I assume you came here for help, but it is going to take a little time to wrap my head around all of this."

I wanted desperately to sink into the wooden floorboards, but I couldn't let Jake take all the blame. I had willingly followed his lead because I loved him.

"We didn't plan for any of this to happen, Uncle Ned. We just didn't want anything disturbed. It seemed almost sacrilegious being there. Those drawings were not for us. They were a visual history of the aborigine tribe who lived here. You said yourself that you heard stories about it when you were a child."

Uncle Ned looked at me, but some of the harshness in his countenance had faded. "So I did, but I never quite believed old Ishmael. It sounds like you have already made up your mind as to what you plan on doing about the paintings, but we can't just pretend that gold veins don't exist when one man has already been killed."

"Don't beat the kids up for making a choice they thought was right," Aunt Nora came to our defense. "They are young! We didn't make the best decisions when we were their age either."

"Youth has nothing to do with this, Nora. The kids purposely chose not to tell us something we had every right to know. We might have had a plan in place if they had, and John Sutter might not have lost his life. Now, all we can do is try to stop any further violence. I don't suppose you know if Trevor mentioned it to anyone. Sutter found a single gold nugget in his field. That is not an excuse to kill him unless finding something more was expected, and the cave you just mentioned certainly applies. I can't believe it has been here all along and no found it before you did."

"Trevor didn't say anything," I abruptly interjected. "I'm not even sure he knew what we were talking about when we went into the room with the gold flecks in the walls. It was dark, but I will ask him about it tomorrow when I pick him up from school."

"By then it might be too late," Uncle Ned said. "I called John's widow after you left, Jake. She said there were dozens of men swarming all over her property, and they wouldn't leave when she asked them to. She was so frightened she called the police in Edna, but there isn't a lot they can do except send a couple of deputies to check things out. It could turn into an all-out war if what you just told us has already been discovered. There are as many ways onto our land as there are people, and no one is more persistent than a man looking for gold."

"We should be okay for a few days," Jake offered. "There are dozens of miles of unforgiving land between here and the cave."

Uncle Ned looked across the table to where Aunt Nora was quietly sitting. "Not if they decide to go over the top. What do you think we should do, Nora?"

She appeared to be in a state of shock. "I'm still trying to digest what we have just been told. To think there might actually be gold on Hawkins' land is a little mind-boggling. It would solve so many problems, but you know how I feel about what we did to the aborigines, Ned. Whatever is in that cave belonged to them first, and we have no right to disturb it."

"Always my voice of reason," he said. "And I agree that what our ancestors did to the aborigines was appalling, but that might not be our most pressing problem. That cave is too close to Sutter's property. Not that I wouldn't mind being a millionaire, but we don't even know if there is anything beneath the surface. What if it is fool's gold, not the real thing?"

My hand went to the stone in the necklace Jake had given me for Christmas. Even after all that had gone on between us, I still wore it underneath my shirt. It seemed like my last link to him.

Jake's brow ceased as he caught my eye.

"The gold veins are real," he said. "I had one of the rocks I took out of the cave made into a necklace for Brylee for Christmas. Oscar Beltram in Edna confirmed its authenticity, but it doesn't mean we have a genuine gold mine on our hands. It only means there are trace elements there."

"Like you really believe that," Uncle Ned mocked. "Did you tell him where you found it?"

"He didn't ask and I didn't say."

"But that doesn't mean he won't remember and start to speculate in light of what Sutter found. It is too close geographically to be a coincidence. Do you happen to have that necklace with you, Brylee?"

I undid the clasp around my neck and handed the necklace to Uncle Ned. I had never intended for anyone to know that I wore, especially Jake. It would only complicate the already impossible situation between us.

"This is more than a speck," he said, looking it over carefully before handing it to Aunt Nora. "But I suppose you could have picked it up anywhere. I just don't like the idea of prospectors so close to our property, especially now that someone has been killed. Still, jumping to conclusions about what is and what isn't known right now might be a little premature. Why don't we concentrate on a plan to preserve the drawings and give everything else a day or two to calm down?"

No one cast a descending vote, so it was decided that Jake would take Uncle Ned to the cave while I drove into Edna to get Trevor for the weekend. I would ask him about mentioning the caves existence before we got home.

"Do you think we did the right thing by telling them?" Jake asked me on the drive home. "I have never seen Ned so upset."

I looked out the window into the eerie darkness that surrounded us. Nights in the outback were so different than they were in L.A. where artificial lighting illuminated everything.

"Can you really blame him?" I queried, not taking my eyes from the passing scenery, even though it was hard to make out anything but shadows and outlines. "We withheld a certain truth from him. Our reason for doing so don't really matter any more and . . . ."

"Secrets only damage," he finished for me. "But I really didn't see the harm in keeping it to ourselves. And I sure as hell didn't want a lot of hot-headed and greedy prospectors snooping around the ranch. I only took you there because it was something special, and I cared about you."

Cared! That implied something that was already in the past. The cave with the drawing and flecks of gold had not been kind to me thus far. It was where Jake had told me that if I didn't want him in my life in a more committed way, he would find someone who did.

"Let's not talk about that right now," I told him. "We can't change the past, but we can work together to solve this latest problem. I just wish Asum and his family were still around. He is Ishmael's son, and I knew him when I was a child. Maybe he could give us a few ideas about what the aborigines would want. If nothing more, he would know if the cave went all the way through the mountain."

"I would accuse you of trying to avoid talking to me about anything personal if I didn't feel the same way," he responded. "This land isn't mine to sell, give away or get rich from, but I think the tribes who lived here before we came should at least be able to voice their opinions about what happens to the drawings. And if those veins of gold ever lead to something big, I am more than certain they can be accessed from a different direction, if that is what we all decide to do. We could even set up some kind of foundation for the aborigines."

"That sounds nice," I said, looking at the outline of his profile in the near dark. "I know we have to move forward, but having more money to make life easier isn't my main concern right now. I don't want to see any more people get hurt. Mr. Sutter should not have been killed defending his own property."

"As you just said, Brylee, we can't change what has already happened. I am not even sure we can stop what has already been set in motion. Gold fever has to burn itself out naturally."

When we got back to the ranch, Jake excused himself while I went into the house to finish baking the pies. I wanted to believe that everything would be okay. But if Jake was right, this might only be the beginning of the worst adventure of my life. He didn't come back inside before turning out the bunkhouse lights, and I went to bed with more than a few unanswered questions swirling around in my head.

Chapter 9

I woke up the next morning much later than anticipated with an inordinate amount of work to do before I left for Edna. I hadn't slept much. Visions of violence and unrest had replaced the more peaceful dreams I had been having since learning that LeAnn had chosen to embrace the gospel.

Restful slumber was a miracle in itself because my nocturnal imaginings were usually about Jake and Beth, and the horror of losing the man I loved because I hadn't been willing to give him the time he needed to change—change that was coming about anyway. The letter he had left for me proved that, but I still hadn't been able to tell him when I found it. Not that it would matter since far too much time had already passed.

I had left the pies cooling on a rack before going to bed, but when I walked into the kitchen there was a huge slice of apple pie missing. A hastily scribbled note sat beside it on the counter top.

"I'm sorry for eating some of Trevor's pie, but it looked too good to resist, and it tasted even better. Be safe driving into town. I should be back about the same time you are. Give

Emma and LeAnn my love, but don't say anything about our discoveries just yet. Neither of them needs anything more to worry about right now."

Before leaving the house, I took the note to my room and buried it in one of my drawers where Trevor would not find it.

My little brother looked like he had grown an inch taller when he came running out of the gray, brick building with the double red doors, talking excitedly to some of his friends. School had been good for him. He had literally blossomed socially during the weeks he had been living in town. Was it fair to take him back to the ranch once the baby arrived? The outback was a great place to visit, but not such a great place for children to be raised. They needed the association of their peers in order to thrive.

He ran straight into my arms, his backpack falling to the ground so he could hug me a little tighter than he had in the past.

"You came," he said as I hugged him back. It would take time for me to regain his trust, but I could accept that. Confidence in another person could not be rushed once it had been broken.

"Of course I did, Trevor." I said, looking directly into his eyes. "I am not going to leave you again no matter how sick I get. I'm afraid you are stuck with me pretty much forever."

"Are we going to Macca's and a movie before we go home? I am awfully hungry," was his only reply.

He picked up his backpack while I opened the door so he could climb inside the Land Rover. He used a booster seat so he could see out of the window. We would have to get a car seat for the baby before we could take her home.

"I was thinking we could have dinner at the ranch tonight. I baked pies and have steak unthawing in the fridge, but I have some fruit snacks and a granola bar you can eat on the way home. I will drive as fast as I can."

He started to laugh. "You can't cook them yourself. That is a man's job."

"Oh, really," I said, slipping in behind the steering wheel. "I will have you know I am turning into a pretty good cook."

"I was only teasing," he said, looking a little sad and as he tore open a package of fruit snacks. Apparently, he was learning more at school than just facts and figures. He was learning how to rag like other kids did and that was something he had never done before. "Will Uncle Jake be there? I miss the times we used to spend together."

I took a deep breath to clear my head. That was one thing I could not promise him. Jake was involved with Beth, and we were entering another volatile situation not of our own making. But none of those things needed to be mentioned until something had been decided.

"As far as I know, he will be there," I told him with a stellar attempt at keeping my voice light and a smile on my face in case he noticed my reflection in the rearview mirror. "But he and Uncle Ned had a few things to do today. You know what it is like on the ranch. You can't plan anything for certain."

He looked out the window and waved to his friends as I pulled the car away from the curb and onto the street.

"It looks like you have made more friends."

"They're cool," he said. "But I still miss Copper and Newton and the others. Are they still okay without me?"

"They're fine. I have been taking care of them personally, but Newton isn't a calf any more. He is almost full-grown. I think you will be very surprised when you see all of them. Both animals and children can grow a lot in two weeks time."

Emma had cookies and milk waiting for us when we stopped by to get Trevor's duffle bag. He ran directly to the kitchen when we got there, but I pulled Emma aside. If anyone knew the latest gossip around town, she would. She had lived in Edna her entire life, and as the owner of the best diner there she was privy to things few other people knew about.

"What have people been saying about Mr. Sutter's death?" I asked. "It is such a tragedy."

"And only the beginning of more trouble," she answered. "The police have no idea who did it. Edna has been crawling with lowlife ever since the word got out about the possibility of finding gold. We all think Ruth should move away from the ranch until the dust settles, but she refuses to leave her home. I can understand that in a way. After all, she and John lived there for over forty years, but I am still very worried about her safety."

"Can't the police doing anything?"

Her shoulders moved ever so slightly upwards. "They can try, but the outback has its own set of rules. John wouldn't have been killed if he hadn't been trying to defend his own land. Men—like the ones I have seen in town the past few days—aren't going to let an old man with a rifle get in their way. They know the law can't touch them out there."

"But it's not right," I countered. We might be living in the twenty-first century but life never seemed to change all that much in *sunburned country*. "People have the right to defend what is theirs."

"I agree, but the unscrupulous people of the world won't let a little thing like law and order stop them. We are living in a recession like the rest of the world. People are losing their jobs and homes as much here as anywhere else, and desperate people do desperate things."

"Still, I don't understand how anyone could think they would get away with cold-blooded murder. The gold—if there really is any—will have to be mined and that costs a lot of money."

"Apparently, John found more than a single nugget plowing a new field on the edge of the mountain."

"But only one has been mentioned," I said.

"That's only because Ruth was smart enough not to reveal to the police, or anyone else, that her husband had been finding them for weeks. Not huge ones like the one that caused all the ruckus, but a whole bag of smaller ones."

I swallowed back a lump that was threatening to choke me. "How would you know that?"

Her brief smile was instantaneous. "Ruth worked for me at the diner years ago."

Of course she had, I mused. Nearly everyone in Edna had worked for Emma at one time or another.

"And we have remained fast friends. She needed someone to talk to and knew I would never say anything. The problem is that she doesn't know what to do now. If she keeps her secret it might all go away on its own, if she doesn't . . . ."

"But you told me. Why?"

"I'm not sure, except that I felt you needed to know. You are closer to the situation than I am, and you could be there to help out if she needed it. Her children have all moved away. Naturally, they will come back for the funeral and will insist that she return with one of them, but I don't see her doing that. She has lived in the outback her entire adult life, and it is where her husband will be buried—in the family plot with the rest of their Sutter ancestors."

In my unsolicited opinion which I was not about to share, Ruth Sutter was being incredibly foolish for not telling the authorities or being willing to leave, but I understood how she felt. For better or worse, the outback was my home too. How much gold there was in the mountain, I wasn't sure. But in light of what Emma had said, it likely wasn't a fluke that we had seen traces of it in the cave. If men were already swarming over Ruth's ranch, it wouldn't be long until they were on ours as well.

We left her home after I had spent a few minutes with LeAnn. She still looked happy, but I knew she listened to the news and word about John Sutter's death would be all over it. She asked if I knew anything new, but true to the promise I had made to Jake, I told everything was fine where we lived.

Trevor and I stopped at the store for a few supplies before the long drive home. I was worried about keeping a conversation going in my present state of mind, but I needn't have been concerned. Trevor was tired and slept most of the way there.

Jake had the grill out and lit when we got back. He looked both worn-out and upset, but I couldn't talk to him about anything until Trevor went to bed. It was going to be a long evening of pretense.

"It looks like I timed that just right," he said, taking the package of steak out of the fridge. "I was going to put some potatoes in the microwave, but I saw that a potato salad had already been made."

"I figured we would all be tired," I said, placing a few plastic bags on the counter top. "I wanted our meal to be quick and easy."

"Can I cook the steaks, Uncle Jake? I am a lot taller now."

Jake smiled at me from across the kitchen. "I guess you are," he said. "Why don't you get the big fork, and we will get these bad boys grilling. I haven't had anything to eat since morning."

Jake really was remarkable, I thought as I began putting the purchased groceries away. Why hadn't I noticed it so much sooner? He loved his family, and we had nothing to fear as long as he was around to protect us.

Trevor said he wasn't tired after dinner, so we put a movie in the DVD player to watch. I made some buttered popcorn and got three sodas out of the fridge for us to drink. It was the first time we had ever done that with Jake, and I hoped he wouldn't be bored with a Pixar animated feature.

Trevor piled a stack of pillows on the floor in the den and lay down on them. Jake sat beside me on the leather sofa. It was an intimate, cozy situation, but I refused to let my true feelings show. Jake had Beth in his life now, and I would never come between them.

So I just sat there beside him with only the bowl of popcorn separating us. I loved him with all my heart and wanted him in my life, but that could never happen now, and I had to accept it.

The movie started, and *Cars II* immediately captivated Trevor's attention, but I couldn't keep my mind on it. Still, regardless of my awareness of Jake's presence, I managed to laugh at the appropriate times so my little brother would think I was enjoying it.

Jake looked relaxed and content as he pushed the knob on the side of the sofa that turned his section into a recliner. I wanted to do the same thing with mine, but instead I just curled my feet underneath my body and leaned away from him. It was my one attempt at self-preservation.

But Jake must have been too tired or preoccupied to notice because he closed his eyes not long after the movie started. I didn't want to wake him, even when Trevor turned around to get more popcorn and saw him sleeping.

"Let's not bother him," I whispered. "He's had a very long day."

Trevor was okay with that. He filled his popcorn bowl again and went back to watching the movie while I watched Jake sleep. I desperately wanted to kiss him, but that would only confuse Trevor, and I might not get the reaction I wanted.

When the movie was over, I walked my little brother upstairs to read him a story while he fell asleep.

"Brylee," he said as he made himself comfortable underneath the sheet with Copper beside him. "Will things change a lot when the baby comes home?"

"Of course they will," I told him, sitting down on the bed with a book in my hands. "We are learning and growing every day. That's the way it is supposed to be. We would get totally bored if they didn't.

"Are you sure," he asked. "All people talk about any more is the baby. Maybe they won't want me after she is born."

I put my arms around him and let the book fall to the floor. He had been through so much the past few months, and it wasn't over yet.

"We will always want and need you and so will the baby. You will be her big brother and teach her how to do so many things. But most of all, you will want to keep her safe."

"But I still don't know how to be a big brother," he said with concern.

I looked down at him with nothing but tenderness. Trevor would grow into a remarkable man. He had strength, courage and an open heart—all qualities I wished more adults had.

"You will do just fine," I told him. "Things may seem a little overwhelming right now, but once Jackie is born you will know exactly what to do."

"Can she sleep in my room?"

I smiled and pulled him even closer. "I'm not sure your mother would allow that. A baby is a big responsibility. She has to be fed, changed, bathed and burped. She won't be able to do anything by herself, not even hold her head up on her own for a few weeks. Can I tell you a little secret? I am kind of scared about having a new baby in the house too. I have never been around one before."

His eyes flew open. "You haven't? But you are older. You should have seen lots of babies."

"I have seen babies, but I have never taken care of one. So you see, you are not alone in wondering what is going to happen when baby Jackie gets here. But I can promise you one thing, we will just love each other more."

He leaned back against his pillow while I retrieved the book from the floor.

"I want to do something extra special for Jackie," he said.

"You already bought her first toy and a mobile."

"Something bigger than that. I want to have everything ready for her when she comes home. Can we get my old crib from the attic and set it up in mum's room? I know where my baby clothes are too. She can wear some of them."

"I think that is an excellent idea, and we can do it tomorrow. Do you think we can wrestle that crib down the stairs by ourselves and set it up?"

"I know we can! I have grown a whole lot just like Newton. In a few months, I will be in the third grade."

I didn't want to say anything about school. Once the baby was born, he would be back at the ranch, and things would go on as they always had. It was homeschooling, boarding school or living with strangers. I was glad I wouldn't be the one telling him that public school was a thing of the past.

I read him another story, and he fell asleep. I could have sat by his side for hours, but I needed to tell Jake what Emma had said. We could be heading towards far more trouble than any of us had anticipated.

He was in the kitchen drinking a cup of coffee when I walked back down the stairs.

"You shouldn't have let me sleep. I missed all the movie," he said.

"We can watch it again sometime," I responded, sitting down across the table from him. It was a far less intimate situation than it had been in the den where all the lights had been turned off so we could see the TV screen better.

He took another sip of coffee. "I will hold you to that, and I am glad you came down. I want to keep you informed about what is going on because I might need your help."

"I am always here for you," I told him, unaware of how personal my declaration was until the words slipped out. "I mean, I will do anything you need me to do."

"I like the way you said it the first time." His smile let his dimple show. "And I am glad you will have my back, especially now that things are heating up."

"Are they really that bad? Emma said there were a lot of strangers in town, and people think Ruth should move into Edna."

"That would be the safest thing for her, but I don't think anyone will bother her as long as she doesn't take a stand like her husband. I hope you can remember how to handle a gun."

"I do," I responded. "But I don't believe in bloodshed, and I could never hurt someone intentionally."

"You might change your mind if they threatened the people you love. What would you do if someone came after Trevor?"

"I don't know," I said, looking down at the table.

"Well, I do. You would give your life for him just like I would and sometimes that means doing unthinkable things."

"But shooting another person! Do you really think it might come to that?"

"It already has. John didn't shoot himself. The hills are crawling with men. Ned and I took the plane up after we got back from the cave. He is every bit as worried as I am."

"So what are we going to do?"

"Well, for one, you are going to stay out of it. Ned and I can take care of things around here. He is planning on leaving in the morning to see if he can find old Ishmael's tribe. He believes that old aborigine might know a lot that can help us. They were never into material things, but that doesn't mean they don't know a whole lot about the mountain."

"But Ishmael deserted his family when I was a baby and never came back. I doubt he is even alive now. And it is highly unlikely even Asum could be found, and he has only been gone a little over five years."

"Ned seems to think he can do it, and I don't see that we have many options left. We certainly don't have much time. Things could explode at any minute, leaving us in one bloody hell of a mess. If even one tribe member that used to inhabit this area could be found, learning more about those drawings would not be the only benefit. I have my suspicions from exploring numerous caverns inside the cave, but only an aborigine would know if veins of gold are more than surface deep and if the cave has entrances on both sides of the mountain. Personally, I think it's worth a shot."

My mind was spinning in circles of confusion and doubt.

"I don't know, Jake. Those are a lot of suppositions. What if the tribe can't be found, or what if they are and no one will talk to him? We might not learn anything that could help us, and it might mean that Uncle Ned isn't here when we need him."

"I know it's a long shot, Brylee, but I don't see what harm it could do."

My fears were raging but I had to let some of them go. "Probably none, but if people really are swarming all over the mountain, like you just said, we might be forced into making a few decisions long before he gets back."

I should have told him what Emma said about the extra gold nuggets John Sutter had found, but I wasn't sure that it really mattered. Besides bringing even more fortune hunters to the area, it might mean an end to Ruth Sutter's life.

"Nora's already on that!" Jake said, stopping my unwanted thoughts. "We talked when we got back earlier today. She is going to the courthouse and historic society first thing Monday morning to see what our options are about having the cave declared an historic monument of sorts."

"That sounds like a good idea, but I don't really know what it means."

"It means it might be a way to keep the drawings protected."

"Not if someone goes into any of the other rooms," I countered.

"I'm not saying it is a solution to everything, but it might stop the cave from being disturbed."

"It should only matter that the cave is on our property."

"In a perfect world it would, but rightful ownership won't stop men from trying to take what isn't theirs. I have seen plenty of them flying supplies into the outback. They have no regard for anything, other than getting rich. It is an illness like gambling or alcoholism. They can't back away from it on their own, and they won't ask for help."

I understood what Jake was saying but were those drawings, or even the possibility of finding gold more mine, really worth risking another life to protect? Maybe we should contact the authorities ourselves and tell them what we knew, or maybe we should just close the entrance permanently. Money could buy a lot of material comforts, but it could not bring anyone back to life.

Chapter 10

Jake was in the kitchen when Trevor and I went downstairs for breakfast the next morning. He had made coffee and was scrambling eggs in a frying pan on the stove. There was a stack of buttered toast on the counter next to him.

"I hope you slept well," he said. "I thought we could take the bikes out to Loon Lake. There might not be any fish, but it is still pretty to look at."

"We were going to get things ready for the baby," Trevor said with a frown. "She's gonna be here real soon now."

I was surprised at his reluctance. He had never been hesitant about doing anything Jake suggested before, and the ranch had always been the center of his universe. But if Jake noticed anything unusual about his comment, he didn't let it show.

"I'll tell you what, sport," he said as he turned the burner off. "You and Brylee come for a ride with me this morning, and I will help you get things set up for the baby when we get back. Uncle Ned said there were some kangaroos over that way. If we are lucky, we might just see them."

That's all it took for Trevor to rethink his plans. To the outside world, Australia was known for cuddly-looking Koala bears and kangaroos, but the chance of seeing one in its natural habitat was decreasing yearly as people pushed the boundaries of civilization. I wanted to see them too, but I had heard that crocodiles liked Loon Lake because of its remote location, and after my brief experience with the Eastern Brown I didn't want to see another dodgy reptile up close and personal. They didn't come near the ranch because the water was so scarce, but like all the other predators they loved the marshland because that was where all the weak and tired animals went to find water and relax.

"I don't know, Jake," I told him. "It might not be safe for us to go out there."

"That's why I always carry a gun," he responded. "Besides, we won't actually be that close to the lake, only on the ridge above it. I' would never suggest going if I thought it might be dangerous. But if you would rather not . . . ."

I looked over at Trevor. His eyes were fixed on me, anticipating my answer. I didn't want him being afraid of the outback like I had been. It was our home, and we needed to learn how to coexist with all the animals that inhabited it, dangerous or otherwise. Besides, if there was anything I had learned over the past few months about Jake, he would never take Trevor where he couldn't protect him. And the lake was in the opposite direction from the cave. There would be no people prowling around out there.

"No, the lake will be fine," I said, smiling at my little brother. Things might be rocky between Jake and me, and we might be on the verge of another catastrophe, but Trevor deserved a little normalcy before everything came crashing down again. "What about taking some lunch? I bought bread yesterday, and there is plenty of lunchmeat in the fridge. I even have chips, pop and a package of Oreos in the pantry."

"And potato salad," Trevor reminded me. "That's my favorite."

By nine, the chores were done, and we were on our way. I didn't feel threatened when Trevor wanted to ride behind Jake on his motorbike while I took the food on mine. I was getting more proficient after herding sheep, but I didn't know how to get to where we were going. And even if I did, I would be somewhat slower than Jake in getting there. Besides, I was used to following his trail of dust.

Loon Lake was blue, clear and beautiful when viewed from the hill where we stopped. Although it was small, the marshland surrounding it extended for miles in three directions making it lush and green when everything else in the outback was suffering from the over abundance of sun and lack of moisture. It appeared so peaceful and calm with white birds flying overhead that I wished we could go swimming, but looks were often deceiving since people rarely went there and wild animals called it home.

Jake laughed when I didn't get off my bike immediately like he and Trevor had done, but my mind was always churning with one thought or another, and today was no exception.

"I promise you it is safe here," he said. "Crocs don't climb hills unless they are really hungry, and I haven't seen any snakes up here either."

"You could have gone all day without saying that," I told him, looking down at the hard-parched earth underneath my feet. "I am not fond of anything that slithers along the ground or builds webs. It is much safer in L.A. All you have to worry about there are earthquakes and fires. Exterminators take care of everything else."

"You aren't wishing you were back in the United States instead of here with us, are you?"

I looked over at Trevor who was investigating an anthill. He knew that Ben and me were no longer together, and he was definitely aware of the tension between his uncle and me, but he didn't need to know details. He had enough adult problems to deal with until his mother was back on her feet and everyone could come home again.

"No, I don't wish I was there." I hung my helmet over the handlebars and got to my feet. "But you can't blame me for being a little nervous. After all, I am a girl, and girls are supposed to be afraid of things."

"Not you," Jake said as he opened the pack on his bike and took out some binoculars. "You are the most altogether lass I have ever met—most of the time—and I promise we won't go anywhere near the lake. We can see everything we need to from here."

He walked over to Trevor and put his hand on his shoulder. "Why don't we head over to the ridge and take a look around."

I didn't feel snubbed at being left out of his invitation because I knew he was only trying to make it up to Trevor for falling asleep during the movie the night before. And in many ways, it made our close proximity easier. Being near him and talking to him as we had done in the past, only made the present harder. I wondered if he had called Beth this morning. She wouldn't be happy if she knew we were spending the day together.

Hearing a sound overhead, I looked up into the cloudless, cerulean sky to see a flock of colorful cockatoos land in a tree. I had to smile. Birdlife was plentiful in the outback. One never knew what species might be seen, and the panoramic view was breathtaking. From the top of the hill I could see red-colored sand dunes, a silvery oasis, and a distant tree line of green that spread upwards over a small hill with just a hint of color that represented wildflowers like the ones Jake had brought to me such a short time ago.

My stomach did a flip-flop when I looked in his direction. He was standing on an outcropping of rocks with his hands on Trevor's shoulders and pointing down towards the lake at something I was too far away to see. A mist clouded my vision, but I blinked it away. Life was so different out here. People lived hard and fast because they had to. Beauty and danger were often synonymous because people took so many unnecessary risks, and one ever really knew when the next tragedy would occur, like John Sutter's death.

Not that things like that didn't happen in Sydney or L.A. One saw accounts of muggings, shootings and deaths from every imaginable cause on the news each day, but it was a rarity when the person involved was known. Out here, the homesteaders counted on each other for survival, even if they lived miles apart and rarely saw each other. And now that people believed there might be gold in the area, no one was safe. I would be glad when Trevor was back in town. I couldn't endure it if anything happened to him.

But even experiencing all I had since coming home, I was glad to be away from a skyline that was often so smoggy I could barely tell one building from another. Sometimes my life there with Ben seemed like a dream, and I didn't know why I was thinking about him now. I hadn't heard from him in months. He might even be married to Jennifer and expecting a child of his own by now.

I wanted his happiness always but couldn't help wishing some of that same kind of contentment would rub off on me. I was trying to do what was right, and yet I was still miserable inside despite many resolutions to look only for the positive and bright. Perhaps what I had shared with Ben was a once-in-a-lifetime occurrence since I doubted there was anyone in all of Australia who could make my real dreams come true.

I spread a blanket on the ground and sat down on it to think, listening intently for the slightest bit of noise that might suggest I wasn't alone. I had grown quite accustomed to monitor and thorny devil lizards, even wombats and quolls, but they still startled me when I wasn't expecting to see them.

Australia was my home and I never wanted to leave it again. I just hoped my newfound faith was strong enough to sustain me through whatever might be coming. This outing seemed like the moment of calm before for the next storm erupted.

"I saw them," Trevor shouted as he ran down the incline towards me. Uncle Jake told me to come and get you so you can see them too."

"Where is your Uncle Jake?" I shielded my eyes from the bright sunlight. I hadn't been sitting down for long, but during that time they had moved away from the rocks to a spot on the ledge that was covered with brittle, dry grass that crackled when they moved and a few shrubs whose needles must have been at least an inch long.

"He's right up there." Trevor waved his hand in the air. "But you have got to hurry, or they might be gone."

When I looked in the direction he was pointing, I saw Jake standing no more than 50 yards away, his hand motioning for us to come quickly. We hurried to where he was waiting, and he handed me the binoculars.

"They are right beyond that tree," he said, resting his hands on my shoulders like he had done with Trevor and leaning close while he practically whispered in my ear. It was hot outside, but I felt goose bumps as his warm breath caressed my skin.

"There is a mother, two little Joey's and a bigger one that has to be the father. You don't see them all together that often. The mother is usually responsible for raising the babies on her own."

I tried not to notice his strength, and the feel of his hands so close to the sensitive part of my neck, but I couldn't. His nearness made me dizzy, and I had to remind myself to keep breathing, or I might keel right over into his arms.

"I wish I had a camera," I told him, trying to steady myself so my head would quit spinning. "This is amazing."

"You haven't seem amazing yet," he said. "There are so many things I wish I could show you. This country is the most picturesque one on earth. You should see it up north where everything is green as emeralds and the rivers and streams are so swift and clear you can see your own reflection."

"I think I would like that," I whispered back but wasn't sure he heard because Trevor was pulling on his arm.

"I want to see them again, Uncle Jake," he was saying. "I wish we could take them home with us."

"I do believe that is against the law," Jake told him as he backed away from me.

I handed Trevor the binoculars. Our moment of closeness was over much too soon, just like all the others.

"And even if the law permitted it," Jake continued. "They would never be happy on the ranch. This is their home."

Trevor let out a resigned breath of air. "I know, but it would still be cool. Wait until I tell my mates at school that I saw them. They will be so jealous because they all live in town."

Trevor put the binoculars to his eyes again and looked down at the little family of contented-looking kangaroos in the tall brush not so far from the lake. It was hot, and they were lying quietly, not jumping around like I was sure he wished they would do. It was a serene and picturesque sight, but I knew it wouldn't last long. Australia might not have many large predators like other countries, but the ones it did have were deadly.

He watched them for a few seconds longer and then declared that he was hungry and ready for lunch. "Maybe we can come back and see them again after we eat," he said.

The chance of seeing them again was remote. It would only take a single movement in the surrounding brush to send them hopping away. But Jake had done as promised and Trevor had seen kangaroos in the wild. If I could just rid myself of the feel of his hands on my shoulders, I might be able to enjoy the rest of the excursion. Fortunately, it didn't last long once we had finished eating. The kangaroos were gone and Trevor was ready to go home.

When we got back to the house, I put our picnic things away while Jake and Trevor went to the attic to get the crib. It had been taken apart for storage, but every panel was there, and the hardware for putting it back together had been secured in a baggie and tied to one of the wooden bars.

By the time I had the kitchen back in order and a few dishes washed, Trevor came running to tell me that Jake had asked him to get the toolbox from the shed because he needed things that were not in the drawer by the stove. I smiled as he literally raced across the floor and out the back door letting the screen door slam shut behind him. He was happier than he had been in months.

"Thank you for today," I told Jake when I walked into LeAnn's bedroom to see if I could do anything to help. He was standing near the fireplace with the front panel of the crib in his hands.

"It was my pleasure," he replied, giving me a weary smile. "I wanted today to be special. I have really missed having that little bloke underfoot every day."

I smiled back. It was an easy, almost natural thing to do when I could rid my brain of everything that had happened between us the past few weeks.

"So have I, but it is going to feel very strange when LeAnn, Trevor and the baby are all here. I have never been around an infant before."

"Really," Jake said. "What about your cousins?"

Suddenly, I felt very foolish. I wanted him to see my strengths not my weaknesses. Even if we were never a couple in the traditional sense, we would still be spending an inordinate amount of time together .

"I was only four when they were born, and we never spent much time together anyway. There was always so much work to do."

He looked at me with what I knew was compassion. We'd both had sad and lonely childhoods. Perhaps that was why we understood each other so well, despite our obvious differences.

"You will do great," he said. "Babies just need a lot of love. I learned that after Trevor was born when LeAnn couldn't take care of him."

"I had forgotten about that," I told him as I subconsciously pulled my bottom lip into my mouth. "Now, I really do feel dumb. You must be a pro when it comes to babies."

"I wouldn't go that far. Trevor was easy. I changed him when he was wet and gave him a bottle when he acted hungry. They really don't have a lot of needs unless they get sick. I think LeAnn has half-a-dozen books on how to take care of everything from colic to teething tucked away in a box of Trevor's baby clothes in the attic. I could help you find it if you like."

Trevor came scurrying into the bedroom with drops of sweat running down his cheeks, interrupting our conversation. His timing never ceased to amaze me—always appearing when I was at another crossroads and trying to decide if I should follow my heart or my head. He wiped the moisture away with his arm.

"I got it, Uncle Jake," he panted, lifting the dust-covered box from his side where we could see it better. "Mum is going to be so surprised when she brings Jackie home from the hospital."

"Jackie?" Jake asked. "I didn't know your mum had already picked out a name. I didn't even know the baby was a girl. Maybe I need to get into town more often so I won't be left in the dark when it comes to my own family."

HIs comment surprised me since he was with Beth now, but oh how I wanted to tell him about all the things he didn't know—like his sister meeting with the missionaries. If both she and Trevor were baptized, he would be the odd-man out instead of me. That might give him something new to think about, or it could push him away completely.

"You are way too quiet," he said, looking over the top of the crib at me after he and Trevor had secured the side panels to the headboard. I had been watching them without offering to help.

"I'm sorry," I told him. "I was just thinking about how the only constant we seem to have in life is change. Is there something you need me to do?"

He gave me an odd look.

"We blokes can finish putting the crib together, but I thought you were going upstairs to find that box of baby things. If I remember correctly, most of the stuff in it is yellow or green. We didn't know Trevor was going to be a boy until the day he was born. Isn't that right, sport? It's a good thing we didn't buy a lot of frilly things. You would have looked a little strange in ruffles."

"Mum would never put me in a dress," he promptly replied as his brow furrowed and his lips formed a pouty smile. That's how I knew he understood that Jake was only teasing him.

"I wouldn't say never," Jake continued. "Have you never seen your christening gown? It was the frilliest one your mum could find."

"That's not true."

Trevor planted his feet defiantly on the floor as his bottom lip began to quiver. Apparently, he had never been told about being christened.

"Your Uncle Jake is just playing with you," I hurriedly said, hoping to mitigate any damage. Trevor might be learning how to have more fun, but he was still a very sensitive child. "All babies in the Catholic Church wear a christening gown when they are baptized and presented to the congregation. I'm sure you even have Godparents."

"Do I, Uncle Jake?"

"As a matter of fact you do. Your Uncle Ned and Aunt Nora were given that responsibility."

"What responsibility?" he asked.

"Godparents promise to take care of you if anything happens to your parents," I told him. "Uncle Ned and Aunt Nora are my Godparents too."

He looked more than a little confused, and who could blame him. It was a lot to take in when religious training had been totally neglected. To my knowledge, he had never been inside a church from the time of his christening until I had been allowed to take him with me.

"Does that mean Uncle Ned is in charge of me now that father is gone?"

"No, Trevor," I said. "They only step in if both of your parents are gone."

"Like you and Uncle Jake because you don't have any parents at all."

I looked at Jake for help.

"Listen, sport," he said. "I know all this talk is puzzling. Your mum took care of me after our parents were killed, and your sister is an adult."

"Why can't you and Brylee be my Godparents? You are a lot younger than Uncle Ned and Aunt Nora, and I know you better."

"Well," Jake said, looking over his shoulder at me. "I am not really sure you can fire Godparents, but your sister and I will always be here for you, and for Jackie."

"Promise?" he said, putting his hands on his hips and looking at us with determination in his eyes. "Brylee already left when she said she wouldn't."

I wished the floor would open and swallow me. I hated that my own confusion had caused me to break the only promise I had made to him, but I couldn't undo it. I could only do better in the future.

"Hey, cut your sister some slack," Jake said. "It wasn't exactly her fault for getting sick."

Oh, how I wished that were true and Jake did not feel it necessary to cover for me. There was no one to blame for my mistakes but me because I had voluntarily chosen to run away instead of facing my problems.

"I am very sorry for doing that, Trevor," I responded, before Jake said anything more that might require a further explanation. "I was being selfish. I hope you can forgive me someday."

"I forgive you," he said with a sigh. "I know big people have problems too."

I crossed the short distance between us, put my arms around him and kissed his upturned cheek.

"You are an amazing little brother. And yes, everyone has problems, even kids, but adults should be able to handle their issues better. And children should be allowed to be young and carefree for as long as possible."

Jake cleared his throat. All this talk about problems and broken promises was noticeably bothering him.

"So, how about all that baby stuff?" he asked. "I'm sure we will have to wash everything before the baby can use it."

"It's not the baby, Uncle Jake," Trevor clarified. "Her name is Jackie."

"So it is," he said. "But if we don't get busy, she will be in high school before we even get her crib set up."

I hurried to the attic. It seemed safer than staying where I was. It didn't take long for me to find the large plastic tub of baby things and carry it from the attic to the bedroom where they were making sure the mattress wasn't damaged and would still fit snugly inside the crib bars. Trevor sat beside me on the floor while I pulled up on the lid until it popped open.

Inside were bibs and *onesies*, blankets and sheets. There was also an assortment of clothing for baby boys that I was determined my little sister would not wear, except in an emergency. As I took the last item out of the container, I suddenly remembered that my mother had packed away some of my baby things too. If I could find them, there would certainly be a few items Jackie could wear, even if they were nearly twenty-five years old.

Thinking about my life as an infant brought to mind the fact that I had slid right through my own birthday a few days earlier without mentioning it to anyone. LeAnn was in bed trying to keep my baby sister safe until her due-date arrived. Aunt Nora was dealing with Molly and everything she wanted to accomplish before the newlyweds moved north. Jake and I were estranged, and Trevor was too young to do anything about it. But suddenly all the talk about Jackie coming home made the pain erupt because no one was there to celebrate the anniversary of my arrival on earth. Most certainly, my father would have remembered, but he had been gone for nearly three-quarters of a year.

"Excuse me for a minute," I said, rising to my feet before the tears came. "There is something else I need to find."

Trevor was busy looking at teething rings and rattles, and Jake was tightening screws now that the baby crib was standing on its own, so neither of them made a comment. I ran back up the stairs to the attic, pausing only a moment before opening the door as I thought about saving my baby things for the daughter I hoped to have one day. But that notion passed swiftly, as did my self-pity at having a special day no one had acknowledged.

My new sister would soon be coming home, and that was a joyous thing. Two babies could easily wear the same things I had. It wasn't like they would be worn out. All a newborn did the first few months of life was eat, sleep and grow. Spending exorbitant amounts of money on clothing that would only be worn a time or two was wasteful, and she would always be in need of new things to wear as she grew older. I was fairly certain most of the clothing I had worn as a toddler onward had been given to Aunt Nora when the twins were born, and it was doubtful she had anything left after the flood unless it had been stored in her attic.

And so our day came swiftly to an end. It had been perfect in almost every way. We had seen a family of kangaroos and assembled the baby's crib. We had even gone through the clothing Trevor and I had worn as infants, picking out just the right things for Jackie to wear. I had washed, dried, folded and put them into the drawers of the changing table Jake had brought down from the attic so it could be cleaned up too.

Trevor and I made a list of all the things we thought the baby would need besides clothing and blankets when she came home from the hospital, but since this was a new experience for both of us, we decided to get input from both LeAnn and Aunt Nora before heading off to any stores. It wasn't hard to convince him not to tell his mother about the preparations we had made at home because he loved surprises.

But I still had deeply-rooted concerns about everything turning out as we hoped it would. LeAnn was close enough to full term that if Jackie arrived now she should be okay, but there were never any guarantees. LeAnn was almost forty-five, and that put both her and Jackie at risk for any number of things.

I had been praying each night and morning for their safety, as I did for Molly and her baby. I didn't feel jealous like I had before my brief time at Emma's beach house when I had unwrapped Ben's gift and realized just how blessed I was, despite all the trials that continued to plague me. I only felt sad that I wasn't bringing one of God's children into the world like everyone else. It was hard waiting on his timing, but I was learning about patience and that had to be a good thing.

Trevor went to bed that night without coaxing. He was worn out from the day's activities, but before retiring, he helped me secure a sheet over the mattress pad. Then he placed the bear I had purchased for him on top of the powder blue blanket he had chosen to be folded at the end of the crib. Jake hung the mobile of small Australian animals to one side where the baby could see it when she opened her eyes.

I couldn't imagine how small a baby must be to fit into the clothes we had put in the drawers of the changing table. Sometimes the thought of being a mother and not knowing how to take care of an infant scared me almost as much as the thought of never being a mother at all did. I tried to concentrate on the fact that God had a special plan for me— one I likely would not know about until it happened.

"Thank you for all your help today," I told Trevor after reading him a story. He was struggling to keep his eyes open, so I kissed him goodnight and told him I would see him first thing in the morning.

Then I stood quietly by the side of his bed until he fell asleep. I simply could not believe how important he had become to me. What had gone so wrong between my parents had left me with incredible gifts—two little half-siblings I would love and cherish forever because we shared some of the same Hawkins' genes.

Chapter 11

Jake was waiting for me in the front hallway when I went downstairs to turn out the lights and secure the house for the night.

"Could I talk to you outside?" he asked. "I wasn't completely truthful with you last night or this morning."

He opened the front door, and I stepped into the warm night air. But as a light breeze hit my bare arms I shivered. This day really had been too good to be true, and now that illusion was about to be shattered.

I folded my arms in front of me, wishing I could shield myself from what was coming.

"It's not that bad," he said, almost laughing when he looked at my insolent stance. "It is just something I know you will not approve of, and I wanted to give Trevor a special day before getting into one of our fights."

"You don't sound like it is nothing, and we don't fight about everything."

"So I exaggerated a little."

I fought back unsolicited tears. Why couldn't life be like it was in the movies? I wanted us back together, or I wanted to get over him so I could actually be happy instead of just pretending. The past ten months of almost constant turmoil had been exhausting.

He reached out and touched my arm. "Come sit by me on the swing. We haven't had a real talk in a long time."

But I refuse to be coddled or have my feelings redirected. I was scared and uncertain about the future with or without him in it.

"Just tell me what you have to say, and then I will decide if I am going to sit down."

He took a cigarette out of the pack in his shirt pocket, but instead of lighting it, he put it back.

"You have every reason for not wanting to trust me or let me back into your life. I don't have the best track record with women."

"Beth doesn't seem to mind, and she did catch the bridal bouquet."

"That is a bunch of nonsense I refuse to be part of. Besides, this isn't about my personal life, unless you have changed your mind about us."

I felt trapped, but I wasn't sure this was the right time to bring up finding his letter. What he had to tell me might change everything again.

"I am still somewhat confused after all that has happened the past few weeks, but least we seemed to be getting along better today."

"That is only because I decided this day would be a pleasant one for Trevor. He needs to know that his uncle and sister can get along for a few hours, even if they aren't doing much speaking otherwise."

"I agree," I responded, choosing to look at the floorboards instead of his face. "Trevor is the only person who really matters right now."

"Then we are not at odds about everything. I wasn't sure you would be willing to go with us today, but this bloody feud between us has to stop when Trevor is around. He takes everything much too seriously."

"Bloody feud!" I thought. He was the one who had set all the ground rules by taking up with the first woman he saw after telling me he was tired of waiting around.

"I think I have already shown you that I am willing to try," I replied.

His eyes narrowed. "So you have. I was just making sure you thought it was worth it. I know I am the last person you want to see right now."

The conversation was becoming distasteful. If it didn't end it soon, it would erupt into name-calling and false innuendos. I had to make sure that didn't happen since Trevor had an uncanny knack of surfacing every time we tried to have a private conversation.

"That's not entirely true!" I said, willing my voice to remain level. "I wouldn't want to come face-to-face with any of the men Emma described as being in town the past few days. They scare me, especially knowing that one of them was likely responsible for John Sutter's death."

"Point taken, but I really wish you would reconsider staying in town until this whole bloody mess blows over. I can't be around to protect you all the time."

"I have already told you I can take care of myself. Besides, you have more important things to do with your life."

He grunted. "I suppose that's one way of looking at it."

The aggravated look on his face made me wish I had the courage to tell him that somewhere along the way I had fallen head-over-heels in love with him and was now willing to give him a chance, but pride kept that secret locked away deep inside where he could never use it against me for a second time. If he no longer had romantic feelings for me, it was a little too late to express mine for him.

His eyes continued searching mine in the half-light from the lone light bulb on the front porch. But when I didn't say anything to contradict him, he took my silence for agreement that nothing had changed between us.

"I won't waste any more of your time, Brylee. I just wanted to tell you that I am heading up to the cave in the morning. I plan on staying there until Ned gets back. I know you can take care of things here without my help. I have seen you do it plenty of times."

The heaviness in my heart was overwhelming. What he was proposing was stupid, but I still couldn't bring myself to own up to my unwanted feelings. He was a grown man who lived by his own set of rules, and he wasn't about to change now.

"I will take whatever supplies I need with me," he continued without pausing. "Just send Ned up there when he returns. Someone needs to protect that cave until we know how things are going to play out, and it might as well be me."

Suddenly, his insanity erased my desire for self-preservation. We might not have a future together, but we were still part of the same family. If he wasn't going to think about his own safety, then I owed it to everyone who cared about his well-being to remind him of the obligations he might be throwing away.

"That would be a very foolish mistake," I said. "It isn't safe."

His jaw clenched. "Then give me a reason to stay and not just because Trevor and LeAnn need me. I am tired of trying to have a serious conversation with you because it always ends with your commitment to the church you joined. After all that has happened between us, it shouldn't matter as much as it does, but for some damned reason I can't seem to let go."

As much as his admission startled me, it didn't change anything, except increasing my guilt for not being able to come clean about everything. "Maybe it's because I still care about you, Jake, and there is no way of knowing who or what might be waiting for you on that mountain."

"Then tell me why you care and be honest about it. You are not a little girl anymore, Brylee. You are a grown woman and should be able to decide a few things for yourself. It wasn't easy for me to tell you how I felt, even in a letter, but I did and was immediately rejected for all my efforts."

He stood less than a foot away, and it would be very easy for me to throw my arms around his neck and feel his heart beating in time to mine, but he had moved on with a waitress from the diner and she loved him too.

Was it right for me to destroy what they had when I wasn't sure I could follow through on what I wanted for myself? Jake deserved better than that, and so did Beth. I would be a fool to lay my heart at his feet when everything around us was so uncertain. Our minds needed to remain free from personal issues until our most threatening crisis was over.

"It's just so complicated, Jake," I said. "All I want is for you to be happy, and if Beth makes you happy."

"Damn it all to bloody hell," he stormed. "This is getting us nowhere. Everything about living is complicated, but you can't keep running forever, Brylee. One of these days, you are going to look back and see that no one is coming after you."

He turned around and walked away. I stood for the longest time where he had left me too numb to move. Something was definitely wrong with me. I couldn't continue to use my membership in the church as an excuse for keeping everyone at arm's length if I ever wanted to do more than live in other people's shadows.

There was no point trying to sleep. If I was going to die from a broken heart, I might as well be awake when it happened. So I went into the den, turned the computer on and tried to find out everything I could about gold mining in Australia. If Jake was going to risk his life to save something, it needed to be the paintings, not a few traces of what might be nothing more than streaks of a precious substance in one of the chambers of the cave.

My search yielded little that would help me in our present situation since surveyors had not yet been brought in to see if we had anything to worry about, but I did find out where most of the aborigine tribes were living. Not that it would be easy for anyone to find them, even Uncle Ned, because they roamed extensively with the availability of food and water.

Sometimes I felt like I might as well join one their tribes and wander aimlessly the breadth and depth of the continent I claimed to love. It would be better than continually crying over spilled milk. Not only had I lost Jake as part of my life, but my continual indecisiveness had cost him the opportunity of hearing the truth and then deciding for himself if he wanted to be part of an eternal family.

Jake needed to understand that I truly loved him and would give him whatever time he needed to learn and decide if he really wanted to be with me, not just for now but for always. If it really didn't matter any longer because his feelings for Beth ran deep, then I needed to know that too. It was the only way to bring closure so I could accept the inevitable. Living with games and secrets was no longer possible.

My decision made, I left the safety of the den and walked outside into the early morning air. It was still dark, barely after one in the morning, but I knew Jake never slept until sunrise if he had something to do. I took a deep breath hoping to quiet the rushing flood of emotions that were taking over. I was going to tell him that I loved him, and then all the complications my lack of commitment and indecisiveness had brought could be sorted out. If he still had feelings for me, I would put my arms around his neck where they belonged and feel his warm breath as his lips sought mine.

I had been over-thinking our situation far too much instead of relying on the spirit to guide me. Telling Jake that I loved him didn't mean I was automatically risking my eternal salvation. It only meant that I was opening another door and letting the man I loved into the light. He needed to know when I had found his letter and how deeply it had touched me.

So with a prayer in my heart, I knocked on the bunkhouse door. No lights were visible from the inside, but that only meant he must still be sleeping. So I knocked again, a little louder.

"Jake, it's Brylee. I need to talk to you. Will you let me come in?"

The silence that accompanied my plea was oppressive. What if he didn't want to talk to me? Or worse, what if he had already left believing I had never really cared about him?

I rapped a third time, and then tried the doorknob. It turned easily and the door swung inward.

"Jake," I loudly whispered. "I am sorry for the way I behaved. I have something really important to tell you. It's about the letter you left me."

I took a step inside the dark room but knew without even looking around that he was gone. He hadn't even waited for it to turn light. My eyes glistened with tears as my hands flew to my mouth before my moan of lost hope became audible. He must have gone to the cave on horseback and hadn't taken much of anything with him. I would have known if he had returned to the house for food, or if one of the vehicles on the ranch had been started.

What if something happened to him while he was gone, and I never got a chance to tell him what was in my heart? I already had a lifetime of regrets over the way things had turned out with my parents and Ben. I didn't want the same thing to happen with Jake, but sometimes it really was too late to undue all the damage that had been done.

I went back to my room and fell down on the bed, not even removing my clothes. I had been given a second chance and had blown it. Why couldn't I seem to make up my mind about anything until it was too late? Tears of disappointment and frustration filled my eyes, but they didn't fall. I stayed that way for the longest time and then forced myself to take a shower and go back down the stairs. Trevor would be stirring soon, and I needed to be ready to make it through a day of worship and worry without any sleep.

I was nursing a cup of hot cocoa when he walked into the kitchen dressed in his Sunday best. I had no desire for food, but a growing boy had to eat, and I had promised myself not to ruin his day by being in a negative, fearful mood.

"Is Uncle Jake going to have breakfast with us?" he asked as I halfheartedly scrambled a few eggs and put some bread in the toaster. "I want to ask him if we can go to the lake again next weekend. I need a picture of the kangaroos to show my new mates at school."

"Your Uncle Jake rode up to the cave very early this morning," I responded, knowing exactly what I must do next. "You haven't told anyone about it, have you?"

Trevor looked disappointed. "I wouldn't tell anyone. Uncle Jake told me not to."

I sat down at the table with him. My stomach was upset and my head hurt like crazy, but I would force a few bites of egg down anyway.

"I knew you hadn't," I said. "It's just that there have been some strangers around lately, and we are trying to figure out what they want."

"I could stay here with you instead of going of going to school if you are scared. I know mum would understand."

My fingers touched his. "I love you dearly for caring so much, but you need to go to school. That is where you will learn everything you can so you will be extra smart when you help us run the ranch in a few years. Do you think Jackie's going to love living out here as much as we do?"

"Maybe even more," he said. "She will have both of us to play with. I used to get lonely sometimes before you came home."

Oh, how my heart went out to him, and I almost cried. He was Christlike in both his thoughts and actions, and I wanted the cares of the world to pass right over him, but that wasn't part of God's plan. We were meant to have trials because hard times strengthened our character—at least that was what my mother used to say whenever I complained. But I now understood that faith was what really carried us through difficulties, even the ones we created for ourselves.

"I used to be lonely too," I told him. "My mother was sick a lot and there was seldom any laughter, but you and I will change all that. We will make sure our little sister has the happiest childhood ever."

"Can she go down the slide on the hill with us when she is big enough?"

"The slide you and I looked for when we got swarmed by insects? Even if we found where it used to be, it could take forever to rebuild. It hasn't been used in a very long time."

Trevor smiled like the Cheshire cat from *Alice in Wonderland*. He was definitely keeping something from me.

"I told Uncle Jake about it."

"You did?" I asked, wishing the pain in my heart would lessen. I had been so foolish and blind when it came to him. "When was that?"

"The day you left. He said he would find it for us."

"And did he?"

"Yes, but I am not supposed to tell cuz it's a surprise. He has already fixed most of it and said he would have the rest of it done before Jackie gets here."

"But why would he do that?" I asked as the frown lines deepened between my eyes. That was after he thought I had rejected him on every level that really mattered. "It had to be an awful lot of work."

"Because I told him it made you sad to see it all broken."

I walked over to the kitchen sink and looked out the window in a southerly direction. In the distance, amongst all the dry grass, was a small line of silver that extended from the top of the hill clear to the bottom. It was gleaming in the early morning light. How had I not seen it when I walked nearly every inch of the compound, but then I suppose I had never looked up.

"I can't believe it," I said as tears of appreciation and regret nearly choked me. Jake would not have spent time working on the slide in the heat and the bugs if he didn't still care about me. I had to get to him as soon as possible and tell him how I really felt—nothing left back because I was frightened and unsure of the outcome. No one had ever done something so unselfish for me. "It must have taken him forever."

"I helped too," Trevor said, and the next second I felt his small hand in mine.

I leaned down and kissed his upturned cheek. "You are the most awesome little brother in the world. How can I ever thank you?"

He grinned with satisfaction. "We were going to finish it the weekend we went to the wedding. Don't tell Uncle Jake I told you. He wanted you to be surprised."

Surprised! I mused on the long drive into town. Jake's thoughtfulness and kindness put me to shame. I wanted to be living as Christ had done by following all of his commandments, but Jake was the one who really knew how to love and forgive. I simply had to be given the chance to show him that I could do those things too. Even if it was too late for us, it was a lesson I desperately needed to learn.

Chapter 12

After the church block ended, I asked President Downing if he could set up an appointment for me to get my Patriarchal blessing. I knew it wasn't like a psychic telling my fortune. I had to be spiritually prepared to receive it, but I had read Ben's blessing and knew it was time for me to learn more about what God expected from me. I had been a member of the church for over eighteen months but had never done much to increase my testimony.

He escorted me into his makeshift office, and I told him what I wanted to do.

"That is a big step, Brylee, and it will bring a lot of comfort. Do you mind if I ask what made you decide to get it now?"

I knew he had been given the gift of discernment so there was no reason to be evasive with him.

"I am at another crossroad and don't exactly know what to do. I thought getting it might give me some direction."

"It can certainly do that, but there may be things in it that are hard to appreciate or understand given our mortal situation."

"I thought it was meant to help me make better decisions," I responded.

His glance was filled with both compassion and understanding. "Have you read someone else's blessing?"

"Just Ben's. It told him so many wonderful things about marriage, having a family, and always being faithful in serving the Lord. It also said he was one of God's most elect children."

"And your blessing could say many of those same things. It will tell you more about yourself, your gifts and talents and maybe give you a warning or two. It can only be understood with the gift of the Holy Ghost. It will be yours alone and should not be shared with just anyone."

I looked across the desk at him. He was such a kind and spiritual man. He often cried in Sacrament meeting when someone bore testimony of the Savior and when I talked to him, he listened with his heart just as he was doing now.

"President Downing," I said, after mulling a few things over in my mind. "I know I have been hit and miss attending my meetings, and you are probably questioning if I am seriously committed to the gospel. It's just that living so far away, and with so many family issues, my time isn't always my own."

"How are LeAnn and Trevor doing?"

"For the most part, really quite well. I'm sure you are aware that LeAnn is seeing the missionaries."

"I am. She will be a strong member once she decides to join the church, and I noticed that Trevor was here with you again today."

"He loves coming. I think living in town the past few weeks has been good for him. He is making new friends and feeling much more confidant."

"That's what I like to hear, but what about you? How are you dealing with all the change?"

"Not as well as the rest of the members of my family. My own issues seem to have taken control of my life so completely that I have failed to give service to anyone, and I know that is what ministering to others is all about."

He smiled and that made more tears form. I could feel the Savior's love so completely when I was around others who believed as I did, but I needed to feel that way when I was alone because that was how I spent most of my time now.

"I think you have that covered," he said. "The most important service we will ever give is within the walls of our own home. The Lord loves you, Brylee, but I think he has been waiting for you to decide what it is that you really want, and what you are willing to do to get it. There is a great work for you to do right here in this branch—if your heart is open to it."

I was listening intently. I hadn't been told that the Savior needed me since I had been called as a Primary teacher with Ben right after joining the church. I missed those little children dreadfully. Perhaps that was part of the reason I had felt such an instant bond with Trevor, other than the fact that we shared the same father.

"My heart is open, President Downing. I'm just not sure what I am supposed to do with it."

"I think I might have something that could help. I was going to have Brother Miller set up an appointment but since you are here now, we are reorganizing the Relief Society. Sister Miller has been called as the new president, and she would like you to be her first counselor."

"What?" I gasped with shock as a tender feeling I had not felt for a very long time flooded my soul. I knew most of the women in the branch by name since there were not that many of us, but I had never considered the possibility of leading them. What direction could I offer? I was a struggling, single female who had only been a member of the church for less than two years.

"I don't know what to say," I finally uttered. "I feel so unworthy and unprepared. Are you sure?"

He smiled. "None of us are truly worthy of any of the blessings we receive, Brylee. But that is not what God requires from us. He only asks for a willing heart and hands ready to serve others. He will supply everything else.

"Oh, I want to serve him more than anything else in the world," I sobbed, my heart so filled with gratitude that I could barely see him through the tears. I reached for another tissue from the box on his desk. "But I don't know what to do."

"Sister Miller will call and explain your new responsibilities, and we will sustain you in Sacrament meeting next week and set you apart. I know this may seem overwhelming right now, but the Lord will help you meet the responsibilities of this new calling, as well as your many challenges at home. Now, why don't we start the process of getting that Patriarchal blessing for you?"

My intention had been to talk to him about my relationship with Jake, but the unexpected calling had been such a surprise that everything else just slipped from my mind. God needed me! It was such an important concept to internalize, but why had it come when so many things in my life were in chaos?

Before leaving his office, I ask for a blessing. He called one of his counselors into the room to help him with it. My heart was incredibly tender as consecrated oil was put on my head and the anointing sealed. Then Brother Mitchell, Margaret's husband, prayed that I would have the clarity of mind to make the decisions that were right for me both now and throughout eternity. He stressed the fact that Satan was very real and would use every persuasion in his arsenal to distract me from the important things in life so I would lose my way, but by recognizing where truth resides, I would be kept from temptation and sin and would be able to accomplish the mission I had been sent to earth to complete.

I felt like crying out with joy when I walked out of our small building into the sun a few minutes later. So much of my testimony had come from leaning on Ben, but now I was beginning to build one of my own from the experiences God was giving me. I couldn't worry about things that had not happened yet, or beat myself up over the past. I needed to focus on being an example of faith and humility to the women in my branch, and if I fulfilled my new calling in righteousness, I would have the answers to my problems when I needed them.

As always, Emma's lunch was wonderful—roast beef and potatoes with chocolate cake for dessert. I wasn't terribly hungry but ate what I could. There was so much to think about. I wanted to share my calling with someone so it would feel more real but knew it should be kept private until the members of the branch had sustained me.

So, I tried to keep the conversation light, but Emma saw right through my attempt at hedging. And when she pointedly asked if anything was bothering me, I told her that I hadn't slept much the past few nights. That was certainly true, but I couldn't bother her with the reasons behind my insomnia. She had enough to worry about with LeAnn, the baby and Trevor. She didn't need to worry about Jake's safety and what was happening at the ranch too. That was my responsibility.

It was nearly dark when I got back to the ranch. I had been without sleep for so long I felt completely disconnected from my body but still managed to get the cores done before curling up in a chair in the den with Copper in my lap to attempt reading the *Ensign* Emma had sent home with me. But I hadn't even made it through the first presidency's message when my eyes closed. I didn't open them again until the sun was beginning its assent into the sky the next morning.

The fact that I had been able to sleep at all surprised me, but I accepted it as one of God's tender mercies in giving me a few hours of relief from the turmoil that continued to swirl around me. I took a quick shower to help clear my head and then fed and watered the animals again. I tried to think uplifting thoughts, but I was more than a little worried about Jake. He was alone in the outback with few supplies and finding my way to him might be impossible, even if I had the courage to try. One hill looked pretty much like every other one, and I had only been to the cave once. Uncle Ned knew how to get there, but he was gone on what I hoped would not turn into a total waste of time. I felt helpless, and the only thing I could think of doing was to pray.

So, I fell to my knees and rested my elbows on a kitchen chair before pleading for guidance. I needed some of that wisdom I had been promised in the blessing Brother Mitchell had given me the day before. I needed to know that my family would be safe and that the fear and unrest brought by the undesirables who were openly walking the streets of Edna in hopes of finding gold that did not belong to them would dissipate before anyone else got hurt. But nothing remarkable happened, and I soon rose to my feet with the realization that God expected me to make a few decisions on my own.

I wasn't sure I knew how to do that, especially when the stakes were so high, but I couldn't sit back and do nothing either. I washed the few dishes in the sink, straightened what I could in the house and then walked out to the slide Jake had rebuilt for me. It was gleaming brightly in the early morning sun, but seeing the amount of work he had already done on it only make me feel worse because we were no closer to solving the difficulties between us than we were the day he had taken Trevor and me to the cave.

That had been one of the most difficult days of my life. I wanted Jake to know that I really cared but expressing my feelings had never come easily—except to Trevor and Ben who made it almost effortless. But in retrospect, I had to admit that Ben had done most of the giving in our relationship. He had told me numerous times that he loved me before I was able was able to say those same words in return.

And it wasn't because the feelings weren't there, but I had grown up with two disillusioned parents who never held hands or kissed each other in my presence. My father was always gone from the house working, and when my mother wasn't resting or doing some kind of handwork, she sat at her piano playing the same sad songs over and over again. Loving people might come naturally, but expressing that love was a learned behavior. Perhaps if my parents had communicated the way my father and LeAnn did, I might be living a much different life.

But as Aunt Nora always said, "You can't cry over spilled milk. You just have to clean it up and go on."

Well, I had certainly spilled enough milk when it came to relationships and didn't know how to clean up any of it. But instead of dwelling on my weaknesses like I usually did, I retraced my steps to the house, turned on the computer and soon discovered from the words of the prophets and apostles that it isn't always the big things—like Jake rebuilding the slide for me—that showed how much one cared. It was the little acts of service and kindness given over a lifetime that made any love eternal. The thought of leading other women when my own life was nothing more than one disaster after another was absolutely terrifying.

But as I contemplated what I had read, I realized that I did nice things for Trevor and LeAnn because I no longer felt threatened by them. I had accepted them as part of my life, asking nothing in return, and that made loving them easy. My feelings for Jake still scared me because they were so strong and kept changing. He couldn't give me the kind of life I wanted, and his involvement with Beth was nothing less than reprehensible if he didn't care about her the way he should, but I still felt drawn to him and needed to know that he was okay.

I stood up and walked over to the window that looked out on the front porch. I couldn't keep waffling in my desires, or I would drive myself crazy again. I had been willing to give us a chance before he rode off to the cave, but how did I feel about him now that some of the dust had settled? I was supposed to set a good example for others by living the gospel, and I wouldn't be living it very well if I turned my back on my yearning for a temple marriage and accepted life with a man who wasn't even sure he believed in God.

On the other hand, I couldn't just abandon him because our lives were inseparably linked if we both wanted to stay on the ranch and be part of LeAnn and the children's lives.

Suddenly, a light seemed to dawn. If I couldn't have what I thought I wanted, I would simply have to make do with what I had. Jake and I had learned how to be friends once, and we could do it again if we were both willing to try. Anything was better than leaving things the way they were now, and with God's, nothing was impossible. I was finally starting to understand that.

So, I baked some chocolate sparkler cookies. They were his favorite, or at least that was what he told me. I was tempted to go into the bunkhouse and clean until everything was spotless, but realized in time that it might seem more like criticism of his housekeeping skills than a genuine act of service and caring. I momentarily thought about washing and waxing his truck, but if I didn't do it the right way, he might get upset. Men loved their pickup trucks!

Later that morning, I picked up the phone to call Aunt Nora before I remembered she had gone into town to see if there was any legal way of protecting the cave from outsiders until Uncle Ned came home, and we had time to decide what we were going to do.

But the more I tried to keep my thoughts focused on other things the more they returned to Jake. He was at the center of everything because he had been the one to find the cave and knew the most about what it contained. He should never have gone up the mountain to protect the drawings. They had been on their own for decades, and if there were more than just gold flecks in the cave, there was nothing we could do about it anyway. I suddenly started to question his motives, but thought better of it. If he had only wanted to get away from me, he could have gone elsewhere.

After a quick lunch, I went to the barn and got a bucket of nails and a hammer and started re-hanging some of the boards on the side of the barn that had come loose during the flood. I was grateful we had sustained so little damage, but after seeing everything so sparkly and new at Uncle Ned's, I almost wished we had more than just a desire to update and make repairs. Everywhere I looked there was nothing but work waiting to be done.

I talked to Trevor after school. He asked if Jake had returned to the ranch, but I told him he hadn't without adding an explanation that would lead to more questions. My little brother had only a passing interest in the cave at present, and that was the way it needed to stay.

Besides, there was no reason to believe Jake wasn't simply enjoying nature. He had been a bush pilot for better part of his life and knew how to take care of himself. I was just unsettled because of our most recent clash and wanted to make things right with him again.

But despite my resolves, restlessness overtook me as the evening hours drew near. I really had expected Jake to come back for more supplies since he had taken so little with him when he left nearly 48 hours earlier. I was trying to read in the den when the phone rang. Aunt Nora was on the other end.

"How are you holding up?" she asked. "This whole affair has left me feeling just a little bit loco."

"Did you find out anything useful in town?"

"I'm still here," she replied. "And the only thing I found out was that city officials keep hours the same way doctors and bankers do. The courthouse was closed today and so was the historical society. I will head over to both of them first thing in the morning, and I won't leave until I get some answers."

"Have you heard from Uncle Ned?" I asked, hoping that something productive would come out of the day.

"Not yet! But I didn't expect to. It's hard to track down a man on a mission."

I thumped the toe of my boot against the bottom of the desk. "Tell me about it! Jake rode up to protect the cave until Uncle Ned gets back. I think it was a stupid, idiotic thing to do, but he wouldn't listen to reason."

There was no way I could tell her that he had gone there early just to get away from me.

"When did he leave?" she asked, and the concern in her voice was evident.

"Some time early Sunday morning. He was gone before I woke up."

"Did he take any guns with him?"

"I'm sure he did, but why do you ask?"

"I don't want to alarm you, but there have been reports of gun fire in the mountains. I know Jake can take care of himself, but I don't like the idea of him being anywhere near that cave right now. A couple of men brought in a few chunks of rock that looked like they could have some gold in them. There is a huge article on the front page of the paper about it. I fear that every crazy bloke in Australia will be on their way up there before Ned even makes it home."

I felt the heat rise to my face and my heart begin to race at the same time. Gunfire could mean anything with all the wild animals in the outback and Jake knew how to take care of himself, but . . . .

"So what should we do?" I asked.

"There's not much either of us can do right now—except wait and pray—but I do need you to do something for me."

"Anything," I told her.

"Could you ride over to the ranch and gather the eggs and make sure all the animals in the barn have enough food and water for another day? I might not make it home until tomorrow night."

"Say no more! I'm on my way. Is there anything else?"

"Just leave a couple of lights on in the house and make sure to lock up. There is an extra key in the top drawer by the phone. I always thought it was stupid to secure doors since unscrupulous people won't let that stop them from breaking in, but this the first time something like this has happened in the thirty-plus years I have lived here, and quite frankly it has my nerves on edge."

Her uneasiness made mine even worse, but it was unwise to borrow trouble in such a tumultuous time, so I did as she asked and was still back home before the sun disappeared and the stars came out. I would call her the next afternoon to make sure she had not run into additional issues in obtaining the information we needed to make more informed decisions, and I would make sure all the animals on both homesteads were cared for until life got back to a semblance of normalcy again.

But falling asleep that night did not come easily. My mind was filled with visions of violence and death that had nothing to do with the relative tranquility at the ranch. There was no reason to believe that Jake was doing anything more than watching the cave's entrance or perhaps doing some additional exploring—other than the fact that he had not returned for additional supplies when I figured he should have. But listening to Aunt Nora's rendition of what was happening in town had heightened the fears I had been fighting all day.

What if Jake was in trouble with no one to cover his back? I couldn't leave him out there alone. I had to make sure he was safe and find a way to convince him to come home until Uncle Ned returned, and we could sit down together and figure out what our next move should be.

But how to find him was the question without an answer. I was smart enough to know that I could never make my way to the cave in the dark, but at first light, and after the chores on both ranches were done, I would get on one of the motorbikes and go looking for him. And when I found him, I would tell him just how insensitive he was for being a stubborn man who refused to listen to anyone, and who had given Aunt Nora and me more to worry about.

My decision made, I packed cookies, crackers, cans of stew and fruit, a can opener, some utensils and matches into the backpack I planned on taking with me on what I hoped would not become a rescue mission for either of us. Then I filled two large jugs with water and put them in the freezer so the ice could melt during the day and we would have cool water to drink when I found him. I secured the first aid kit I had made during the flood in the compartment underneath the back seat of the motorbike, just in case it might be needed.

After that was done, I took the key from my father's desk drawer and opened his gun case. I stood immobile for what seemed like hours debating the enormity of the task I was about to undertake. I hated guns, even the small one LeAnn loaned me when Jake and I went to round up the sheep, but what if I found myself in a situation where defending myself was necessary? I had already checked her room, but she must have put the small, silver pistil some place safe when she found out she was going to have another baby.

Glancing at the selection of guns my father had learned to use as a child, I instantly realized that a rifle would be useless because of its size, but there were several revolvers among his collection.

I removed the smallest one from its nail, carried it to the desk and laid it beside the computer keyboard. "Dear Heavenly Father," I prayed with my hands clasp together and my head bowed. "Please help me to know how to safely use it if I must."

When no intervention came, I booted up the computer for a second time that day and began an Internet search. The gun on the desk in front of me was a Beretta model 87 Cheeta. The name meant nothing to me, but according to the site I was on it was easy to use.

I went back to the gun case and looked for the size of bullets I needed. In ways, I hoped I would not find any, but a full box lay underneath the peg the gun had been hanging on.

Following the diagrams on the website, I made sure the safety was on before inserting enough bullets to fill all the chambers. It was insane when I thought about it logically and would give Jake a good laugh since I wasn't sure I would even be able to pull the trigger, but maybe its presence on my person would scare an opponent away. I could either stow it away in the backpack along with everything else I was taking, or carry it in my shirt pocket for easy access. I would even leave a message on Aunt Nora's home phone and a detailed explanation of where I was going on the kitchen table. And hopefully when I returned, it would not be alone.

Chapter 13

I tossed and turned until I heard the first morning bird sing. It was still dark, but the sun would be peaking its head over the horizon before I got the chores done and made it to the place where I would have to start climbing—if I could even find the beginning of the tail that led up the mountain to the cave. I would have taken my horse like Jake had done, but I wasn't the least bit confident about where I was going and didn't want to take any chances with Rupert's safety. I would ride as far as I could on the motorbike and go the rest of the way on foot.

I braided my hair so it would be out of the way but didn't bother with makeup. Even waterproof mascara had little chance of staying fresh where I was going, and having it burn my eyes as the day got warmer and the sweat slid down my cheeks was plain loco. Then I pulled on some jeans, heavy socks and the long-sleeved shirt that had belonged to my father. I had found my old hiking boots in the attic while looking for clothing I had worn before running away the first time. I would definitely need them today.

After filling an extra canteen with water, I got the backpack that was crammed full of supplies out of the hall closest. I had put it there for self-preservation in case Jake came home unexpectedly. He would only be annoyed because I had not trusted him as I should.

The gun sitting on the kitchen table filled me with horror, although it didn't seem nearly as sinister as it had the night before. I almost left it behind, but at the last minute decided to slip it into the backpack with everything else I had collected the night before, including the box with the remaining bullets. It could easily slip out of my pocket as I rode over ruts and through gullies that would rattle my teeth if I didn't take them slowly enough.

The forecast said there was little chance of rain—as usual—but I still stuffed a packaged tarp and solar blanket into the backpack before zipping it shut. One could never be too careful when traveling in the outback. I tucked my father's utility knife into my pant's pocket before leaving a message on Aunt Nora's phone and a note in the middle of the table. Then I crossed the kitchen floor, turned out the lights and locked the back door.

I felt more than uneasy about my plan when backing the motorbike out of the shed. I had said my morning prayer asking for strength and safety in finding Jake, but I had never taken off on my own like this before. My trips into the ever changing and often hostile outback had been planned in increments—going a little farther each day but always knowing how to get home on my own before nightfall.

This journey into the unknown was far different from that, and I was only attempting it because Jake had been gone much too long. I knew the general direction and might even be able to find the stream—hidden from eyes that were none too prying—that trailed down the mountain from the falls in front of the cave. If I followed it uphill, I should eventually find Jake safe and would simply explain that I was worried about him having enough to eat. But that wasn't the way he had taken Trevor and me to the cave. He said the climb was too difficult and he had found a much easier way to get there. It was longer but much less arduous.

So, with a heart racing and less than the amount of confidence that might be needed, I climbed on the motorbike and turned the key in the ignition. In no time at all, I was speeding down the dirt driveway—the dust flying up behind me like a small tornado. Right before I got to the highway, I took a sharp turn to the left on the back road we used to get to Uncle Ned's part of the ranch when we were in a hurry.

Arriving at his homestead, I took care of the animals left in my charge, and then focused on a large outcropping of rocks near the top of the northern-most mountain. I knew we had gone that way while herding sheep for shearing, but had been so wrapped up in the importance of making the right decisions concerning my tempestuous relationship with Jake that it had left little time to think about anything of a more practical nature.

While it was a pleasant morning for a ride, I knew the trip across the meadow could be treacherous, and I would have to slow down considerably if I wanted to keep my bike under control. Rocks, shrubs, rodents and other small animals, even undersized washes, could cause the most experienced biker to crash. It was all about expecting the unexpected before it happened. I was getting better with that, but the outback was not a place for a girl who had any misgivings about surviving anything Mother Nature threw her way.

If Jake had just come home for more supplies like anticipated this ride into unfamiliar territory would be unnecessary. But he hadn't returned, and Aunt Nora's news about gunfire two days earlier had left me with an uneasiness that refused to go away. With any luck, I would pass him coming down the mountain while I was going up. He would say something caustic, or even mean, that would be upsetting but it would be far preferable to what I might discover if I ever made it to the cave.

Jake simply had to be okay, I told myself as the bike bounced up and down over uneven terrain. He was a man's man and used to taking care of himself. Wasn't it the thrill of adventure and excitement that drove him to become a bush pilot in the first place? He was used to making difficult decisions and defending himself in the face of danger. I was just being a meddlesome woman in love with a man who no longer wanted her.

That thought alone almost caused me to turn around, but I couldn't worry about a negative reaction to my interference until my fears had been put to rest. I was only doing what LeAnn would expect if she knew what was going on. So I continued on my way trying to watch where my bike was taking me, but the tall, yellow, dust-ridden grass made the ground impossible to see.

I hadn't remembered the mountain being so far away when we had been herding sheep to Uncle Ned's ranch, but increased anxiety has a habit of stretching minutes unmercifully and swarming bugs and fear of crashing didn't help. When I got to its base, I glanced down at my watch. It was only ten o'clock in the morning, but the worst of the trip lay ahead. When listening intently, I could hear the sound rushing water coming from somewhere above my head but finding the stream took close to an hour. The dry brush was thick and insect filled and there was the constant fear of poisonous spiders and snakes whose homes I was disturbing.

Tears and prayers were continual as I chided myself for even attempting such a difficult journey without the needed knowledge or preparation, and for not riding Rupert. It might have taken us longer to reach the base of the mountain, but he could have sniffed out water far faster than I had found it and climbed at least part of the way up the mountain with me on his back. Now, I would have to make it on foot since there was no trail a motorbike could follow on either side of the stream that in places appeared to be little more than a trickle.

I shoved back more thoughts about the likelihood of having picking the wrong place to climb, scribbled a note on a napkin and tucked it underneath the front seat of the motorbike with just the edge of it showing. Anyone who found the bike by chance, or design, would see what I had written. Purposely, I had not included anything about the cave, only that I was climbing to the mountain summit and if I didn't come down, I hoped someone would try to find me. I signed it with my name, date and time of day.

Then I slipped the key into my pant's pocket, forced my arms through the backpack straps and started to move upward. I listened intently to the sounds around me and every so often scratched a large X on a tree trunk or piled up a few rocks so I could find my way back more easily. My sense of direction was horrid, and I had the distinct feeling that I had bitten off far more than I would ever be able to chew on my own.

If nothing more, marking my path gave me something to do and made me more conscious of my surroundings. Snakes and lizards and all kinds of creepy, crawling things I didn't want to touch slithered across my path at unforeseen intervals, and wild animals I didn't want to meet unexpectedly lurked where they could not be seen until they were ready to pounce. I swatted at flying insects and bugs until my hands and face were spattered with blood. I would look like a pincushion before making it home again.

Maybe Jake was right about the need for more than a single self-defense class and plain common sense, I contemplated while pushing dry, prickly brush away from my face and trying to keep from tripping over obstructions along the water's edge. Guns, like the one inside my backpack, were for protection and I should quit being so afraid of them. They wouldn't hurt me or anyone else as long as I didn't try to use them. But if I did brandish one, I had better be ready to pull the trigger.

It seemed like I had been climbing forever when I actually heard the sound of more than just trickling water. Sweat was pouring from my brow and my legs, back and shoulders throbbed unmercifully from carrying such a heavy load, but the noise of chattering birds let me know that my destination was near. I could only pray it was the right stream and cave because I had seen no sign of Jake or anyone else taking the path I had chosen. I wanted to race forward but low-hanging vines and thick ground cover that twisted and curled beneath my feet made rapid movement impossible.

None-the-less, I cried out with relief when moist soil began sucking at my boots. It was more of a threat to me than any of the dry brush I had already walked through since its life-giving properties attracted most everything. I wasn't particularly worried about wild animals, except for dingoes that traveled in vicious packs, but they slept during the day and hunted at night so I should be safe for now.

My voice was dry and raspy, but I still tied to sing. It helped me feel less alone, and every so often I called out Jake's name. When he didn't answer, there was no choice except to keep moving upward over slippery rocks and under branches that hung too close to the earth. I was hot, dirty, miserable, and still being eaten alive by things I could not see. Even the mosquito repellant I had sprayed so lavishly over my clothing and on my face and neck did little to keep the mostly invisible beasties from trying to take big chunks of my flesh.

The sun was moving into the afternoon sky when I heard what sounded like a horse whiney. I stopped walking and listened intently. When I didn't hear it again, I opened the canteen and took a drink of water. It had a slightly metallic taste, but it was cool and did much to sooth my parched throat. Then I grabbed a handful of crackers before putting the straps of the backpack around my shoulders again. The muscles throughout my entire body were now throbbing.

"Where are you, Jake?" I asked the trees and shrubs that encircled me, even though I knew they could not answer. "I have traipsed up this bloody mountain in the heat and the bugs and look like I have been through an explosion. You better have a darned good reason for not letting me know you were okay."

And then I sighed and resumed moving, but I had gone no more than a few feet when I heard the noise again. It was definitely a horse, Jake's horse, unless there were other people on the mountain. And even if there were, maybe they could help me find him.

"I'm coming, General," I shouted as I slipped on a rock and found myself face down on the ground.

General was a stupid name for a horse, I decided as I got to my feet. The front of my body was covered with foul-smelling mud and I was in a fetid mood, more from frustration and fear than from being in any real physical pain. When I found Jake, I would let him know that only a woman in love would come looking for him when she had no idea how to get to where he was.

When I found General a few minutes later, I saw that he had wound his reins so tightly around the tree he had been tied to that he was unable to reach the water. He had worn a deep rut in the ground trying to free himself before collapsing to the ground, and there was dried blood underneath the leather strap that would cut off all air if it got any tighter.

"It's okay, General," I told him, dropping my backpack to the ground and patting his soft nose. "You have gotten yourself into quite a muddle here."

He snorted, shook his massive head and tried to get up on his hoofs, but he was virtually held captive by the leather that had barely begun to fray even after being rubbed so violently against the tree.

"You've got to stay calm or I can't help you," I said in a voice I hoped was reassuring, but when I looked into his large black eyes I could see only terror. He was looking over my shoulder, and I suddenly felt every hair on my body bristle.

I slowly turned my head. Less than fifty feet behind me the biggest crocodile I had ever seen was emerging from the edge of the water. They weren't supposed to be this high in the mountains, but it had been an exceptionally dry year after the flood. My body went stiff with horror. The sound of my voice must have startled him, and it would only take moments until he was upon us. But I couldn't run and leave General to be its next meal, and even if I cut his reins with the knife in my back pocket I could never get him on his feet in time.

The crocodile was on the ground and nearly racing towards us with its huge teeth gnashing in anticipation of the delicacy it was about to devour. I instinctively reached for the gun in the pocket of the backpack. Impulse told me what to do. I held it out in front of me and pulled the trigger, but the bullet missed its mark and that only seemed to make the beast more angry.

I rose to my feet and fired until all the bullets were out of their chambers. I wasn't even sure if my eyes had been open, but one of them must have hit its mark. Just as the crocodile reached General with its razor-sharp incisors it dropped to the ground, but the gushing of blood from General's left front leg told me that I had not killed it in time. Jake's horse needed immediate medical attention and all I had with me was a makeshift first aid kit and no idea what I was doing.

Without conscious thought, I slid to my knees in the rotting leaves and foul-smelling muck, shaking violently, the gun still gripped tightly in my hands. The body of the crocodile was still jerking spasmodically around but its eyes were closed, and I knew it could not inflict any more pain. Tears welled as I opened the backpack and took out what few useful items I had brought with me. I would not let this turn into the fiasco I had been part of the day Newton was born and his mother died.

"I am so sorry, General!" I sobbed as I kicked the crocodile's head away with my foot. Blood was flowing from two bullet holes in its body, but I didn't care. It had hurt Jake's horse, and it would have killed at least one of us if I hadn't stopped it first.

I washed the wound clean with water from the canteen I had been carrying over my shoulder and covered it with a heavy antiseptic I had found in the bathroom at the ranch. Then I wrapped the lesion with gauze and went to work untangling the reins from around the tree. I couldn't leave General where he was. If there was one crocodile in the stream there might be more, and the smell of fresh blood would attract any scavenger in the area.

"It's going to be okay," I said again as I tried to get him on his feet. He seemed to have given up the will to fight for either his freedom or his life after being gouged and had not even tried to fight back while I was treating his wound. It was deep but the crocodile's teeth had not hit an artery or a bone. He would likely need stitches, but he was going to get off that mountain alive.

"Come on, General," I encouraged, pulling helplessly on the reins as my body went through spasms of anxiety and relief. General was a huge horse and there was no way I could move him unless he was willing to help. Trust had to be earned, and I had never spent any time with him. I had never even been on his back.

"We've got to find Jake," I continued as my efforts brought no results and tears streamed down my cheeks, smearing the dirt, debris and blood underneath. I might have wiped them away if I had not been so consumed with the task at hand. "He never would have left you alone if he wasn't in trouble himself. Please try to get up. I know it hurts, but I can't leave you alone to find him."

While I was still pushing, prodding and pleading, General suddenly decided to rally, and with another snort and a whip of his head he was soon standing on his own. I patted his nose fondly.

"I will lead you out of here, General," I promised. "And nothing will hurt you again."

I meant what I said but was in what seemed like an impossible situation. I feared letting go of his reins because even injured he might bolt and finding him would not be easy in unfamiliar territory. But I couldn't tie him around the tree again either. He was traumatized and hurt, but if I took him back to the ranch it would mean giving up on Jake who might need my help even more than his horse did.

Leaving this place of horror with the remains of a truly horrid predator at my feet was logical enough, but there was a reason Jake had not taken General further up the mountain. So I pulled the horse towards the stream where he lapped at the water voraciously while I tried to think. I even called out Jake's name again, but if the consecutive gun shots had not brought him running then . . . .

I forcibly stopped my thoughts because hope and prayer were all I had left. General was favoring his leg considerably while I looked around the area with fresh awareness now that the current threat was behind us. Further up the incline I saw Jake's saddle draped over a large rock. I shooed a large, grey-green bird away from it once General had finished drinking but decided to leave it where it was.

Crushed undergrowth near the edge of the stream indicated the beginning of a trail that led upwards and when I looked in that direction, I knew I was much closer to the top of the mountain than I thought. I could even see the outline of the waterfall as its droplets sparkled in the sunlight that was visible between the leaves on the trees.

"I know you don't want to walk, but it isn't far and we have to find Jake."

My heart went out to the injured animal. General was mighty and fierce on his own, but tied to a tree with a heavy leather rope he was helpless as a baby.

I opened the backpack and gave him one of the apples I had brought with me. He looked so grateful I almost fed him the other one. But if Jake was okay—not just detained—he might enjoy it too. I had to believe this was the worst I would find, regardless of the feeling of doom that had settled in my stomach after killing the crocodile.

My soul was filled with trepidation and fear as we followed as closely as was prudent the stream from which the crocodile had emerged. The rivulet was too shallow for them to live in so what had brought this one so far up the mountain? Perhaps it had been carried away from its natural habitat and gotten lost when the floodwater rerouted everything but the sturdiest trees a few months earlier. That made sense if it had been injured and needed recovery time, and it also meant that the likelihood of seeing another one was minuscule. Unfortunately, it did not mean that other carnivorous animals that mostly left humans alone would not come to finish off its remains.

I was so lost in my musings that I tripped over a protruding branch but didn't go down. I looked back at General whose bridle I had secured around his neck and was holding tightly in my hands. I could not let anything else happen to him. Jake would never forgive me if I did. His limping was so pronounced I slowed our pace even more. It couldn't be that much farther to the cave because I was almost out of mountain.

But if I was so near the top, where was Jake? He should have heard my screams, but   even if he hadn't the sound of falling water would not have muffled the firing of my gun six times. Was it possible that there was a fork in the stream and I had somehow missed it? The idea was preposterous! I was grasping for straws because that was my only recourse if I wanted to stay focused.

I stopped to take a drink of water from the canteen. Then I called out his name again, but there was still no answer. The pressure of my heart beating became more pronounced as each step forward brought me closer to a reality I might not want to face. Jake had to be alive. I had to tell him that I loved him and was willing to give us a chance. I simply could not endure my indecisiveness if it was too late for that.

I called out his name a few more times while we were climbing. I was totally exhausted, and the rush of adrenaline from shooting the crocodile was starting to wear off. If I didn't get to the cave soon, I would have to sit down and rest. Then another thought infiltrated my consciousness. What if Jake was okay, but my constant shouting had brought corrupt and possible murderous men over the crest of the mountain? My desire to set my mind at ease might only bring further danger to all of us by giving our location away.

There was so much I didn't know about living in the outback. Crocodiles were supposed to inhabit the lower marshlands, and people were supposed to help each other, not steal from and kill them. Why hadn't I believed Jake when he told me it wasn't safe to wander away from the ranch?

My actions had been incredibly foolish, but I had saved General's life and could not turn back now. At least I had proven my ability to use a gun if the need arose, albeit with it with less than sterling accuracy. I had returned it to the pocket of the backpack, but not before reloading the chambers. I would not be unprepared again, and I would have Jake teach me more about using a firearm once we were all home again.

Just then, I rounded a slight bend and saw the falls. It was even more spectacular than I remembered. Specks of sunlight had transformed the cascading water into a shimmering rainbow, and the trees surrounding it were all tall, majestic and green. There were still spots of yellow, pink and lavender where wild flowers had bloomed profusely just weeks earlier. It nearly took my breath away. Jake was right. We had an obligation to protect this grandeur of nature along with the drawings inside. It was on Hawkins' land, and no one had the right to destroy it.

"Jake, it's me," I called out as I hesitatingly tied General to a tree near the water where he could graze and drink freely. I hated leaving him alone outside, but there wasn't room in the cave for him. Besides, once I found Jake we would all be on our way down the mountain together. I would not let him stay here any longer without me, and I had no intention of remaining myself.

Gnawing fingers of fear washed over my body as I stepped into the stream bed. It wasn't like Jake to be inside, even during the hottest part of the day. I glanced down at my watch as water splashed around my ankles and moved upwards until my jeans were wet to my knees. It was after four in the afternoon. I had been climbing relentlessly for nearly six hours. No wonder I could scarcely put one foot in front of the other.

"Jake, are you in there?" I questioned out loud as I came to the cave's entrance. It was dark inside, so I removed the flashlight from my backpack and let the bag drop to the ground. I was too tired to bend down and pick it up.

I waited a moment until my eyes became adjusted to the dimness before calling out his name again. He had definitely been here. His bedroll and saddlebag were lying on the floor of the cave, but he was nowhere in sight.

"Answer me, Jake," I almost screamed as tears of frustration and dread slid down my cheeks again. This wasn't the time for playing hide and seek. I was too tired and emotionally drained to deal with child's play.

"Jake, it's me, Brylee."

When he still didn't respond, I started off towards the back of the cave where I knew the entrance to the chamber of drawings was, but if he wasn't there, I wasn't sure where I could look.

The white outlines reflected in the beam of light I cast towards the walls were in sharp contrast to the ghostly and heavy blackness surrounding me. As I stood contemplating what my next move should be, what sounded like a faint moan reached my ears. While I had never been afraid of the dark, I had a healthy respect for things I could only hear.

But even in my elevated state of emotional fright, I would have run towards the sound if the height of the passage leading in the direction from which it came had not prevented me. I dropped to my hands and knees and began crawling, literally digging my hands and the toes of my boots into the moist earth to push myself forward faster.

"I'm coming," I sobbed as the beam of light guiding my way cast eerie shadows everywhere. I heard the rush of wings around my face and the scuttle of tiny feet, and felt sticky substances each time I put one hand in front of another, but I didn't slow my pace. Whatever might be coming at me now in the dark had been in the cave with Jake. I had nothing to fear except how I might find him.

And then I was in another small chamber and knew why he had not answered my calls. He way lying on his back with the front and sides of his shirt caked in dried blood. He didn't move or even open his eyes when I shinned the light directly at him.

"No!" I cried out as I propelled myself towards him. I was too frightened to even think about trying to stand.

When I got to his side, I touched his arm. It was cold and clammy. I checked his wrist for a pulse, and after several attempts found one. It was weak, but at least there was still a measure of life inside. A cursory glance gave no indication of broken bones, but I knew he had been shot. Blood was everywhere, especially on the ground around him.

I rocked back on my knees as wave after wave of nausea nearly made me wrench. I couldn't leave him where he was, but I would never be able to drag him through the tunnel I had just come through by myself. Like General, he was much too big to move, unless he was able to help me.

"Oh, Heavenly Father," I cried out. "He can't die here! Not like this! Not now!"

It was then I remembered the canteen of water that still hung around my neck. I sat down on the dank, pungent earth beside him and gently lifted his head until it was resting in my lap.

"Jake, can you hear me?" I asked again. He moved ever so slightly in my arms, and an involuntary sob escaped from between my parted lips.

"Do you think you could drink something?"

It was a stupid thing to ask. I knew that the moment the words slipped out. If he had been without water for over two days his internal organs would be shutting down. That was just as lethal as a gunshot.

He moved again, so I opened the canteen and held it to his lips until a small trickle of water came out. He sputtered, letting most of it slide down the sides of his mouth.

"My side," he whispered. "Damned encroachers shot me."

"I know it, love," I said as my face contorted with more tears. "But I am going to get you out of here. You need a doctor."

"Can't make it. I tried."

I leaned my head down until my chin was resting on his forehead. He was burning up with fever—that meant infection had set in. If we didn't get help soon, it would be too late for any rescue measures, and I was determined not to lose him on the mountain after what I had just gone through trying to find him.

"Yes, you can!" I stated with more resolve than I felt. "We are going to do it together. You will not die on this mountain today."

He moved again.

"So you kinda like old Jake now that he is on his way out of this life."

"I have always liked you, Jake," I inadvertently cried out as tears of regret and sorrow streamed down my cheeks. "I liked you more than I ever wanted to, more than you will ever know. And you are not going to leave me now. I will get you out of here if it is the last thing I do."

"That's my spunky, Brylee. I am glad you are the last person I get to see—figuratively speaking anyway. What day is it?"

"Tuesday afternoon."

"Then I really am a gonner. I got shot nearly three days ago and have lost more than a little blood. Hell, even I am smart enough to know that if a bullet isn't removed promptly, infection alone will kill the poor bastard who got hit. Now, be a good girl and look for my bottle of whiskey. I seem to have misplaced it, but it should be around here somewhere."

I didn't want to give him any whiskey, but I knew it would dull the pain, if only momentarily. I also knew that alcohol, when applied directly to a wound, had properties that could slow down or kill infection. Jake was right about the time frame, but I wasn't about to give up hope yet. I had found him alive, and that was one miracle that could never be discounted. I might just as easily have found him dead.

It only took a moment of searching the small cavity before I found his bottle of whiskey less than three feet from where he was lying. It was nearly full. I helped him drink some to edge off the pain, and then I poured what I dared over the hole in his side.

"Damn you to bloody hell," he snarled, reaching for his side while he rolled away from me. "I already told you I won't make it off this bloody mountain, and you dump out the only friend that can help get me to the end of this miserable existence."

I was unnerved by his outburst but not offended. At least he was fully conscious now. That had to be a good sign.

I reached out and ran my fingers down his cheek. He didn't pull away again.

"I'm sorry for hurting you and for wasting some of your precious whiskey, but it's not your only friend. I would not have gone through what I have today if you didn't mean a whole lot to me. Now, quit being a bloody baby, and let's figure a way out of this mess. I will not let you die in this horrible cave, and if you will not come with me willingly then they will just have to find two bodies instead of one when a search party finally come looking for both of us."

"Have you lost your freakin' mind?" he snapped back. "You don't have to die just because I am going to."

"You are not going to die, Jake Johnson," I responded, not sure how to get him to believe in living again when he had likely spent the past few days dwelling on what it would be like to no longer exist. "You are not a man who gives up on anything."

"I gave up on you."

"Well, you shouldn't have!" I was shaking with fear and anger, but at least we were finally having a real conversation. "Don't you know how much I love you? You are an incredibly bullheaded and insufferable man and you infuriate me beyond belief at times, but that only makes me love you more."

"No kidding," he whispered as he slumped back into my arms. "If I had known it takes me dying to get you to admit how you really feel, I would have done this months ago."

"That's not funny," I replied, choking back another onslaught of tears.

"Oh, I think it is the perfect irony. The girl I have loved since the first day I saw her—with a defiant look in her eyes and a hammer in her hands—actually loves me back. Now, do you suppose you could give me another sip of whiskey, if there is any left. Before I was only numb, now I hurt like hell."

I put the bottle back to his lips while I held his head steady so he could take another swallow.

The person I had been a few days ago would have balked at enabling his desire for alcohol because it went against what I believed and wasn't good for him, but something had changed during the hours I had been searching for him. I had finally come to understand that love cannot be hurried or changed. It might sneak up unexpectedly and unwanted, but once there, it was nearly impossible to resist. My accepting Jake for the person he was now, not the person I wanted him to be, was the only way change would ever happen.

He had never tried to force me into doing anything against my will. He had even walked away so I could quit torturing myself over a simple decision that had been too difficult for me to make. How could I fault him for anything? If he didn't make it out of the cave alive, another drink of alcohol wouldn't matter, but my inflexibility most certainly would.

"That's better," he said, letting his head fall back into my lap. "I'm not feeling the least bit hammered, but the pain isn't as bad as when you tried to kill me a few minutes ago."

"I didn't mean to hurt you," I said as my hand found his. "I just thought it might help. You were pretty much delirious and burning up."

"Always practical, and as impetuous as ever, aren't you."

"I'm not sure how to take that," I said, lifting his hand to my lips and kissing it.

"It doesn't matter," he whispered, and I felt his arm go limp. "Maybe you should go for help. I'm certainly not going anywhere, and I don't want you to sit here and watch me die."

"I'm afraid that is not your decision to make," I countered. "I won't leave you alone. There has to be some other way."

"Unless you can sprout wings and fly out of here with me on your back, I don't think we have many alternatives."

I knew he was right, but what if something final happened while I was gone? Could life be so unfair as to take him away from me now that I had finally found the courage to tell him what was really in my heart?

"Come on," he said, trying his hardest to smile in the faint light given off by the flashlight I had brought with me. "I don't want the woman I love sitting here watching the life drain out of me. I have seen it happen too many times, and the result is always the same. You and I both know that going for help is the only chance I have."

I wanted to refute his assessment of the situation, but knew the score as well as he did. He would be dead in a matter of hours if we did nothing but wait.

"Isn't there anything else I can do?"

"There is something," he said, his voice weak with exhaustion.

"Just name it!"

"You could give me a kiss—a real kiss like the one I hoped we would share on the beach. I need something to remember you by."

"Don't say that," I whimpered. "We will have lots of time to make memories, happy ones."

"I hope you are right," he sadly replied. "I would almost give that religion of yours a real go—even after everything that has happened between us—if I thought it would give us more time together."

"Don't say something you don't mean, Jake. Not now."

"Oh, I mean it alright. I would do just about anything to hold you in my arms . . . ." His voice trailed away, and I knew there was very little time left.

"Maybe it's time I held you," I said, fighting back a cold sickness that was threatening to engulf me in a darkness even more dreadful than what we were in now.

"Maybe," he whispered.

So I gathered his shoulders and head in my arms, and when our lips touched, I knew I had finally gotten it right. They were cold and very dry, but he responded with every ounce of strength he possessed.

"I knew you still cared about me, despite all your protests ," he whispered. "And your kiss just proved it."

"Don't try to talk," I said. "You need to conserve your strength."

"And you need to go before . . . ." His voice trailed off and I thought for sure I had lost him, but he rallied one more time. "Go on! Get out of here! I'm not going anywhere, and I promise to still be alive when you get back. I love you Brylee Hawkins, forever and always, no matter what that means."

"It means just what you said—forever and aways," I replied, kissing his lips again.

If I didn't leave now, I never would. So, fighting back my fear of him dying before I got back, I lay his head carefully on the ground, and then covered him with the solar blanket I had brought. I knew it would bring little warmth without the sun rays to get it going, but maybe it would give him added hope. I made sure the canteen of water and what was left of his whiskey was close by where he could reach it. There was no sense worrying about food. He would never be able to eat it anyway.

"I love you, Jake Johnson," I said, and then I kissed him again before crawling back through the passageway that led into the cave with all the drawings. He didn't say anything, but then he didn't have to. The depth of our shared kiss had assured me that he had never stopped loving me, regardless of the amount of time he had spent with Beth.

Chapter 14

Jake's horse was standing where I had left him by the edge of the stream.

"Come on, General," I told him. "I know you're hurt, but Jake is hurt worse, and we have to get help for him."

I took his reins and pulled him down the mountain after me through the brush and trees that ripped at my clothing and skin. When we got past the place on the stream where the dead crocodile lay, and I knew no major obstacles would stand in our way, I climbed on his back and gave him the lead.

I wouldn't say he actually ran down the mountain, but it certainly felt like he did. I just hung onto his mane and prayed that he wouldn't fall. It would mean certain death for all of us since no one knew where I had gone. But providence, destiny or God's tender mercy was with us—even Jake would have to give credence to that—because we made it to the bottom of the mountain without incident.

General was hot, sweaty and panting by the time we got to the open meadow, but instead of jumping off his back and onto the motorbike, I let him gallop all the way to Uncle Ned's. Then I swung his reins three times around the hitching post by the watering trough before running up the wooden stairs into the house. I dialed 911 as soon as I unlocked the door and reached the kitchen—grateful the house key had been left where it was easily found.

"What's your emergency?" The person answering the phone asked.

I explained the dire situation and how we needed help fast.

"Let me connect you with the emergency room chopper."

It seemed like an eternity before a medic picked up. I repeated what had happened.

"I know where Ned Hawkins lives," he assured me. "We can be there in twenty minutes. but I'm afraid we need to get much closer than that if we are going to get to him in time."

Suddenly, I remembered the outcropping of rocks just above the cave. They were nearly white. Anyone who had flown over the area would recognize them, and even if they didn't, the cave was on the other side of the mountain from where John Sutter had been killed, and everybody in town knew about that. I might not know exactly how to get to it from over the top, but I hadn't come this far to wimp out now.

"How much area do you need to land?" I asked.

"Just enough to set the runners down."

I told him what I had been thinking, hoping it would be enough.

"Perfect," the medic said. "We will check out the coordinates during the flight. Maybe you could turn on some lights at the ranch so we will know where to land so you can go with us."

And turn on lights I did! Nearly every light in the house and barnyard was blazing by the time I heard, and then saw, the chopper coming. It was 9:15 pm. I had been away from Jake for nearly four hours. I hadn't taken the time to speculate as to why Aunt Nora wasn't there to greet me, but I had thrown some hay to the animals that needed it and made sure they had enough water to drink. I had even called the vet to see what I needed to do for General. He gave me a few specific instructions and promised to be there at first light, even if no one was at the ranch to meet him.

"Dear God," I prayed again as the chopper came in for a landing. "Please let Jake be alive when we get there."

After the blades quit rotating, one of the medics opened the door and jumped out so he could help me climb in.

"I'm Prentice and this is Richards," he shouted when I was sitting on the floor in the cargo space behind them.

I nodded my greeting since the rotating blades above my head made it almost impossible to hear anything he was saying. There was a gurney and a duffle bag. That was all I could make out in the dark.

"We checked things out and think the ridge might just be large enough for us to land on." Prentice shouted as Richards turned the chopper in the direction the mountain. "I don't suppose you know if we can make it to the cave from the top. It looks like a bloody steep drop."

I hadn't wanted to think about what we might have to go through to enter the cave from above, but since we were already on our way, I knew they wouldn't give up.

"The cave is located behind a waterfall. I'm not sure what that means, but there has to be a way around it."

"If there is a way, we will find it," he responded. "I really am sorry about your friend. There have been more than a few reports of gunfire, but this is the first injury we have encountered."

He didn't say anything about John Sutter. I figured it was his way of keeping me focused so I wouldn't fall apart and become totally useless. But I was having a difficult time thinking about anything but my newfound love for the man who lay dying in a cave trying to protect something that few people would even care about.

The medic named Prentice spoke again. "You said he had been shot in the side, Miss Hawkins. Do you remember which one?"

"The right, I think," I replied. "It was dark and rather hard to tell. There was blood everywhere. He had a fever and kept slipping in and out of consciousness. What does that mean?"

"Let's just take it one step at a time, Miss Hawkins. We won't know anything for sure until we arrive. Are there any details you may not have mentioned? Anything could be helpful in assessing the situation more accurately."

I pushed the palms of my hands into my forehead trying to remember the particulars of finding Jake, and more than grateful that Prentice was still acting positive. From the sketchy information I had already given, it was doubtful that either of my companions thought this would be anything more than the removal of a body.

"I poured some whiskey over his side thinking it might help. He said it hurt something awful."

Prentice stifled a laugh. "I can only imagine! But at least he was still feeling pain. How long has it been since you last saw him?"

"Over four hours. It took a long time to get down that mountain."

"And you came by horseback. I would say someone has been watching over you. Those mountains aren't easy to navigate. I'm just glad we don't have to take the same route you did."

I knew he was calculating time, something we may have already run out of.

"Will we make it?" I asked. "He was barely conscious when I left."

"We will do our best," he replied.

But what if his best wasn't good enough? It had been far too long already. Even someone without a smidgen of medical training knew that.

"There's the ledge," I called out when the light on the nose of the helicopter illuminated it. I was on my knees in the cargo area in an instant since there wasn't enough room to stand erect.

"You have a good eye," Richards said, lowering the chopper to the ground as the blades stirred up a heavy haze of dust.

Prentice opened the door for me. "We will have to take the stretcher. You said he isn't able to walk, and there is some kind of tunnel to get through . . . ."

"That's right," I interrupted, dropping to the ground. I inhaled deeply to help get my bearings and then turned on the industrial grade flashlight I had gotten from Uncle Ned's house. The area around us lit up inharmoniously, but I was no longer afraid of what could not be seen. I heard the sound of rushing water from somewhere below the ridge and would let that be our guide.

"This way. It can't be far," I called out, more than a little anxious to be on our way. They were busy retrieving a stretcher and a bag of medical supplies from the chopper. I frowned at my own impatience. They were doing their job, and I needed to stay out of their way.

"I think we're set," Prentice said when they were standing on the edge of the precipice beside me. "Why don't you lead the way?"

The rocks were jagged and slippery in the cool mountain air, and the way down much steeper than I had anticipated. I slipped several times, but grabbed at trees and shrubs with my bare hands to keep from falling, no longer caring if they were ripped to shreds as long as we got to Jake in time.

The men were struggling just as much as I was to remain upright, and I heard a few curse words as they followed along behind me. I wished I knew exactly where I was going, but I had never been to the top of the mountain before and coming towards the cave from over the summit was far more difficult than coming from the valley below. I prayed there were no sudden drop-offs. They might be impossible to see in the dark.

But it wasn't long until we were in the small clearing in front of the waterfall.

"This is a hell of a place to get shot," Richards said, quickly surveying his surroundings. "I'm surprised you were even able to find your way here."

"I've been here before," I replied. "Jake is in one of the smaller chambers."

I didn't care what they saw as we walked behind the waterfall letting the mist soak through the outer layer of our clothing. All that mattered was Jake.

I called his name the minute I was in the first cavern, but there was no answer. The walls of the cave looked even more sinister than I remembered as the light I held out in front of me cast demonic shadows that appeared to dart and dance everywhere. I let it guide me into a second chamber, and then I got down on my hands and knees and crawled through the passage that led to the cold, enclosed room where I had left Jake. The medics crawled through after me, but getting the stretcher through the narrow tunnel wasn't easy. They would have to push and pull it on the ground in order to get Jake out.

He hadn't moved since I left. I half-stumbled and half-crawled to where he was lying so still and lifeless.

"Jake, wake up," I pleaded as I fell to my knees beside him. "I've brought help. We are going to get you out of here."

"Stand aside, Miss Hawkins, so we can get to him," Prentice instructed.

I backed away, willing myself to be calm. Jake didn't move as a cursory examination began.

"I've got a pulse," Richards finally said. "It's weak, but let's bag him and see if we can get him to the hospital."

All the emotions and physical exertion of the day were suddenly overwhelming, but God has a way of giving strength when needed, so I held the light steady while the medics worked. Once they had an IV started, they rolled Jake onto his side so they could get the stretcher underneath his body before strapping him down. He still hadn't made a sound—not even one expressing pain. In a way, I knew that was a blessing. I just hoped we had made it in time.

"You go first with the light," Prentice told me. "And we need you to carry this bag. It's going to take all of us working together to get him out of this cave and up that mountain in the dark."

I didn't say anything. I just got on my hands and knees and crawled back through the tunnel, dragging their medical bag behind me. Sharp noises, and a few curses I knew were not meant for my ears, let me know they were doing their best in getting Jake to safety.

"Don't let me lose him now," my mind petitioned our Eternal Father as I waited for the medics to get him through the tunnel and into the room where all the drawings looked down at me as if to say that this was exactly what we deserved for disturbing a place where white men were not meant to be. The idea that the Rainbow Serpent I had told Trevor about could actually exist chilled me, but sitting in the suffocating darkness with so much antiquity around me, it was easy to believe in most anything, even the paranormal and bizarre.

My relief was immense when both medics and stretcher made it out of the cave. I stood to the side and shinned the light on the rocks that led from the stream bed to the summit of the mountain where the chopper stood ready to take us to town. The distance to the top seemed much greater than it had coming down, and Jake was a solid, muscular man well over six-feet tall. The men carrying him were no lightweights and would have little trouble traversing level ground, but his dead weight would make upward progress over uneven terrain slow, and there was nothing I could do to help.

So, I simply took the lead and moved as slowly as needed, making sure the light I carried was focused on them so they could see the loose rocks and tangled branches. The men with me were in excellent physical condition—they had to be considering the area where we lived and the kind of assistance they were forced to give—but they slipped and stumbled every few steps, forcing the stretcher to the ground. Jake's face looked a lifeless and chalky white, but I was almost certain I saw a grimace when his body slammed into a boulder they had been unsuccessful in climbing over.

I finally pulled myself onto the ledge and sank down on the rocks to wait. My strength was nearly spent, and there wasn't a single inch of my body that did not hurt. I hadn't eaten anything, with the exception of a couple of crackers, for nearly twenty-four hours and had consumed very little water, but I couldn't think about myself just yet. Jake's needs had to come first.

Prentice jumped in the chopper and opened the door to the tail section. "Pass him on up," he shouted down to his partner, but Richards was already lifting the front end of the stretcher so it was level with the opening to the cargo hold.

I wanted to help but knew I would only be in the way. These men were dedicated professionals, and they didn't need me telling them how to do their jobs. Jake was soon inside, and Richards slammed the door shut.

"You will have to ride up front," he said. "But don't worry. Prentice is one hell of a medic. If anyone can keep your friend alive until we get to the hospital, he can."

"Thank you," I told him as I fastened the safety strap in front of me.

"Don't thank me just yet. Getting him out of that cave may have been the easy part. We won't know the extent of his internal injuries until the doctor has him on the operating table, but I will radio ahead and tell them what we know."

He secured his headset before the blades of the chopper began whirling, and then turned the chopper in the direction of town. Prentice had his back to me as he hooked Jake up to a series of monitors. Their constant beeping and flashing symbols were distracting, and I wanted to ask a million questions about what they were testing, but I remained silent. Jake needed their undivided attention. I would learn soon enough if something went wrong.

I tried to listen while Richards told the dispatcher what he could about Jake's condition, but his terminology left me with more questions than answers. I looked behind me only one additional time during the relatively short flight. I couldn't see Jake's face, but I touched his shoulder. If I could only pass some of my strength to him! He simply had to know how much I loved him.

The lights surrounding the heliport pad at the hospital in Edna were bright when we landed. Two orderlies were waiting for us and shielded their faces from the rush of air our landing stirred up. They opened the cargo door, and Prentice positioned the stretcher and the tubes that were keeping Jake alive towards them. The stretcher was lowered to the ground and put on a gurney. A nurse who had come with them took charge of the IV bag.

"How's the patient?" one of them asked.

"Gunshot wound to the right side. He's been unconscious since we got to him."

I couldn't hear anything more. They were running towards the door leading into the emergency room and gave no thought to me.

"I don't know how to thank you," I told Prentice and Richards as I paused momentarily before following Jake and the orderlies inside.

"It's our job," Prentice replied, almost smiling at me. "And I really hope he makes it. I hate it when bad things happen to good people."

"We'll have to file a police report since there was a shooting," Richards interjected. "But the authorities shouldn't bother you with questions until morning. Is there someone we can call? You shouldn't have to wait this out alone."

"I'll be fine," I told him. "All I care about is knowing Jake will be okay."

"This may be a small town but we have a bloody amazing hospital staff. They have to be good with some of the cases we bring in. But I have to admit that tonight was a first. One of us could stick around for a while if it would be helpful."

"Thank you," I said again as we stopped in front of the admitting desk. My knees were trembling so badly I had to grad hold of the countertop for support. I didn't know where Jake was. He had been taken behind closed doors by the time we got into the building.

"Have those cuts and bruises checked out," Richards said as he turned his attention to the nurse who was handing him a clipboard with papers on it. Prentice was busy talking to a man in white coat. I could only assume it was the surgeon who had been called in to operate.

I wanted to be with Jake but knew regulations would be strictly enforced. Someone would talk to me as soon as they could. I sat in the nearest chair, clasp my hands together in my lap and waited. The ticking of the clock on the wall was deafening. Had I been there under any other circumstances, I might not have known it was even there, but my heightened emotions intensified every sound and movement. I jumped at each new voice or door that cracked open. The medics who had brought us from the cave were busy filling out reports. I hoped they were right in saying that no one would interrogate me tonight. I was in no condition to answer questions until I knew our rescue mission had been successful.

After what seemed an eternity, a curtain parted and I saw Jake being wheeled out of a cubicle and towards a set of double doors that led into the main part of the hospital. I ran in his direction hoping to get a glimpse that would tell me if he was still alive, but a nurse prevented me from reaching him.

"Not now," she said, grabbing my arm. "He's on his way to surgery."

"But I need to tell him something," I protested.

"I'm afraid that will have to wait, but I can assure you that he is in the best possible hands. I understand you have been through quite an ordeal yourself. My job is to make sure you get the attention you need." She propelled me away from the doors through which Jake had disappeared. "You have some pretty bad abrasions."

"I'll be fine," I told her, struggling in vain against her grasp. I was close to my breaking point, and I pitied the person who was around when that happened.

"Try not to worry. He will be in surgery for several hours," she said, releasing her hold on my arm but not allowing me to move away from her. "You can help best by giving us some information."

"What kind of information?" I asked as she picked up a clipboard that was sitting on the counter and led me to a corner of the waiting room where we both sat down. "I already told the men who helped us everything I know."

"And that has been very helpful, but I'm afraid we don't even have his last name yet."

"Johnson," I responded, pressing in on my temples. My head felt like it was going to explode. The fluorescent light was much too bright after the darkness of the night. "He's foreman of Hawkins' Enterprises."

It felt weird saying that, but it was true. None of us would be able to do our jobs without him. He was the one person who had the strength and the knowledge to keep us from going under.

"Are you his next of kin?"

Her question surprised me, even though it should have been expected. It would not be easy explaining why both of us were on that mountain when there was so much we wanted to keep from becoming public knowledge.

"No," I said. "He has a sister, but she is going through a very difficult pregnancy and can't get out of bed."

"Well, we won't bother her tonight, if we don't have to. Do you know if Mr. Johnson has any allergies to medications or anesthetics?"

I couldn't answer her question. I couldn't even tell her his age or birth date. I knew so little about the man I claimed to love. Why hadn't I paid more attention to the little things while I had the chance?

"Do you know how long it will be until we hear something," I asked, ignoring her latest question about his medical history.

"It could be several hours, or even longer, depending on what they find."

"But he will be okay as long as the bullet didn't hit any major organs."

"I can only tell you that he has lost a massive amount of blood and has yet to regain consciousness, but I will be happy to take you to the chapel as soon as I have one of our other doctors check you out."

Arguing with nurse Gravel, as her name badge indicated, was pointless. So I gave her my medical history while she led me into an examining room and told me to undress and put on the unbecoming gown that was already on the table. Then she left me alone while I removed tattered and filthy clothing that would never be worn again.

It didn't take long for the attending doctor to knock on the door. He was young with fine features and sandy-colored hair.

"I'm Dr. Hilde," he said with a pleasant smile. "I understand you've had quite the day."

"Something like that," I told him, not feeling the bit least receptive to his bedside charm. "Have you heard anything about Jake Johnson? He was brought in with gunshot wound . . . ." My voice trailed off. It was useless to ask for more information when we had just arrived.

"All I can tell you is that he's in surgery and it will likely take most of the night. In the meantime, why don't we see what we can do to get you back on your feet. Someone will keep you updated and make sure you get to see him as soon as possible. I understand he owes his life to you."

"He would have done the same for me," I muttered, climbing onto the table while Dr. Hilde looked over the notes Nurse Gravel had already made.

I wanted to see Jake again. I wanted to see his dark, brooding eyes, the way his lips turned up at the corners when he smiled, and I wanted to hear his voice. I wanted to tell him over and over that I loved him and wanted him in my life for always. The details that had kept us apart no longer seemed important. There would be time to sort everything out once he was better.

The doctor completed a thorough examination, talking cheerfully about nothing of importance. I knew it was his way of trying to calm a patient on the verge of hysterics but still had trouble staying focused, even when he told me that I was severely dehydrated and would need stitches in the palm of my left hand.

The bruises and abrasions that covered my body were deep, and many of them had barely begun to show. He assured me that I would look like I had been through a war for several weeks but should suffer no permanent damage—as long as the lack of water and excess physical exertion had not adversely affected any of my organs. He wanted me to stay where I was for the next few hours so I could be monitored.

I thought he was being overly cautious but was wise enough to understand that I would be of no help to Jake if I didn't take care of myself now. So I lay my head down on the hard, metal bed and quit arguing.

"I'm sorry I don't have anything more fancy for you to wear," nurse Gravel said as she handed me some clean scrubs. "I will show you where the shower is, and once you are finished, I will see you back in this room. Dr. Hilde will stitch up your hand, and I will take care of everything else."

The warm water burned as it slid over my tired, bruised and bleeding body and turned from clear to an ugly shade of brown before going down the drain. I was exhausted mentally, physically and everywhere in-between, but I would do the same thing over again right now if it meant saving the life of someone I loved.

Still, I knew I didn't deserve any of the credit. God had led me to Jake. Everything about the day had been divinely orchestrated from finding General before the crocodile did to landing the helicopter on the top of the mountain in the dark and getting the man I loved to the hospital. If Jake survived, he would have to admit there was a God because his rescue could not have happened any other way.

Dr. Hilde gave me a local anesthetic so I wouldn't feel anything as he stitched up the gap that extended from wrist to index finger on my left hand. I had no idea when, where or how I had cut it.

"I'm afraid you will be left with a scar," he said as he worked and I kept my eyes averted. "That gash was pretty close to the bone. I'm surprised you didn't feel it immediately. From the way it looks, it must have happened hours ago. We'll give you antibiotics and a tetanus shot just in case you are not up-to-date. I would say your friend isn't the only one who received a miracle today."

"We were blessed, but honesty, all I could think about was getting Jake to safety," I told him.

"The two of you must be very close."

"Sometimes," I responded, forcing the weariest of smiles. "But I would be lost without him."

Dr. Hilde patted my arm. "Well, you can rest assured that he is getting the best care possible, but I am more worried about you right now. Your heart is still racing, and we need to push fluids and electrolytes into your system until we know everything is going to continue working the way it should."

"I feel fine," I protested. "I'm just a little tired but can assure you that I am not going anywhere as long as Jake is here."

"I figured that might be the case," he responded with a knowing smile. "Nonetheless, you need to concentrate on your own healing right now. Your body is still running on adrenalin but the crash is coming, and it is my responsibly to make sure you suffer no long-term ill effects. It only takes a few hours for the kidneys to start shutting down."

"But it was only one day."

I had been put in a semi-upright position so the doctor could work on my hand, but I leaned back when the full realization about what he was telling me hit home. I didn't feel fine. My entire body ached, and the pain in my hand where he was pulling the flesh together was awful, even with local anesthetic. But dwelling on my discomfort was impossible until I knew what was happening with Jake.

"Miss Hawkins," he said, looking at me with both compassion and understanding. "I know you saved a man's life today and want to be awake when he gets out of surgery, but it could be several hours before we know anything. I won't admit you as a patient, as long as you agree to lie here and rest. I have ordered an IV and expect it to be empty before you even try to get on your feet again. Do you understand what I am saying?"

I nodded, suddenly feeling as if I didn't have the energy to lift my head.

"Good," he said, patting my arm again. "I have asked the nurse to treat your other abrasions and give you a sedative. I'm afraid I can't do anything about the bruising. You must have one hell of a story to tell."

"I guess I do, but I don't want a sedative," I replied, trying to smile. "I want to stay awake."

"It's only a mild one, and I promise to let you know the minute we hear anything about Jake."

"You promise?"

"Cross my heart," he said. "I'll keep you updated."

Nurse Gravel came back with an IV bag and a long, ugly needle.

"This might hurt for a second, but I will be as gentle as I can."

She lifted my arm and tied a rubber cord around it. Then she thumped on a vein while I made a fist with my hand. I had to look away when the needle was inserted. Suddenly, I was feeling very queasy.

"I think I'm going to throw up," I said as bile from my stomach rose to my throat. She held a basin to my mouth as I wrenched several times with very little coming out.

"I am so sorry," I told her as she handed me a tissue so I could wipe the spittle from the corners of my mouth.

"Don't be sorry," she said. "It's all part of being a hero. I will give you something for the nausea. It should let up a little once you have some fluid circulating in your system again. Dehydration and heat stroke are very serious conditions."

By this time, I understood that both the nurse and doctor knew what they were talking about. I had never felt so sick, but I would not allow myself to give in or give up. I had to be both awake and lucid when Jake got out of surgery.

Chapter 15

I must have underestimated the strength of the sedative and my complete exhaustion. When I opened my eyes again, my wounds had been taken care of and my hand bandaged. A different nurse was checking my vitals and the amount of fluid still in the IV bag.

"What time is it?" I asked, trying to raise myself up on my elbows. I was almost too weak to move and noticed that the sides of the hospital bed had been pulled up so I wouldn't roll off. I felt helpless as a kitten and almost started to cry until I remembered what had brought me here.

"Please," I said, looking at the nurse whose face seemed to loom so menacingly above me. "I need to know about Jake Johnson. Is he out of surgery? Is he okay?"

She smiled. "The answer to both those questions is *yes*. I was just coming to tell you that he is in recovery, and all his vitals are stable."

My uninjured hand flew to my mouth as my nose began to tickle and my throat became tight. I had never felt such relief. "When can I see him?" I managed to ask.

"Not for a while," she replied. "But right now, you have some work of your own to do."

She squeezed the skin on my hand and foot and then watched until it had returned to normal.

"The doctor has ordered another IV. You are still dehydrated, and I would imagine a little hungry. Do you think you could take a few sips of broth?"

"I will do anything, if it means getting out of this bed sooner. Jake needs someone with him when he wakes up."

"You do know that it is against hospital regulations for anyone, other than immediate members of the family, to be in the ICU with a patient."

Nurse Jennings, as her name tag read, was only trying to follow the rules, but apparently she didn't understand what we had been through. I intended to clarify the situation because no one was going to keep me away from the man I loved.

"We are family," I told her as defiance set my jaw in a firm line. "Jake's sister was married to my father until he died a few months ago, and she is confined to bed with a difficult pregnancy. So you see, there isn't anyone else who can be with him, except for my nephew who is only eight. You can check things out if you really need to."

"I don't think that will be necessary, Miss Hawkins," Nurse Jennings relented. "I just wanted to make sure you understood the rules. What you did for him was truly heroic, and people need loved ones around during recovery, even if they are not fully aware of their presence."

She rubbed some Vaseline on my dry, chapped lips.

"I must look awful," I said, not even bothering to move.

"You will look like an angel to him when he wakes up. A slightly bruised and beaten angel who sacrificed a great deal to save his life. I have only heard bits and pieces of what happened, but love, you accomplished the miraculous."

"Not me," I told her. "I was only the instrument God used for his own miracle."

Nurse Jennings brought a hairbrush and the supplies needed to brush my teeth after I had swallowed a few sips of broth. My stomach had settled considerably, but I knew it had more to do with finding out that Jake had made it through surgery than with the condition of my body. I was still unable to sit upright without feeling dizzy.

"Give it some time," she said as she brushed some of the tangles out of my hair. I was glad I'd had the foresight not to let it hang loose when I went looking for Jake. Scissors would have been the only remedy after what we had been through.

I couldn't imagine what my face must look like now. When I showered a few hours earlier there was a huge bruise on my right cheekbone, and I had counted seventeen deep scratches and dozens of insect bites in the few places that had not been burned by the sun. But I was alive and so was Jake, and whatever lay ahead would be faced together.

Dr. Hilde came in to check on me a few minutes later, bringing an older doctor who was still dressed in surgical scrubs with him.

"You're looking better," he said as they both stepped into the small cubicle where I tried to push myself more upright in the hospital bed. "I've brought Jake's surgeon, Dr. Turret, to answer any questions you have. You see, I do keep my promises to my patients."

"Thank you," I responded, grateful that he had followed through but not sure what I was going to ask.

"Fire away," Dr. Turret said.

He looked tired. I wondered just how long he had been working on Jake. Other than knowing the sun was now up, I had no idea what time it was.

"I had a hundred questions when we got here, but the only thing I can think of right now is thanking you for saving his life."

"I wish I could say it was my skill as a surgeon that got him through this, but as a God-fearing man, I know who gets the credit for this one. There is no way that young man should have made it off that mountain alive. The loss of blood alone should have killed him days ago."

My brow furrowed. "But he's going to be okay?"

"The next twenty-four hours will tell. The bullet lacerated his appendix and lodged in his spleen. We were able to get it out and do some repairs, but the infection is a different story. We are pumping antibiotics into him as fast as we can, but his full recovery lies in God's hands. Are you a religious person, Miss Hawkins?"

I inclined my head. "I certainly am!"

"Then a few extra prayers wouldn't hurt. I will have a nurse wheel you to the chapel when you feel up to it. I know it's a good place to pray."

I thanked him for his kindness, but I didn't need to be in a chapel to pray. Since joining the church, I knew I could pray at any time and in any place. God was always there for me, and he did answer my prayers in his own time and way.

With Jake safely out of surgery, my world slowly started to fall back into place. I needed to let family know what had happened before they heard it on the radio or television. Aunt Nora would be frantic with worry when she got home and found every light at the ranch turned on and Jake's wounded horse in the barn. At least I'd had the presence of mind to put him in a stall with hay and water available before the helicopter arrived, but I had no way of knowing if the vet has made good on his promise.

General would need medical attention not only from the crocodile's bite but any other damage caused by racing down the mountain and across the meadow with me on his back. I couldn't bear the thought that something final might have happened to him during the night. He was loyal, brave and strong and Jake would be lost without him.

As for Emma and LeAnn, they would never forgive me for keeping what had happened from them. By all rights, Jake should have died on that mountain, but he hadn't and the repercussions from his ordeal would likely haunt us for a very long time.

There would be a thorough police investigation. That meant questions from every possible source, including the media. This was just the kind of event that made the early morning news. I was surprised that we hadn't been bombarded with reporters, cameras and police already.

So, despite not wanting to deal with any of the fallout, I pushed the call button that was draped over the bar at the side of the bed. In a few moments, Nurse Jennings parted the curtains and stepped into the small enclosure. I was surprised the hospital appeared so silent after all the commotion of the night before.

"Is there a phone I could use? I need to contact family."

"Of course," she said. "There's a phone on the other side of the curtain. Let's see if the cord is long enough to reach you."

She deftly pushed back the barrier. Then apparently changed her mind and kicked the lock on the wheels of my bed that kept it in place.

"I think I will just move you closer to it. We've cleared everyone out of this area. The doctor didn't want you disturbed by police or reporters until you were stronger."

"Have they already been here?" I asked.

"Oh, land, girl," she said. "They have been swarming the place since the helicopter landed last night. You have become quite a celebrity, and they want answers. Dr. Hilde won't be able to keep them away indefinitely."

I looked up at her in confusion.

"You mean he protected my privacy on purpose?"

"He believes in his patient's recovery first, but now that you are awake and stable he would have to get a court order to keep them away. No names have been released, but the media is certainly running with the story."

I thanked her for her kindness, and she put the phone in my hand after helping me sit upright so I could punch in the numbers myself.

There were only two phone numbers in Australia I knew—other than the one at the ranch—Uncle Ned's and Emma's. I decided to try Aunt Nora first, but when she didn't answer I left a message explaining what had happened and asking if she could check on Copper and the other animals at the old homestead. Copper had plenty of water and food, but she also had a habit of tipping things over when she got excited or frustrated. Fortunately, the other animals were in the corral by the barn so they would be okay for a day or two on their own, as long as the watering troughs had something in them and the fences remained intact.

My next call was to Emma. She answered after the second ring. It was six-thirty in the morning.

"Hi, Emma," I said, trying to make my voice sound less husky than it really was. My throat still felt like it was filled with fully puffed cotton balls, but I wanted to ease her into what had happened as gently as I could.

"My goodness, have I ever been worried about you!" she exclaimed. "And Trevor has been beside himself since you didn't return his call yesterday. He cried himself to sleep last night saying you had promised to never leave him again. What's going on?"

"It's complicated," I volunteered, knowing that everything in life was complicated until one got to the point of sorting things out.

"Lay it on me, and don't sugar coat anything," she responded impatiently. "I have been listening to the radio since I got up this morning, and all they have been talking about was some miraculous rescue in the outback. I'm supposing you were involved in that since I have been calling the ranch non-stop for the past hour. Where are you anyway?"

There was no point in evading the truth. It would only make her angry. "I'm at the hospital. Jake got shot."

Her intake of breath was sharp, and I hoped my news had not caused a sudden heart attack or stoke. Emma appeared to be in excellent health, but she wasn't exactly young. I hurried on with my tale.

"I found him yesterday. The doctor operated last night. He is still in recovery, but I should be able to see him soon."

"Praise the Lord for that," she said, reverting back to her childhood religious training.

Her way of expressing deep emotion made me smile, but there was nothing humorous about the condition Jake was in. It would be touch and go for the next twenty-four hours or more.

"Just how bad is he?" she asked.

"Bad enough," I responded.

"That's just a polite way of saying he might not make it. What is it you aren't telling me?"

"The bullet hit a couple of organs, but they were able to get it out."

"Heaven help us all!" she exclaimed. "I knew the lunacy that comes with even a hint of gold would not end with John Sutter's death. But what in the world was Jake doing to get shot?"

"He was just in the wrong place at the wrong time."

It wasn't my right to tell her about the cave, the drawings or the gold veins. Not that I believed she would tell anyone, but she didn't need anything more to worry about with LeAnn, Trevor and trying to run her cafe. Uncle Ned would be back soon, and hopefully he would have some of the answers we needed to stop the growing madness.

"You don't sound good," she said. "I'm coming to the hospital as soon as I get Trevor out the door to school."

"That's not necessary," I assured her. "You are the first person I will call when I know something more."

"And just what do you propose I tell LeAnn? She watches the news religiously. They haven't released names yet, but it doesn't take a genius to figure out who was involved once they start talking about where it happened. Jake knew better than to get involved in something that didn't concern him."

Oh, how I wanted to tell her that he had been protecting aborigine drawings in a cave that might contain gold, but it all seemed so pointless now that he was fighting for his life. He shouldn't have been on that mountain. He should have been home at the ranch with me.

"It's a long story," I told her. "Once Jake is well, he can tell you all about it."

The words nearly stuck in my throat. What a horrible price secrets and deceptions bring. If we had just been upfront with everyone perhaps none of this would have happened.

"But it doesn't make any sense," Emma mused, and I could picture her brow furrowing. "Jake is a smart man and would never knowingly put himself in danger."

With those few words, all the stress associated with the past few days suddenly exploded like the doctor said it would.

"It's my fault he was shot," I blurted out as more tears came. "He was angry with me because I refused to tell him how I really felt. I didn't think he would leave before daylight."

"What nonsense are you talking about now?" Emma demanded.

I took a deep breath to bring back rational thought. "Just how much do you already know, Emma?" I asked.

"Only what they have reported on the news. A man was rescued from a cave on the other side of the mountain from John Sutter's place. That only means one thing. Jake found something other people want, and it is not the drawings Nora has been telling us about. You have no idea what this means."

"I think I do," I told her. "Jake didn't shoot himself, but I am not sure the assailant got inside the cave. His gear hadn't been touched, and there was no sign of a struggle."

"Oh, my," she sighed again. "I wish that made me feel better, but it doesn't. I have seen what happens when men get gold fever. This isn't going to stop until that mountain has been stripped of everything it contains."

"I hope you are wrong, Emma, but we can't worry about any of that right now. We need to concentrate on Jake's full recovery."

"I wish I could be as optimistic as you pretend to be, but I suppose we can only deal with one problem at a time. What did the doctor say?"

"That the surgery was successful, but the loss of blood was great and the amount of infection . . . ." I gulped back a moment of unadulterated fear. "The next twenty-four hours are crucial."

"That's what they all say, and I suppose it's the bloody truth," she responded. "I just don't know what to tell LeAnn. She is going to want to know everything."

"You don't have to lie to her, Emma. Just tell her that Jake is stable and in good hands. There is baby Jackie to think about."

"I'll do what I can," she said with resignation. "But the two of you have a lot of explaining to do. You shouldn't have been on that mountain either. What on God's green earth possessed you to go there?"

"I needed to find Jake."

"But why? I knew you were concerned about him when we talked on Sunday, but you couldn't have known he had been hurt."

"Call it divine inspiration if you like. That is certainly what I am doing. He took so little with him and when he didn't come back . . . ."

"You don't have to finish, love. I see where this is heading. The two of you have always had a strong connection, but it's more than that now, isn't it?"

Denying my newly discovered feelings would be a bold-faced lie since I had already expressed them to Jake, and even in a state of near delirium he had told me that it had been love at first sight for him. And when our lips touched, my entire being had come alive.

"I do love Jake, Emma, and with all my heart. I just didn't realize it until I saw him lying so helpless on the ground and knew how easily I could lose him."

"Sometimes God has to give us a little push in the right direction, but I will still be stopping by the hospital this morning to see for myself how both of you are doing."

"I'm fine, really," I lied, not wishing to upset her any further. "Just a few scrapes and bruises—nothing serious. But I have been trying to reach Aunt Nora. Do you know where she is?"

"She stayed here again last night. Nora is one of the strongest women I know, but this whole situation with the drawings, the possibility of gold, John Sutter's murder and Ned being gone has depleted nearly every ounce of her get-up-and-go. Molly's condition hasn't helped any either. She's sleeping on the sofa in the front room. I'll get her for you."

"Maybe you shouldn't wake her."

"And have one more person in this family upset because they have been left in the dark?" Emma said with conviction. "I don't think so! It is not in my nature to keep secrets, but both Nora and I agree that LeAnn doesn't need to know any more than necessary about the conditions at home."

"You have done so much for us, Emma," I said as salty tears made my cheeks sting. "We will never be able to make it up to you"

"I don't expect praise or adoration, Brylee. You are family. That is the only thing that matters to me. Have you called the branch president? He needs to know what is going on."

"I was hoping you could do that for me."

"Consider it done," she said. "I'm sure he will be there as soon as he can to give both of you blessings. Now, I am getting Nora for you."

A few seconds later, I heard Aunt Nora's heavy breathing.

"My God, Brylee! Emma said Jake has been shot. I knew this mess with the cave wasn't going away any time soon, but I never expected anyone else to get hurt. I'm on my way to the hospital as soon as I gulp down some coffee. I promised your father I would look after you. He will never forgive me for letting either one of you get hurt."

There was little point in defending past actions. She was like a Pit Bull when it came to protecting family.

Chapter 16

"**Are you ready to** see Jake?" Nurse Jennings asked after I hung up. "I just heard that he is conscious and has been taken to the ICU."

"Oh, yes," I told her as my body began to tremble with fear and anticipation. I had never seen someone I cared about in the hospital before, except my father, and I loved him in a very different way.

"I thought you might be, but I have a few conditions. You go there in a wheelchair with your IV attached, and you don't try to stand on your own. You are still in our care until the doctor releases you."

I nodded my compliance, even though I didn't fully understand her concern until I had been put in a wheelchair and pushed to the ICU. By the time we arrived, I was woozy and light-headed, but if I betrayed how I felt I would not be allowed to stay.

My eyes sought Jake's face the moment the door closed behind us, and I couldn't restrain my cry of anguish when I saw how pale and fragile he looked in the gray dawn. He was hooked up to several monitors that were no less intimidating than the ones on the helicopter and bags like the one attached to me were pushing fluids and antibiotics into his body. One of them was filled with blood.

"Don't let his appearance frighten you. He is doing amazingly well considering what he has been through."

She wheeled me close enough to the bed that I could reach out with my uninjured hand and touch his face. It was still flushed and warm, but he blinked open his eyes when my fingers moved down his cheek.

"Hey, beautiful," he whispered. "I must be dead or dreaming to have you here by my side."

His tender confession opened a floodgate of fresh tears, but I didn't even try to wipe them away.

"You are very much alive, and I couldn't survive if I lost you."

"Thanks to you, I just might live to see a few more days."

My fingers found their way to his lips. They were as dry and chapped as my own, but they curved into the faintest smile.

"You had better see a ton more days, Jake Johnson. You don't know how scared I have been."

"I think I might have a slight idea. The last thing I remember was thinking that I would never get to see you again, never get to hold you in my arms and kiss those amazing lips."

"They are pretty burned like the rest of my face, but I would kiss you a million times if I could," I replied, wishing he did not have to see me the way I looked now.

"And I would kiss you right back if I didn't feel like a freight train had run over me."

He closed his eyes, but I knew he was just resting because his chest was still moving slowly up and down.

"Is he okay?" I asked Nurse Jennings who had moved to the door to give us more privacy.

"He will be in-and-out like this for a day or two. The doctors are keeping him heavily sedated so his body can heal."

"But I can still stay with him? I don't want him to be alone."

She smiled. "I will have to check with both of your doctors, but under the circumstances, I doubt there will be any problems, unless you stop taking care of yourself."

"No more heroics for me," I assured her, looking over at the man lying so still on the hospital bed. What I had said was true. I would never leave Jake alone again—even knowing I would have to face Beth's wrath first.

"He is a lucky bloke to have you watching his back."

"I'm the lucky one," I told her. "I have been given a second chance to show him how much I care."

It only took a few minutes for her to obtain permission for me to stay in Jake's room—at least until he was fully conscious. I had been forthright about LeAnn's delicate condition and my relationship with Jake. We might not be related by blood, but we were family. For better or worse, we would always be part of each other's lives.

While I waited for the promised recliner so I would be more comfortable while waiting for him to awaken again, a different nurse informed me that Aunt Nora was in the ICU waiting room demanding to see for herself that I was okay. I knew she would not leave until I had talked to her—and she would not be allowed into his room—so I told Jake that I would be back in a minute or two. His eyes were still closed, and I was fairly certain that nothing I said was registering on a conscious level, but that didn't matter as long as he was still with me physically.

"This is unbelievable, Brylee," she said, getting to her feet the moment I was wheeled into the more secure waiting room with my own IV pouch hanging from a rod beside me. It would have been a news frenzy had I been anywhere else in the hospital, but I could see a uniformed officer standing outside the door. Obviously the police felt that added security was necessary until the perpetrator was caught. "You said you were fine."

"I am fine, and doing much better now that I have seen Jake."

She clasped her hands together as she stood looking down at me. "I thought you might have a few scratches, but I never expected to see you like this. What happened to your hand?"

I slid the bandaged hand underneath the light blanket that had been spread over my knees. "I don't know, Aunt Nora, but it's fine, really! Just a few stitches."

"I wish you and Jake had never found those damned cave paintings."

A man who had been sitting quietly in one corner, stood up and flashed a police badge in our direction. "What paintings?" he inquired, approaching us. "I am Officer Riley and have been assigned to the Johnson case. Are you the young woman who found him?"

I looked up at the police officer who was getting a small notebook and pen from his shirt pocket. He was of medium height with brown hair and blue eyes, nothing distinctive, except for the uniform he was wearing. I wondered just how much he already knew about the cave, the drawings and the gold veins in the walls. Prentice and Richards had most certainly given their full reports by now, and it wasn't a stretch to believe they had seen far more than they should have.

"I'm Brylee Hawkins," I told him. "I found Jake Johnson yesterday, but he is still in critical condition and I am afraid there isn't much I can tell you."

"I am very much aware of Mr. Johnson's condition, Miss Hawkins, but his testimony is vital to our finding out who did this to him."

"I have no idea what he knows about his attacker. He was in no condition to give a description when I found him."

"But you may have noticed something that might help. Was anything out of place? Any evidence of someone else having been there? Signs of a struggle perhaps?

"I had only been to the cave once," I responded, looking at Aunt Nora for help. "And had just killed a crocodile to save his horse. I'm afraid I was already in a state of shock by the time I made it to where he was."

I felt Aunt Nora's hand on my arm. "I think my niece has told you everything she knows, Officer Riley. She is the most honest person I know, but she has been through a bloody ordeal of her own. Just look at her!"

"It's all right, Aunt Nora," I said, suddenly finding a new reservoir of strength. "I want the person who shot Jake to be found and will help any way I can."

"We have a couple of leads," Officer Riley continued. "But we have to work fast. Once word leaks out that Mr. Johnson is still alive, the men responsible will be gone, if they aren't already."

"But that means whoever did this will go free!"

He looked at me with more compassion than before. "Most of the perpetrators in cases like this are never prosecuted. It has been over three days. That is plenty of time for someone to cover his tracks or completely disappear."

Aunt Nora planted her hands on her hips, her eyes flashing with anger. "But it has to be one of the same men who killed John Sutter."

"The ones we have in custody were already behind bars when Mr. Johnson was shot. That doesn't mean they weren't involved, but unfortunately, neither of them are talking."

"So, you are telling us you have nothing to go on?"

"We have the bullet that was taken out of Mr. Johnson. It is being compared to the one obtained during Mr. Sutter's autopsy, but it is highly doubtful it will be a match. My partner is doing a follow-up interview with the medics who brought you in last night, Miss Hawkins. Maybe if you tell me more about this cave Mr. Johnson found it might give us a lead."

"What has the cave got to do with anything?" Aunt Nora demanded.

I understood her reluctance to say anything that would bring more people to Hawkins' land, but I doubted that what we knew would remain a secret for long. And for all practical purposes, there was no one left to defend anything in our part of the outback. It was fair game for whomever got there first because the police had their hands full with one homicide and the man who had shot Jake.

"It's okay," I said. "Jake found a cave behind a waterfall on our property a few months ago. It is filled with the most amazing aborigine paintings. We just wanted to protect them from people who might not care if they got destroyed. The cave is through the mountain from Mr. Sutter's ranch."

"That explains a lot," he said. "If there is gold on one side of the mountain, it only stands to reason that there will be gold on the other side. Did you find any evidence of that?"

I didn't want to give him any more information, but my choices were limited if I wanted the man who had shot Jake to be caught.

"We saw flecks of what might be gold on the walls of a chamber, but it was minimal at best."

"But if someone came over the mountain after what was found on Sutter's property, it is conceivable they may have assumed that Mr. Johnson had struck it rich and was only protecting what was lawfully his."

"It wasn't like that," I told him. "All we were concerned about was the paintings. We didn't even know if it was real gold."

He raised an eyebrow as if he didn't believe me.

"Just a minute, officer," Aunt Nora said with more than irritation in her voice. "You make it sound like it was Jake's fault for getting shot. I can assure you that he was only there to protect the paintings. You can ask Ned Hawkins about it when he returns. He is scouring the outback right now trying to find the aboriginal tribe whose ancestors drew them."

"I am not questioning anyone's integrity," Officer Riley said. "I am just trying to piece together what happened. Mr. Johnson might not have been there for the gold, but other men obviously were."

"Then you need to find them," Aunt Nora said with finality.

"That's what we are trying to do, but we have very little to go on unless there is something else you can tell us, Miss Hawkins?"

"I didn't see anything," I assured him. "I wish I had."

He closed his notebook and returned it to his shirt pocket.

"In that case, I will be back later today to see if Mr. Johnson is able to answer a few questions."

"Thank you," I told Officer Riley before he left the waiting room.

"Well, I don't care what he says, Brylee," Aunt Nora stormed. "There has to be some way to prove who did this. I am just so damned mad right now. I told Ned before he left that he needed to stay here instead of taking off on a brainless errand to find some old aborigine, but men always think they know everything."

"I doubt Uncle Ned's presence would have kept Jake away from the cave. He wasn't even supposed to be there that night, but he was mad at me. We'd just had another fight."

Aunt Nora frowned. "I think you and me need to have another little chat about priorities and honesty."

I grimaced. How I hated secrets, and I had been part of a huge one in the guise of protecting the people I loved.

"There really is gold in that cave, isn't there?" she whispered as she slumped into a chair less than a foot away from me. "That's the real reason Ned went to find old Ishmael or Asum. He wanted to find out who has the legal rights to that cave and everything in it."

"No, Aunt Nora," I said. "Our only goal was to preserve the paintings. What would we do with gold? It would cost a fortune just to prove there was enough to worry about."

"No one gets shot over ancient paintings on cave walls. I wish you had never found that bloody cave."

"We couldn't predict what was going to happen," I told her. "We don't even know if the man, or men, who shot Jake found the cave. He could have been anywhere on that side of that mountain. We might be worrying for nothing."

"You really think he was shot somewhere else and was capable of dragging himself inside that cave?"

"Maybe. We won't know anything for sure until he can tell us."

"Well, I hate playing the devil's advocate, but even if your theory proves factual, once this news starts to circulate there will be hundreds of people swarming all over those mountains. None of us will be safe on our own property again."

"We have to believe the police will figure out who hurt Jake and killed Mr. Sutter. I didn't see any evidence leading me to believe that anyone had been inside the cave except Jake."

"What about the medics? They aren't stupid, and they listen to the news."

"It was dark, they were busy and we didn't go inside the chamber where flecks were found. Besides, what choice did we have? Jake would be dead if they hadn't gotten there in time."

"I can't imagine what you went through trying to find him," she said. "But if it was Ned instead of Jake trying to protect the drawings I would have done the same thing, only I have no idea where the cave is."

"Just be glad you don't," I told her. "Nothing good can come from going up there again. Even if gold is found, there is very little we can do about it."

She clasp and unclasp her hands for a few moments before speaking again. "I am sorry for being difficult, but this whole situation has me on needles. I talked to the chairman of the board of directors of Edna's Historic Society yesterday. They want to send some anthropologists from Sydney to authenticate the drawings. Once that is done, they can declare the cave a historic landmark. That would give it some protection. But if they find gold, everything will change."

I touched her weathered hand. There were tears in her eyes. Most people viewed Aunt Nora as being a little scary, but inside she was just as tender and fearful as everyone else.

"We can't do anything about the past, Aunt Nora, and I have no idea what the future will bring. All I know is that no drawings or supposed gold veins are worth what happened to Jake and Mr. Sutter. Maybe we should just blast the whole thing shut. That way, no one else would get hurt."

"I would take the dynamite up there and do it myself if I believed a single explosion would solve anything," she replied. "But that would be a bloody, stupid thing to do since, like you said, we really don't know anything yet. Besides, Ned has to come home sometime, and despite my irritation with him for going off by himself on some fool's errand, he will know what to do. I'm usually not so emotional, but with Molly and the baby it is just a little too much to digest."

"I know how you feel, but we have to be strong for each other," I replied.

"Then tell me everything you know about what really happened on that mountain, Bryee, and don't leave any of the details out. We are way past withholding information simply because we don't want to upset or bother anyone."

So, instead of returning to Jake's room as quickly as planned, I explained to her all that had happened during the past twenty-four hours—the impression I'd had that Jake was in trouble, the ride into the unknown, killing the crocodile, finding Jake alone and dying, and the sudden realization that love might not conquer all but life was certainly worth little without it. And then there was the agony of leaving him in the cave and not knowing if he would still be alive when I returned, the ride down the mountain on General, the miraculous airlift, and the surgery that had hopefully saved his life. She listened patiently without asking any questions until I had finished.

"You are a stronger woman than I am, Brylee Hawkins," she said. "Before you know it, you will be on every talk show from Sydney to Perth. *Young woman from outback kills croc while rescuing man she loves.* That's the stuff legends are made of."

"I don't want to be a legend!" I scoffed. "I would prefer it if no one else ever knew what happened. All I want is for Jake to get well."

"I know you do, love, and I am right there with you, but there might not be much you can do about the publicity once the news service gets hold of it. Stories like yours always seem to take on a life of their own."

"You are the only person I've told, Aunt Nora, and I am not leaving Jake's side until he can go home with me."

"My lips are sealed," she responded, drawing her fingers in front of them. "I just wish your parents were here to see what a remarkable young woman you have become. They would be so proud of you."

"I hope so. I certainly messed up enough while they were both alive."

"You can't blame yourself for anything that happened while you were a child. Parents are supposed to lead and direct their children, but sometimes they just don't have the necessary skills."

I looked down at the highly polished, speckled tile floor as fresh tears clouded my vision. There was so much to be grateful for, but coming to terms with past blunders wasn't easy, especially when loved ones were involved.

"I am not proud of keeping so many secrets, Aunt Nora. Jake and I should have told you and Uncle Ned about the cave weeks ago, and LeAnn is going to hate me when she finds out that I didn't call her about Jake when I first got back to Edna."

"Ned and I aren't children. We understand your reluctance in talking about the cave. As for LeAnn, she might be upset for a while, but I think she will forgive you once she knows he is going to be okay."

"But that's just it! No one knows if he is going to make it."

"God does, Brylee, and I doubt he would have brought Jake this far just to let him die during recovery. You just need to have faith."

"I do have faith, Aunt Nora," I told her with complete conviction, ashamed that I needed to be reminded of something I knew for myself. "It's just hard seeing him lie there so helpless and knowing there is nothing I can do but wait."

"But that's where you are wrong, Brylee. Jake knows how you feel about him now. Just allow that love to work its magic. There is no stronger medicine in the world."

"There you are," I heard a familiar voice say as Emma walked into the waiting room to join us. I looked up at her in confusion. It was barely seven-thirty in the morning, and Trevor didn't leave for school until well after eight.

"Now, don't get all worried on me. Trevor is with LeAnn, and she can shoo him to the bus practically as well as I can. I just told them I had an important errand to run. She doesn't watch the news until after he leaves anyway. That gives me time to return with a more accurate report before she goes ballistic."

"Then I will leave the two of you to visit," Aunt Nora said. "I want to get back to the ranch and see if the vet took care of General. I will call you later with a full report. Just don't give up on anyone, and that includes my wandering husband."

She gave me a quick peck on the cheek, touched Emma's arm and left us before I had a chance to say anything more than thanks.

"Your aunt is a remarkable woman," Emma said, rocking back on the heels of her well-worn shoes. "She will make a fine member of the church one day, but that is not why I'm here. I simply had to see how you were doing with my own eyes. Not that you don't look like you have been through a bloody combat because you do. Notwithstanding that, you are alive and so is Jake. Those are true miracles. Has he regained consciousness yet?"

"Only briefly. He thought he was either dreaming or dead because I was with him."

"That boy loves you a great deal and has for a very long time. That is why he will fight to get well."

"Do you really think so? We have so many issues to work through, and we haven't even talked about his relationship with Beth."

"We've had this discussion before, Brylee. What Jake and Beth had wasn't the real thing. She will have to accept that eventually."

"But I don't want to see her get hurt. I know what it feels like to lose the man you think you are going to spend the rest of your life with."

"And you also know that life goes on and you work through whatever you have to. What happens to Jake is in God's hands. What happens between the two of you, well, let's just say that we have our agency and can decide certain things for ourselves."

"But it seems so unfair! Why does one person's happiness always seem to come at the expense of someone else's?"

"Because life wasn't meant to be easy, and it certainly wasn't meant to be fair. If it were, we would learn very little and never have a reason to exercise greater faith."

"I do have faith," I told her, just as I had told Aunt Nora only minutes before. "Maybe I'm just tired."

"That is certainly understandable," she responded, sitting down in a chair and putting her handbag on her lap. "I am not going to ask for some lengthy recitation of things you most likely want to forget, but I needed to see for myself that you were okay before I talked to LeAnn. She will be devastated when she finds out what happened."

"I'm sorry I didn't call earlier, but everything happened so fast once we got to the hospital."

"Chastisement is not why I am here either. I know what it's like to be in the hospital. I just wish you hadn't felt it necessary to go through everything alone. You have a family who really cares about you and Jake."

"I know that," I said. "I just didn't want . . . ." my voice trailed off.

"To upset people before you knew something for sure? I get that, but it is a new day and people will have to be told. What exactly did the doctor say about Jake's condition?"

"Nothing that I haven't already told you. He is stable at the moment, but the next twenty-four hours are crucial. It could go either way."

"Then I guess all we can do is wait and pray. I talked to President Downing. He will be here as soon as he can."

"You don't think it matters that Jake claims not to believe in God?"

"The God I know and trust with all my heart never forgets any of his children, regardless how tough, self-sufficient or atheistic they believe themselves to be. A blessing is just what he needs. I even called the temple in Sydney and had your names put on the prayer role. I think we could all use a few extra prayers right now."

The way she said it caused a new set of alarms to go off in my head.

"Has something else happened?" I asked.

"Nothing for you to worry about, but I need to get back to the house. LeAnn has been having false labor pains the past couple of days and I worry about what might happen when she finds out Jake is in the hospital."

"I should be the one telling her."

"Not on your life, Brylee Hawkins! She would take one look at you and fall completely apart. No, it is best if I handle this for now. You will have plenty of time to sort through all the details once Jake is fully on the road to recovery."

"I am sorry for putting you in the middle of such a mess."

She rose to her feet and placed a kiss on my forehead. "I am exactly where I want to be. Now, get back to Jake's room and try to get some rest. You need to be well so you can be there for him. I will make sure Trevor and LeAnn are taken care of."

She took a missionary copy of the *Book of Mormon* out of her purse and handed it to me. "I thought you might like having this with you to read. There will be some long hours to get through over the next few days. I just wish I could be here with you, but Trevor and LeAnn need me more than you do right now. Is there anything else I can bring you?"

"No. Aunt Nora said she would bring what I need from the house when she goes to check on Copper and the other animals. I'm afraid I have been somewhat remiss in taking care of that little dog lately."

"Some things can't be helped. I will talk to Nora about bringing Copper into town to stay with us until both you and Jake are out of the hospital. I will also answer as many calls as I can from the house. I know people from church will want to help out, and I am afraid Beth will be on her way here the minute she figures out it was Jake on that mountain."

I wriggled my mouth. Beth had every bit as much right to be with Jake as I did considering their relationship, but that was something I didn't want. Our time alone on the mountain had forged a bond I hoped no one would ever try to break.

"Don't look so worried," Emma said. "I can handle Beth, and I will do it in a very kind way. Besides, they won't let her see him as long as he is in the ICU. That should buy both of you a little time to make some very important decisions. Things can change quite rapidly once the adrenalin quits pumping."

I knew she was right. We were all in a heightened emotional state, but I doubted my feelings for Jake would change once his full recovery began. They had come on very slowly, and there was nothing I would not do to protect or take care of him. If that wasn't the beginning of true love, then I didn't know what was.

The nurse who had wheeled me to the waiting room retuned not long after Emma left.

"I hope your visit went well," she said. "But I think it is time for you to get some rest."

"It went longer than anticipated," I replied, wondering how many times she had checked to see if I was still occupied. "Is Jake doing okay?"

"Nothing has changed with him, but there are a bunch of reporters in the lobby downstairs who want to talk to you. You have become quite a celebrity."

I hated the way the people used the term, implying that a person had done something of worth to be recognized. I had only been following my heart.

"Jake getting well is all I want," I replied.

"Then let's make it happen," she responded as she pushed me towards double doors that swung inward. "Reporters don't like to give up, but as long as you stay in the ICU, they can't get to you. I just hope your family can avoid them. This is the biggest story Edna has seen for more than a decade."

Chapter 17

I understood that no one could assure me Jake would make it. His life was in God's hands now but I still felt totally helpless just watching him sleep, especially when my own IV was removed around ten. With nothing to do but wait, it was a pleasant relief when President Downing and Brother Smyth arrived later that morning to give both of us blessings. People in hospitals were used to priests and last rites and were more than open to other religious figures that might bring added comfort to their patients.

"You have had quite an adventure the past couple of days," President Downing said after he had shaken my hand. "How are you doing, aside from the obvious?"

"I can't complain. Jake made it through surgery, and his doctor is hopeful he will have a full recover."

"That is good news. I have to tell you that Emma's call this morning was quite a surprise. I have been watching the news, naturally, but had no idea you were the young woman responsible for such an amazing rescue."

"It's something I really hope to forget one day," I responded as visions of Jake's lifeless body in the suffocating darkness of the cave came flooding back.

"I can appreciate that," he said, unaware of how truly traumatic the past few days had been. "Do the police have any leads?"

"Not really, and I wasn't much help. All I could think about was getting Jake off that mountain."

"Maybe he can give them some useful information once he is fully awake. I want you to know that everyone in the branch is praying for both of you, and the Relief Society will see that meals are taken to Emma's for the next few days. There will also be someone available to sit with LeAnn and take care of Trevor if Emma is needed here."

"Thank you," I told him as tears flooded my eyes yet again. I had never been the recipient of so much love and kindness, and it was hard to take everything in.

I watched as Brother Smyth poured consecrated oil on Jake's head and sealed the anointing. Then I listened intently as President Downing gave him a most beautiful blessing. He identified him as being one of God's most choice sons and promised him a full recovery in due time.

My own blessing was slightly different. I too, was promised a complete recovery, but I was also assured that I would feel peace of mind during the coming days. And if I continued faithful and prayerful, I would know what God expected of me and would have the courage to make the right decisions when they arose because things were not always as they seemed.

They left soon after that since it was the middle of a work day, and then the long hours of waiting began. Jake's eyes had not opened again, but I had heard somewhere that the subconscious knew what was going on, even if there was no outward indication. So, I read to him from the book that had transformed my life beginning with the opening sentence. "I, Nephi, having been born of goodly parents . . . ."

Doctor Hilde came back later in the day as promised and was very pleased with my progress, and the nurses who checked on Jake every hour always asked if I needed anything. They were very aware of my reluctance to be cornered by reporters until I was ready to let the public know my side of the story.

I was enormously grateful for the kindness of everyone at the hospital, but it was the outpouring of love from my branch family that kept tears of gratitude flowing. Not only had the Branch President and Brother Smyth taken time to give us blessings, but Sister Miller, the Relief Society president I had just been called to serve with, sent a potted plant with a card expressing her love, concern and willingness to perform any necessary task whether it was in Edna or back at the ranch.

But I was most surprised when I got a call from the desk in the ICU saying I had a visitor and it wasn't a reporter, so I could come to the waiting room if I felt so inclined. I hated leaving Jake alone but when she told me who was there, I didn't hesitate.

Margaret Mitchell, whom I had met the first time I attended church in Edna, was waiting for me with a milkshake in one hand and a book by Dallin Oaks in the other.

"I won't stay long," she said, and I noticed there were tears in her eyes as she handed me what she had brought. "I just had to let you to know that you are loved, and there are a lot of people praying for both of you. Did you know that everyone is talking about what a brave woman you are?"

My eyes sought the floor as I frowned. Why couldn't other people understand that bravery had nothing to do with it? Neither did skill or luck. Heavenly Father had been directing me, or I never would have found Jake at all.

"I wasn't brave!" I said after taking a deep breath. "I was scared to death and still am."

"Oh, dear," she said with a heavy sigh that let me know her concern was real. "It was thoughtless of me to bring up all the talk around town when you must be frantic with worry about Jake. LeAnn told me he was her brother. I have been to see her at Emma's a couple of times. She is so enthusiastic about the gospel and the new baby."

"LeAnn has certainly taught me about patience since finding out she was pregnant, and it was very kind of you to visit her. Despite some rather harsh setbacks since my return we have been abundantly blessed."

"Even if Jake is far from being well?"

My smile was more pensive than one might expect. "President Downing's blessing promised him a full recovery. I just don't know when that might be."

"And what about you?" she asked, trying very hard not to stare at my bruised, sunburned and scratched face or bandaged hand. "You have been through a terrible ordeal. The rumors about what happened on that mountain are certainly flying, but then you know how small towns are. If there isn't something sensational to talk about people get bored and start inventing stories to pass the time. How did you ever manage if even a portion of what I have heard is true?"

"Divine intervention and a remarkable horse."

"Now you have peaked my curiosity, but you don't have to talk about it unless you need someone to listen."

"I'm still trying to put the pieces together," I told her, feeling oddly comfortable being with someone I knew I could trust who had no direct involvement with our latest family drama. "But somewhere during the day I killed a crocodile and rode a horse bareback down a mountain."

"Oh, my," she replied. "You really are a heroine. I never could have done that."

"Quite honestly, I'm not sure how I did it either."

"You must really care about Jake to risk your own life like that."

"I do care, more than ever imagined, but I would have done the same thing for anyone in trouble."

I quit talking and took a sip of the chocolate milkshake. It helped quiet the burning in my throat but did little to relieve my still troubled heart. So much had changed during the past few days. Until I saw Jake lying in that cave and barely breathing, I had never truly acknowledged the depth of my feelings for him. I would walk through burning coals and not give a single thought to my own well-being if it meant getting him to safety again.

Margaret reached out and touched my arm. "I am sensing that you more than just care about him. Do I detect a little love there?"

"More than a little," I admitted. Come what might, I had to give Jake a chance and allow him time to discover for himself whether or not he could accept the truth as I had done. If that happened life could be wonderful, but if it didn't I would have to learn how to live without him again. "Only I have been too scared and confused to admit it. Nearly losing him made me realize just what an amazing man he really is."

"I hate it when that happens," she said with a smile. "I tried so bloody hard not to fall in love with my husband. He was riding with a biker gang who spent their weekends in the outback drinking, smoking, cussing and doing who knows what else. They would come into the diner every Friday night and Sunday evening."

"Emma's diner?"

"Naturally! I think nearly every girl in Edna has worked for her at one time or another."

"I wish I had known her when I was young," I replied. "She has come to our rescue in so many ways. Not only does she have both LeAnn and Trevor living with her, but she has become a real grandmother to me."

"That doesn't surprise me. Emma may not have had children of her own, but she treats everyone she meets like family."

"You sound like you have been there."

"Oh, I have! She has more wisdom than anyone else I know and is not afraid to share it if one is willing to listen."

"Did she help you solve your problems?" It was an impertinent thing to ask since I didn't know Margaret that well, but somehow I felt she would understand.

"That she did, by listening and making comments I would not have tolerated coming from anyone else. She never told me what to do or said '*I told you so*', but she made me look inside for the answers I needed."

"What about your own family? I know you grew up in the church and were close to them."

"I still am, but it wasn't easy being the only daughter of the first branch president in Edna. Everyone expected me to be perfect, and what did I do? I got involved with a biker who had never set foot inside a church his entire life."

"But it turned out okay!"

"Not without a lot of heartache for everyone involved. My family moved north right after I graduated high school. I had already met Errol and was afraid I would never see him again if left town, so I convinced them to let me stay here and work for Emma. She let me live in this little one-room apartment above the diner."

"And she knew how you felt about Errol?"

"She knew I would find a way to stay here with or without guidance, so she basically volunteered to look out for me."

My interest in her story was increasing since it had so many similarities to mine. "But weren't you afraid of losing your eternal blessings by getting involved with a man who didn't believe as you did?"

"I was terrified of losing everything I held dear. I knew I could never marry someone who wasn't committed to Christ, but I couldn't forget about him either. We had this most amazing connection from the day we met. I felt like I had known him forever and could see into his heart—even if he claimed he wasn't sure he had one—and soon found that it was made of pure gold."

"Wow!" I said, realizing that was the same conclusion I had come to about Jake. He was a little rough around the edges, but his heart was solid and good. "How did you get past all the fear so you could give him a chance?"

"Every time I got scared, I reminded myself that our lives were in the Lord's hands, but it was the longest three years of my life. I was miserable when we were apart and afraid I might fall from grace when we were together. The odds were so against us. For every girl who took the same chance I did, a dozen had major regrets. It is very easy for a man to change on the surface, but once he gets what he wants, old behaviors come flying back."

"But you and Errol seem amazingly happy together."

"That's because I made him work harder for me than for anything else in his life. We made it because I knew Satan was tempting me to give in before the time was right. If I had done that, there would have been nothing left to salvage. He needed to learn that it was my beliefs that made me the person I was. Only then was he ready to investigate the church for himself."

"I'm glad he decided to join."

"Me too, but it didn't happen without a whole lot of tears and pleading with God on my part. Errol was determined to live his life on his own terms. That meant doing what he wanted when he felt like it. He didn't want to be controlled by anything. And let's face it, what we believe isn't exactly endorsed by a world that equates sin with pleasure and good times. I wasn't sure he would ever give up being part of the world."

"What changed his mind?" I asked without thinking.

Her smile was heartfelt and sincere. "I suppose he finally figured out that he wanted more than wild weekends with his mates. I had moved home with my parents for a few months to see if I could get over him. When Emma told him I was gone and wouldn't be coming back, he went off the deep end—carousing around with every woman he could find."

"That must have hurt you deeply," I responded, thinking back to my own experience with Beth and Jake. Betrayal was one of the worst feelings ever, and mine was far from being over.

"I have never been in more pain. I must have looked at my cell a thousand times a day wanting to call him and hoping he would call me. Emma let me know that he was still alive, but that was about it."

I almost hated to ask the next question but couldn't seem to stop myself. "How long were you separated?"

"Almost six months! I knew I couldn't see him again until I was strong enough to find him with someone else and not fall apart myself. I was working as a bank teller when he came into my life again and apologized for being a bloody fool who had let the best thing in his life slip right through his fingers."

"But how did you know you could ever trust him again?"

"At first, I wasn't sure I could, but we promised to take things incredibly slow and see if what had been lost could be regained. He cut his hair, quit riding with his gang and began attending church with me. The most important things in life cannot be rushed, and I had to decide if I had what it took to wait on God's timing and accept what he knew was right me. I am just grateful it didn't mean another breakup because I can't imagine my life without Errol in it."

I wanted what she had found more than ever, I decided as I sat vigil at Jake's bedside watching the numbers flash on the monitors and making sure that the steady movement of his chest as oxygen filled his lungs never stopped.

Before the sun left the sky and the moon came out, Aunt Nora called to say that everything was okay at both homesteads, and that the vet had been out to treat General. He would be good as new in a few weeks and she would keep her eyes on him until I was able to do it myself. She had fed and watered the animals on our part of the ranch and had taken

Copper home with her. She would make the drive back to Edna the next morning with the things I needed.

Emma dropped off get well soon cards Trevor had made for us, and President Downing stopped by again before visiting hours were over just to see how we were both doing.

The hardest part of the day was answering a call from LeAnn. She broke into tears the moment she heard my voice.

"You have to tell me everything, Brylee, or I am coming straight to the hospital. I don't care what anyone says. If Jackie decides to come early, then she will just have to do it."

I took a deep breath to calm my nerves and decide exactly how to explain what had happened without giving her more cause for alarm. LeAnn was in no condition to hear the particulars, even though she wanted to. I brushed Jake's arm with the back of my injured hand before moving away from the bed.

"There is no reason for you to come. Jake is still sleeping." I couldn't tell her that his doctor had induced a coma-like state to promote healing and no one was sure how long it would take for him to wake up. "And I promise I won't leave his side."

"I should be so angry with you for not calling me last night, but I know you were just trying to protect me and Jackie. However, I expect a few honest answers now. What in the world was Jake doing on that mountain? Nora said he had discovered some cave with a lot of ancient drawings in it but that is no reason for him to get shot, especially by men who were looking for gold."

I wished I could tell her the entire truth, but Uncle Ned and Jake needed to weigh in on what we shared with anyone else, and neither of them was available right now.

"Exactly what did Aunt Nora tell you?" I asked.

"Not nearly as much as I have the right to know since the ranch is part of Trevor's legacy too. I get it that the cave is on the other side of the mountain from Sutter's ranch, and that

Jake was there looking after the drawings, but why would someone shoot him over that?"

"I wish I could give you an answer that makes sense," I replied, biting my lip because I hated so much to be lying again. "The police are conducting a thorough investigation. I talked with them earlier myself, but there wasn't much I could add to what they already know. They promised to keep us in the loop."

"That doesn't make me feel any better, but I will trust you for now because I know you love Jake, despite the way he acts most of the time. Besides, I am not exactly in a position to be pushing my weight around."

"Emma said you were having false labor."

"Just a few twinges now and then. I refuse to let Jackie arrive before her due date."

"Smart girl," I replied, glad that we had found another topic of conversation.

"I don't feel very smart right now, but I do understand my limitations. Just promise me that you will never give up on any of us. I know you have been through a lot since coming home but once this is over, maybe things will fall into place for a while."

I sighed with my own longings. "I hope so, but for right now, let's make a deal. You take care of my little sister, and I will take care of your little brother."

"Done!" she responded, before I even had time to cross my fingers. "Has there been any change? I know Emma hasn't told me everything because she is worried about both the baby and me."

"There is nothing new to report. He hasn't opened his eyes since early this morning."

"But he will open them again, won't he?"

I hesitated only slightly before telling her about the blessing Jake had received earlier in the day. Since she had decided to investigate the church it might give her some of the hope she so desperately needed.

"A few weeks ago that would not have made a difference," she said. "But after reading the book Emma gave me, I know there is a reason for everything that happens in life."

"You have no idea how relieved I am to hear that because beliefs are such a personal thing, but I have been reading the *Book of Mormon* to Jake today. I think at some level he knows I am here and understands what he is hearing."

"I'm sure of it, Brylee," she replied. "I have learned so much lately about the reason for having to endure even the most horrific trials. I would give anything this world has to offer to have Jack back, but knowing I will see him again and we can be a forever family makes the separation easier."

We talked for a few minutes longer before I heard Trevor say my name. He was on the extension in the kitchen, and he sounded both confused and sad, regardless of the fact that he was trying to be brave.

"I am sorry you got hurt, Brylee, and I am sorry about Uncle Jake, but when are you coming to see me? You promised not to leave me again."

"I didn't exactly leave you, and I hope you can understand that I need to stay with your uncle until he gets better since there is no one else who can do it because he is in a very private place. I will call you everyday and see you as soon as I can. I love the cards you sent."

"Emma said they wouldn't let me see anyone because I am too young. That's why I made them, but it's still not fair."

"Nothing about this is fair, Trevor, but I think it helps us understand just how much we love each other and how precious life is."

"Does your hand hurt bad? Emma said you got stitches."

"My hand is fine, but I need to ask you something really important. Can you keep an eye on your mother and baby

Jackie for me? We don't want our little sister coming any sooner than she should."

"I guess so," he relented. "But I still want to come to the hospital to see you and Uncle Jake."

"And we will make sure that happens, but it might be a few days."

I was considering my own appearance, in addition to Jake's condition. Hearing that I had been hurt was one thing. Seeing the extent of my injuries was something else, especially for a confused little boy. It was better if we could keep him occupied with other things until Jake regained consciousness and I looked somewhat more human.

"But I want to talk to Uncle Jake now?" Trevor lamented.

I could hear the tremor of fear in his voice again, and it made me sad because there was nothing I could do to erase it.

"He's sleeping right now. That is the best way for him to get better. But I need you to listen very carefully to what I say. If anyone asks you what happened, all you have to tell them is that you don't know anything. Do you understand?"

I was suddenly very afraid for him. If the media or police started to question him, he wouldn't know what to say and might reveal something he shouldn't?

"I don't want to talk to anybody," he retorted. "I just want to go home."

"We all do," I told him. "But we have to be brave for a few days longer. You might hear a lot of conflicting stories when you go back to school tomorrow, but don't let them worry you. Just concentrate on your mother and Jackie and let me worry about everything else. Can you do that?"

In my mind's eye, I could see the lines between his eyes deepen like they always did when he was thinking really hard.

"Did you really find Uncle Jake in that cave and get rescued by a helicopter?"

His unexpected question made me smile, even though the muscles in my face still throbbed.

"I did! And do you know what the most amazing thing was? I rode General bareback all the way down the mountain without falling off."

"Weren't you scared?"

"I was a lot scared, but General knew just what to do. I think he deserves a few extra apples and carrots, don't you?"

"A whole truckload of them," he said before becoming very quiet again. "Will you come and see me tomorrow, Brylee?"

I wished I could tell him yes but my leaving the hospital wasn't a good idea as long as reporters were still looking for a story. Even I might say something I shouldn't, and I didn't want my face plastered all over the news. My story was private and it belonged to only Jake and me.

"I will tell you what, Trevor. If I can't come to you, maybe Emma can bring you to the hospital to see me. We can visit in the waiting room."

"Promise?" he asked.

"I promise," I replied.

He seemed content with that, and I hung up my end of the conversation without talking to Emma. I hadn't slept well for several days now and could feel my body beginning to crash, just as my emotional state had done earlier in the day.

I slept on and off in the recliner by Jake's hospital bed in the semi-light coming into the room through the cracks around the doorframe and window, but every strange sound caused me to jump. Even the almost imperceptible beeping of the pumps that kept him alive awaked me—a persistent reminder that time was passing and nothing about his condition had changed.

A nurse came in to check his vitals every couple of hours. She was always pleasant and had a word of good will, but she could never tell me what I most wanted to hear. That Jake would soon wake up with his mind clear and his body healing the way it should. I prayed continually that he would open his eyes and give me one of his wonderful, heartwarming smiles, but he didn't. His promise of a full recovery was certainly going to test my convictions because all I could think about was what I would do if he didn't make it.

Still, despite my misgivings and fears, I tried to remain optimistic as the hours dragged slowly onward. It was what God expected of me, and every time a negative thought surfaced, I took Jake's hand and held it while reading to him from the scriptures about the trials Nephi and his family had to endure in building a boat so they could travel to the Promised Land and all the challenges that came after.

Oh, how I wanted my own promised land with Jake. He was a good man and I knew God loved him, but if he had only said what he did about wanting to change because he thought he was dying, we would never get a happy ending like Margaret and Errol Mitchell.

Doctor Hilde, who had treated me in the emergency room, came into Jake's room with the surgeon early the next morning during rounds. I was surprised to see him since my second IV had been taken out the day before, and I had never been admitted.

"Jake Johnson is one lucky man," he said to me as the surgeon looked at the incision he had made two nights before and checked vitals. "You haven't left his room, have you?"

I was suddenly aware of my less than attractive appearance—all the scratches and bruises on my face and arms —along with the fact that I had showered but had not fixed my hair or applied any makeup. I was still wearing the scrubs Nurse Gravel had given me, and Dr. Hilde was an attractive man who was not wearing a wedding ring.

"I must look pretty awful, but my place is here," I told him, trying to hide the hand that he had so carefully stitched together. "Someone familiar needs be here when Jake opens his eyes, and I am all he has right now since his sister can't get out of bed."

I didn't mention Beth. They might have been seeing each other, but he needed me. He had said that much on the mountain and again when he opened his eyes. I had to believe I was where he wanted me to be.

"You are a compassionate and understanding woman," he said. "In addition to being both beautiful and brave. I would ask you out for a drink and dinner if I didn't know that your heart was already taken."

"Thank you," I said. "And I just might say yes, to dinner anyway, if circumstances were different."

His smile made him even more attractive. "Understood. Just be careful not to get your hand wet until I take the stitches out next week?"

"Perfectly careful," I replied. "One of the nurses brought me a bread bag and a few rubber bands so I could shower. It looks rather strange but it works."

He patted my arm. "Bloody good, but don't hesitate to call if you need anything, and I expect to see you in my office early next week so we can see how that hand is doing. I know there will be a scar, but I am pretty good with a needle. How's the pain? I could add a refill to the prescription . . . ."

"No need for that," I interjected, suddenly realizing that I hadn't needed so much as an aspirin since receiving my blessing.

Doctor Turret was moving away from the bed, so I excused myself and turned my attention to him.

"How is he doing?" I asked, hoping he had something positive to say.

"His condition is still stable, and his fever is going down. That means the antibiotics are working. We have been keeping him heavily sedated so his body can heal faster, but if . . . ." He stopped as if trying to decide what to say next. "Well, let's just see what the next few hours bring. I will stop by a little later today, but you can always have someone reach me if needed."

He replaced the clipboard on the end of the bed and walked out of the room. He didn't have much of a bedside manner, but then he was a surgeon and probably didn't did need one.

Aunt Nora came around noon. I went out to the waiting room to meet her, grateful that both Jake and me were protected from desperate reporters. She brought several changes of clothing and my makeup bag so I could return the scrubs and put on a little mascara if I felt the desire to. She also brought a metal box from the bunkhouse. LeAnn had told her it was where Jake kept all of his important papers.

"I felt just awful invading his personal space," she said. "But LeAnn said you might need his medical records."

"I'm sure they will be helpful," I said, crossing the waiting room floor to give her a hug. I had eaten the food meant for Jake and was fairly certain Dr. Hilde had arranged it so I wouldn't have to find something on my own. Just the few calories available were reversing the effects of dehydration and heart exhaustion and I was feeling decidedly stronger.

She hugged me back. "I have been so worried about the two of you. I hope you don't mind that I called the kids. I felt they had a right to know."

"We're family," I told her. "We have to be there for each other. How is Molly doing?"

"She says she is getting fatter everyday, but Evan is a gem. He waits on her hand and foot. I just hope she doesn't wear him out before the baby comes. I can hardly believe I will be a grandmother in a few months."

"And you will be a wonderful one. I don't suppose you have heard from Uncle Ned?"

"I could just strangle that man for picking such an awful time to disappear."

She walked over to the window and looked down at the cars in the parking lot. I followed her. It was impossible to tell just how hot it was outside through the tinted windows, but the hospital had air-conditioning, and it felt good after my day on the mountain in the heat.

"How is Jake doing?" she asked, turning her head towards me. "And don't leave anything out. I need to know where this mixed-up family stands."

"The doctor says he is sable and the antibiotics are working, but it is still just a waiting game."

She made a scoffing sound. "I think it's more of a ploy to keep family members pacified so they won't contemplate suing."

"I'm sure they are doing everything they can, Aunt Nora. Real healing is in God's hands."

"Don't I know that!" She made the sign of the cross. "And his hands are large enough to hold everyone. Damn!" she suddenly swore. "The news truck just pulled up. Reporters called the house three times this morning. I will give them credit for determination, but they need to learn when to give up. I'm just glad Emma said they haven't been bothering her too much. I guess they think she doesn't know anything."

"That's a good thing, but do you have any idea what we should do?" I asked.

"Nothing! Unless you are ready to talk to them."

I intuitively backed away from the window when I saw a man holding a microphone climb out and look up. "My story is my own. I just want to be left alone."

"So they haven't gotten to you yet?"

"The nurses at the desk have been screening both my calls and my visitors. I only leave Jake's room when I know it is safe."

"Then go back and be with him. I will deal with them."

"Are you sure?" I asked as she moved in the direction of the door leading into the outside hallway.

"Quite sure! Like it or not, I have dealt with them before. They just want a story. I will tell them that you are both resting comfortably and I will let them know when you are ready to talk. Maybe I will throw in a little about General and his recovery, if that's okay with you. If there is anything reporters like more than suffering humans it is heroic animals. That angle should hold them for a few hours."

I wasn't sure that drawing attention to any of the details surrounding what had happened was wise, but her interview became the lead story on the five-o'clock news as she shared her beliefs that innocent people, who had been the victims of violent crimes, should be allowed privacy while the authorities looked for the perpetrators. In her own commanding way, she had given us the reprieve from the media we needed. Whatever rumors were flying around town would just have to be tolerated and then dealt with when the time was right.

"My goodness," Emma said around seven that night when she brought Trevor to the hospital to see me. He was clinging to her hand when they entered the ICU waiting room. "I have always respected Nora, but I never knew she was such a force to be reckoned with. Ned Hawkins certainly got a jewel when he found her."

"So you saw the television report," I said as I hurried over to them and pulled my little brother into my arms. The visit would be brief out of necessity, and I wanted to make the most of it.

"Saw it," she said. "I have half a mind to call the station and demand they replay it at ten. The world needs to see that victims have rights. They should be no more at the mercy of the press than they were at the hands of the evil men who harmed them. But you do know that they aren't going to give up? People like happy endings, but they like drama and violence even more."

"They will have to wait a very long time to get anything from me," I told her. "Much of what happened on that mountain was personal."

I escorted Trevor to the sofa where no one would see him if they walked down the hall. I just hoped anyone who joined us would be too wrapped up in their own struggles to pay any attention to ours.

Once we were both seated, he looked up at me and frowned. "You said you weren't hurt bad, but your face is all buggered up."

I smiled at his use of adjectives, wondering if he even knew what modifiers were. "I know it's not a pretty sight, but I am doing a whole lot better now that you are here. How was school today?"

"Boring! But it got a whole lot better when I got home. Did you know Aunt Nora brought Copper to stay with us until you and Uncle Jake are ready to go home."

"That sounds like a fine idea to me."

I looked over his head at Emma who was smiling. With everything she had already taken on, she didn't need a frisky puppy underfoot.

"But you have to promise that you will take care of Copper yourself. She needs to be fed and watered every day and taken for a walk when you get home from school."

"I promise, Brylee," he said. "Emma won't even know Copper is there. Aunt Nora bought a new leash so she can't get away when I take her outside but it's kinda girly. It has fake diamonds on it."

I had to fight back the laughter. School really had done wonders for Trevor. He was beginning to act and talk like every other boy his age, but his mention of fake diamonds set my raw nerves on edge.

Emma gave Trevor a dollar so he could get something from the vending machine across the hall from where we were sitting so we would have a moment of privacy.

"Just to be on the safe side, we won't stay long," she began. "But I need to know how Jake is really doing. LeAnn is a basket case. She cried all morning, saying she was totally useless. I understand her frustration, but I don't know how to help her, poor girl."

"I'm afraid I don't either since there has been no change in Jake's condition. The doctor is keeping him heavily sedated, but I have to believe he will wake up soon. Have you asked her if she would like a blessing of comfort? That is the only way I have made it through the past—I don't even know how many hours."

"We talked about it last night, but she said she wasn't the one who needed God's blessings."

"You and I both know that isn't true. She and Jackie won't be out of the woods until after a safe delivery."

"I'm afraid the complications surrounding her own condition have been moved to the back burner as the old saying goes, but I don't want you to worry about anything because I have it covered."

"Come on, Emma," I said. "What else is bothering you?"

She gave me a funny look. "I wish I didn't have to burden you with anything more, but Beth has been calling the house non-stop all day because she can't get through to Jake at the hospital. She is horribly upset because she isn't allowed to see him."

"That's understandable considering their relationship," I replied as a heavy feeling of nausea returned to the pit of my stomach.

"But it gets worse, Brylee. She has already been here once and has threatened the nurse on duty saying that she will go to the administration if she isn't allowed to see him by morning."

"No one will approve that request. She's not family."

"Her relationship to Jake might not matter. Her parents are wealthy and influential people who have done a lot for the community."

"You're talking about bribery!"

"Call it what you like, people with money get results. I'm not saying it is going to happen. I am just giving you a head's up."

"So she knows I'm here?"

"Everyone in town does. The media has a habit of blabbing everything they know and half of what they don't. I haven't said anything to her, except what little I know about Jake's condition, but I am surprised her calls haven't been transferred to his room."

"Maybe the person taking them decided it was unnecessary since he couldn't talk," I replied.

"Perhaps, but you need to be prepared. Things could get ugly. She really loves him and believes he loves her back."

"Why did it have to turn out this way?" I asked, wishing Beth would voluntarily disappear. "I never wanted to get involved in their relationship."

"I'm afraid that ship sailed long ago, but this is between the two of them. If Jake led her to believe something that wasn't true, then he needs to be the one to fix it. Until he is able to do that, you have to stay out of it. Just be pleasant if you have any contact with her, but for heaven's sake don't let her intimidate you into thinking you have done anything wrong because you haven't."

"But she loves him and has had far more intimate contact with him than I have."

"That depends on how you define intimate. The kind of sharing that leads to permanence doesn't always happen in the bedroom. Beth is somewhat spoiled but she is basically a good person who has loved Jake since she was in high school. But like I told you before, he has never been interested in her that way."

"He's been sleeping with her, Emma!" I exclaimed a little too loudly.

"I can't condone what he has done, but I do understand it. Maybe his brush with death has given him a clearer perspective when it comes to the really important things in life."

I hoped she was right. What little he had said to me in the cave certainly indicated soul-searching, but deathbed repentance didn't mean much unless it could be followed by action. I wouldn't know how he really felt until he was fully conscious, and there was no guarantee that would ever happen.

Jake was still sleeping when I returned to his room, but I told him about my visits with Aunt Nora, Emma and Trevor in rather subdued tones anyway. I didn't care if people thought I was crazy because I knew he heard my voice. I didn't confide my concerns about Beth, or his not so chivalrous behavior towards her. He was only doing what all men who had not committed themselves to Christ did, enjoying the advances of an attractive female.

Officer Riley, who had questioned me the previous day, had not returned to the hospital. It was an open investigation and time was crucial, but then he already knew I could not tell him anything helpful. I desperately wanted the men who had hurt Jake to be caught, but the relative quiet of the evening gave me a chance to tell the man I loved exactly what was in my heart.

The box Aunt Nora had brought sat on the nightstand by his bed unopened. It took all my willpower not to lift the lid, but I couldn't invade Jake's private life unless I was invited, or unless more vital information about his personal life was needed.

His condition remained the same for the next two days. I only left his room when family came to talk, and then I was very careful to make sure that neither reporters nor Beth were waiting in the hallway where they might try to get inside the ICU waiting room.

Jake's waitress, as I still referred to Beth when I was by myself, sent two huge bouquets of flowers with notes attached. I would have preferred having the flowers given to other patients and the notes tossed in the trash, but that wasn't my call to make. Jake needed to straighten out their affair before we could even think about moving forward with a relationship of our own.

Thankfully, she had not followed through with her threat about seeing him, but it was still difficult to keep my thoughts from dwelling on what could happen when his care was no longer under such strict supervision.

I developed a profound respect for Aunt Nora and Emma during the time I spent waiting for Jake to wake up. Their ability to protect all of us was nothing short of miraculous. Emma took calls from nearly everyone in town and was able to satisfy their curiosity without giving anything of importance away. While she was doing that, Aunt Nora took care of the work on both ranches and came into town every other day so she could check on us in person. Uncle Ned had not returned and we were all concerned about him.

We needed a sign of hope desperately, but all we could do was pray.

Chapter 18

Early Sunday morning, about four, Jake's eyes started to flutter, and he groaned. I jumped from the chair that had never been more than a few feet from his bed.

"Hey, you," I said, brushing back the hair from his forehead while my heart beat so rapidly I thought I might faint. "I thought you would never wake up."

I blinked back tears of joy as his eyes began to slowly, but steadily, focus on mine. He tried to reach up and touch my arm, but his hand dropped instantly back to the bed. I leaned over and took it in mine.

"I'm weak as hell," he whispered. "How long have I been out?"

"Four days," I responded.

"And you have been with me the whole time."

"Where else would I be?" My voice cracked with emotion as I realized that my long, lonely vigil might actually be over. Jake was awake, his mind was clear, and he was talking to me. "I had to make sure they were taking good care of you."

"You have never been a very good liar. They would have taken care of me anyway. What made you stay?"

The directness of his question surprise me since I thought he would be groggier, and I wasn't sure how to respond. What if he didn't remember telling me that he loved me?

"You know why!" I said as my chin started to quiver. "No one should have to go through what you have alone."

"I hope that's not the only reason."

He looked openly honest and completely vulnerable, and I knew I was seeing a side of him that was   rarely revealed.

"So you remember what happened in the cave?"

"Bits and pieces mostly," he replied. "But how could I ever forget this most remarkable woman rescuing me. I want to hear all about that, but not before you tell me if you really meant what you said about loving me. Or were you just saying it because you thought I would be dead before you got back?"

I bent over and kissed his lips. I had kept them soft with Vaseline, and they were healing just like mine.

"Does that answer your question?" I asked.

"Only partially! I want to hear the words again. That was the only thing that kept me   going after you went for help. I knew I couldn't die before I found out if you really had been there, or if it was just a dying man's apparition."

The time for playing games and hiding true feelings was over. God had sent Jake back to me, and I had to give him—and us—a chance.

Nonetheless, it was difficult to speak through a sudden rush of emotional longing, but I did it anyway—tears, sputtering and all. "You are the most infuriating man I have ever known, Jake Johnson, but God help me, I do love you."

"And I love you. Now, give me another kiss before I close my eyes again. I can't tell you how sleepy I am."

I did as instructed and he was asleep before I stood upright. I could hardly wait to tell everyone what had just happened. Not the part about love because that was still very new and tender, but that he had awakened and completely lucid.

By mid-morning, Jake was asking for something to eat.

"I could get used to seeing your face every time I open my eyes," he said. "You truly are the most phenomenal woman alive. I still can't believe you made it back to the cave. I had made my peace with never seeing anyone I loved again."

"But that wasn't what God had in mind for you," I told him, standing by the side of his bed and looking into his deep, dark eyes.

"Are you sure it wasn't just good karma?" he chided.

I brought his hand to my lips before replying. "Absolutely positive! Nothing about that day was anything short of miraculous. I even shot a crocodile as it was about to attack General and then rode him down the mountain to get help. I truly believed I had known pain and regret before, but nothing remotely comparable to that moment when I saw you in that cave. I thought I had lost you forever. Your saddle and everything else is still on the mountain. I will go back and get everything as soon as you are better."

He had been trying to push himself up in bed but sank back after my brief recitation of what I most remembered about that horrific Tuesday. I hoped I hadn't pushed him into a setback, but he just grasp my hand more tightly and started to laugh. Granted, it wasn't the kind of laugher I was used to hearing from him, but he was definitely finding humor in my almost unbelievable tale.

"I'm not sure which I find more difficult to believe. You riding General without a saddle or you killing an unfortunate crocodile."

I pulled my bottom lip into my mouth. "He wasn't a poor crocodile! He was trying to hurt General, and I had to do something."

"So my little city girl has become a genuine outback Aussie."

He looked at me with such tenderness I started to cry. How could I tell him that General had lost a huge chunk of his leg, and I had ridden him down the mountain anyway?

"Come here," Jake said, wrapping his fingers around my wrist. "I'm sure my breath smells awful, but I could definitely use another kiss."

I dried my eyes, leaned over and did as instructed, not once but twice. I would have added a third kiss just to make sure I wasn't the one dreaming, but we had some crucial things to discuss. Now that he was awake, there would be more than just the media to deal with.

"Do you feel up to talking about what happened?" I asked when our lips parted. "The police have been here asking questions I couldn't answer."

He shook his head and let in sink backwards into the folds of his pillow. "I don't remember a whole lot, except that I was walking around outside the cave when I heard a noise. I looked up and saw two men with rifles pointed right at me. I told them they were on private property and needed to leave, but all I got for my trouble was a bullet in the gut. I wasn't close enough to get a good look at either of them, but one man had a limp, and they weren't from around here."

"You're sure about that? The police haven't had any solid leads, and the men they suspected of killing Mr. Sutter were in jail."

"That doesn't mean they weren't part of the same group of gold hustlers. They were determined to push past me, but I got off several shots before collapsing. I'm pretty sure I hit one of them."

"But that's important, Jake. The police could check hospital and clinic records. All gunshot wounds have to be reported, and he would have needed help."

"They can try, but I have a feeling those men were long gone by the time the sun came up the next morning. I'm pretty sure they thought they had killed me. It's one thing to be trespassing, but it's quite another to add murder to what I can only assume is a long list of run-ins with the authorities."

"You said they weren't from around here. How did you know that?"

"Because I'd heard that accent before when I was flying provision up north."

"Then that's probably where they are from."

"Don't look so hopeful, Brylee. If they've gone north no one will ever find them. There are plenty of places in the outback where the law doesn't exist."

"So they are just going to get away with it? What if they come back?"

"That is highly unlikely. I'm not even sure they saw the cave. I was on the bank beside the falls when it happened. I had just built a campfire, and it was still dark outside. By the time I came too and made it inside no one was around, and everything appeared to be just as I had left it."

Since I believed what Jake had remembered would help—even if he thought the perpetrators were long gone—I called Officer Riley to report that he was awake and had told me that he'd been attacked by two men, one of them with a limp, and he was fairly certain he had hit one of the when he fired back before going down. The fact that they could be from the north might also help narrow the search.

"I wish we had known this sooner, Miss Hawkins," he said. "None of the men we have interrogated had a limp and no gunshot wounds have been reported, but that doesn't mean someone we have already talked to isn't aware of the men you described. If we can round them up again we might learn something, especially if we let them know that our witness is awake and can identify his assailants. I will stop by the hospital in about an hour to take Jake's statement. I'm glad he is going to make it."

"Me too," I said. "His condition could easily have gone the other way."

Jake continued to improve. The police took his statement in the early afternoon and arranged for a sketch artist to construct drawings that could be released to the media. It was a long shot since it had been over a week since the incident occurred, and he wasn't sure he could recall any features with much accuracy, but it was all we had. Maybe someone had seen them and would come forward. No mention was made of placing a guard at his door, and I hoped that would never become an issue.

I called LeAnn as soon as Jake felt strong enough to talk to her. I tried to leave the room so they could speak in privacy, but he refused to let me move from his side.

"You aren't going anywhere," he said as he took the phone from me. "We are in this together, unless you have already changed your mind now that you know I am going to live."

I leaned over and kissed his forehead. "I haven't changed my mind, but we still have a lot of things to work through."

"Save that thought," he said, and I could hear LeAnn's excited voice in the background.

"Is it really you?" she was sobbing into the receiver. "I have never been so scared. I simply could not survive if I lost anyone else."

"Well, I guess it takes more than a bullet to wipe out Jake Johnson," he said as his lips brushed the tips of my fingers.

I let them talk without interrupting. My heart was filled with undeniable gratitude for life, love and second and third chances. We really were not here by chance. I felt sorry for anyone who believed that.

After evening rounds, Jake's doctor felt he was well enough to be moved out of the ICU to a regular hospital room. I was thrilled with his recovery but saddened by the thought that I would no longer be the only person allowed to see him. I liked having him to myself and knew that he wasn't strong enough to handle a whole lot of unnecessary drama. That included dealing with Beth. She would descend on him like a vulture the moment he was no longer protected by a series of double doors.

But I didn't mention my concerns over his former ladylove. He had read the cards included with the flowers but hadn't shown them to me. I knew he was trying to figure out what to say, and I had worries of my own to consider.

Being moved from the ICU was the first step towards being released, and that meant making additional adjustments when it came to our living arrangements. He wouldn't be able to do much for weeks, and someone would have to take care of him. I wanted to be that person but with LeAnn confined to bed at Emma's, it would mean taking him home by myself. A few weeks earlier it would not have mattered as much, but now that we had declared our feelings for each other people would become more watchful, and I needed to set a good example for the women in my branch. We discussed our situation briefly during our last night in the ICU.

"Nothing to worry your pretty head about it," he said with a wicked twinkle in his eyes. "I won't be able to get into much mischief for at least another week or so and by then, LeAnn, Trevor and the new baby are sure to be home."

"You think I am being silly, don't you?" I responded.

"I think you are the woman I am head over heels in love with and I never want you to change. I like knowing that you have principles even love can't shatter."

"How can you even say that after the way this near fiasco started? We had been fighting as usual, and you could have died on that mountain."

"We've never had a real fight, love. That comes with throwing things and physical confrontations. Ours have been disagreements and if I hadn't survived, it would have been my own bloody fault for never listening like I should. What I did was stupid. You don't have the corner market on that."

I loved that our conversations now had substance and shared trust instead of fault-finding and groundless accusations. I could only pray it would last.

We both sleep off and on until morning rounds began and we were told that someone would be moving his bed to the ground floor around ten. I showered and made myself as presentable as possible and then began carrying flowers and potted plants to their new home for the next few days.

"Just a minute," he said as I moved towards the door with my last load.

I turned back with alarm. "Is something wrong?"

He winked at the pretty nurse that was unlocking the wheels on his bed. He had tried to convince her that he was ready for a wheelchair at least, but she was sticking with the orders Dr. Turret had given.

"Nothing! I'm in great hands. I just need another kiss before we leave. Things won't be the same downstairs."

"Are you afraid I won't kiss you anymore because there will be too many people milling around?"

"That thought never crossed my mind, love, but it won't be like it the last twenty-four hours. I almost dread leaving this room because it means life will shortly be back to normal."

"I'm not sure normal is a word that could ever be used to describe our lives," I told him in jest as I moved towards him and placed a kiss on his upturned lips. "And we will just have to make sure that some things never change."

"You got that right," he replied, pulling me down towards him until our lips were touching again. I loved this new side to our relationship, but he was correct in his assumptions about leaving the safety of the ICU. No matter how hard we tried, some things would never be the same again.

I was organizing a few articles of clothing in a dresser drawer when his first visitor arrived. It was Beth, naturally, and she had a huge bouquet of red roses in her hands and didn't see me because I was partially hidden behind the door when it opened.

She was beautifully dressed in a pink sundress with her hair curled around her face and a generous amount of makeup covering her almost flawless skin. She looked radiantly beautiful! How could any man resist her? I looked down at the drab clothing I was wearing for the third day in a row. I looked like a scullery maid.

"My, God, darling," she said, racing to his side as fast as her stiletto heels would allow, and putting the roses on the nightstand before kissing him soundly on the lips. "I have been sick with worry ever since I heard you had been shot. I tried to get in to see you, but the horrid nurses wouldn't let me past the barriers that kept us apart. They said only family was allowed until you woke up, but you should never have been left alone. With LeAnn in bed and Trevor too young, they should have permitted your girlfriend to be with you. I tried to tell them that over and over again. How are you feeling? We have so much to talk about. I missed you dreadfully."

I watched the proceedings from the corner of the room almost shell-shocked at what was going on. I had tied to forget about Beth the past few days, but she hadn't forgotten about Jake. He looked almost as shaken as I felt.

"I'm glad you came to visit, Beth," he said, not even attempting to make her feel welcome. "But there is something you need to know."

"Whatever it is, it doesn't matter, love?" she said, leaning over to kiss his forehead and stroke the hair out of his eyes. "I don't care about anything except the fact that you are getting well, and I will be able to take you home soon."

He looked in my direction, and her eyes followed his. I could see the malice in them before her next words were spoken.

"Oh, it's you!" she smirked. "Emma told me you were here to help out since he is family and all, but I can take over now.

I'm sure you have lots of work to do back on the ranch. After all, that is where you are most needed."

For a split-second, I didn't know what to say. This conversation did not need a third party, and I was tired of being humiliated by someone who didn't even know me. Jake had a lot of explaining to do. He had been thoughtless, careless and a little naïve if he thought they had both entered the relationship with the same expectations.

"I will leave the two of you alone," I said, moving around the door. "There are a few calls I need to make anyway."

"You don't have to go," Jake said.

"Why not?" Beth asked, stopping me from beating a hasty retreat. "I know you are grateful that she rescued you, but I'm your girlfriend."

Jake reached up and took her hand. "About that, Beth. I never meant to hurt you, but we both know that we didn't get together for love."

She started to cry. "But what about all the nights we spent together and the way you treated me? No man does that unless he really cares."

My face flushed scarlet as the pain in my heart intensified. I knew they had spent two nights together, but she made it sound like they had been together almost constantly. Could I have really been so stupid and blind as to believe that Jake really loved me when he had been so attentive with someone else?

"I do care about you, Beth. You have been a great friend, but getting together was a mistake on my part. I truly am sorry," Jake said as I slumped into the nearest chair, my legs no longer able to support my weight.

"It wasn't a mistake," Beth sobbed, clinging to his hand. "We were good together. You said that yourself."

"And I meant it, but I never said that I loved you and wanted our relationship to be anything more than it was. I thought you understood that it was one of mutual comfort and need. We can't go back to the way things used to be. Too much has happened since then."

"It's her, isn't it?" She glared in my direction. "So the prim and proper cold fish has finally warmed up. She will never be able to give you what I can."

"Don't talk about Brylee that way," he told her. "She has nothing to do with this."

"Oh, I think she has everything to do with it. She saved your life so now you think you are in love with her. She will just break your heart again, only this time I might not be there for you to run to."

"It isn't like that, Beth."

"Bloody hell it isn't! Things like that happen all the time. People get emotional during a crisis and say things they don't really mean. Everything will look different once you are back on your feet and remember all the amazing times we shared. You're to want them back."

"No, I won't," Jake said with a slight shake of his head. "What we shared was special, but I happen to be very much in love with Brylee. Nearly dying didn't change my feelings. It merely confirmed what I knew all along but was too stupid to admit."

"What about her?" she spat in my direction. I knew she was taking inventory from the cuts and bruises on my face to the way I was sitting slumped down on the chair. There was no way I could compare to her. "Does she feel the same way about you?"

"Yes! Despite everything I have done to hurt her. I am not a good man, Beth. I use women and cast them away. You will do so much better without me."

"Maybe I like complicated men," she responded. "I have loved you since I was a child. That was why I didn't go away to school like all my friends. I knew that someday you would come to me."

"Is that what you really want, Beth, a man who cannot commit because his heart is with someone else?"

"That could change. You just need more time to forget about what happened on that mountain. Gratitude only goes so far. Haven't I shown you that I am always there for you? I could help you forget about her again."

"That's not going to happen because I won't let it."

Quite suddenly her whole countenance changed. She was no longer begging for another chance. She was so angry I could feel the hatred in the room. She wiped at the tears on her cheeks with an index finger while turning on a spiked heel and taking a step away from his bed. "I hope the two of you rot in bloody hell because it is what you both deserve." A few more indignant steps and the door slammed shut behind her.

Jake and I looked at each other for the longest time without speaking. Our newfound joy had just been shattered, and I wasn't sure we could pick up the pieces and move on. Beth may have entered their relationship under false hopes with no promises, but she was devastatingly hurt. No one deserved to have her life ripped apart in front of the other woman. I should have made myself leave the room while I could.

"I'm sorry you had to witness that," he finally said. "I want to be a better man, but Beth and I do share a certain history."

I could see the pain in his eyes, but I couldn't go to him, even when he held out his hand to me.

"I don't know how you can say that so calmly. Beth is very much in love with you."

"And I'm sorry it had to end like that, but I told her from the beginning that it wasn't love for me. She said she understood and it didn't matter."

"But it did matter to her, Jake, and it matters to me. I know the world thinks sex outside of commitment and marriage is okay, but someone always gets hurt."

"And I hurt her. I get that, but you have to believe that I never meant for it to happen. She's a good kid. I should never have let things go as far as they did." He took a deep breath and slumped back on the pillow beneath his head. "I went to the diner after our blowup in the cave. I had to get away from the ranch, and I needed a comfortable place to think. Beth invited me back to her place for a drink."

I closed my eyes and chewed down on my lower lip. I knew what it was like to be used and abused and then tossed away. Jon had seen to that.

"I thought I had lost you forever, Brylee. I needed to be held and reassured. Don't try to tell me you have never felt like that."

"You know that's exactly how I felt that night on the beach after Ben and I broke up, but comfort didn't lead to sex."

"Only because I respected what you wanted. If you had given me the least bit of encouragement we likely would not have left that beach all night."

"Do you really believe that sex, or making love as you so casually label it, solves everything? Unless it happens in the right place, at the time, and with the right person, it is just an act any animal can perform."

I was being both bitter and accusing as I leaned back in the chair and put my forehead in the palms of my hands. I was no good at confrontations. I loved Jake with all my heart, but I could not excuse what he had done, even if Beth had been a willing participant.

"I would change everything if I could," he said. "And you have every right to hate me."

"I don't hate you, Jake," I said, risking everything by looking over at him. "I knew Beth was in love with you that day we ate at the diner."

"Then why didn't you say something?"

"Because every girl we met that day was falling all over you. I couldn't see the attraction, but most assuredly did not want to become one of them."

"Come here," he said with a smile, extending his hand to me again. "You were never like them. You were so far out of my league I felt like an ant ready to be stomped on. The only way I could be around you was by throwing barbs. I have made a million mistakes in my life and have done a whole lot of things I am not proud of. But finding you was a miracle, and I don't want to lose what we just found because of my misspent life. I love you—and only you—and promise to spend the rest of my days trying to make you happy. Please give me another chance to prove that I can be a man who is worthy of you."

"No more waitresses!" I said, sitting upright. Admitting our faults and sins was the first step to repentance. I had found that out for myself not that long ago.

"No more waitresses or anyone else," he responded.

I rose to my feet. How could I condemn him for acting like any other red-blooded man when he didn't know what I did? The gospel brought clarity only when it was accepted.

"And from this point on, we will always be honest with each other?"

"Scout's honor."

I took a step towards him. "I might still get angry because of what happened."

"And I will keep reassuring you that it will never happen again because almost losing everything has given me more than a desire to change. It has brought hope for something greater than I have ever known before."

I crossed the distance between us and his fingers closed over mine.

"It won't be easy for us," I told him. "We both have a lot of baggage and some pretty clear expectations."

"I wouldn't have it any other way."

He put my hand to his lips and kissed it. "You never did tell me what happened to your hand."

"That's because I don't know, but it did take a whole lot of stitches."

I tried not to think about Beth during the next few hours, but it was impossible. Girls in the world were not protected by church standards like I had been the past two years. So many of them bought into the false belief that sex was just something one did because it felt good or was expected. Consequences were never a major consideration, unless they came with certain complications—like Molly's unexpected pregnancies.

But that approach to living did far too much damage. Aunt Nora and Uncle Ned were the exception since few couples stayed together for over thirty years with or without making holy vows. But I still feared for my cousins because NJ was like a kid in a candy store around women, and Molly had married a man who might not be the father of her child. Nonetheless, sins being forgiven and slates wiped clean was a fundamental part of the gospel of Jesus Christ. That was what had initially attracted me to it, and I had committed to share what I knew with others. I just hoped my fledgling testimony was strong enough to keep living by precepts I knew were true.

Chapter 19

Uncle Ned returned later that day after having spent a week traveling through the outback looking for a tribe of aborigine's who did not want to be found. His was tired and mad at himself for leaving at such a potentially dangerous time. He came to the hospital to see Jake that evening.

We were just returning from a short walk up and down the hall. Jake was gripping the stand with the IV that was still pumping antibiotics into his body, and I was helping to hold him upright. His hours in the cave after being shot and his subsequent operation and medically induced coma had left him weak, but I appreciated the time we had together. It would not be the same once he was back on the ranch and had recovered enough to start doing things on his own.

Our decision to take things at a snail's pace, even before Beth's visit, seemed more important than ever. What she had said about him loving me because I had saved his life was worrisome. Emotionally driven situations had a way of imploding once safety was restored, and giving in to things that were not right would make a train wreck of what we were trying to build.

"We have to be two of the dumbest blokes in the outback," Uncle Ned told Jake as soon as he was back in his hospital bed.

"I leave on a bloody fool's mission, and you get yourself shot. We should have paid more attention to the women in our lives. Not only are they two of the prettiest girls in the country but they happen to be the smartest ones too."

I was standing next to Uncle Ned. He put his arm around me as his eyes misted with tears. "I am just so proud of you, Brylee. I don't know how you got Jake off that mountain. A grown man could not have done any better."

I smiled up at him. "I had more than a little help from above and a whole lot of motivation down here."

His laughter, that sounded just like my father. filled the room. "It's about time the two of you quit dancing around your feelings for each other. A blind man could tell you belong together."

"We were a little slow," I admitted.

Jake looked over at me, his smile warming my soul. "And we wouldn't be together now if some bloke had not fired a few rounds at me. Your niece is the bravest and most incredible woman I have ever known—despite my putting her through incredible nonsense since the day we met—but I wouldn't be here today without her. Nonetheless, it is going to take some time to get back in her good graces once I get out of this place."

"Now that you mention it, I'm afraid I will have my own list of *'honey-does'* when I get back to the ranch," Uncle Ned interjected. "Nora isn't too pleased with me right now, but she will come around now that everyone is safe."

"We might be okay for the moment," I mused as I listened to their cheerful banter, but we were far from having anything settled.

"I hope so, Uncle Ned, but we still don't know what to do about the cave, and it is highly unlikely the authorities will ever find the men who killed Mr. Sutter and tried to kill Jake."

"Sometimes the best advice is to leave things alone, Brylee, but I do have a scrap of news. I stopped by the police station on my way here and they have a lead on a man who was treated for a gunshot wound in Kimberly."

"But that's over fifty miles away."

"I know it's a long shot, but a guy with a bullet in him and another one with a limp would be pretty hard to miss, especially now that a sketch of them has been released. I just wish I had seen them myself."

"I hope they get put behind bars," Jake admitted. "But even more, I wish people would just forget that the mountain might have a vein or two of gold running through it. Nothing good ever comes from trying to get something for nothing."

"Well, maybe this will help," Uncle Ned, said, pulling the latest edition of Edna's newspaper out of his back pocket. On the front page was a huge headline *No Gold in Mountains*.

My brows furrowed in confusion. "I don't understand, Uncle Ned. All three of us saw gold deposits in the cave."

"True enough, but you have to remember that thanks to Jake getting shot no one else seems to have been inside that particular cave. Sutter's side of the mountain has been thoroughly searched with nothing out of the ordinary found. Maybe the man who shot Jake thought he would have better luck approaching it from a different way. The rumor now is that John found that nugget someplace else but was killed before disclosing the true location. It could have come from anywhere."

We were making too many assumptions. If there was any truth behind what Emma had told me about John Sutter finding a number of small nuggets in a newly cultivated field, this was only a small reprieve. I should have mentioned it to both Uncle Ned and Jake but figured the news media controlled almost everything and they seemed to believe it was over.

"What about Aunt Nora contacting the historical preservation society?" I asked. "If they get into the cave to look at the drawings then all this craziness will start again."

"Then we have to make sure that doesn't happen," Jake responded. "I, for one, don't have to be shot a second time to know when it is best to leave well enough alone."

"I couldn't agree more," Uncle Ned added. "I don't want strangers traipsing all over our land, and I doubt the aborigines will ever be back to claim what is rightfully theirs."

"So you were unable to find them . . . ."

"No exactly, I found their tribe but Ishmael and Asum weren't there. I left a message about contacting me, but we all know that likely won't happen. They are nomadic by nature, and material assets mean nothing to them. It is all about becoming one with both family and nature."

"So that leaves us right back where we started from."

Jake looked over at me. "I wouldn't say that. I think the aborigines have it right about family, nature and personal beliefs trumping monetary advantages. I could have died on that mountain and lost you forever, Brylee. I am not willing to take that chance again."

His tender admittance touched my heart and drove away some of my fears because I didn't want to risk losing him again either.

And so we decided to do nothing about the cave, the drawings, or the gold veins—at least for the present. When or if the time came to reveal what we had found, a plan would be in place for doing so. Until then, we would go on with our lives the way we always had, trusting that things would turn out the way they were meant to.

Jake was going to be released from the hospital on Friday, possibly before if there were no complications. I had arranged for both of us to stay with Uncle Ned and Aunt Nora for a few days. Despite his remarkable recovery, I was afraid for his safety at my hands because I had never nursed someone back to health before. Even after my father's return from the hospital not long before his death, LeAnn had been the one to take care of him.

Jake laughed when I admitted my fears but did not discount my feelings. We were heading into uncharted territory and he knew that I didn't want tongues wagging about our being alone at the ranch. Besides, I think he was as worried as I was about what Beth might be saying now that she knew about our budding romance. A woman scorned always posed a threat until she found someone new, and even then there were no guarantees that she would not seek revenge.

But if we had known what was going to happen a few hours later, we might have saved ourselves a lot of unnecessary worry.

Emma called at eleven on Tuesday night to say that LeAnn was in labor, and she was on her way to the hospital with both mother-to-be and Trevor since he could not be left alone. Jake had been resting when the phone rang.

"The baby's coming," I said, nearly knocking the pitcher of water off the bedside table in my eagerness to tell him the news. "They're on their way right now. Are you ready to be an uncle again?"

He looked at me and laughed. "I guess I will have to be since that little one has finally decided to make her appearance, but isn't it still a little early?"

"Only a week or so," I said, suddenly realizing that I still had a promise to fulfill.

"What's wrong?" Jake asked when he saw a frown appear on my brow. "You are supposed to be excited, but you look more like you have lost your last friend."

"I completely forgot that LeAnn wanted me to be her birthing coach and we haven't even practiced."

"There's nothing to it," he replied. "You just tell her to breathe and let her squeeze your hand. At least that is what I did while we were waiting for Trevor. Your father was late getting to the hospital but made it for the delivery."

I hadn't thought about the truth surrounding Trevor's birth for a long time. And even though I had forgiven everyone involved, it still hurt knowing that my father had betrayed both my mother and me.

"I shouldn't have reminded you of that," Jake said, noticing my reaction.

I leaned down and kissed his parted lips. They were so much softer than when I found him in the cave alone and dying.

"No more walking on egg shells," I told him. "We can't change the past, and while I may have a few belated reactions over certain things, I have a feeling the future is going to be pretty spectacular."

He caught my arm as I turned away. "I can't tell you often enough how sorry I am for all the pain and heartache I have caused, but I promise to spent the rest of my life making it up to you. All I want is for you to be happy."

"I am happy," I told him as I kissed his lips again. "And you don't have to make any promises, except that we will always be honest with each other. There have been too many secrets and all they do is destroy."

"I can do that," he said. "Just don't expect me to be perfect. I've had way too much practice doing things the wrong way, but then I never knew what truly loving someone could do for a heathen's ability to change until I met you."

"What about Wendy?" I asked, no longer afraid of the ghosts from his past.

"Puppy love! But you had better run along now. We don't want LeAnn upset because her birthing coach isn't there to meet her when she gets to the emergency room door. Maybe you and I will be the next ones waiting for one of heaven's little miracles, after Molly delivers that is."

I had been thinking a lot about that myself, but now was not the time to discuss all of the things that needed to change if having children was to be part of our future. What if I wasn't being fair by demanding so much? He had agency to choose just as I did, and that could not be compromised regardless of how much I wanted us to spend forever together.

"We can talk about that later," I told him. "Right now, we have a new member of our family to greet and don't want LeAnn any more stressed than I know she already is. Are you sure you will be okay without me?"

"I will never be okay without you again but know you have responsibilities that won't always include me. Maybe Emma and Trevor can keep me company while you're gone. I know he is too young to be on this floor. But heck, rules were only made to be broken."

I was standing just inside the emergency room doors when Emma pulled up in her car. She never ceased to amaze me. For being eighty-plus years old, she had the energy of someone twenty years younger. She would be lost when LeAnn and Trevor left her home to go back to the ranch once Jackie was born. I hurried out to greet them pushing the wheelchair I found in the hall.

LeAnn thrust the car door open with her foot. "I tried to hold off coming until morning, but Jackie is determined that it has to be tonight."

She was having trouble standing, so I pulled her upright while asking if she had alerted the doctor?"

"Yes," she said as another contraction made her double over in pain. She gripped her swollen belly and screamed as I eased her into the wheelchair. When I looked up, a nurse was running towards us.

"I can take it from here," she said, turning the wheelchair towards the hospital and leaving us standing beneath the awning.

Trevor had been charged with making sure a small suitcase got to the hospital with them. It was clasp tightly in both hands and he looked terrified.

"Is mum going to be okay?" he asked. "She keeps screaming."

I knelt down on the driveway in front of him while Emma drove away to park the car. "I think that is the way it's supposed to be. Jackie has to let her know when she is ready to be born or the trip to the hospital might not be made in time."

He seemed to accept my explanation. The truth was, I had no idea what was supposed to happen, except from movies and TV shows that tended to simplify most everything.

"Come on," Emma said, soon joining us in the warm night air. "I don't know about the two of you, but I am ready to be a grandmother—an adopted one—but a grandmother none-the-less."

After a brief examination, LeAnn was wheeled to the maternity ward. I told Emma that she and Trevor should go home and try to get some sleep because it might be a long night, but she didn't take my suggestion to heart any more than Trevor did. They both wanted to be there when baby Jackie made her arrival.

I asked the nurse on duty if Trevor could visit with Jake because he wasn't sleeping but as anticipated, her answer was a firm "no". The hospital had regulations, but she did find a pillow and blanket so he could curl up on a sofa and sleep while they waited. Emma had brought her crocheting and was determined to have the edging on the pink afghan finished before the night was over.

So I gave both of them a kiss and hurried into the room where LeAnn was still letting her discomfort be known.

"I'm sorry for being such a booby," she said as the nurse checked her blood pressure again. "But I don't remember it hurting like this with Trevor. You don't think there is anything wrong with the baby do you?"

"She will be fine," I replied before she could say anything more. "You are in the best possible place, and your doctor is on his way."

"I hope he gets here soon because I feel like pushing again."

She squeezed my hand so tightly I felt like I might join her in screaming. Even in her weakened state, LeAnn was much stronger than she looked.

She was in labor for an additional three hours before Jackie finally made her debut. I had never witnessed anything so frightening, yet beautiful. I saw my little sister before her mother did. She was slimy and red and looked like a wrinkled, old woman, but she was the most beautiful baby I had ever seen with lots of dark, brown hair and piercing blue eyes.

"You can tell the two of you are sisters," the doctor said as he cleared the baby's airway and cut the umbilical cord. He had learned all about our unusual family dynamics during the months LeAnn had been in his care. Jackie let out a lusty scream.

"Well, LeAnn," he said as he placed the squirming newborn in her arms. "You have done bloody well. Your baby is perfect."

LeAnn was sobbing with joy as tiny fingers wrapped around her thumb. "But she is so little. Are you sure she is going to be okay?"

"We will check her out, but from what I can see you have nothing to worry about. I have a feeling this little girl is going to keep all of you on your toes for a very long time."

"Thank you, Doctor Arnold," LeAnn said through tears of delight. "You will never know how grateful I am for all you have done for both of us."

"You are the one who did all the hard work, LeAnn," he said. "Jack would be very proud of you."

"I hope so," she replied, kissing Jackie's head as the baby snuggled into her arms. "This is one gift I could not bear to lose."

"There will be plenty of time for bonding once we get this little angel cleaned up. I think you know the drill," the doctor told her as a nurse removed the baby from her arms. "And once we are done here, we need to get you settled in a room. I do believe there are some people anxiously waiting to hear the news. Why don't you go and share it with them, Brylee?"

I knew he was politely ushering me out of the delivery room so they could take care of necessities, and I was fine with that. I had seen enough of the birthing process to know I wasn't quite ready to become a mother. I wondered if Molly knew what she was getting into.

I kissed LeAnn's forehead. "Congratulations on having the most beautiful baby in the world. She's absolutely perfect."

"She is, isn't she?" LeAnn whispered, raising her head so she could get another glimpse of her daughter before she was taken away. "And thank you for taking care of my little brother. You know how much I wanted to be there for him."

I brushed a lock of blonde, damp hair from her forehead. "We both had something important to do and with God's help, we do it."

"But if you hadn't found him . . . ."

"I did, so there is no reason to let that trouble us any longer. You have an amazing, new daughter who needs you."

She suddenly pulled me down close to her.

"Brylee, I have something important to tell you." Her voice was little more than a whisper so no one else would hear. "Your Father was here when Jackie was born. I saw him standing next to the doctor. He was smiling so warmly at me. I am not going crazy, am I?"

Her belief in all she was learning humbled me. "No," I replied, gulping back a sob of my own. "I know it can happen that way when people are really in tune with the spirit and each other. I felt his presence but didn't get to see him."

"He was so beautiful, although he would die all over again if he heard me say that. He was dressed in white, almost glowing. It's like Emma has been telling me. Our loved ones know what is going on in our lives, even if they can't be here. It is all part of being an eternal family, isn't it?"

"Yes!" I told her. "I think we have some very important work to do before our own lives come to an end. I want us to be part of the same family forever."

"Even Jake?" she asked.

"Especially Jake. I cannot begin to tell you how much I love him."

"You don't have to tell me in words. Your actions say everything, and I know he feels the same way about you because he told me so on more than one occasion."

"Ladies," the doctor impatiently stated. "You will have plenty of time to catch up and we still have a few things to do."

I didn't need to be asked a third time to leave. "I will see you in a little while," I told my stepmother who by now had become a very dear friend.

Trevor was still sleeping when I got to the waiting room. Emma looked up from her crocheting when she heard the door close behind me. I was wiping tears of joy, love and contentment from my eyes. She got to her feet immediately.

"Is everything all right?" she asked.

I put my arms around her and gave her a hug. "Everything is perfect and we never would have made it to this moment without you."

"So both LeAnn and the baby are okay?"

"Absolutely! The doctor had to ask me to leave the delivery room twice, I'm afraid. It was an incredible experience watching a new life come into the world. They are cleaning the baby up now and doing whatever they need to with LeAnn."

"Praise the good Lord," she said, sitting down in her chair again as if her legs were too weak to hold her upright any longer. "I have quit asking God why I wasn't allowed to be a mother. But after a lifetime of waiting and questioning his judgment far more than I should, he has given me the next best blessing possible. I have all of you in my life and could not be happier."

I glanced over at Trevor who had not yet awakened. I knew about unexpected blessings and had certainly received my share the past year. "Do you think we should tell him Jackie is here?"

"Let him sleep a while longer. There is nothing to see until they get the baby to the nursery anyway. I just hope he isn't too disappointed. All he has been talking about is taking the baby home and playing with her. I am afraid he doesn't fully understand that an infant is incapable of doing anything more than eat and sleep the first few weeks of life."

"Oh, but she can smile, Emma. I saw her doing that when LeAnn pulled her into her arms. It was like she knew exactly where she was supposed to be."

I sniffed back tears of tenderness and joy. How I wanted a child of my own, but as Emma had said, sometimes God's plans for us were quite different than our own.

"As for my little brother," I said before another wave of self-pity could wash over me and destroy the beauty of the moment. "We will just have to keep him occupied with other things. I know having a baby around is going to be a big adjustment for all of us, and I don't want him to feel like he is getting lost in the shuffle."

She smiled her agreement, but from the sudden look of sorrow in her eyes I knew something was bothering her.

"What's wrong?" I asked.

"Nothing important," she said, dabbing at her eyes with the handkerchief she always had tucked up her sleeve. "It's just that I didn't get the baby's blanket finished in time."

I knew there was more to it than that but didn't want to pry. Emma was a very private person and would let me know what had changed her countenance when she was ready.

"Do you mind if I tell Jake about the baby?" I asked as her fingers began working again with the string that sat in a ball in her lap. "I won't be long."

"Take your time," she responded, "We aren't going anywhere. When Trevor wakes up, I will send someone to find you."

I kissed her cheek before leaving. There had to be some way of making sure she never felt alone again. An idea was forming in my mind, but I needed to talk to both LeAnn and Jake before saying anything.

The man I loved had his eyes closed when I got back to his room. The change in our relationship was like floating on a white, fluffy cloud during a bright summer day, but I was still afraid that cloud had a few holes in it. If Jake never accepted the gospel's message of hope and salvation there would be no permanence for us, but I had put our lives in God's hands. He knew what was right from an eternal perspective while I was still having trouble seeing beyond the moment.

"Hey, there, handsome," I said as he opened his eyes. "Did you miss me?"

He laughed and held out his hand. "I missed you from the moment you left. Is the baby here already?"

"Already," I chided. "It has been over four hours but Jackie is finally here, and she is beautiful."

"What about LeAnn?"

"Exhausted, but thrilled to have her daughter arrive safely. The doctor said she would be in recovery for a while but we should be able to see the baby in the nursery soon, if you are up for that?"

"I am almost good as new," he said, trying to push himself upright in bed and then lying back with a groan. "Well, maybe not completely reenergized quite yet, but I don't want you to think you have fallen in love with a complete invalid."

"I have fallen in love with the perfect man. I just wish I could take your pain away. Do you need me to get a nurse?"

"I don't need anything but you," was his kind and thoughtful reply.

The hand on the clock had moved very little when I received word that baby Jackie was now in the nursery. Jake decided to walk there instead of being pushed in a wheelchair so his condition would not upset Trevor who would be seeing him for the first time since the shooting. But he leaned heavily on my arm as he looked through the glass window at the single infant tightly swaddled in a pink blanket with the name Hawkins above her head. Everyone made the right comments about her being a true gift from God and how tiny and precious she was, but it was Jake's personal question that made my pulse race and my face flush scarlet.

"What do you think, Bryee? Can you see a little person like that in your future?"

Trevor looked up at us in confusion. "Brylee can't have babies. She isn't even married yet."

Jake winked at me. "I was just talking about the future, Trevor. Don't you think Jackie looks a lot an awfully lot like your big sister?"

"Only cuz she's got brown hair. I thought she would be bigger."

I put my hand on his shoulder. "She did come a couple of weeks early, and her legs and arms are tucked snuggly in the blanket making her seem even smaller, but she will grow much too fast."

"It is an absolute miracle," Emma said, wiping the tears from her eyes again. "It will be so lonely in that old house once all of you have gone back to the ranch."

"But I thought you would be glad to have some of the peace restored after having your home filled to overflowing with Hawkins' the past few months."

She smiled sadly. "You made it seem like a real home again, and it hasn't felt like since my husband died."

"Perhaps there is something we could do about that if you agree to become a permanent member of this rather strange and mixed-up family."

I had already talked to Jake about my idea. He thought it sounded like the perfect solution to our most pressing problems, and we both agreed that LeAnn would feel the same way we did.

"There is nothing I would like more, Brylee," she said. "I am an old lady who always figured I would die alone, but that doesn't seem like a bloody desirable option anymore. I have grown to love all of you so much."

"Then come out to the ranch with us. I can't possibly take care of everyone by myself. And with Jake laid up for a while, I will have more responsibilities than ever."

We all watched as Emma's countenance changed from sorrow and loss to complete elation.

"I suppose I could come out for a few weeks," she said with the proper amount of reluctance to make it seem as if it had not been her secret desire all along. "But just until everyone is back on his or her feet."

Trevor gave her a huge hug that cemented the deal. "I am ever so glad you are coming, Emma. Your food tastes so much better than Brylee's."

"Oh, really," I told him, faking my disappointment. I was a horrible cook and getting better, but with Emma's help I might just be more than tolerable by the time Jake and I were ready to move on to the next stage of our lives.

Thinking about the possibilities of what the future might bring made me almost giddy with expectations and joy. After months of adversity it truly felt as if a heavy fog of darkness was finally lifting. God was keeping his promises, and now I needed to keep mine.

Chapter 20

On Friday morning, Jake and LeAnn both signed their discharge papers, and we left the hospital in two vehicles. Aunt Nora had come into town to help transport all of us back to the ranch. She had even gone to the store and picked up everything she thought a new baby would need. The back of her Land Rover was piled high with plastic bags filled with things for the makeshift nursery and the groceries we would need for the first week at home.

"I hope I got everything, LeAnn," she said when we stopped at Emma's to make sure nothing had been left behind and the house was secure since no one would be living there for the next few weeks.

LeAnn smiled demurely bringing a new softness to her face. In fact, everything about her countenance seemed more refined and serene. I knew that hearing about the gospel and accepting its message of love, hope and peace was as much responsible for the change as having a new baby to love. I just prayed the same thing would happen with Jake.

"You shouldn't have gone to all the trouble," LeAnn responded." "But we could never be able to do this without you, Nora. Family is everything! I feel like I have been born again the past few days."

She smiled in my direction, and I knew she was recalling my father's visitation during Jackie's birth. I hadn't told anyone, not even Jake. It was her experience to share if she ever felt like doing so.

"I am going to miss this house and all the people who came to call," LeAnn told Emma as she glanced inside the bedroom where she had lain on her back for the past few months. "I am afraid your accommodations at the ranch won't be nearly as nice but the hide-a-bed in the den is really quite comfortable."

I had offered Emma my bedroom upstairs, but she had declined saying that she needed to be on the main level to help out during the night without disturbing anyone else's rest. I didn't have the heart to insist that we do it any other way. I had watched her with Jackie at the hospital. If love was ever born in heaven, it was between the white-haired dynamo that had cared so unselfishly for our family and the dark-haired infant who nestled into her arms the moment she was cradled there.

But I wasn't exactly happy when Emma handed her car keys to me and insisted that I be the one drive it to the ranch. She was used to taking it around town, but the open road frightened her. I would have preferred sitting in the back seat with Jake and holding his hand, but since LeAnn had just delivered a baby and was still in a highly weakened condition, that left Aunt Nora and me to do the driving. Jake would not be allowed to operate any moving vehicle until he was cleared to do so by his doctor.

I went outside to talk to him while the others finished up in the house. He was lying down on the back seat of Aunt Nora's Land Rover. Some of the packages had been moved to the trunk of Emma's car to make more room for him. His eyes were closed, but he opened them when he heard my approach.

"I didn't mean to disturb you," I said, feeling just a little uncertain how to act now that we were away from the safety of the hospital. "How are you feeling?"

"Like bloody hell, but anything is tolerable as long as you are with me," he said as I sat on the edge of the seat so I would not have to look down at him.

We would work on his language later but right now, I just wanted to bask in the joy of being together. "Do you think people are surprised that we have become a bonafide couple?" I asked.

He placed a kiss on my eager lips before replying. "I think what surprises them most is that we have waited so long to admit our feelings for each other. LeAnn came to see me yesterday while you and Trevor were taking a walk. She said you are the best thing that has ever happened to me, and I had better not bugger anything up or I would be answering to her."

"She really said that?"

"And more! I simply cannot believe how much she has changed from the woman who ran away because she could not accept Jack's death."

"I'm sure Jackie is part of the reason. She looks so much like my father."

He frowned and brought my hand to his lips. "It's more than that, Brylee. Something deep inside of her has changed, and it's not just Jackie. LeAnn is peaceful and calm, and I can assure you she wasn't like that with Trevor. I have never seen her quite like this before."

Oh, how I wanted to tell him that LeAnn was investigating the Church of Jesus Christ of Latter-day Saints and liked what she was learning, but that was not my story to tell. I could only lead by example and pray that someday Jake would see the light for himself.

"You're awfully quiet," he said a moment later since I had not responded to his statement like I usually did. "Is there something you are not telling me?"

It was a fair question, but I couldn't answer it without betraying a confidence. Would he feel like everyone he loved had betrayed him when LeAnn told him what she was considering?

"I was just thinking about all that has happened the past year," I replied as a way of bypassing a very uncomfortable topic. "Sometimes I think change is the only certainty in life."

"You have certainly had a bloody rough go of it since you came home," he said. "And I am sorry for all the times I was unkind. You didn't deserve any of my rantings."

"You have nothing to apologize for, Jake. I wasn't very nice to you either."

His eyes were so intense and filled with both longing and compassion. How could I not have noticed the man behind the tough exterior sooner? But I had made up my mind to hate him and it had taken something truly life-altering to make me see how foolish I had been.

"You know what a therapist would say if he heard our story, don't you, Brylee?"

"No!" I challenged, liking this new Jake immensely. He was unpredictable but so easy to be around. "What would a therapist say?"

"He would call it foreplay."

The color rushed to my cheeks. Sometimes unpredictable was unnerving when the same thought was shared.

"I like it when you blush," he said. "It makes me realize just how innocent and amazingly special you are."

"I'm not exactly innocent. I wish I was."

"Compared to all the women I have known, you are completely without guile. But that's a good thing, and it makes me feel more like a real man because I want to protect you."

"You don't have to protect me, Jake. You just need to love and cherish me."

"I have been doing that for a very long time, love. But I still question if you ever would have admitted to loving me if I hadn't come so close to dying?"

My lips curved into a smile. "I had already decided to tell you how I felt. I was just waiting for the right time."

"I guess impending death qualifies for that. I still can't believe everything you went through to save my life. My, God, Brylee, you killed a crocodile!"

Yes, we would definitely have to work on his language.

"And I would do it again in a heartbeat! I love you, Jake Johnson. Finding you in that cave so close to death was the biggest wake-up call of my life. I want to be with you forever and always."

"Forever is a long time."

"Not when you love someone as much as I love you."

Trevor pulled the car door open and stuck his head inside. "What are you doing?" he innocently asked.

My embarrassment at almost being caught kissing Jake brought me back to the present in a hurry.

"I just wanted to make sure your Uncle Jake was okay before we began the long drive home. You will look after him, won't you, Trevor?"

He put his hand on my shoulder as if he knew something I didn't.

"I will take care of him, Brylee. You don't have to worry."

I looked over at Jake, but his face gave nothing away. "We have it covered, don't we, sport?"

"I'm not sure I like the sounds of that," I told both of them as I moved towards my little brother and away from the man I loved, but Jake caught my arm.

"What do you say, Trevor?" he asked. "Do you think we can get your sister to give me a kiss before we leave? The sooner we get on the road, the sooner I will be able to stretch out on my own bed and let her wait on me for everything."

"Not everything," I said, wishing Trevor would look away so I could kiss him in private. But when he didn't, I gave Jake a quick peck on the cheek.

"You can do better than that," he said. "We don't have to hide how we feel about each other any longer. Trevor likes the idea of us being together."

"You talked to him about it?"

I was glad Jake felt so open with everyone, but it would take me a little longer since I had spent the past eleven months telling everyone how much I detested him.

"I will see you at the ranch, Trevor," I said as I got to my feet. Aunt Nora was already climbing into the driver's seat, and Trevor hurried around the vehicle so he could ride up front with her. I had tried to persuade him to come with me, but the thought of riding shotgun was too compelling and he really wanted to be with his uncle.

"Don't be afraid to love him," Aunt Nora whispered in my ear as I bent my head to tell her to be safe. "He is a great bloke and would do anything in the world for you."

LeAnn started to cry the moment she stepped through the front door into the ranch house. "We're home, baby girl," she said, putting Jackie's carrier on the hallway floor. "Your father would be so thrilled if he was here to greet you."

Tears clouded my own vision as I came into the house behind her carrying the first load of baby things. "I am so sorry for all you have gone through, LeAnn. This has to be a rather bitter homecoming."

"It could be so much worse," she replied, smiling over her shoulder at me. "I have wonderful friends, two beautiful children, a safe home, the promise of being with your father forever, and my brother is going to live. Under the circumstances, life can't get much better than that."

I stopped in my tracks. This was the second time LeAnn had mentioned her desire to be affiliated with the church so we could be part of the same forever family. I wondered if anyone other than Emma and me knew of her plans.

"I haven't told Jake how I feel, or what I have been doing all these months besides resting, if that is what you are thinking," she continued. "It's not going to be easy. He sees no need for religious conviction and that is mostly my fault."

"I don't understand," I told her. "You have always been very tolerant when it comes to what people believe."

"That was easy when it didn't affect me directly. Your father and I sort of skirted around religion all the time we were together. We knew what we were doing was wrong, but we couldn't seem to stop ourselves. You made us see our relationship for what it was when you came home."

"I didn't mean to be judgmental, but the whole thing came as such a shock."

"I imagine it did, just as your coming home shocked us. I always knew it could happen but after so many years, I sort of figured we would never see you again. Trying to make things right was incredibly hard on your father."

The implications of her words stung deeply. My appearance had turned their entire world upside-down, and I had been too consumed with my own shock and abhorrence to even consider what my presence had done to them. They had every right to resent or even hate me.

"You are far more forgiving than me," I said.

"But you didn't do anything wrong, Brylee. You found the truth and it worked for you. Our own guilt was what made us so reluctant to listen. It was like staring at our reflections and not much liking what we saw. But you never made excuses or backed down. You continued to do what you believed was right, even though every member of your family, excluding Trevor of course, made you feel like you would never belong here again."

"Not everyone is against me now," I said.

"No, they aren't," she responded with a bright smile. "I just hope that one day my little brother will understand too. Forever means very little unless it can be shared with the people you love. As long as your father was alive, I didn't have to think about life after death."

"And now you know that the time you had together will never be enough."

"Exactly, but we have to believe Jake will eventually understand what we do. He was so young when our parents died, and I had to work to put food on the table. That meant he learned how to fend for himself, trust his own instincts and control where his life went. He is bloody afraid to let God into his life for fear things will fall apart like they did when Wendy betrayed him with his best friend. He vowed never to allow himself to need anyone again."

I felt gooseflesh rush up my arms and legs. Was she trying to warn me that Jake might not be capable of making a long-lasting commitment, regardless of what he had said? If that was what she really believed, why hadn't she said something before I let everyone know that I was in love with him? It would have been the kindest thing to do.

She must have noticed the stunned look on my face.

"I didn't mean to make you worry," she said. "Things are different now that he has found you. He really is trying to let you in. It's just not that easy for him."

Her words were reassuring, but a seed of doubt had been planted, and I wasn't sure what it would take to pluck it out and make everything right again.

"But let's not talk about disheartening thoughts any longer," she continued, bringing me back to the present. "This is a joyful day. My new baby is home where she belongs, and my brother's life is out of danger. I am just hoping your mother will forgive me one day. I never meant to break up her family, but if what Emma and the missionaries claim is true, the Savior's atonement covers even the vilest of sinners."

"I know she will, and Emma is right," I responded, placing my hand tenderly on the top of my baby sister's dark hair. Nothing good ever came from dwelling on the past or trying to predict the future. All we had was this day. "Time and family—whatever its source—coupled with clarity, faith and repentance have a way of changing everything. I never knew I could love anyone quite the way I do my little sister and brother."

"What about my little brother?" she asked as she lay Jackie down in the crib we had set up in the master bedroom. "He has loved you since the day you arrived, and all that talk a few moments ago was just my way of saying that I am scared to bring up the subject of religion right now. He needs to be much stronger first."

I blinked back the mist that was making my world fuzzy. I could not afford to let doubt creep into my world when it had just started to right itself.

"I love him so much," I told her as I looked down at the sleeping baby. "I just never knew how much until I almost lost him."

"But love isn't always enough, is it?" She took both my hands in hers and looked intently at me. "Please don't give up on him because you have a loving support system now. He will come around just like I did."

"I hope so," I told myself as I looked around the master bedroom that had been turned into a nursery. LeAnn wasn't warning me, she was simply letting me know why Jake was fighting religion so rigorously. Perhaps once he knew where all of us stood, he would be more willing to give our beliefs a chance.

"Thanks being such a good friend, LeAnn," I told her. "We have come a long way since that day in the lane. I was so determined to hate you, but now I understand why my father loves you so much."

"Your father had the most tender heart of any man I have ever known. You are very much like him that way."

"We sound like a mutual admiration society," I said, trying to hide how much it touched my heart to be likened to my father. "But I do want you to know that I will always be here for Trevor, Jackie and you. Jake too, if that is what God has in mind for us."

Aunt Nora came into the bedroom just then and dropped a number of shopping bags on the bed. "I thought the two of you must have gotten lost. Trevor took Jake to the bunkhouse, but he is asking for you, Brylee. I think he feels better with you around."

"I will check on him once we get everything into the house," I told her as I pulled back the bedcovers so LeAnn could lie down while Jackie was sleeping. "Then I suppose we should start thinking about what we are going to eat."

"Emma is way ahead with that," Aunt Nora replied. "She is already in the kitchen putting things away and deciding how to reorganize so she will know where to find what she needs. I can't believe you convinced her to come way out here. She will have this place running like clockwork in no time at all."

We settled into a routine much faster than I thought possible with two additional people in the house. Emma seemed to be everywhere work needed to be done, and I worried that she would burn out before the first week was over. But the truth was, we would never have survived without her. She got up with the baby at night when she only needed to be cuddled, and she had meals on the table before anyone had time to ask what was for lunch or dinner. I tried to keep up with the laundry and make sure she never had to climb the stairs, but most of my time was filled with outside chores, conversations with Uncle Ned over what had transpired during the time I had been at the hospital and spending time with Jake.

I had decided not to question his love for me, or the commitments we had made to each other, unless something happened that made it impossible not to ask difficult questions. I was happy for the first time in almost a year and wasn't about to go looking for trouble until it landed directly at my doorstep.

With Jake unable to do much more than get himself to the house for meals, I was pretty much left alone to run the ranch. Trevor was a lifesaver in so many ways. His animals were fully grown and would be put out with the rest of the sheep and beef cattle once the new offspring were born and they had been counted or sheered, but he seemed to accept not having them around without reservation. It was almost as if he had unknowingly assumed the responsibilities our father's legacy had reserved for him, and I wasn't going to deny him that feeling of importance. So I let him assume whatever tasks he felt capable of completing—always under my supervision—once his school lessons were done.

He loved everything about the ranch and ran errands for me almost constantly. I had to be careful not to overtax him. He was still a child and needed to play.

That was how we discovered our shared fondness for the slide our grandfather had built—the one he had helped Jake restore when I had deserted everyone because I had yet to understand that the process of living could not be rushed. I had managed to replace the last few boards along the sides while Trevor was at school. While my work was far from professional, at least no one would get hurt as long they didn't hang on too tightly as they came sailing off and landed in the sparse, dry grass.

One particular morning when we were heading towards the barn to feed the animals we noticed it shimmering in the early morning light.

"Have you been on it yet?" I asked my little brother.

He looked up at me quizzically. "No! There hasn't been anyone around to take me."

"Well, there is now," I told him. "Why don't we go up there as soon as Newton and the others have breakfast? I think it might be the perfect day to try it out."

"What about Uncle Jake? He wants to go with us and it was supposed to be a surprise."

His sensitivity to other's feelings made me smile. Most children only thought about their wants and desires. Jake would not be able to climb the hill for weeks, but Trevor needed a break from our new routine of all work and no play and quite frankly, so did I.

"It could be our secret," I told him.

"Isn't that like a lie?" he asked.

I looked down at him with a clarity that shamed me. To him, everything was still black and white, not shades of gray like it was for most adults. That certainly included me, especially when I was trying to protect the people I loved.

"Then why don't we ask him what he thinks? You do know that he won't be able to go with us for a long time."

"I know he was hurt really bad, but he is getting stronger. He says so every time we play checkers."

"I'm glad you are spending more time together and am very sorry things have been so chaotic lately."

There was no need to recite platitudes about life being filled with challenges we would someday understand or making more promises that would only be broken. Trevor had already seen more than his share of adult disfunction.

"It's okay," he responded. "We are all home now."

"We certainly are," I replied, wishing I had his depth of compassion. "Just never forget how very much you are loved and how sorry we are for hurting you."

We went to the bunkhouse together after chores were done to take Jake his breakfast instead of walking with him to the house.

"Now, this is a surprise," he said when we knocked and then entered the two-room dwelling with a tray that had toast, juice and scrambled eggs on it. He had been making his own coffee in the bunkhouse and was sitting in a chair next to an upright lamp drinking a cup of it. "Is there some reason my meal is being catered this morning? The two of you look like you have something to say."

"Oh, we do, Uncle Jake," Trevor said, unable to keep his excitement from showing. "Brylee and I have something very important to ask you."

I put the tray on the small kitchen table and then crossed to Jake's side.

"Is that so," he said, pulling me down so I could give him a morning kiss. It was much less ardent than the one I knew we would be sharing later on in the day, but Trevor didn't need to see grownups falling in love. He had accepted our new relationship without question, and that meant a great deal to me. But I was still getting used to the idea of public displays of affection around family. With Ben it had been different because it was his family, not mine, seeing us establish ourselves as a couple.

"So what is it?" Jake prodded. "You know you can ask me anything."

I bit the inside of my bottom lip and tried to smile. What we were asking was easy when compared to a discussion about religion and even LeAnn was avoiding that.

"We want to try out the slide, Uncle Jake, only we know you want to go with us since you were the one who fixed it."

Jake leaned back and laughed. "Is that all? I was afraid one of you wanted to run away and join the circus. I understand one is going to be in Sydney in the next few months, and I thought I would see about getting us tickets."

"Could we really go?" Trevor's eyes brightened at the prospect. "I have never been to a circus before."

"I went to one when I was a kid and think it is only fair that you see one too," Jake responded. "We could get a couple of rooms at a hotel and make a real holiday of it. I think we could all use one."

Trevor was suddenly solemn. "But what about mum, Jackie and Emma? I know they will want to go too?"

"I have already cleared it with your mum. Jackie is too young to travel, and Emma said she has seen plenty of circus's and needs to be here where she is really needed."

My own excitement had faded almost as rapidly as Trevor's but for a very different reason. What would others think if we took a holiday together? Couples did it all the time, but they didn't respect certain acts of intimacy the way I did. Wagging tongues would only make my new calling more difficult and jeopardize my desire for Jake to see life the way I did.

He seemed to sense my hesitation and the reason for it.

"Not to worry, my sweet Brylee," he said. "The doctor hasn't cleared me for any strenuous activity. You will be perfectly safe for another few weeks anyway."

The implication behind his words was lost on Trevor and I was grateful for that, but the very human side of me could hardly wait for the time when we could really be together.

"Can we go, Brylee? I want to ever so bad."

The earnestness of his question brought me out of my reveries in a hurry. How could I refuse based on the possible opinions of others? Nothing would happen unless I allowed it to. Besides, I had never been to a circus either, and the thought of seeing elephants and trapeze artists excited me every bit as much as it did my little brother.

"I don't see why not, provided it is not too much for your uncle," I told him. "We don't want a relapse."

"There aren't going to be any relapses," Jake insisted. "I have been confined to bed long enough and have a whole lot of living to do. Now, why don't the two of you give me a few minutes to eat and get dressed? Then I will go with you to the base of the hill and see which one of you makes it down first."

It was a magical morning in so many ways, and Trevor chattered on about the circus as we fought our way up the hillside through dry, brittle grass that was tall enough for even the most timid snake to seek refuge in. I went first, checking each footstep and bringing my feet down with such force that insects literally scurried or flew away. I didn't want to see the inside of the hospital ever again, and I certainly didn't want to see anyone else that I loved get hurt.

When we made it to the top with nothing more serious than a few insect bites and the sweat dripping into our eyes, we looked down to see Jake waving up at us. LeAnn and Emma had joined him and their eyes were shielded against the ever-present Australian sun. It was in the high 90s, but that was cool when compared to the triple digits that would come in the next few weeks. Another summer was on its way, and I could hardly believe that I had been home for over a year

"Are you ready?" I asked Trevor who was looking anxiously at the slide that seemed to go down forever.

"I guess so," he said. "Are you sure it's really safe?"

I remembered my first time and the hesitation I'd felt. It had been with our father and he had secured me tightly in front of him, cautioning me not to touch the sides of the slide while we descended. The friction alone would easily burn my hands. He should be here to share this experience with Trevor, and with Jackie when she was old enough.

But he wasn't here! He would never share any of those firsts with his younger daughter, and he would miss out on so much with Trevor. I was certainly learning that God moved in mysterious ways to put people in the places they needed to be. I would never have made the decision to come home on my own but was glad I had. I might not be able to replace my father, but I could make certain my younger siblings knew everything I did about him.

"I'll tell you what, Trevor," I said. "We will go down together and I will hold you in my arms just the way father held me. But you have to promise not to touch the sides of the slide or your hands could get hurt."

I knew he didn't need to be remind a second time. Trevor was an obedient, loving child. Regardless of their many faults, LeAnn and my father had taught him well. He would be an amazing man when he got older, as long as we didn't discourage him from embracing life in a good and honorable way.

I pushed the yellow-brown grass out of the way and sat down on the slide, pressing my tennis shoes against the sides so I wouldn't begin my descent before I was ready. Truth be told, I was a little bit nervous myself. I hadn't been on the slide for over fifteen years and some phobias never go away, like my childish fear of heights.

Trevor sat down in front of me and nestled back in my arms with his hands folded tightly in his lap and his legs fitted inside of mine. I put my arms securely around him. I wanted this to be an experience he would always remember with pleasure.

"Here we go!" I shouted as my legs moved inward and we were sailing downwards, the heavy air pulling at our faces. Trevor was shrieking with delight for the full 30 seconds it took to get to the bottom. I braced my feet for the sudden impact with the ground, and then it was over. Our bodies lunged forward but did not separate as we came to an abrupt stop at the bottom of the hill. Both LeAnn and Emma were applauding our accomplishment.

"That was fun," Trevor breathlessly exclaimed as soon as he got to his feet. "Can we do it again?"

And so we did, not once, but half a dozen times until I was too tired to even think about climbing the hill again. I collapsed on the blanket LeAnn had brought out from the house, along with a pitcher of cold lemonade and enough glasses for everyone.

"I think I am getting too old for that," I told her as she placed an ice-filled drink in my hands. "It is always so much fun to come down, but that trek up the hill is a killer when one is out of shape."

"I like the shape you're in," Jake said with smile that made me blush. I had never seen him so relaxed. Maybe his near-death experience had softened his heart enough that he was ready to feel the spirit. He was certainly different than the angry man who had stormed away from the ranch and nearly died in a cave trying to save something that belonged to another civilization.

"So, here is where the party is taking place," Uncle Ned said as we heard the screen door slam shut behind him. "I hope you don't mind that I showed up uninvited, but Emma told me where you were. I don't know how you convinced her to come, but she bakes the best deserts in the county."

She had gone into the house to check on the baby, and he had come out balancing a large piece of blueberry pie in one hand and a glass of milk in the other.

"You are always welcome in our home, Ned," LeAnn said, patting the lawn chair beside her. "Did you get a chance to see the baby? She has grown so much she is almost out of preemie clothes."

"She's a real beauty," Uncle Ned told her. "Jack would be getting his shotgun ready if he was here."

I fixed my gaze on the dry grass beneath my feet. We made every effort not to talk about my father around LeAnn. She was doing amazingly well and we didn't want another setback.

"He sure would but I guess that will be my job. or Trevor's if he is still around when she gets old enough to even know boys exist," she said, surprising me with her calmness. "The only thing I know for sure is that Jack is up in heaven watching over all of us."

Uncle Ned cleared his throat, and I knew he was at a loss for words. He believed in an afterlife of some sort, but I wasn't sure he had ever thought about trying to define what it might be like.

"What brings you over here this early in the day?" I asked to help fill the awkward silence that had descended like so many others did. "And don't tell me that you just stopped by for some of Emma's pie, not that it isn't an excellent excuse."

"Nora would kill me if she knew I was indulging this early in the day," he replied. "But I thought it was time we had a face-to-face about our ranching enterprise."

"Is something wrong?" Jake asked.

"Nothing serious, except that you picked a hell of a bad time to get yourself shot. You know better than anyone else where the animals are most likely to give birth. I hate it when they need help and I don't know about it."

Jake's body language let me know just how restless he really was, despite a show of relative acceptance .

"Just for the record, Ned, I did not ask to get shot any more than you asked to come back empty-handed when looking for that tribe of aborigines. Bloody inconvenient setback is how I choose to look at it."

"Point taken," Uncle Ned responded as he took another bite of Emma's pie. "But what I didn't tell you is that the men I was looking for were last seen not too far from your old stomping grounds."

"You mean up north where I used to fly supplies to the miners? I thought they had vacated that area years ago."

"Apparently, they are back. Once you're back on your feet maybe we could fly up there together and look around. I would like to get this matter of the cave settled permanently."

"It has been settled," LeAnn interrupted. "We are going to leave everything alone and hope no one discovers what we know. There has been too much violence already."

The color on Uncle Ned's face deepened dramatically. "But it's a powder keg just waiting to explode, LeAnn. Who is to say that the medics evacuating your brother didn't catch a glimpse of what was there, and we already know the secret Ruth is keeping about the gold nuggets allegedly found on their ranch. The media may claim there is nothing to be found but we all know a gold-siting never really dies. It just goes underground while the unscrupulous regroup."

"It's doubtful the medics noticed anything," I interjected. All this talk about the cave was making me tense and stressing LeAnn. Trevor had gone into the house to convince Emma that he needed his own piece of pie, even though it wasn't time for lunch yet. "It was pitch black, we didn't go near the room where the flecks were, and they were incredibly busy and more than a little tense after all the crawling and maneuvering. I can attest to that."

"Brylee's right," Jake said as I moved to his side. "If they had seen anything, they would have said something by now. We just need to put the whole incident behind us and get on with living. If you need me to take you up in the plane, I would be more than happy to do it."

"Not without your doctor's approval," LeAnn told him. "I can go with Ned on horseback or motorbike. Jack and I used to work together on everything before you came to our rescue. I know where the animals are most likely to be."

"Who is being unrealistic now?" Jake scolded. "You are in no condition to be traipsing all over the ranch. Besides, you have Jackie to think about, and I promised your husband I would take care of you."

"Well, you can't do that forever," she retorted. "You have someone more important to take care of now, or have you forgotten about the girl you love."

"I haven't forgotten anything," he replied, taking my hand and squeezing it. "But when I make a promise, I do so intending to keep it."

We were getting nowhere rapidly and I looked to Uncle Ned for help, but he had his head down and was devouring the last of his pie.

"I can go," I said, bringing an abrupt end to the brother-sister confrontation. "I may not know where the animals are, but I can sure as heck help Uncle Ned find them. And I can help him round up the sheep for sheering too. Both of you just need to sit back and relax and let us do it. That's right, isn't it, Uncle Ned."

He inclined his head in agreement, although I wasn't sure he considered my help even remotely adequate. Herding sheep with Jake the previous year and knowing how to set up a financial ledger hardly qualified me as a viable rancher. Still, we all understood that neither Jake nor LeAnn would be able to help until they had fully recovered. I would be Uncle Ned's right hand man for as long as necessary, and everyone else would just have to get used to it.

Uncle Ned came in his pickup truck to get me the next morning. I had called him the evening before to say that I wanted to get an early start. That was true enough since the morning hours were the most pleasant and productive, but my main reason for leaving before the sun came up was to stop a confrontation with Jake. He was a man of action and being confined to the bunkhouse was making him testy. He had lamented his inability to take care of the people he loved for hours the previous day. I was afraid he might insist on going with us, but I was even more afraid that I might not be able to stop him.

"Ready to go?" my uncle asked as I climbed into the passenger seat. "I wish there was another way of doing this, but for the time being, it looks like it truly is just you and me, kiddo. Nora wants to head up to Brisbane and check on the kids. She missed helping them move with all the hospital stuff and is feeling rather disheartened."

"I hate that our problems kept her from going. I know how much she was counting on it."

"Life had other plans for all of us, apparently, but she will be on her way in a few hours. Kinda wish I was going with her."

"And that is exactly here you should be. If all this with Jake had not happened, I would insist on it."

"I keep waiting for life to get back to the way it used to be," he retorted. "This past year has been a bloody bugger for everyone. I bet you wish you had never come home."

"Only in some ways," I replied without further elaboration.

It was a long and discouraging day. We rode Uncle Ned's motorbikes and scoured hundreds of acres through swarming bugs, stinging insects and temperatures too warm and dry for comfort looking for animals in distress and only found one. I figured that was a good thing since we saw dozens of cows and their new calves foraging for food in the lower pastures, but each animal lost meant thousands of dollars in profit gone because they would not bear offspring again. Raising sheep in the outback was a risk. Raising cattle was just plain loco.

We heard the sound of labored mooing when we stopped to knock back a drink of water, but by the time we made it over the next ridge, the calf was dead—lying unceremoniously on the ground with its umbilical cord wrapped tightly around its neck. Its mother was still struggling for life, but Uncle Ned knew she would not survive and put a bullet in her head to stop the suffering.

Had we been closer to the ranch, he might have considered hauling her back to the ranch to be butchered. But it would take hours to come back with a tractor and front end loader, and by then the meat would be spoiled. He would return later, dig a hole and bury her. It was either that, or leave her for the dingoes to tear apart.

I had watched from the sidelines dry-eyed. This was what happened when ranchers had to rely on motorbikes or horses to check on cattle that roamed freely over a nearly five-thousand acre ranch now that it had been incorporated. If Jake had been able to take his plane up, he would have found the cow in time to save both mother and offspring. But I couldn't fault him for getting shot. I held responsible the coward who had left him to die.

Trouble was, we might never know who it was. Officer Riley had called a few days earlier to say all their leads had run dry, and while the case was not being labeled "*unsolved*" and put in the dead pile there were other more pressing matters that demanded police attention. He had promised to keep us appraised of any new developments.

Uncle Ned dropped me off at the ranch before dusk.

"Looks like you are going to get an earful tonight," he said as we watched Jake come out of the bunkhouse with a determined and less-than-friendly expression on his face. "I told you we should have given him a head-up this morning. Something tells me he doesn't like his woman becoming overly independent."

"Jake isn't like that," I replied. "He knows I can take care of myself."

"That's not the point, Brylee. Real men want to take care of their women. It makes them feel masculine and strong. I still hate the fact that Nora has to work as hard as I do, but she has been right by my side for over thirty years and I don't know what I would do without her."

"I have never heard her complain."

"She wouldn't. That is just the kind of woman she is, but I still wish she could dress fancy and sip tea like all the other ladies she will be rubbing shoulders with when she goes to see Molly and Evan."

"Really, Uncle Ned," I laughed. "Can you see Aunt Nora balancing a teacup and eating biscuits? It's not who she is."

"Well, maybe it should be," he responded as Jake's hand came to rest on the outside of the passenger door.

"Are you going to sit in that pickup truck all night?" he asked as he pulled it open and extended his hand to help me out. "You might as well come on up to the house for supper, Ned. Emma has it ready to put on the table, and she will only be upset if you don't stay since she knows you will be batching it for the next few days."

"Women," Uncle Ned lamented as he climbed down to the ground. "But I wouldn't miss one of Emma's meals for anything. What's she fixing? Meat loaf, pigs in a blanket, Emu, lamb leg roast or pea and ham soup? Makes my mouth water just thinking about all the delectables that woman can concoct."

"Couldn't tell you," Jake said slapping him on the back in a manly way as we all moved in front of his truck. "But I heard something about pavlova for dessert."

"Say no more, I am on my way."

"We will be there directly," Jake told him, placing a restraining hand on my arm. "I need a moment or two with my girl."

While Uncle Ned disappeared up the stairs leading to the veranda, Jake pulled me to the far side of the truck and kissed my waiting lips. I was filthy and needed a shower but mighty glad he didn't seemed to be as upset as I thought he might be.

"Well, love," he said, brushing a strand of hair from my eyes. "I have been waiting all day to do that."

"You have," I queried, running my hands over his strong, broad shoulders. "I thought maybe you would be angry with me for leaving this morning without saying goodbye."

"I was, but I know why you did it. You were afraid I would insist on going with you and we'd have another bloody row, but I promise you that I will not do anything stupid. I need these bloody stitches out so I can show you just how much I love you."

The wicked twinkle in his eyes made my heart race. I missed him every second of every day when we were not together. We had been taking things slow and easy but now that he was starting to feel better, he might not be content with just snuggling. He was a man's man and knew just how to make a woman feel both desirable and beautiful, even when she was covered with sweat and dirt.

"Jake Johnson," I said, pushing myself just far enough away that I could see his face clearly. "I do believe you are trying to seduce me."

He nuzzled my neck with his chin sending chills down my arm. "My sweet, Brylee, there is nothing I would like more than to sweep you into my arms and carry you to the bunkhouse where I would make mad, passionate love to you all night long, but we both know that can't happen just yet."

"You're terrible," I told him, giving him a quick kiss, which he returned only too willingly. "Can't you see that this girl needs a shower and a good meal before she can be tempted?"

"I could take care of that," he replied, but I suddenly felt the lightheartedness of the moment disappear.

Jake did know how to take care of a woman. He had been doing that very thing with Beth just a few weeks earlier. I had tried to forget everything they had shared, but it was incredibly hard knowing that I would not be his first, second or even third lover when the time came. I had never been with a man before, except for being raped. What if I my response was inadequate? He would be horribly disillusioned and might even regret wasting so much time on me.

"What's wrong?" he asked, tilting my chin up with his thumb so I couldn't look away. "You know I would never force something before the time was right. I respect you too much for that."

I tried to smile, but my bottom lip began to quiver. "I know the past is over, but that doesn't stop me from worrying. You know my history and I am not exactly experienced in . . . ."

He pulled me protectively into his arms.

"Don't you know what an incredible find that makes you, love? The women I have been with might know all the right moves because they have experienced them over and over again but if the heart and soul isn't involved, it is just a pleasurable encounter. I can hardly wait to take you in my arms and love you for all the right reasons."

"Even if I don't know what I am doing?"

"Especially if you don't know what you are doing. That means I can show you things you have never experienced before. That is just about the sexiest thing I can think of."

"But what if I am so scared because of what happened that all I do is cry?"

"Then I will kiss your tears away. That guy who hurt you was an animal and your scars run deep, but I promise never to pressure you for anything until you are completely ready."

"I'm not sure that is being fair to you. You have known so many exciting women."

"None as exciting as you are. I love you, Brylee. That makes all the difference in the world to me."

During the weeks of Jake's recovery, nothing would have made me happier than holding my baby sister, playing with Trevor, learning how to fix some of Emma's mouth-watering meals or simply sitting on the porch swing with the man I loved. Basking in the peaceful enjoyment of feeling totally connected to someone else was a heady experience. I had loved Ben as completely as I had known how at the time, but we had never weathered any storms together. We had simply fallen in love, believing that our lives would follow the course we had planned. When it didn't, we simply called it quits.

With Jake, nothing had gone smoothly. We had fought and bickered and laid blame at each other's feet more times than I could count, but we had grown to trust and respect each other in the process. We still had a long way to go but I believed we could survive just about anything because we already had.

We spent what time we could holding hands as I walked him to and from the bunkhouse, stealing kisses when I thought no one was looking, playing games with the family and gazing up at the stars while we each contemplated what the future could bring. We never discussed upcoming plans, unless they involved the ranch or our family. To do so might destroy the peace and contentment we were experiencing, but we both knew the day would come when we could no longer ignore our differences. That thought terrified me because I knew I would never back down, and I doubted he would either.

So we lived our blissful life of make-believe, pretending that we had already resolved the issues that had kept us apart in the past. He continued to recover from the gun shot at home while I took on the responsibility of making sure the ranch stayed solvent until he was well enough to help me. I had already been through the spring months when calves and lambs were born, sheep sheered and some animals sold, but my father had been there to represent us in the decision process.

Now that he was gone and the two ranches had been merged, it would become a joint ruling. How could I make an informed assessment without knowing everything about the operation I was supposed to be heading? That worried me greatly. From careful observation, I had learned that my main responsibility was checking on a portion of the herds daily, mending broken fences and safeguarding flocks and herds as much as humanly possible. That seemed an impossible task since their main predator, the wild dingo, could jump like any dog and when running with a pack could easily destroy a hundred sheep in a single night.

My father had taught me during the precious time we had spent together that there were six main areas on the ranch where the animals congregated. The water from the main river flowed into smaller tributaries, forming miniature lakes that stayed wet most of the year, even when there was very little rain. But they weren't always assessable by horse or motorbike. That was why Jake's plane had become such a valuable asset. He was able to fly them over areas they would never be able to see otherwise.

But the doctor had told him a full six weeks of recovery was needed before even thinking about flying again, and I wasn't about to send him into a relapse. He and LeAnn were feeling guilty enough not being able to help out, so I turned to Uncle Ned. He was always willing to lend a hand but with Aunt Nora visiting the newlyweds, he was busier than ever with his own part of the ranch. Relying on him to take me places had become a tremendous liability since it cut in half the amount of territory we could cover in a day.

After expressing my concerns and assuring him that I would not do anything foolish, he drew me a map of the combined ranches, giving me location markers so I could find my way to the herds and back, along with a heavy dose of warnings about not going off by myself if I wasn't carrying a gun and feeling confident enough to use it.

He explained in graphic detail that the various oasis where the cattle and sheep liked to wander were also the homes to every other wild animal in the territory, eighty percent of them indigenous to Australia. I knew about snakes, spiders, scorpions, lizards and dingoes, but he assured me that I could also run into feral pigs and wild cats, numbats, quolls and Tasmanian devils that had been reintroduced to the mainland. I should never allow myself to feel overconfident because of their small size or laid back manner. They had razor sharp claws and teeth that could cut through bone.

And if that wasn't enough to make me want to stay home after my experiences with the Eastern Brown and crocodile, he talked to me about how easy it was to get lost when there was nothing but rolling sand dunes and a few tall gum trees to help determine my location. If I got into trouble, even by falling into a wash and spraining my ankle there would be no one around to help. That was why so few men lived in the outback. The country was some of the most beautiful on the planet with its red rocks, gray trees, colorful wildlife and skies that seemed to extend indefinitely, but it was also desolate and dangerous to even the most experienced rancher.

"You make me wonder if I will ever survive out here, Uncle Ned," I told him after his lengthy narrative. We were sitting in his office taking a short break while Aunt Nora was still gone. "I didn't have to worry about things like that in Los Angeles."

"My intention was never to scare you," he replied, leaning back in his chair and studying me intently as his fingertips danced on the desktop. "And I know you can take care of yourself after rescuing Jake from that cave. Hell, I don't know of any other woman on the continent who has killed a crocodile, but it doesn't stop me from worrying. I have known men who lived out here for decades and through some fluke of nature lost their lives. I just don't want that to happen to you."

"I don't want it to happen to me either, but the work still has to be done. We can't afford to lose any more animals."

"What happened with that cow and calf was inevitable. Do you really think we could have helped them, even if we had gotten there sooner?"

I sank back in my own chair. "I know there is nothing I could have done on my own. I am trying, but sometimes wonder if I will ever be strong or resourceful enough to make any difference out here. Maybe father made a mistake including me as part of his legacy. Everyone else seems to handle things so much better than I do."

"You can't expect to pick up where your father left off. He had been ranching his entire life."

"And I didn't learn a single thing about it while growing up."

"You never had much of a chance, but make no mistake now. Your father would be incredibly proud of all you have accomplished since coming home. You didn't have to stick with his plan but you did, and you will learn everything else that is needed in time. We lose a dozen or more cows and calves like that every spring—always have, always will—and that doesn't include the number of animals we never find."

"I don't see how you manage at all!" I suddenly exclaimed. "One major catastrophe could wipe out everything."

"And it has, Brylee, more than once. Only a few of the most stubborn ranchers are willing to risk everything to stay here. The key is keeping enough money in the bank to pay bills in case there is a really bad year. Did your father ever tell you about the time Old Ishmael, Asum's father, took the two of us young blokes divining for water? We must have been about eight and ten. He dragged us nearly twelve miles holding his forked stick in front of him—chanting and watching it for any sign of movement—which never came that trip, in case you are interested."

I smiled. "I'm interested in everything you and father did."

"Well, we came over this hill, and you will never believe what we saw. A pack of bloody dingoes had wiped out an entire herd of ewes and their babies. Must have been close to two-hundred head just lying there on the blood-soaked ground, writhing in pain. Some of the lambs had been ripped clean out of their mother's wombs. Tore them all to hell! Blood and guts everywhere, and not a damned thing anyone could do about it. Old Ishmael just shook his head and said it was nature's way of taking care of its own, and *carking it,* in his lingo, was just as important as being born. Never could understand that logic, but then the true aborigine never gives a damn about material things. He trusts Mother Nature to provide what is needed. So, I guess I'm just saying that if you think you will ever get rich living out here, you are bloody misguided. This is an intolerant land, and it has wiped out more than a few ranchers. We have just been lucky so far."

"Then why do you stay?" I asked. "It sounds more like a crap shoot than making a living to me."

"Because it is all I have ever known and for some reason, it is the only life I ever wanted after blowing a whole lot of time and money on my own riotous living. You will find out soon enough if you are meant to stay here."

"But I made a promise."

"So you did, but sometimes things are taken out of our hands, and we have to readjust our thinking. That's why I pushed for incorporating the two ranches. We stand a much better chance making it together than alone in this economy, provided you and Jake can make a go of it."

I swallowed back a sudden burst of unease. So much depended on Jake and me being able to live and work together. What if we couldn't resolve our issues and had to call it quits for good? What would happen to our family then?

"We're both committed to doing our best," I told him.

"That's good because I am getting too bloody old to do this on my own any longer and my offspring have no desire to lend a hand. Your father kept all the pastureland, and I got the serviceable land where we planted grain and hay. Someone, besides Jake and me, needs to know how to harvest those crops if one of us isn't around to do it."

"I could do that, if you would show me how," I volunteered. "I might not be as good as Jake, my father or even a hired hand but at least I . . . ."

His laughter cut me off mid-sentence. "I was hoping you would say that. Otherwise, I might have been forced to insist that you give it a try. Crops won't wait just because people aren't able to take care of them and with Nora gone, someone has to drive the tractor. The first crop of hay is almost ready for cutting."

I swallowed back more apprehension. My bravado had been premature since I had never been on a tractor, let alone a bailer, combine or thresher and that was the equipment Uncle Ned used. Still, if Aunt Nora could do it, then so could I. Living a more refined life like the one I had with Ben was already outside my control. I might as well go for broke when it came to keeping the commitment I had made to my father.

During the next few days, I rode out to check on as many animals as I could in the morning, always carrying a gun and hoping I would never see anything like the situation with the ewes Uncle Ned had described. I hated death, especially when it was unnecessary, but understood that managing my reaction to the unthinkable and praying for strength to endure would be my best mantra for the upcoming months.

In the afternoons, while I watched Uncle Ned overhaul harvesting equipment, I picked his brain on the best way to ensure a successful spring season since that was the time when most of the cash flowed into the ranch's accounts. He gave me solid advice on how to pick the best time for selling animals and the merchants who would give us the best price for wool. But everything still depended on the economy. People could not pay what they didn't have.

He taught me the fundamentals of how each piece of equipment ran and how to maneuver it out of the barn and into the fields. He even explained how the twine ran through the bailer and what to do if it got jammed during the bailing process. It was more than I ever imagined learning and wasn't sure I could follow through on a complete process without becoming an even greater burden, but Uncle Ned was a patient man. He went over everything until I was confident enough to try it on my own—even reassuring me after I nearly tipped over a tractor by getting the tires too close to the side of an unstable wash.

While I was busy with outside chores and unexpected responsibilities no one else could help with until fully recovered, I was unaware of how rapidly things inside the ranch house were changing. LeAnn had quit smoking after first learning she was pregnant with Jackie, and once she decided to investigate the church she gave up alcohol, coffee and tea. That meant Jake had to fend for himself in those areas when they had always been available before. I often caught him watching us with a puzzled look as we sat around the dinner table and tried to confine the conversation to areas of living that would not cause undo stress or another confrontation.

"What gives?" he finally asked me one night when we were sitting together on the porch swing, hands interlocked, underneath a mantle of brilliant, shimmering stars. "This place is so quiet it is making me nervous. Do you realize we haven't had an emergency for nearly a month?"

I leaned over and kissed his cheek. Oh, how I loved his profile, the firm set of his jaw, his prominent cheekbones and the curve of his delicious-looking lips.

"That is a good thing, isn't it?" I asked.

"It's fantastic, but there is something peculiar going on. I just can't seem to put my finger on what it is."

"Maybe it's just having new people in the house."

"It's more than that," he replied, taking my chin in his hand and gently forcing me to look at him. "Everything, and I do mean everything, has changed since you got here. There is not a drop of alcohol in the fridge. I have to brew my own coffee if I want anything other than instant, and my sister and Emma are always whispering about something I am not privy to."

"I don't know what to tell you," I said as a sudden rush of hope made my head begin to swim. I wanted desperately to divulge LeAnn's desire to join the church, but that was her secret to share when the time was right. "I really haven't been around that much lately."

He looked into my eyes with complete love and tenderness, making me feel worse than awful for withholding something that might change our entire family dynamic. The conflict I felt inside caused me to involuntarily shiver.

"Are you cold?" he asked.

Willing myself not to overreact wasn't easy. "I'm fine," I assured him as he drew me closer into the shelter of his arms.

"Then tell me what is going on around here. I feel more like a bloody outsider every day."

"Maybe it's because you are surrounded by so many women. It's you and Trevor against LeAnn, Emma, Jackie and me. We have pretty much taken over the entire house."

"I have been around gaggles of women before, and it is more than that. It's like the whole atmosphere has changed. New music is always playing. Different pictures are being hung on the walls, and everyone is reading from the same book—the one you read to me while I was unconscious in the hospital."

"If you were unconscious, how did you know what I was reading to you?"

"Don't try to sidestep the issue with me, Brylee Hawkins. I don't know how I know, I just do. I have this strong feeling that every one of you is heading somewhere else and leaving me behind. I even overheard LeAnn talking to Emma about some kind of baptism. I thought it was about Jackie's christening until they mentioned that Trevor might be doing it too. That makes no sense since I know for a fact that he was christened after he was born."

"Why didn't you ask LeAnn what was going on? I'm sure she would have told you."

"And let my sister know that I had been listening to their private conversations? She has no tolerance for eavesdropping."

"She would understand that you were not doing it intentionally."

"Damn it, Brylee," he said. "I thought I could get a straight answer from you. Didn't we promise each other that there would be no more secrets between us?"

"It isn't my place to talk about someone else's business," I told him, wishing I could somehow put his mind at ease.

"So you admit that something is going on."

"I am not denying or confirming anything, Jake. I promised to be honest with you, but this is something you really need to talk to LeAnn about."

His arm slipped from around my shoulders as his head fell into his hands.

"Well, I will be gob smacked," he said. "You and Emma have convinced LeAnn to check out that church the two of you are affiliated with. I should have put everything together long before now, but I have been too busy trying to recover from getting shot. Emma is the one you met up with in town on Sunday morning before LeAnn went to stay with her, isn't she? I can't believe I was so bloody blind. All of this hospitality and kindness was just part of some calculated scheme to get at my sister when she was too fragile emotionally to resist."

I was offended by his accusations but how could I explain that neither Emma nor I had much to do with what was happening in LeAnn's life? The Spirit was testifying the truth to her heart, and she was accepting it of her own volition.

"No one is trying to exclude you from anything, Jake, but people are free to make their own choices. Isn't that what you are always telling me?"

"This is different," he said. "Your father would be very upset. Don't you remember how he reacted when you first told him what you had become involved with? He was not a happy man."

"But he didn't withdraw his love and support, regardless of the fact that he disagreed with me. I know he sees things quite differently now."

"You can't possibly know that! No one can say with assurance what happens after we die, even those who claim to come back from the dead have varying accounts that can never proven. There might be nothing more than a big, black hole."

Oh, how I wished that the Holy Spirit could touch his heart, but that would not happen until he was ready to let it in.

" I know you have your own reasons to doubt what I say, Jake, but I do know what happens after we die—just as I know where we came from and why we are here in the first place. It is all about creating eternal families and being with them and our Heavenly Father forever. We are his children, every one of us, and he loves us unconditionally."

He looked sadly over at me. "I wish I had your faith, Brylee, but I have seen too bloody much of life to believe that God—if he really does exist—can love all people equally. There is just too much evil and despair in the world. Why can't he just be satisfied with people who are trying to do their best? It shouldn't matter what religion they embrace."

"Oh, Jake," I said, putting my arm around his weary shoulders. "I wish I could take away all of your confusion and help you truly understand, but life doesn't work that way. If we are always looking for the negative, that is the only thing we will ever find. But if we look for the good, we will find that too. That is why I found you."

"Well, you sure got a bloody prize there! I am not some God-fearing saint like Ben and right now, I am just about the most useless bloke in the universe. I can't even help the woman I love take care of this ranch."

His remark cut deeply. I hadn't thought about Ben for a long time, and it wasn't Jake's fault he had been shot. If I hadn't pushed so hard when it came to what I wanted, he would have waited until morning to go to the cave.

"You can't blame yourself for any of this, Jake, and you will be back on your feet in no time."

He snorted his difference of opinion.

"You don't know what it's like, Byrlee. I have never been laid up a day in my life, and it's killing me."

Platitudes about a rosy future would do no good when he was stuck in such a dismal present, but I couldn't just sit there without saying something reassuring. "You will be doing those things again before you know it. Your body simply needs time to heal."

"And just how long is that going to take?" he asked, running his hand through his hair. "Everything is going to bloody hell around me, and there isn't a damned thing I can do about it."

"You can be yourself and know that I love you. You are kind and gentle, strong and independent and truly the sexiest man I have ever met, and I want to be with you forever. This life will never be enough."

Sheer sorrow returned to his eyes. "That's where things still get fuzzy for me. Marriage is over when we die. All this talk about eternal families isn't healthy because none of it is going to happen."

"But it can, Jake!" I said without flinching while I reached out to him. "That's what LeAnn is learning. She and my father can be together forever. They just have to want it badly enough to make and keep certain covenants."

He brushed my hand away from his arm.

"Don't you think that I would do just about anything to have you in my life forever? I can't imagine the sorrow I will feel when one of us is gone, but there is no us being together after we die. It is a cold, cruel fact and one we have to accept."

I reached out to him again but instead of taking me in his arms as he did each evening before we retired, he simply got up and walked away. I sat there alone in the moonlight for the longest time wondering how the hole in my cloud had gotten so large that I would eventually fall right through it.

I cried myself to sleep that night. I had been so certain Jake would come to accept what I had when he saw the positive way the lives of the people around him were changing, but he was fighting the truth with every fiber of his being. Satan and his millions of minions were behind it. They didn't want him to be happy because that would be one less human spreading their lies that living for the moment was the only thing that really mattered.

Chapter 21

The next morning, which just happened to be Sunday, I arose early so I could drive into Edna for a meeting with the Relief Society presidency before the two-hour block began. Everyone else was staying home. Jackie was too little to be taken out, Trevor didn't want to miss out on anything with his baby sister, and Emma refused to leave them alone, regardless of the fact that Jake was just a few yards away in the bunkhouse.

He hadn't been anywhere since leaving the hospital and hadn't mentioned taking his plane up since the morning Uncle Ned came to visit when Trevor and I were trying out the slide. I was worried that he was either too depressed, or still too ill, to be thinking clearly. I would ask him about talking to the doctor as soon as this latest strain to our relationship lifted. He hadn't come out of the bunkhouse to say goodbye, and I hadn't wanted another argument on my mind while preparing to take the Lord's sacrament.

"I am so happy you have accepted the calling, Brylee," Sister Miller, the new Relief Society president said as she extended her hand in my direction. "You have become quite a celebrity these past few weeks."

Smiling wasn't easy as I found a place at the table where another sister, with the last name of Gorman, was already sitting. She must have moved into the branch quite recently because I couldn't recall ever seeing her before.

"It wasn't like that," I replied, looking down at the hard, dark surface. "I only did what had to be done."

"Just how many of us do you think would have killed a crocodile?" Sister Gorman asked. "I have lived in Australia my entire life but have never even picked up a gun, and the outback is one place I only want to visit."

I was definitely part of a dying breed of women who could make do without all the conveniences and distractions of modern living. We were still waiting for a tower to be built close enough that cell phones could be used at the ranch.

"I suppose it has its drawbacks, but I cannot imagine living any other place now that I'm back," I told her.

"Your determination to give it a go out there after living in a big city like Los Angeles leaves me speechless," she replied. "I have always wanted to visit the states. Don't you miss all the nightlife and glamour?"

"Not really," I told her. There were a few things I missed about living in the United States like the beach and the weather, but most of its attraction was gone now that Ben and I were no longer together. "I was much too busy working and going to school."

"That's too bad. Do you think you will ever go back?"

I was just about to tell her that I doubted I would ever return when Sister Miller cleared her throat and began speaking.

"Why don't we get down to business since we have so little time. I understand another member of the Hawkins' family may be joining us soon. We would like to organize a baby shower for LeAnn, if you think she would agree. I know she is unfamiliar with most of the sisters in the branch and it would be a perfect way for her to get acquainted."

I assured them that I would talk to LeAnn but couldn't give them a definitive answer until then. My stepmother was shy and even less inclined to being singled out than I was.

We concluded our brief meeting without further talk about me or my family. I was glad Jake's name hadn't come up because I wasn't sure what I could say about him without crying. I wanted what we had to grow into something permanent more than anything else in the world but even after everything we had been through, he was still vacillating when it came what he felt capable of doing. He was waiting for me on the veranda when I got back to the ranch later that afternoon.

"I would have flown you into town," he said as I walked up the wooden stairs to the front door of the house.

It had been an emotional day. I had been sustained during Sacrament meeting and then set apart after the block. Everyone had congratulated me on my new calling and told me how great they knew I would be, but I wasn't so sure. My blessing had filled me with a greater desire to serve God and be a righteous example to the sisters I had been called to serve, but my personal life was still in such turmoil. How could I help anyone when I couldn't even help myself?

"That's okay," I told him. "I needed time alone to think."

He stepped out of my way so I could walk past him to the hanging swing. My knees felt like soft rubber. I would have to be sitting down if this conversation turned out to be a reenactment of the previous one.

"I'm sorry for being a bloody jerk last night," he said, closing the distance between us but instead of sitting beside me, he leaned against the wooden porch railing that was much in need of paint.

"You were just expressing how you feel, Jake. I can't blame you for that."

I looked up at him. There was nothing but gentleness in his eyes. He ran his hands through his hair—a mannerism that had come quite endearing to me.

"There is just this huge elephant standing between us and I don't know how to get past it. I know you love me, Brylee, but I think you love this new church of yours more."

"I don't love it more," I told him. "But it is the only way I know of that I can be with the people I love forever."

"But that's just it, Brylee. Don't you think that if two people really love each other the God you believe in would allow them to be together, even if they didn't belong to a specific religion?"

"It's not just a religion, Jake," I said, motioning for him to sit beside me, but he didn't move from his resting place against the railing. "It is a total way of life. I haven't told anyone about this yet, but I was called to a new position of leadership today. I have been asked to help guide other women in becoming closer to Christ. It is an absolutely daunting responsibility, but one I take very seriously."

"And one I am sure you will be very good at, but I still don't see what that has to do with us."

I wanted to say something reassuring, but God's laws were unchangeable. If I wanted to return to him, I had to be willing to make certain sacrifices. How could I set a righteous example and still merge my life with that of an unbeliever who had no desire to change? I couldn't have it both ways.

"Do you really think this is easy for me, Brylee?" he continued. "I want to be with you so much I am in constant physical pain, but I can't talk about the way I really feel because it isn't what you are willing to accept. How can I fight something that can't be seen or felt? I do understand your need to believe in something, but why can't you just believe in me? I am standing right here in front of you. All you have to do is reach out and I will never leave you alone."

Oh, how I wanted to do just that, but I couldn't turn away from God just because I had chosen to fall in love with a good man who either couldn't or wouldn't give what I had wholeheartedly embraced a chance.

"I do love you, Jake, with all my heart," I said, reaching out my hand to him. "That's why it is so important to me that we are married at the right time, in the right place and don't do anything to mess it up. I know that seems inflexible, but it is only because I believe so strongly that this life isn't just about doing what makes us feel good. It's about working through challenges, making sacrifices we don't fully understand, committing to something and not wavering, and about learning to love the way the Savior does."

He sighed and sat down beside me, but he didn't take my hand or put his arm around me. He just looked out across the driveway towards the barn and bunkhouse. There was so much work that needed to be done if we wanted the buildings to remain standing for generations to come.

"I am trying to understand your need to believe in something greater than this life, Brylee, but I can't seem to do it. We can't be assured of anything that cannot be seen."

I was so weary of fighting with him over something that should be so beautifully simple to understand but our deadlock was as solid as it had ever been, even after our declarations of love and wanting to be together.

"Some things in life have to be accepted on faith," I finally said. "Don't you ever say a little prayer for safety before taking off in your plane?"

"I believe in my own ability, and the plane's integrity, to get me to where I need to go. It hasn't failed me yet."

The look in his eyes told me that his heart was filled with confusion and sorrow. He wanted me but liked his life the way it was—uncomplicated and controlled. If he even attempted to see things differently, he would have to let some of that go.

"I don't want to fight with you again tonight, Jake," I told him. "I wish you could give what I believe a chance, but I know that might be asking too much right now. I will be gone for the next few days with Uncle Ned getting the sheep to his ranch. I want to leave my copy of the Book of Mormon for you to read, if you would be willing to do that."

"I am not a reader, Brylee. You should know that by now, and I am fairly certain that reading some book isn't going to change how I feel about religion. I may not be a good Catholic bloke who goes to confession every week, but I don't think I am a bad person."

I stared into his downcast face. Maybe I should just let things go until he was really well again. It was obvious he didn't have the strength for our continual confrontations either, but I couldn't seem to do it.

"What are you so afraid of?" I asked. "I would never force anything on you. I just want you to understand where I am coming from. Eternal marriage and a forever family is just part of it."

"That's what scares me the most! I love you with all my heart, Brylee, but I know we will never move forward unless one of us is willing to compromise on all these bloody beliefs that don't make any sense to me. Since I know you will never back down, that leaves me to make all the concessions. It shouldn't be that way."

"No, it shouldn't," I admitted, sliding off the swing and kneeling on the wooden boards in front of him. I placed my hands on his cheeks so he couldn't look away.

"I don't know where to go from here, Jake. I have never loved anyone the way I love you, but what you said is true. There are certain things I can't negotiate on, and I would never expect you to accept something you don't believe."

He took my hands and removed them from his face. He looked totally defeated.

"So this is how our story ends. We won't have a future together unless I surrender to everything you want, even if it isn't for me?"

The blood rushed to my head, and I had to lean back on my heels to steady myself. It had only been a little over a month since I had found him in the cave and declared my love. Life was so cruel! If I hadn't joined the church, Jake and I would be together, but I might never be with my family forever. Oh, what a beating my faith was taking. If I remained true to my baptismal covenants, I would lose the man I loved. If I didn't, I was risking the eternity I so much wanted.

"I don't want it to be like that," I quietly admitted.

"So everything you said to me in the cave and since was a lie."

The light coming from the single bulb that hung on the side of the house cast a shadow across his face, but I could have sworn there were tears in his eyes.

"Nothing was a lie, Jake. No matter what happens between us, you will always be the love of my life."

He brushed my cheek with the back of his hand and then kissed my lips. I wanted to throw my arms around his neck and kiss him over and over again until we could think about nothing but our love for each other, but it would only postpone the inevitable. Unless one of us was willing to change, we would always end up back at the same impasse.

He looked at me for a moment longer and then got to his feet and walked away. I didn't see him again before leaving for Uncle Ned's early the next morning.

Aunt Nora greeted me at the door and invited me in for breakfast. She had returned from visiting Molly and Evan the day before so she would be around to help with the sheep shearing process. Uncle Ned was sitting at the kitchen table finishing fried eggs, toast and bacon and washing it all down with hot, black coffee. I wondered how he could eat so much first thing in the morning, but he worked hard all day and seldom snacked between meals.

"I'm not much of a breakfast eater," I told her, hoping she would not detect the depth of emotional torment in my voice. It was a good thing I would be gone for the next few days. Maybe it would give everyone at the ranch time to think more clearly. So much had changed in little more than a year. It made me wonder how God could orchestrate so many details at the same time, but mostly it made me wonder if Jake would still be at the ranch when I returned.

I couldn't blame him if he left and never came back, or even if he returned to Beth. She adored him and while she might still be angry over being dumped, I knew those feelings would vanish the moment he reappeared in her life. He was a man women could not help but love. Despite his arrogance and need to be right, there was a tenderness and attentiveness about him that defied description, and I knew my heart would never be the same again after giving it to him.

Working with Uncle Ned was pleasant. His cheerful banter kept me from dwelling on personal problems for long stretches of time. His voice sounded so much like my father's that if I closed my eyes I could see him riding his black horse, Thunder, with his back straight and the horse's reins wrapped lightly around his wrist. He had been as much at home on his horse as he had been in the ranch house where he had been born and spent his entire life.

"You're lost in thought," Uncle Ned said our second day out when we had stopped to take a drink from one of the canteens we were carrying with us. I still hadn't gotten used to the metallic taste but it was better than nothing when the dust was so thick in one's throat that it felt like the bottom of a cochy's cage, making it almost impossible to swallow.

"I was just thinking about father," I told him as tears of regret tickled my nose. I wriggled my lips to keep from crying.

"I feel so cheated because I never really got to know him, except for a little at the end. He loved this life so much, and I don't want to disappoint him."

He took off his hat and wiped the sweat from his brow with his shirtsleeve.

"I don't know how to convince you that your father never blamed you for anything. He loved you from the depths of his heart, and I truly believe he was only hanging onto life in hopes that you would come back to him."

I stared ahead and frowned at the dry foliage that kept the sheep and their predators from sight. Why couldn't it just rain, not like it had a few months earlier when the flooding had nearly destroyed my aunt and uncle's home, but just a nice gentle mist that would settle the flying dust and bring some color back to the undergrowth. I was sick to death of being hot, dirty and tired, and seeing nothing but red sand and gray-brown foliage everywhere.

"I am grateful for the time we had together," I assured him as I reined in on my horse, Rupert. He didn't like being kept from going where he wanted—most usually to a place where the grass was much more palatable. "But I never really got to know him like Trevor did. I shouldn't feel jealous because he had the kind of relationship with our father I really wanted, but sometimes I just can't help it."

Uncle Ned let out a heavy sigh, but he didn't glance in my direction. "I loved my big brother dearly, Brylee, but he wasn't always easy to be around. He made mistakes just like everyone else and ran away from things he didn't want to deal with. You just need to count your blessings that you got to know him at all."

I wanted to ask him for an explanation, but he was through with remembrances. We didn't speak of family for the next few hours. Even when we made camp at night, Uncle Ned drank his coffee and smoked his cigarettes in silence. I didn't complain. I was dead tired of chasing sheep who had no desire to be herded, and my heart was in so much pain over the possibility of losing Jake forever that it was easier to remain silent than crumbling into a heap of tears and regret in front of someone who could never understand that I was purposefully walking away from love. He would think I had completely lost my mind, and I was beginning to wonder if he might be right.

Even during the shearing process when I could have gone home at night, I opted to stay with my uncle and aunt. We worked eighteen-hour days and since NJ had not come home to help, and Jake wasn't able to, I was given the responsibility of making sure the sheep were herded into the shed when it was their turn to be sheared and then driven into the far pasture once the process was complete. Uncle Ned was working right along with the rest of the shearers, and Aunt Nora was taking care of everything else.

I was becoming a real cowgirl, maneuvering my horse in and out of animals with my hat on my head and tan, leather gloves covering my hands. I tried not to think about the previous year when Jake had been with me. We ad spent most of our time bickering, but that was better than the enmity that existed between us now. I should be reaching out to him but had no idea what I could say that would make any difference.

I was fairly certain Aunt Nora and LeAnn had been in touch because her eyes filled with compassion every time we were together at meals or in the shearing shed. But the only thing of a personal nature we discussed was Molly and the baby that would be arriving in a few months. Uncle Ned made it abundantly clear that he wasn't packing his bags and moving north the minute the child arrived, and even Aunt Nora seemed more connected to the ranch than she had been when first learning about becoming a grandmother. Maybe she had finally realized that her children had lives of their own and didn't need her like they had when they were younger.

I talked to Trevor and Emma only once when I went into the house during the middle of the day. Emma told me how big Jackie was getting and how much she loved being there to help take care of her. Trevor talked about his animals and how he wished I would come home at night so we could do something together. Neither of them said anything about Jake, and I was afraid to even mention his name. I had the sick feeling that he was gone—that I had asked too much of him and he had finally given up—but putting into words what my actions had cost all of us was impossible until my fears were confirmed.

I didn't return home until Saturday night. Everything had taken much longer than anticipated. Not that the shearers hadn't worked equally as fast as they had the year before, or that it took us longer to round up all the sheep, but I hadn't taken into account the extra time it would take to help Uncle Ned with his portion of the operation and all the cleanup.

I had ridden to places on his property I had never even known existed—places closer to the big river where the marshes were teaming with life, and not all of it desirable. My father had definitely given him the most fertile part of the original ranch, and while I hated sounding petty, I was grateful we had already signed papers of consolidation. It would eventually prove more profitable for all of us since had the better ground, but we certainly had the most.

LeAnn was sitting on the veranda swing rocking Jackie and singly softly to her when I arrived home, hot, grimy and emotionally and physically drained.

"I'm glad you are back," she said. "We have missed you."

Her words were welcoming, but the look of pity and compassion in her eyes made my heart lurch.

"He's gone, isn't he?"

I sank down onto one of the lawn chairs and looked down at the wooden planks beneath my feet. They had been worn smooth by generations of Hawkins' feet passing over them. If I looked at her, I would most certainly cry.

"I'm so sorry, Brylee," she said. "I tried to get him to see reason, but he feels like he has been betrayed by everyone he loves. He just packed his bag and left. Trevor is brokenhearted and so are Emma and me."

Not a muscle in my body moved as I sat like a granite statue for the longest time. Life no longer mattered. Jake and I had spared like gladiators, but we had also let the barriers down so we could fall in love. How was I going to survive without him? He stimulated every part of me, making me feel complete and whole. Now, he was gone. I had driven him away and in doing so, had destroyed everyone's lives.

"None of this is your fault, LeAnn. It's mine," I finally replied as I stared blindly out towards the bunkhouse whose dark windows were more than menacing. "I never should have pushed so hard about the church when I knew he wasn't ready."

"No one blames you for taking a stand, Brylee. My brother is a complicated bloke and doesn't always make the best decisions when it comes to matters of the heart. It is easier to run away than face obstacles and challenges. That seems to be part of the Johnson genes."

"But I didn't even give him a fighting chance. I just let him know that no matter how much I loved him it would never be enough unless he believed the same things I did."

"You know what you need to be happy. That is not a crime."

"It is if it drives someone you love with all your heart away."

"A few months ago, I would have backed my brother completely about all this religion stuff being nonsense, but losing your father has made me re-evaluate everything."

"Did you tell Jake how you feel?"

"I did! Unfortunately, it wasn't the best timing on my part either. When I told him that I was investigating the church because I knew it was the only way I could be with your father again, he simply threw his hands in the air and said that he knew when he was no longer wanted or needed—even by his own family. He doesn't see the church as keeping us together; he only sees it as tearing us apart."

The beat of my heart landed with a thump. We hadn't considered his needs nearly enough. He had been trying to recover from an almost fatal gunshot, and we had been hitting him with concepts and unwanted disclosures that had pushed him over the edge.

"I don't suppose he is ever going to forgive us after this," I said. "I can only imagine how lonely and betrayed he must feel."

"No one was trying to betray him, Brylee, but I do understand how he feels. We are supposed to be there for each other no matter what. I should have realized how hard it was for him being cooped up at the ranch while you were away doing all the work. My little brother has always been in command of his life, except for two times—losing our parents and losing Wendy. It's hard for him to share how he really feels, but I think at some level he understands that there is something greater than what is visible to the naked eye. It scares the hell out of him because he can't stand being out of control. It is the only way he knows how to survive."

"But you have been able to see that there is more to life than just survival."

"Only because I had more time with our parents and have children of my own who show me very clearly that God does indeed exist. I have also known complete oneness with your father and want desperately to have that again. Jake has never had those connections. He and Wendy had a hot and passionate love affair he thought was going to last forever. When it didn't, he took it as just one more sign that if there was a God, he just didn't care."

"But that's not true!"

"Try telling that to someone who is afraid to feel much of anything because it is usually associated with pain. Jake is a good man, but he is so afraid of being hurt again that he refuses to take any risks that really matter. He knows how to handle his life as it is now, but the thought of change terrifies him, even if he knows it is for his own good."

I leaned back in the chair and looked up into the clear, dark sky. How I longed for my own star to wish on, but that was a fairytale. Life wasn't filled with happy endings just because a person was trying to do what was right. LeAnn's decision to investigate the church was a true miracle. But the daily trials were still soul-consuming, and I was so tired of fighting all the world protested as being good simply because it offered mortal satisfactions.

"How did everything get so messed up?" I asked. "I thought our love would be sufficient to jumpstart any change, but I guess nearly dying wasn't dramatic enough."

She leaned over and kissed Jackie's cheek.

"Sometimes life seems impossible, but we are not going to give up. I hate that my brother ran away from the one woman who could give him what he really needs and wants, but he has his agency just as we do. We have to believe that eventually he will figure things out and come home to all of us."

"But what if he has gone back to Beth?"

Just saying the words made the possibility more plausible. What man wouldn't run back into the arms of a woman who clearly adored him, and Jake was a passionate, impulsive man who only knew one way of dealing with pain—fill it with someone else.

"I have been praying all week that hasn't happen," LeAnn said, interrupting my disturbing thoughts. "Don't get me wrong, Beth is a good girl, but Jake has never really cared about her."

"She can give him love and affection without any conditions. Maybe that is all he is really looking for."

"Not Jake! He needs to be challenged. She accepts him just as he is, selfish, temperamental and uncontrollable. How can that possibly be a foundation for anything except disaster? If they are together he will just keep drifting along, never understanding that the most important things in life seldom come without personal sacrifice and accountability."

"But loving me came with too many conditions."

"Only because you were being honest with yourself. Men like Jake have to be believe they are making their own decisions. The trouble is that they are usually too stubborn to see what is right in front of them. If you had backed down, Jake never would change because he got you on his own terms without making any concessions. That's what happened with your father. You only saw the way it was with us in the end. You didn't live through the years he blamed himself for your mother's death and you running away. And because he blamed himself, he had to blame me because I gave in to him and eventually got pregnant. If we had never become involved, his life would have gone on just the way it always had."

"But you made it! Why can't it be that way with Jake and me?"

"Because we were incredibly lucky, that's all! I was barely seventeen when we met, but I fell in love with him, even though I knew he was married and would never leave your mother. I thought I could live in her shadows until I found out Trevor was coming and then I wanted what she had, a real home and a legitimate family."

"That's what most every girl wants."

"I suppose, but it didn't change the fact that your father believed in the sanctity of marriage, even if he couldn't live it. He told me that from the very beginning. If your mother, God rest her soul, had not died in that accident, I would have raised Trevor on my own."

"I don't believe my father would have let you do that. He was an honorable man."

"Yes, an honorable man who had been unfaithful to his wife. You see we can't have it both ways, Brylee. We always end up paying for our mistakes. If you back down with Jake, you will have to accept the kind of life he has to offer right now, and that would be one without the gospel. Why would he ever consider changing when he already had what he wanted? I think you have known that all along, and that is why you made the only decision you could."

I sat outside on the porch long after LeAnn took Jackie inside to put her to bed. What she had said about my relationship with Jake made perfect sense. By its very nature, change breeds fear. Hadn't I discovered that for myself when I joined the Church of Jesus Christ of Latter-day Saints? I had thought Becky was crazy going to church every Sunday, paying tithing, living what she called the Word of Wisdom, avoiding r-rated movies and going out of her way to be kind and considerate to everyone. But she hadn't given up on me—even though I had been overtly condescending—and she certainly hadn't given me any ultimatums.

True, there hadn't been a romantic component to our relationship. That had only happened when I met her brother, Ben. But even he had never pushed me to accept anything before I was ready. He had been my friend and led me to the truth by example. It was only after I had decided for myself that the church was true and I wanted to be a part of it that he told me how he felt.

Why couldn't I have done the same thing with Jake? It seemed to me that we had done everything backwards by falling in love before we understood how stubborn we both were. What if I never saw him again? Never had a chance to give him the time he needed to decide for himself if religious convictions were necessary to his ultimate happiness? Force in any form was one of Satan's tactics, as was taking away someone's agency. If Jake and I ever found our way back to each other it would only be with God's help.

I called Sister Miller before going to bed. I hated missing Sunday meetings but my entire body ached, especially my heart. It was more unbearable than when I had lost my father. All I wanted to do was crawl into bed and stay there. How would we manage without Jake? We were the most unlikely group of survivors ever assembled. Emma was past eighty, though she never told anyone her exact age. LeAnn had just been through a difficult pregnancy and had Jackie to take care of. Trevor was only a child, and what I knew about running a ranch could be put in seamstress' thimble—regardless of the fact that I had been working tirelessly the past few weeks trying to keep our part in the corporation from falling apart.

It seemed that after all we had endured we were doomed to failure, and telling Uncle Ned and Aunt Nora what had happened would be the hardest confrontation of all. They believed that Jake and I had worked through all the nonsense religious differences brought and were finally together.

Jackie's crying in the early morning hours brought me upright in bed. Since sleep had been minimal at best I went downstairs to see if there was anything I could do to help.

"LeAnn's, it's me," I whispered, wrapping lightly on her bedroom door. I heard the rocking chair stop moving and a moment later we were facing each other.

"I'm sorry Jackie's fussiness woke you up," she said as she brushed at the tears that lined her weary face. "But she senses something is wrong and refuses to nurse, even though I know she is hungry."

I held out my arms, and she placed my tiny sister in them.

"This just isn't working. I have tried to hold everything inside so Emma and Trevor will not be more upset than they already are, but I am terrified that we will never survive with both your father and Jake gone. We can't do all of the work by ourselves, even if we knew what needed to be done."

Jackie snuggled close to me and quit crying.

"See," LeAnn said as fresh tears started to fall. "My own daughter likes you more than she does me."

She retraced her steps and sat down on the edge of the bed. I followed her into the room.

"That's not true, LeAnn," I told her, "She knows you are her mother and depends on you for everything."

"Then why do I feel like such a failure? I can't even provide a livelihood for my children. Your father leaving this house to me doesn't mean much if I can't pay the utilities or taxes."

Light footsteps in the hallway made both of us stop talking and turn around. Emma was walking towards us. She was wearing a bathrobe and her white hair stood up in the back. It was evident that our dialogue had awakened her.

"I'm sorry for waking you up too," LeAnn apologized with such a worn-out sigh that I wondered if everything had become too much for her and she was contemplating another disappearing act herself. That seemed to be standard operating procedure for every adult member of our family when the stress became too much.

"You didn't wake me up. I wasn't sleeping," Emma replied as she tried to cover a yawn with the palm of one hand. "But since we are all up and likely not going to get any more sleep tonight, might I suggest some warm milk and conversation in the kitchen?"

"I don't like warm milk, Emma, and you know it," LeAnn retorted, but she still moved into the hallway. "This is one of those times when a nice cup of strong, black coffee sounds mighty appealing but since I have chosen to give that up, I will have hot cocoa instead."

I followed the two women down the short hallway to the kitchen and sat down at the table with Jackie asleep in my arms. Then I watched as the teapot was filled with water and put on the stove to heat. Emma had a bag of marshmallows already sitting open on the counter.

"I think we have a few decisions to make and I want to be part of them," she promptly stated.

LeAnn frowned. "But what we are facing isn't your problem, Emma. You have already done so much for us."

"Nonsense! You are my family now," she replied, placing her hand on top of LeAnn's as they lay helpless on the edge of the kitchen counter. "I know Jake is gone and that neither one of you is going to talk about what that means for all of us, unless I am the one to bring it up. It is always best to make decisions while there are still options available."

"What options?' LeAnn asked. "With my brother missing in action, we might as well turn the land and the house over to the Aborigine Society. They are going to get it eventually anyway."

"Not if I have anything to say about it," she replied. "We might be women, but we are not helpless. With God on our side, we can accomplish anything we set our minds to. It might just take a little ingenuity to do it."

The two women looked at each other with such compassion and understanding that my thoughts immediately turned to the story of Ruth and Naomi in the Bible. Their circumstances might be slightly different than mother and daughter-in-law but people didn't have to be bound by blood to be family as long as they loved each other enough to stick together through even the worst of times.

"I have been thinking a lot about our situation since Jake left and believe I have come up with at least a temporary fix," Emma continued. "But before I even suggest what I have in mind, I want you to know that I have complete faith in both of you. Women in the outback have always been strong, and the two of you are no exception."

"I don't feel very strong," LeAnn said as she sipped her cocoa. "I feel like shag on a rock. I just want to know that my children will have a roof over their heads while they are growing up. I can't believe my own brother took off the way he did. He knows the dire situation we are in."

My little sister was sleeping now, but I was beginning to understand why she was having trouble nursing. LeAnn was in a horribly volatile state, and Jackie could most certainly detect all the stress and tension in the house.

"I know you are both tired, frustrated and a little heartbroken too," Emma said. "But we aren't going to be evicted tomorrow. The house is paid for, and Ned will get a good price for the wool."

"How can you be so confident?" LeAnn questioned. "Just look around this room! The flooring needs to be replaced, the faucet leaks, and I saw a mouse in the pantry this morning."

"No worries about the mouse," Emma retorted. "He has been disposed of."

LeAnn forced a cryptic laugh. "So we have one less mouse! None of us have the physical strength or the knowledge to do what needs to be done to set this place in order. I can drive a tractor, but I can't fix it. I can nail boards on a fence, but I can't put the posts in the ground so they will stay up. Heck, I can even round up the cattle and sheep, but I can't wrestle them down to be branded. We need a man here to help us, and I am not going to ask Ned for any more favors. He deserves to live his own life without us adding further complications to it."

I listened to their conversation—my guilt becoming stronger with each sentence uttered. Telling Jake how I felt about him was a huge mistake. If I had remained silent, he may have been irritated with me for the rest of life, but he never would have run away from his family, even if he decided to move on with someone else.

"It's all my fault!" I suddenly blurted out.

LeAnn slammed her fist down on the table nearly waking the baby. Her eyes were flashing.

"I never want to hear you say that again! You are not the problem. My brother is a bloody fool for running away from the people who love him—even if we do have some differences of opinion."

"I agree with LeAnn," Emma said, and I saw her chest heave with unspoken emotion. She had been through a great deal in her life—far more than what I had been privy to thus far. "We need to have faith that he will come to his senses, recognize what he has given up and come back. Love is a powerful motivator but in the meantime, we need a plan that will get us through until he does."

"But what?" I asked. "When I look into the future, all I see inside this house is sorrow. And the outside isn't any brighter. What is not already in complete shambles is getting that way in a hurry."

"Then don't look into the future," she told me without hesitation. "Just concentrate on the moment. We can make it through this hour, and the next one, and pretty soon we will have made it through another day."

"But that doesn't bring Jake back, and it doesn't solve our problem in needing more help than we can ever provide on our own," LeAnn said.

"We wouldn't be in this situation together if God did not have something in mind for us to learn," Emma countered. "Have you even considered the idea that Satan is behind some of what is happening? He knows he can best destroy most everything by causing doubts and uncertainty to override both faith and reason. He will do everything in his power to make us believe that bad things are happening because we are better off without Christ's gospel."

"But we know that isn't true," LeAnn said. "I may not be baptized yet, but my convictions are strong enough to assure me that faith is the only thing that will get us through the tough times."

"Then let's cling to that," Emma told her. "If we show Heavenly Father our complete trust in him, he will open the windows of heaven for us."

Her description of God's mercy and blessings for those who truly believed filled my soul with unspeakable joy, but before I could visualize what her words meant for our family LeAnn was speaking again.

"I want to be strong for my children and Jack but literally do not know how to do it."

"May I suggest that we start with prayer," Emma replied. "God can only guide us if we are willing to ask for his help and then really listen for an answer. Besides, I have always been rather fond of the old adage that *it is hard to stumble when on your knees* because I know it's true."

And so we knelt around the kitchen table together. I was incredibly grateful for having these strong women in my life. We came from different beginnings, but we were sisters now and forever. And maybe, with God's help, we could make it. I only knew that nothing would be accomplished if we didn't try.

I managed to sleep for an hour or so before the sun came up and Trevor was knocking on my door.

"Can I come in?" he breathlessly asked.

I knew he had just run up the stairs after finding out from his mother or Emma that I was back at the ranch but still felt a chill as I wondered what could possibly be said that would make things better. I instinctively pulled the sheet around my neck to add extra warmth.

"Of course you can, Trevor," I said with less enthusiasm than intended.

He burst through the door with Copper at his heels. The little dog seemed bigger than she had the week before, but then so did Trevor. They both landed on my bed with separate thumps.

"I missed you," he said, pushing his body closer to mine until I had my arm around his shoulders. He was still wearing the sleeping attire I had given him for Christmas and it was getting too small.

"I was afraid I would never get to see you again. Uncle Jake left right after you did and nobody knows where he is."

When I looked at his upturned face, his eyes were filled with questions I could not answer. "That's what your mother said, but we will do everything in our power to find him."

"How?" he asked. "Uncle Jake has never left us before. Why did he do it, Brylee?"

I kissed the top of his head. The look of grief and loneliness in his eyes matched my own, but how could I explain the reason for his uncle's sudden departure when Trevor was too young to understand that love wasn't always enough?

"Maybe he just needed some time alone to think."

"But that's not fair," Trevor insisted. "Nobody thinks I care that people leave, but I do. Father left! Mother left! You left! And now Uncle Jake is gone. When is it my turn to run away? No one pays attention to me now that Jackie is here, but I have feelings too."

The pain in my heart shifted from its usual focus. Not one of us had been thinking about his needs when we tried to escape our personal problems.

"Oh, Trevor," I sighed, chewing down on my lip before continuing. "Adults do really stupid things and can be very selfish. One day they think they have all the answers and the next day they simply lose their way."

"But that doesn't tell me why Uncle Jake left. Did I do something wrong? He wasn't even better yet. We have to find him, Brylee. We just have to."

I wanted to do just that but had very little to go on, unless I was willing to forgo all pride and contact Beth. And if he was with her, he would not come back willingly just because I asked him too. I had ruined everything without even trying.

"Jake loves you with all his heart, Trevor, and you have brought nothing but joy into his life. I promise to do my best to find him but there are times when people's needs cannot be supplied by the ones who love them most.

Jake had left the ranch in his plane, that much we knew for sure since it was not sitting in its accustomed place behind the barn. It worried me that he was flying when it had yet to be cleared by his doctor, but he had been gone for nearly a week and could be any place in Australia by now.

When I asked LeAnn if she had checked his truck, she told me she hadn't felt it necessary since it was still in the shed, but I needed something to ease my mind so I took his keys from the hook by the back door after breakfast. He would certainly come back for it at some point, but all I found was proof of insurance and licensing information. There wasn't so much as a scrap of paper on the floor or underneath the seats.

That left me with the bunkhouse and LeAnn had already told me that was one place she could not go. She hadn't even tried to contact anyone from his past because she needed to believe he would return the moment he came to his senses, and if he knew she had been trying to track him down it would only complicate what could otherwise be a happy reunion.

I understood how she felt, but it seemed to me that not knowing where he was or what had happened to him was far worse than the truth could ever be.

So while Trevor was busy helping Emma in the kitchen, I crossed the short distance to the bunkhouse in a hot wind that had unexpectedly come up. It tore at my sunburned arms and made them sting, but it was nothing when compared to the pain I felt inside for what my actions had caused my family.

I opened the door and flipped the light switch. The curtains were drawn, and it took a moment for my eyes to adjust to the lack of light provided by a single bulb in the ceiling of the living and sleeping area. His bed was made, but his closet door was open and most of his clothes were gone.

I sat down on the bed and hugged his pillow to my chest. It smelled just like he did, and fresh tears filled my eyes. We had been through so much together during the past twelve months, and my love for him wasn't just based on attraction. It came from deep inside because regardless of our differences Jake had become my best friend and the man I could share anything with—anything but the one thing that kept us apart— the restored gospel of Jesus Christ.

Knowing there was nothing left in the bunkhouse to do— other than experiencing continual waves of both sorrow and remorse—I was about to leave when I noticed an envelope that was partially hidden underneath the refrigerator. It must have blown off the table when the door was opened. I hung back as fingers of fear traveled up my spine, but postponing the inevitable would not make it any less real.

My name was printed in bold letters on the front, and my hands were visibly shaking when I reached inside and pulled out a single, folded sheet of paper.

"Dear Brylee,

"I know I am taking the coward's way out by not telling you in person that I am leaving, but I can't bear to see the pain in your eyes again. You deserve that eternal husband and family you are always talking about. Maybe if I had told you to go after Ben instead of kissing you that night on the beach both of our lives might have turned out differently, but I was very selfish back then and wanted you for all the wrong reasons.

"I spent the entire night reading the book you loaned me, and while it is an interesting story with plenty of practical advice, I find it impossible to believe that some man in the early eighteen hundreds found a gold book of sacred writing in a mountain and translated it from a language no one else had ever seen.

"Maybe it is just the cynic in me, but the truth is that I can't seem to believe in anything anymore. I really do wish I

was the man who could make all your dreams to come true but if I stayed here, I might let my carnal desires override my great love and respect for you. I can't allow that to happen.

"So I am leaving you my bankbook. I have already made arrangements for you to withdraw everything. There's about $100,000 in savings. Use that to hire someone to help out around here. My truck is paid for. You can either sell it or keep it but money isn't exactly necessary where I am going.

"I may not believe in God and forever like you do, Brylee, but I will love you until the day I die. Jake"

My knees were so weak I slumped into the nearest chair where surges of disbelief and horror numbed my entire body. There was only one place I could think of where he would not need any money, and he had spelled out very clearly why he had gone.

How could I tell anyone what he had written? I pounded on my forehead as if that singular demonstration would somehow clear my mind of all the terrible scenes rushing through it. I pictured his body lying in a morgue in some remote part of the Australian outback, covered by a sheet and with no one to claim it. Or worse, lying in the rubble of his plane after it had crashed into the side of a mountain in a place where it would never be found.

When I was finally able to focus, I slipped to my knees. I didn't know what had happened to Jake, but God did. I'm not sure how long I knelt there, or even if I uttered any words, but the next sound I heard was Trevor's voice coming from what seemed a lost oasis outside the bunkhouse door.

"Are you in there, Brylee?" he was calling out as I attempted to pull myself together. "Emma said lunch was ready and you were supposed to come."

"Yes," I responded, forcing myself to my feet. My eyes were dry and that surprised me, but it was hard to cry when everything inside felt dead. I opened the door before he had time to do it himself.

"What's wrong?" he asked when he saw me standing like an effigy with the letter still clutched in one hand. "You are awfully white."

I crumpled the lone sheet of paper and held it behind my back. "It's just the bad lighting. Tell Emma to start without me and I will be there as soon as I can."

His brow furrowed into a deep frown. "Are you sure you don't want me to get mum?"

"No need for that," I told him as I tried to smile and maneuver him back through the open door. "You certainly don't want to upset Emma when you know how she feels about being punctual to meals."

He was reluctant to leave, but he had been taught to obey the adults in his life. So he shook his head and shuffled away, leaving me alone in a tiny strip of sunlight. How could I ever return to the house and tell LeAnn and Emma what Jake had written?

I fell backwards on his bed and curled up in a fetal position. This couldn't be happening! Jake would walk through that door and tell me that he had been wrong about everything. Then he would take me in his arms and smother me with passionate kisses while confirming that he did believe in God and forever and that by working together all of our dreams would come true.

But that didn't happen and a short time later, LeAnn walked in without knocking. Her face was drawn and haggard.

"Trevor said you were sick. What happened?"

I held the now moist letter out to her without speaking. The damning message could not be withheld. Jake was gone, possibly for good, and it was my fault for falling in love with him.

I heard the note crinkle in her hands but couldn't bring myself to look at her. Guilt, in its most debilitating form, was making it hard for me to breathe. How could anyone make so many mistakes trying to live as the Savior had done?

Suddenly I heard her loud intake of breath, and then she was sitting on the bed beside me.

"If my brother wasn't already gone I would put him in a time-out where he belongs!None of this is your fault, Brylee. Jake has been angry at the world ever since he was a child. I used to think he would outgrow it, but he blames God for everything bad that has ever happened from losing our parents and Wendy to losing you. He tries to believe in love, but once he lets someone into his heart that person always disappears."

"Just like I disappeared, figuratively speaking, when I put the church before him."

"Do you love my brother?" she asked, placing her hand on my shoulder as I stared at the faded red curtains hanging in front of the only window in the room.

"With all my heart."

"Then you have to believe things will work out, even with our God-given agency. During the past few months, I have learned that we need to want something so badly we are willing to surrender everything for it. I didn't think I could ever forgive God for taking your father away but he has given me so many blessings, despite all the pain. I have Jackie, Trevor, you, and the promise of being with my family forever. If you hadn't come home and shared the gospel with me none of that would be possible."

"But you have accepted it. Why can't Jake?"

"Other than the answer I have already given, I simply don't know. God is in charge of him now, and whatever happens is out of our hands."

I wasn't sure what surprised me most, her acceptance that Jake might be gone for good or her total belief in God's grace for all of us. My emotions were still too raw to think clearly.

"How can you say that when he is your brother?"

"Because Jake has to find his own way back to us, Brylee, whether in this life or the next. I don't know of any other way to look at it."

"But what about Trevor? I promised him I would do everything possible to bring Jake home. He thinks he is responsible for each one of us leaving."

"I know he does. He was such a happy child until your father died, and then I fell apart and took off. You think you know guilt? Try dealing with running away from your own child who had lost every bit as much as you had."

She was trying to be supportive, but she hadn't driven someone away from his home.

"It's not the same thing, LeAnn. Jake left because I refused to bend on anything. How much more should a little boy have to take?"

"I don't know, but I have been thinking that it might not be such a bad idea to take my children away from the ranch for a while. There are just too many sad memories here."

Her words were crystal clear, but the idea of taking my little brother and sister away for even a short holiday was more than repugnant. This was their home. If anyone should leave, it was me.

"That's a horrible idea," I said as tears that had refused to come earlier began sliding down my cheeks. "There has to be some way of pulling this family back together."

"I don't know what that could possibly be," she responded. "We can't run this ranch without Jake. I have two small children to raise and you deserve to have a life of your own."

"But father worked so hard to keep this ranch in our family."

"I'm not suggesting we do anything permanent right away. I am just trying to decide what is best for my children. The outback is no place for them when there is a civilized world just two hours away. There are far too many dangers, and Trevor was doing so much better when we lived in town with Emma. He even had friends his own age. Is it right for us to deny him a chance to do things with other children? You said yourself how lonely it was for you growing up out here."

"But I only had my mother and father. Trevor and Jackie have each other, and they have you and me and Emma and Uncle Ned and Aunt Nora, and . . . ." I couldn't finish my thought because Jake was gone and might never be coming back.

LeAnn patted my knee as if I was a child. "We don't have to talk about this right now. Come in and eat something. None of us can afford to get sick."

It was an awful day, and I'm not sure how I survived the rest of the afternoon and early evening, but somehow I managed to play a few games with the family before taking Trevor up the stairs and putting him to bed.

"I love you, Brylee," he said, wrapping his arms around my neck as I tried to stand up after reading him one of his favorite stories.

"I love you too," I replied, fighting back another blitz of tears. I was so tired of crying all the time. Why couldn't life just give us a little prolonged happiness occasionally? Even Jackie's presence had not brought the joy I hoped for. A baby needed to feel peace and security and there was very little of that in our mixed up household.

"Now get to sleep. I was thinking about saddling the horses in the morning and riding over to Uncle Ned's. I bet you didn't know that he found a little rabbit that hurt its leg while we were out herding sheep. He has it in a cage in the barn and is trying to nurse it back to health. I know he could use your help."

"Would he let me take it out and hold it? I would be really careful."

"I think that could be arranged. Uncle Ned told me that he could see you becoming a veterinarian when you get older."

"I like taking care of animals," he said.

"And you are very good at it." I pulled the sheet up so it covered his legs. It was too warm for anything else. "See you in the morning, little brother."

My heart was heavy as I walked down the stairs and into the kitchen where LeAnn and Emma were sitting at the table drinking lemonade.

"Is Jackie asleep?" I asked.

"Amazingly enough, she is," LeAnn said. "I hope you don't mind but I shared Jake's letter with Emma while you were reading to Trevor."

The air came out of my lungs through parted lips as I sat down at the table with them.

"I don't want to rehash what we talked about earlier," LeAnn continued. "But we do have to figure out how we are going to run things around here until Jake comes back. I refuse to accept that he meant anything by his note, except that he needed time to get over some of the pain."

"I think he spelled out his intentions quite clearly," I retorted. "Leaving everything behind, except for his plane and his clothes, can only mean one thing."

She gave me an irritated look. "I know you think it's hopeless, Brylee, but you don't know him the way I do. He is headstrong, impulsive and inclined to self-defeating behaviors, but he loves his family and will stay away forever—even if he is upset with most of us right now. That said, I do recognize that we are not super women and need a man around to help."

I rubbed my eyes and tried to concentrate on what she was saying. At least she wasn't as adamant about leaving with the children as she had been a few hours before.

"LeAnn's right," Emma said. "I wasn't raised out here, but even I can see that three women and two children can't take care of things for long."

"So what do you propose?" I asked.

"I'm not sure, but we have to keep things from falling apart," LeAnn respond.

"What things?" I asked because I didn't have the heart to talk about Jake any longer.

"For starters, there is a leak in the waterline going into the barn. I tried to dig it up and fix it, but I am no plumber and the ground is too hard."

"I will look at it tomorrow," I said.

"You aren't getting the point, Brylee. It is not just a broken water line. The tin is coming off the barn roof, we are out of grain and the hay is nearly gone. Every bit of grass on the ranch has dried up because there has been no rain, and it is the beginning of fire season. Add to that horses that need to be ridden, calving that needs to be supervised, hospital bills that need to be paid, and that is just the beginning of the never-ending list I have been compiling in my head."

Frustrating was driving her venting because she had been out of commission for such a long time, but refuting what she had said was impossible because I had seen things that needed to be done too. We really were sinking and if we didn't do something soon, there would not be a ranch left to save.

"I'm taking Trevor over to Uncle Ned's in the morning and will talk to him about what has happened. Perhaps he will have some ideas."

"What we need is another miracle, and I am almost afraid to ask God for more," LeAnn said as both Emma and I looked down at the floor.

Our lives had been filled with miracles the past few weeks. Jake's life had been spared, Jackie had entered the word unharmed and Emma had come to our rescue more times than I could count.

I wanted to stand firm and true, but as I walked up the stairs towards bed that night, I knew I could never let Uncle Ned know just how desperate things were on our part of the ranch.

Maybe LeAnn's first assessment of our situation was right. There were plenty of corporations who would be glad to get their hands on our property and, despite the provisions that had been set in place, any will or trust could be contested and broken if the desire to do so was great enough.

When I opened my eyes the next morning, I wished everything could go back to the way it had been with Jake in the bunkhouse and the rest of us waiting for him in the kitchen so our day could begin, but that wasn't going to happen today so I dressed quickly and headed downstairs.

Trevor was excited to be out of the house and riding our father's horse, Thunder, again. I set the pace as we rode along —a slow canter so I didn't have to worry about him having to rein in a horse that was still too strong for him to handle on his own. For his age, my little brother was an excellent horseman, but we had seen enough tragedy and sorrow to last a lifetime.

He chattered happily all the way to Uncle Ned's. When we got there and the horses had been tied off and watered, he ran into the barn. I stayed by the hitching post trying to figure out what to say about the impossible situation I had helped create by falling in love with a man who should have remained off-limits. A few minutes later, Uncle Ned came out of the barn laughing.

"I swear that boy is just like his father. He isn't afraid of anything."

"Did something happen I should know about?" I asked.

"No, it was just an observation. He has such a bloody fondness for animals and they seem to know intuitively that he is only there to help them."

"My little brother has a very tender heart, and I am afraid the adults in his life have not been very considerate of his feelings lately."

"Oh, Brylee," he sighed as we stood leaning on the fence and looking over the herd of sheared sheep we had decided to sell. "I hope we are not going to have another yak about your father. He was a member of the human race who made his share of mistakes, but it certainly wasn't his fault he got cancer. If every person who smoked got it there would not be bloody soul left in the outback, with the exception of you and certain young ones."

"I'm not talking about father this time," I told him. "I am talking about how horribly the adults in Trevor's life have let him down. Father died. LeAnn left right after he was buried. Then I took off because I was having issues of my own, and now Jake has gone because of me."

"Hold on just a minute," he said, giving me a look of surprised concern. "I thought Jake was still recuperating at the ranch."

"He was, but he took off in his plane while I was gone and nobody knows where he is or if he is ever coming back."

"That doesn't sound like the Jake Johnson I have known for the past six years. He is as honorable and reliable as they come. He must have had one hell-of-a-reason to leave. Did the two of you have a lover's spat?"

"It's more complicated than that, Uncle Ned," I said, looking at the tree-lined mountains in the distance and trying not to cry again. They looked more brown than ever.

"Bloody hell, Brylee, everything in life is complicated. But you still need to have a little faith in other people. Jake is as good a man as you will find anywhere."

"I know that, but we seem to have come to a deadlock over religion."

"Only because you think two people can't be happy together unless they share everything in common? Life would be mighty dull if that was true. Nora is a good, strong Catholic girl, and it is no news to anyone that your father and I are just about as heathen as they come. Don't you think it bothers her that we have been together for over 30 years and have never gotten married? In the eyes of the church, we have been living together in sin for over a quarter of a century. But that doesn't change the way we feel about each other? Hell, no! Nora is my life."

"Then why don't you marry her, Uncle Ned? I know it would make her happy."

"Because I have seen too many miserable marriages that ended in bitter divorce or death. We are together because we want to be, not because some piece of paper says we have to be come hell or high water."

"It doesn't have to be like that."

"Maybe not, but why take the chance. Nora and I have something amazing together and are going to be grandparents. Nothing can compare to that."

I knew better than to say anything more. I had already alienated enough people with my religious fervor. The day of enlightenment and modern living meant doing whatever felt good. People no longer cared about God or what he said— anciently or through modern-day prophecy.

"You have been very lucky," I told him.

"Luck has nothing to do with it! We have worked hard building our relationship and have made hundreds of compromises. That's what you do when you love someone."

"Are you saying I haven't done that with Jake."

"I'm not saying anything but you talk a whole lot about not judging others, yet you can't let Jake into your life because he doesn't believe the same things you do. What kind of a religion tells a person to throw love away because different beliefs are involved? Jake is a man, and he won't pine away after you forever. He will find another woman, or she will find him. Are you ready to live with that?"

I frowned. What did he know that I didn't, besides the fact that my words and actions didn't always match? I was fighting for my eternal salvation. Something Uncle Ned knew nothing about.

"Maybe I am being unfair," I told him. "But Jake didn't talk to me either. Do you know where he is?"

"I could make an educated guess."

My heat began to race, and I gripped the top board of the fence until my knuckles turned white.

"Then tell me, is he in Edna?" I didn't have the strength to ask if he was with Beth. His answer might destroy every shred of hope I had left.

"I haven't talked to him recently, if that is what you are asking, but I can assure you his decision was not made lightly."

"And how would you know that?"

"Because men talk just like women do, only a little more discretely. Jake loves you, Brylee, but he can't fight a losing battle forever."

"It doesn't have to be like that."

"But it does, unless you are willing to make a few concessions. I get it that you want to believe in something, but why let it come between you and the bloke you claim to love."

I wanted to explain, but my answer would only fall on deaf ears. Uncle Ned was one of the best men I had ever known, but he simply wasn't into religion. I had felt much the same way before meeting Becky and Ben, but then I had been willing to listen. Jake wasn't to that point yet.

"So what are we supposed to do, Uncle Ned?" I asked. "LeAnn and I can't even run our part of the ranch without Jake's help, and there is no way the merger we have already signed can work giving you and Aunt Nora more freedom to visit your family."

"Hell, it's probably a blessing in disguise," he said with a hearty laugh. "I can't imagine ever leaving this place for more than a few days at a time, but I do understand that you need someone to help out besides me. I will make a few calls and see what I can come up with."

"Thank you, Uncle Ned. I promise to do everything humanly possible to make things work, and just for the record, I do love Jake with all my heart. I am just not certain that is enough to make him want to come back, if that is even a possibility now."

"Only time will tell," he replied, squeezing my hand in a comforting way. "Men have their pride, but they can't stay mad at the women they love forever. Just ask Nora if you don't believe me."

"I hope you are right," I said, but I had learned over the past long year that love wasn't always enough. If it were, I would be with either Jake or Ben instead of alone trying to mend a totally broken heart.

Chapter 22

The next few days were incredibly hard. I tried to keep my tone light and smile when   Trevor was with me, but avoided prolonged conversations with both LeAnn and Emma. I knew they didn't blame me for Jake leaving, but I blamed myself for not trying harder to be the person God knew I could be—a righteous example of Christlike qualities to my entire family.

Nonetheless, I spent as much time as possible with my little brother because he was grieving another loss he didn't understand too. We worked on the waterline until the leak was stopped. We cleaned out the granary and barn so they would be ready when new crops were brought in. We fed and watered animals, and rode somewhere almost daily to see if any new calves, or their mothers, needed our help. But no amount of work or recreation could fill the hole in my heart because Jake was no longer there. I half-expected to hear his voice or see his face a hundred times a day, but it was nothing more than an illusion. No one at the ranch had heard from him since the day he left.

For my own sanity, I had to believe Jake was okay. If something really awful had happened, we would have been notified. Most everyone in Edna knew something about the Hawkins' family and even if they didn't, Emma was privy to most of the town gossip because her diner was the most frequently visited eating place in town. I was becoming more certain each day that he had gone back to Beth, and that was why Uncle Ned never mentioned his name.

He did, however, find someone who was willing to work for us until a more permanent solution to our problem could be found and brought him to the house so we could meet him.

"You remember Chester Watkins, don't you, LeAnn?" Uncle Ned asked after the man had removed his hat and stepped into the kitchen.

"Of course," LeAnn said, extending her hand in his direction. "You and Jack grew up together, and I believe we met you and your wife several years ago when we went into town for dinner. How is Dottie doing?"

The man with just enough gray at his temples to look competent, but not enough to look old gave her a sad smile. "She passed not long before Jack did. That's why I didn't make it to the wake. You had a little boy didn't you?"

"Yes," she said without commenting on his loss. "And now we have a daughter. She's seven weeks old. Jack never got to see her, but she looks just like him."

"That must bring a lot of comfort," Chester replied. "I know how much he valued family."

LeAnn cleared her throat and for a moment I thought she might cry, but she managed to keep it together. "That he did. I don't know if you've met Jack's other daughter, Brylee. She came back to us from America where she graduated from college. It has been a real blessing having her here this past year."

He smiled in my direction. "The pleasure is all mine, Miss Brylee. Your father brought you to the house a few times when you were small. Dottie would feed you milk and fresh baked cookies while we talked. She really looked forward to those visits since she wanted a girl of her own and never got one. Time certainly has a way of changing most everything."

"Yes, it does," I replied, wishing I felt more like an adult partner in running the ranch than a long, lost child who had run away.

Since there was nothing left for us to say to each other because I had no recollection of those visits, Chester turned his attention back to LeAnn. "I really would like to help out since I know you are going through a rough spot right now. It's what Jack would do if our situations were reversed.

LeAnn's lips twitched. "What about your own place? The last I heard, you were still one of the few ranchers who hadn't sold out to the enemy. It's what Jack always called the corporations who want to absorb everything out here."

"Those vultures are still circling but I refuse each and every offer," Chester volunteered. "My two boys have pretty much taken over the daily operations since Dottie and I planned on a doing some traveling before she passed, but now I sort of wish I hadn't relinquished quite so much control. Not that my boys are trying to get rid of me but a ranch doesn't need three bosses, and I end up with a little too much spare time on my hands."

"I can understand that," LeAnn said. "And I'm sure Ned would not have suggested you talk to us if you weren't perfectly capable, but I would like a couple of days to think about it. This is a huge adjustment for all of us."

"Take all the time you need," Chester responded. "Ned knows where to find me when you come to a decision. I know how hard change is, but I would like to lend a hand of support if you want me."

He looked so contrite and hopeful standing there in his worn overalls that I almost asked if he could start the next day, but it wasn't my decision to make without LeAnn's approval and she seemed to have some serious reservations.

"You could do a whole lot worse than Chester Watkins," Uncle Ned said after he had gone. "Even with all the modern conveniences we have managed to obtain, life in the outback is hard for anyone—man, woman or child."

"What about NJ?" LeAnn asked. "Has he said anything about coming home?"

"Not a word! He still thinks he is going to become some famous marine biologist. I can't really blame him for wanting to pursue his own dreams. That's what the rest of us have done. If Trevor was ten years older, we likely wouldn't be having this conversation."

"Well, he isn't," LeAnn retorted. "And I would never force him to stay out here if he didn't want to. I can't help but think we might all be better off if we found some way out of that bloody will and moved into town. It's so isolated out here and with both Jack and Jake gone, I'm not sure it will ever feel like home to any of us again."

I had been listening from my end of the table without saying much of anything but could not let her observation go unchallenged. The ranch might seem like a futile existence right now but it would always be my home, even if no one else wanted it.

"You said we weren't going to talk about that for a while, LeAnn. Father wanted all his children to be raised out here and even seemingly impossible things can change. You said that yourself."

My vehemence for wanting to remain exactly where I was surprised me. Little more than a year ago I had planned on coming home, making peace with my father and then returning to the states to marry Ben. In many ways, my losses were every bit as devastating as hers, but I was learning to adjust and had no place else to go.

"I understand where you're coming from, Brylee, but I have to be realistic," she said, interrupting my less than charitable thoughts. "And Ned needs to know where every one of us stands. I love this land too but if Jake doesn't come back, there really is little point in putting off the inevitable. Chester might be very knowledgeable and willing to help out, but no one can guarantee he won't change his mind in a month or two. Besides, it just doesn't feel right hiring someone who isn't family."

"Even if it means keeping the ranch for Trevor?"

She frowned. "It's much more complicated than that. When your father died, I didn't just lose my husband and the father of my children, I lost a part of my heart. He made this house what it was and it is so empty without him."

I looked to Uncle Ned for help but his eyes were fixed on the tabletop, so I stood up, walked the few steps to LeAnn's side and put my hand lightly on her shoulder.

"I'm sorry for being insensitive, but I thought it was a comfort being around all the things he loved."

"Unfortunately, it is both a blessing and a curse," she responded. "I keep expecting him to come through that door and join us for a meal. It was easier at Emma's because we had never spent any time together there."

"Perhaps we are premature in making any decisions," Uncle Ned unexpectedly interjected, and I thought I saw a glint of fear in is eyes. "There are other possibilities to consider."

"Like what?" LeAnn asked.

"I might need a little time to come up with them, but I am certain they exist. Rome wasn't built in a day as the old saying goes."

I wondered what possibilities he might find as I walked him to the back door. We needed help now, and if LeAnn wouldn't consider hiring Chester, we were right back where we started.

"What are you really thinking, Uncle Ned?" I asked as the screen door slammed shut behind us. "We can't lose the ranch. I promised father to keep it going until Trevor was old enough to take over."

"Don't start packing your bags just yet," he said. "This ranch has been in the family for eight generations, and I'm not about to lose it before we make it to nine."

"But what about LeAnn? She isn't getting any sleep with the baby, and I am really worried about her."

Uncle Ned lit a cigarette and took a long drag on it.

"I would suggest taking a short vacation to clear her head but in her present frame of mind, I'm not so sure she would come back. My brother made it bloody impossible to do much when he put the house in her name and the land in Trevor's and yours. What does Emma say about all this? She has known LeAnn longer than the rest of us."

My shoulders moved up and then down without conscious thought. "Emma's logic is the only thing holding us together right now. She even suggested selling her house in town and moving out here permanently but that wouldn't solve any of our problems, at least not for very long. We need Jake to survive. It's as simple as that."

"That bloke certainly picked a fine time for a crisis," he said. "Is Emma still living in the den?"

I wanted to ask if he had any leads on where Jake may have gone but knew he wouldn't share anything until he was ready, so I answered his question. "She refuses to take my room upstairs, and I have tried on numerous occasions to convince her she would be more comfortable there."

"Emma is old school. She has worked hard all her life and doesn't see inconvenience as a hardship as long as the people she loves are okay."

"But we aren't okay, Uncle Ned. Every last one of us is a mess and Jackie has picked up on it," I said as I leaned back against the side of his truck. He needed to know just how desperate the situation really was and telling him was my responsibility since I was the catalyst behind all of our troubles. "I haven't been completely honest with you about Jake's leaving. He left a letter for me."

"You don't have to share that with me, Brylee. I understand the need for privacy when it comes to matters of the heart."

"But you need to know that he left everything to me, including his bank account and truck. He said he wouldn't need money where he was going. I am terrified he may have done something stupid and I will never see him again."

Uncle Ned took a few more draws on his cigarette.

"No wonder LeAnn feels so desperate. It is never a good sign when a man gives everything away."

"So you do think something bad may have happened to him? You made it sound like he would be fine a few days ago."

"And for all I know, he is. If he went back to flying supplies into the outback he wouldn't need any money. How hard have you tried to locate him?"

I felt my cheeks begin to tremble. "With LeAnn's assistance I made a few inquiries, but none of the companies he worked for in the past have seen him. It's like he just dropped off the face of the earth and doesn't want to be found."

"But he took his plane?"

"It is the only thing missing other than his clothes. I even called the airport in Edna, but Janet said she hadn't seen him."

Uncle Ned threw the remains of his cigarette on the ground and pressed down with the sole of his boot until he knew it was out.

"Janet might not be telling the truth. She and Jake go way back. If he asked her to keep a secret, she would do it."

"But the outback is huge! If that's where he is, how will we ever find him?"

"He has to be somewhere, Brylee, and now that I know there was more to him leaving than just a difference of opinion between two very hard-headed Aussies perhaps it is time for me to step in. I really haven't done much since we last talked because I figured you and Jake only needed some time away from each other to figure things out. Just convince LeAnn to stay put until I get back to you. We don't need any more runaways in this family."

I rose up on my toes and put my arms around his neck. "I love you, Uncle Ned, but as much as I hate to admit it, sometimes even people like you and me need to accept when enough is enough. I'm sure the aborigines would love getting their land back legally, along with a house to live in."

"That may be," he retorted. "Just don't go including my house with yours. Nora and I built that for our family to enjoy, and I am not about to give it to some native who would rather use it for firewood than a place of residence."

His assessment of their way of life made me smile but true to his word, he left early the next morning to hunt for Jake. Aunt Nora said she wasn't sure where he had gone or when he might be back, only that he had promised to call her each night with an update.

From that point on, the days were almost intolerable and the only person sleeping was Trevor. The rest of us tossed silently in our beds hoping our restlessness wasn't bothering anyone else. But our dark-rimmed eyes, along with the feeling of having to walk on eggshells, was proof enough that we were considerably worried about the future, and more than just a little concerned with the present.

And so we arrived at the first Sunday of a new month—the Sunday Jackie was going to be blessed. I was afraid LeAnn might change her mind about having the ordinance done since she was not yet baptized, but she was wearing the dress I had purchased for her wedding when I walked down the stairs and into the kitchen.

I had already decided to attend church alone if necessary. I needed to make good on my commitments if I wanted the Lord's help in putting my family back together again.

"Good morning, Brylee," she said, placing a box of cold cereal on the table. "Would you mind checking on Trevor in a few minutes? I haven't heard him moving around yet."

"Of course," I replied. "You look very pretty this morning."

"I look like crap, but thanks for being kind," she retorted. "I suppose I can blame my looks on having a baby that isn't sleeping through the night yet. No one needs to know anything else that has been going on out here."

"Most certainly not," I responded, wondering why she didn't want the branch president informed. He had been incredibly kind to all of us and was the one she had asked to bless the baby.

"I just want this to be a happy day," she continued. "Emma suggested we have lunch at the diner to celebrate Jackie's blessing. That way, we won't have to cook when we get back."

"Sounds like a great idea. Have you decided what she is going to wear?"

"I was thinking about one of the little dresses the ladies from church sent out in the mail. They're awfully pretty and she will be too big to wear them before long."

My frown was unintentional but LeAnn saw it anyway.

"Did you have something else in mind?" she asked.

"Sort of," I admitted. "When I was looking through the boxes in the attic, I found the dress I was christened in. I washed and ironed it before you brought her home from the hospital, but I understand if you want her to wear something new."

"Absolutely not!" she declared. "Nothing will mean more to Jackie when she grows up than knowing she wore her big sister's dress on this important day."

I breathed a sigh of relief before hurrying to the hall closet. Perhaps at least one part of our lives was going to be okay since LeAnn hadn't given up on the idea of joining the church, even after all she had been through.

She was still standing in front of the sink when I returned, but instead of handing her the dress I asked a very loaded question. "Have you felt father's presence in the house today because I certainly have."

Her hands fell to her side as she looked over at me. Her lengthy pause before responding filled me with dread. Perhaps I should have been more cautious on such an emotionally-charged day.

"Funny you should ask that since knowing your father will be with us when Jackie is blessed is the only reason I was able to get out of bed this morning. Jack wants us to be a forever family. I know that with all my heart, and simply do not understand how I could even contemplate leaving the ranch when that was where we spent our life together. The pain I sometimes feel is just a reminder of what I can have again someday—if I live worthy of it."

"So you still feel good about the decisions you are making?"

"Good enough to know that I want to be at church with you today and hope you will tell me if I am doing something wrong. Emma says it is very different from going to Mass with Father Francis conducting."

"You definitely won't see any costly robes or ornate furnishings since the building is a converted storefront and the branch president isn't paid to watch over his flock. But one thing I am certain of, you will feel Christ's presence and know how much you are loved."

And so we drove off towards town in the green Land Rover my father had bought when he took me to boarding school in Sydney. I was at the wheel, with Emma riding shotgun, and LeAnn, Trevor and Jackie in the backseat. I tried to smile as I thought about what the day might bring. We would be in church together for the first time as a family, but one very important person was missing.

If Uncle Ned could not find Jake and convince him to come home without Beth or someone else, I would lose far more than the ranch. I inadvertently looked at the mirage glistening on the road in front of me. Some people got their happy endings without having to take a stand. Why couldn't that happen for me?

But even as such an uncharitable thought slipped out, I knew there was still a great deal for me to learn about life, love and human relationships. Things did not always happen when they were convenient, anticipated or even planned. Sometimes they were simply part of God's plan in helping his children return home. I needed to remember that if I wanted a more joyful life.

To be continued . . . .

See Book Five: **Reawakening - Indecision's Flame** for more of Brylee's story.

About the Author

JS Ririe is the pen name for Jan Hill. She spent her youth in the country where she learned to appreciate solitude, making her own fun, and reading romance novels from some of the masters like the Bronte sisters, Louisa May Alcott, Victoria Holt and Phyllis Whitney. She penned her first novel as a teenager but never pursued what is now her greatest passion until becoming the lead witness in a federal case brought against the school district where she taught broadcasting and journalism. Writing Brylee's story as she waited two years to testify helped her through a terrifying time. She lives in Utah and has two children and two living grandchildren who help bring meaning and joy to her life.

A Note From Jan

Thank you so much for reading this novel. I'd love to stay in touch with you. Please consider joining my MAILING LIST so I can send you periodic newsletters about upcoming book releases, special offers and more. The link to sign up for my mailing list is: http://eepurl.com/dCPYVf . I promise that I will not spam you, will not sell your email information and will treat it with care.

One last favor: Your rating/review of this book helps me to keep writing. I would really appreciate it if you could leave a review. It shouldn't take more than a minute or two. You can reach the page directly at http://amzn.to/2BXNSdv

Thank you again,
JS Ririe

www.JanHillBooks.com
For contacting the author: JSRirie@JanHillBooks.com